CORMORANT BAY

CORMORANT BAY

JOAN WILLIAMS

iUniverse LLC
Bloomington

CORMORANT BAY

iUniverse books may be ordered through booksellers or by contacting:

iUniverse LLC
1663 Liberty Drive
Bloomington, IN 47403
www.iuniverse.com
1-800-Authors (1-800-288-4677)

ISBN: 978-1-4917-2224-4 (sc)
ISBN: 978-1-4917-2226-8 (hc)
ISBN: 978-1-4917-2225-1 (e)

Library of Congress Control Number: 2014901573

Printed in the United States of America.

iUniverse rev. date: 04/12/2014

CHAPTER ONE

September 1985

Kara sighed as she searched through her bulging handbag for the emergency supply of Tylenol tablets. *Extra strength,* she noted thankfully upon locating them, *which hopefully will provide faster relief.* Taking a couple of sips of almost cold coffee she grimaced after swallowing the two pills. She disliked taking medication of any kind, but sitting in the waiting area at Gate 6 of the International Terminal at Heathrow Airport, between flights, was not Kara's idea of the most efficient way to spend one's time. It provided an expanse of time to dwell upon matters which had given her the headache in the first place.

Suddenly it felt cool. After the speedy helter-skelter from northern England, starting with the early flight from the local airport to Heathrow airport outside London, it had been a carefully structured journey. There had been little time for reminiscing. Until now! With one flight a day to Los Angeles there was a ninety minutes stop-over at the Heathrow airport waiting for this connection, which hung like a cloud over her head. Kara shrugged into her coat, accidentally knocking the arm of the young boy sitting in the seat beside her.

"Oh, I'm terribly sorry. Are you all right?"

His well-scrubbed face turned to look at Kara. He smiled shyly and nodded his head. She is a very beautiful lady with shining blonde hair tied back with a ribbon and large green eyes that even to his youthful awareness looked as if she had been crying. He had been watching her gazing into space with a sad expression on her face. When she smiled at him, his face lit up. The smile transformed her somber expression, releasing the sparkle in her eyes and showing even white teeth behind sensuously curved lips. Kara's engaging smile was such an intrinsic part of her personality that she hardly noticed the impact on others.

"My name is Kara, what's yours?"

"Kenneth," he responded, "and this is my mum and sister."

Kara looked over and smiled at a nice looking woman about her own age sitting at the other side of Kenneth, with a little girl asleep on the seat beside her.

"Hello. I've just met your son and if I'd realized how delightful it is to meet someone of the opposite sex in an airport, I'd have started much earlier."

She spoke with a twinkle in her eyes. He was a cute little fellow, with big curious eyes. Talking out aloud had broken her dismal thought pattern and that was a relief.

The mother smiled tiredly.

"I'm just getting over the flu, so please forgive my lack of social graces. 'Fraid I'm just not very good company right now and the trip to Los Angeles is looming ahead."

"Can I help in any way?" Kara offered.

"No, thanks, my husband should be here very soon. He went to the Duty Free Shop."

Her less than enthusiastic response was offset by a quick, though weary, smile.

Kara pulled her coat collar up around her neck and settled back on the plastic chair, smiling at Kenneth once more.

Flying was not her panacea of choice. Jet setters could have the firmament to themselves she conceded—she would just be thankful to get back into her normal daily routine. Kara loved her work and that had influenced her greatly in postponing one of the most difficult decisions she had to make in her life. This had taken place just a couple of days before her stay in England was to end, and she was still trying to cope with the extent of it.

In California she was accustomed to running a very large operation that ran smoothly and efficiently, thanks to the groundwork meticulously established several years earlier. She had a sixth sense in its regard, detecting irregularities almost by intuition and Kara had come to rely upon her own sharp judgment in every way. She had come a long way from the days when she was a shy, introverted schoolgirl and, because she was annoyed that the current emotional turmoil could not be resolved, the dratted headache had crept up on her.

Struggling to overcome the gloomy state of mind that enveloped her, Kara pulled a Monthly Planner out of her carry-on bag and flipped through toward September. No time like the present to start getting her life back on track, she concedes. Almost like an omen the pages open at the entries for August. Crammed into the small spaces were buzz words used to condense blocks of time into chapter and verse; "Wisherly beach/Jon," "Coppice Farm/Jon." The painful memories brought back intense feelings and reminded Kara that her headache was gathering impetus. Did she do the right thing? Her mind drifted.

Normally, Kara loved beachcombing. She had done it most of her life, living thirty-five miles from the ocean where her parents had a houseboat. They used it quite frequently. Most of the time it was anchored and the deck and cabin utilized as a beach retreat, providing cooking facilities and sleeping accommodation. The majority of their outings took place on foot or in the small motorboat that was harnessed to one of the houseboat's corner-posts. It was a very casual and uncomplicated lifestyle they led at weekends and holidays. It was the perfect antidote for the stress encountered by her father during his busy workdays as president of his prestigious and vast engineering conglomerates.

On the private strip of beach property, which followed the outline of a small isolated aquamarine bay, "a baker's dozen" houseboats were berthed secluded and completely hidden from view by all but passing planes and birds. The huge sand dunes and rocky cliffs gave Cormorant Bay total privacy. The houseboats, peaceful in their solitude, had been there for years. Before Kara was born, her father and a group of friends decided to seek their own kind of isolation and by a stroke of immense good luck found and purchased the beach property. It was being sold at the death of a widow who had come into the property through her deceased husband. As a farmer's wife living a hundred miles inland she was not interested in an isolated piece of unworkable coastline and had stipulated in her Last Will and Testament that the land was to be sold for whatever price it could raise. The proceeds were to be given to her favorite charity. Kara's father and friends were aware that a road would need to be forged over the primitive path already made by animal trails, to allow vehicle access from the main road. There also would be the cost of constructing access to the beach level. Most of the other bidders were reluctant to invest more money into what would be expensive, but necessary, improvements. It was, after all, just a piece of unproductive land favored with little more than a scenic view and nesting cormorants. Because its inaccessibility proved to be the major purchasing deterrent to the bidders, Kara's father and friends raised their bidding price slightly. This strategy paid off—they acquired the land.

This was the first step. For a few years camping in tents was the only affordable way for the "Ne'er-do-wells" as they called themselves, to utilize their hideaway, paying off their debt in the process. The group, made up of energetic, eager young couples, adventurous and optimistic, was temporarily impeded by the primary financial demands of creating a good, secure lifestyle for themselves and their growing families. However they were sure of their abilities and goals. They were a close-knit clique, with a long association and proven loyalties. As their fortunes improved, houseboats were added to this beach community. Some more elaborate than others, but each characteristic of its owner and each formally named and "christened."

Kara's family's houseboat called "The End of the Rainbow" was chosen by Kara's artist mother, Silvia Olavssen, but others had more playful names like "C. Gull's Landing" and "Just Juxtaposing."

"Much Ado about Nothing" belonged to the Williams' family. Jonathan Williams was born twenty months before Kara and all her life she had tried to catch up to him. Growing up so closely together they graduated from gathering unusual shells on the beach to making and destroying each other's sandcastles. Exploring tide pools and fishing from the shore were natural progressions. In their early teens they were allowed to take one of the small motor boats out of the bay and fish further afield. When they entered high school and their interests differed, both Kara and Jon invited friends to their respective houseboats and they often merged for social activities, but as time passed they saw less of each other; it was not because they had lost common ground, but because they had different pursuits and ambitions. Sometimes one would invite the other to participate in some function or other but, after high school graduation, Kara attended the

University of Durham and Jon and she met only occasionally at the beach.

Kara's parents kept her apprised of what Jon was doing and Kara was always interested in the latest news they had to relay. She was very proud when he was conscripted as Center Forward of the regional professional soccer team and even more delighted when he was recruited by the renowned Manchester United national soccer team headquartered in the midlands. For a few years Jon's star rose. His team went from one victory to another, with Jon the object of the fans' affection and adulation. He could do no wrong.

In an unexpected incident Jon's right foot was vigorously kicked by an opposing player coming up fast behind him during an exhausting and highly competitive game. That debilitating injury ended the soccer career of one of the highest paid and idolized players in the sport. Not immediately, there was hope of recovery during the various surgeries and therapy sessions. After a year, tired and somewhat bitter, with a ruptured Achilles tendon damaged beyond repair, Jon resigned from the soccer league and retired from the world.

For a while Kara saw much more of Jon. He practically lived at the beach, cutting himself off from everyone but his immediate family and the "Ne'er-do-wells." Kara's heart went out to her friend. She was in her final year at university and whenever she was home at school recesses she gravitated to the beach life. She coaxed and encouraged Jon to swim and fish with her and gradually they started walking slowly along the beach again, confiding in each other as they had done all their lives.

Jon would always walk with a limp. Kara would turn her head away when her eyes filled with tears as she saw how bravely Jon struggled to conquer the constant nagging pain that medications only partly desensitized. He would not give in and the distress that flashed into his eyes should he accidentally place his foot awkwardly—or worse, stumble—was almost like a physical blow to Kara. She knew him too well to offer sympathy and once, when he fell face down lengthwise in the sand and stayed there unmoving, Kara forced herself not to rush to his side to comfort him. Instead she said in a pseudo-whining tone, "Come on, Jon, this isn't the time to rest. We have to get back for lunch." She had not realized that she had been holding her breath until Jon turned his head to look at her and for a moment they were youngsters again. With a strained grin on his face he reminded Kara that even though he could not run quite as fast as he used to, he still had a fast right hand for swatting. This was the way they covered their genuine feelings of affection for each other; it was a game they played. The walks started lengthening, though still at a slow pace. They usually kept to the edge of the waterline where the outgoing tide left compacted sand, which made walking a little easier for Jon. He seldom complained and sometimes, involved in absorbing conversations, the two would forget about time. As Jon's limp became noticeably pronounced Kara was guiltily reminded of his disability.

A few times she had suggested that he rest while she went and brought back one of the small motorboats, so that he would not have to strain his foot further. Jon scoffed at this, saying a short rest was all that was needed. He insisted it was no hardship getting back to "The Colony," as they had started calling it. He could manage.

It was with some reluctance that Kara returned to college after spending time with Jon. She took some credit for helping him recuperate and was happy when he said he had decided to go into business for himself. As he was still in the preliminary stages of figuring it out, he would let her know all about it at Christmas when she returned.

* * *

Kara shook her head and looked around the airport lounge. The little boy was looking at her and she wondered if she had been thinking and speaking her thoughts out aloud. He held up a Dr. Seuss book titled "The Cat in the Hat."

"Will you read to me?" Kenneth entreated. "Please."

His mother was leaning back with her eyes closed and a labored expression on her face. Kara looked at her watch, just over an hour before takeoff. How the time flew when one was having fun.

"Why not Kenneth?"

She held out her hand for the book with a cat wearing a red and white top hat on the cover.

"Come and sit on the other side of me and we won't disturb your mommy and sister."

Kara started reading.

Kenneth giggled in the appropriate places and Kara knew he could have recited it himself. His lips mouthed the words. A few pages before the end Kara was aware of someone standing in front of her. She looked up. A man, with a look of amusement on his face, was watching her.

"Hello, Dad! Kara, this is my dad."

A man in the uniform of a naval officer offered his hand.

"I didn't want to interrupt. In fact if I could have found my camera I would have taken a picture. I'm Ken's father, Bruce Tanner. Carry on."

Kara smiled. How could she ignore such a command? She finished the book and handed it back to Kenneth. He smiled and jumped off the chair.

"Thanks a lot, Kara."

He ran along the aisle, leapfrogging onto his father's lap.

Kara closed her eyes.

It was difficult pushing back memories crowding in on her, insistently reminding her of a past she wanted to forget and a future she was not ready to think about.

★ ★ ★

She remembered how excited she had been at the Christmas recess when she had rushed home from university to inform her parents and Jon that she had found the most extraordinary man, who thought she was very special too. Somehow she thought she needed Jon's approval. Roger Algernon Smithers, who would be graduating in June with Kara, had three more years to go before being able to add Juris Prudence behind his name. It was not Roger's looks that had drawn Kara to him—it was the earnestness and eloquence of his viewpoint when debates took place in the general Commons Room of the university. She admired the tenacity of his refusal to back-down under duress and she attributed this to the aura of sophistication he projected. Roger was five years older than Kara and, in growing closer, their discussions turned to more personal observations and topics. This led to an exclusive relationship between them and Kara was romantically captivated. She found it fascinating watching Roger in the simple process of filling and smoking a pipe. It reminded her of the times she had watched her father doing the same thing. Roger's curly brown hair was in contrast to the thinly defined moustache, which Kara found endearing. Roger's slender nose adroitly kept in place tortoiseshell spectacles that gave him a profoundly scholarly appearance. The casually elegant way in which Roger carried his jacket across one of his shoulders pointed to his sense of style. His choice of impeccable clothing set him apart from the rest of the students. Kara was in love.

Roger had willingly agreed to split-up his vacation and spend part of it at Kara's family's beach property to celebrate the advent of the New Year. He insisted that Kara's family formally invite him and they had no problem with this. Their concern was in the suddenness of the news thrust upon them. Kara usually displayed a level headedness beyond her years, and this breach of protocol bothered them.

Most of the "Ne'er-do-wells" celebrated the advent of the New Year at the beach each year and these arrangements were accepted without question by Kara. It was a way of life. Whoever could get there did. They tried to be there a few days in advance to discuss the New Year's Eve arrangements and this left sufficient time to relax, visit with each other or play badminton and quoits on the beach during the day. Listening to music or playing games in one or two of the larger houseboats was the usual night time activity. Last-minute repairs were also done at this time, before the houseboats were battened down and the doors and windows sealed with the specially made fitments before winter and the stormy weather took over. This was when the beach and houseboats were abandoned until the spring weather returned.

It was in this group that Roger, with his cultivated manners and refined diction found that he was completely out-of-place and ill-at-ease. He viewed the primitive behavior of this group of strangers as distasteful and uncouth. He had been willing to tolerate the nonchalant and, to his mind, devoid of purpose daily beach activities, but from an intellectual standpoint he questioned the purpose of squandering time in such a worthless pastime. How could Kara have done this to him? Why had she not mentioned this aspect of her family's leisure time before, even at the time when the last-minute invitation from her parents had been extended? Was she uncomfortable about asking him to join her family in such a lowly setting? This must be the reason, and it was not to his liking. Kara was aware of the high standards and goals for which he was reaching, with the determined intent to attain them.

Roger found Kara's parents to be good sorts, friendly and down-to-earth people, but as for the others here in this confining zoo, he really had nothing in common with them. This put a different light on his intentions. Roger mused that he and Kara had known each other for such a short time that he knew as little of Kara's background as she knew of his. This visit had presented itself as an opportunity to advance to a more personal level with Kara and at the same time make a favorable impression on her parents. Thankfully he realized that at the first opportunity he must extricate himself from a potentially disastrous situation, before a big blunder was made on his part. He wanted no further involvement with Kara or commitment to her.

★ ★ ★

After lunch, the day before New Year's Eve day, Roger cornered Kara in the galley.

"Let's walk over to the breakwater soon."

His bespectacled face was serious and unsmiling. Kara had the distinct feeling of impending doom.

Walking across the sand toward the breakwater promontory at mid-afternoon they spoke desultorily in a somewhat stilted fashion. Kara was tense. Things were not going well between the two of them. Roger had distanced himself totally from everyone, privately complaining to her about the lack of telephones, newspapers and creature comforts like four star restaurants and quality entertainment. He was particularly resentful of the absence of serious, meaningful discussions.

Kara had attempted to provide Roger with background information on how this community had been established in an effort to counteract what he saw as a trivial and boring lifestyle. She could see by his compressed lips and stony stare that he had chosen not to enter into further conversation on the subject.

In silence they reached the craggy projection and sat down awkwardly on huge boulders. Roger made no effort to sit beside Kara. He looked off into the distance and then brought his gaze back to Kara. He took a deep breath and cleared his throat.

'I realize, just as you must too, that coming here was a mistake."

Kara clasped her hands together tightly. This was not a good start.

"It's too bad you didn't inform me of living conditions here before we came. My expectations were obviously on a much higher plain and quite frankly, Kara, I thought yours were too. I'm not cut out to be a beach bum and this lifestyle does not appeal to me in any way—it is not one I would choose."

Kara raised the palm of her right hand to signal a stop to the conversation and interjected crossly, "We don't live here, Roger—this is where we come to get away from all the mundane aspects of life— where we can physically relax and rejuvenate our senses in a secure and beautiful environment with friends. I did mention this to you when you were invited here."

The curled lips indicated to Kara that his impression differed significantly from hers and he was intent upon making sure he was not misunderstood. "One practical factor learned from all this is how little we know each other and how different are our expectations; it is fortunate that this flaw in our relationship has been discovered before further commitment is made."

Kara inhaled sharply, thinking, *Roger hasn't wasted any time in declaring his separation from me. Surely I didn't misinterpret his intentions when he spoke lovingly of a future together just a few weeks ago?*

Blinking away threatening tears Kara asked, "So now that you have come to this conclusion all by yourself, what do you intend to do?" bitterly adding, "Now that your vow to cherish and love me for eternity has fizzled out and died."

A surprised expression flashed across Roger's face. "You are so naïve, Kara. Those words were not a lifetime promise—they were spoken as a manner of speech to convey my growing interest in you and the possibility of a future together."

Sliding off the rock Roger faced Kara.

"Observing this antiquated beach lifestyle in which you are involved has brought the realization that we are quite unsuited for each other. You may find it harsh to accept the single-mindedness of my future goals and plans, but I will not deviate from my pursuit to successfully carry them out—no matter what obstacles stand in the way."

Kara bit her lip. "It sounds as if you have just issued an ultimatum. Do you regard me as 'an obstacle'?"

Roger adjusted the spectacles over the bridge of his long nose before replying. "There comes a time in life when one has to make decisions that sometimes can be regretful to give and painful to hear. This is one of those occasions. Fortunately our incompatibility has been discovered before serious assumptions have been made. You are still very young and inexperienced and no doubt this interlude will have few lasting effects." In an attempt to be sympathetic and lighten the mood, he continued. "You probably won't remember my name in a few months."

Kara fought the tears about to be shed. So their short-lived romance that she had believed to be so perfect had just ended. Shakily getting down from the rock, she turned her back on Roger, wiping her eyes on the sleeve of her blouse.

"So that is it! You came here, into my peaceful world, spouting insulting and sarcastic comments about people I have known and loved all my life; you have spewed your condescending remarks like a coward talking to the wind. I made a mistake and I will never forget it, but you have made a mistake and you will regret it."

Confused and distraught, Kara's emotions swirled and eddied like the undercurrents of the water beneath them.

Roger was her first love and Kara was reluctant to surrender the wonderment and magic that had cast a glow over her life, until this shattering moment.

Striding angrily away from Roger she hurried back to the safety of her beach home, leaving Roger to retrace his steps at his own slower pace. The sun was setting after what was for Kara an interminable journey back. The lights twinkled from the cluster of houseboats, guiding Kara and Roger on their separate, silent return course. It was all over between them.

Kara sat up with a start and looked around the busy airport lounge. The memories had come back crystal clear and vividly. Kara surreptitiously mopped her wet eyelids and blew her nose on a tissue that she pulled from her coat pocket.

"Are you getting a cold too?" a little voice by her side asked.

"No, I don't think so," she choked.

Kara's head pounded. She stood up and threw the straps of her handbag over her shoulder and picked up the carryon luggage. The waiting area had become crowded.

"Will you look after my seat for a few minutes, Kenneth?"

He nodded his head vigorously, lying across the vacated chair to demonstrate claim.

Kara freshened up in the Ladies Room and looked at her watch again. Time seemed to be frozen. She felt as if she could sleep standing up, she was so exhausted. The headache still persisted and she took another Tylenol tablet before returning to the waiting area.

Kenneth was waiting for her. He had another Dr. Seuss book in his hand.

Fishing around in her handbag Kara brought out a British Airways deck of playing cards, which she had purchased on the flight south.

"Why don't you ask your daddy to play "Snap" with you?"

She handed over the packet of cards.

She sat down once again on the reclaimed chair and resolutely closed her eyes.

Kara sighed. It all seemed so long ago and yet she could recall everything minutely, as if it had occurred yesterday. First love did have its toll, she thought wryly.

Roger had appeared so sophisticated and she had succumbed so easily to his superficial savoir faire.

Even now, eight years later, she could conjure up the shock and sense of rejection when Roger, in no uncertain language, had expressed the need to get away from what he called "this provincial retreat" at the earliest opportunity.

Falling asleep that night had been almost impossible for Kara. She mentally retraced and labored over the basically one-sided conversation, which had taken place just hours earlier, trying to put her finger on the epicenter that had triggered this eruption of earthquake proportions in her life. Kara shuddered at the insensitive manner in which Roger had chosen to end their relationship. It had hurt terribly to learn that her love, so freely given, was not reciprocated and tears of disappointment and anguish quietly coursed down her cheeks. It had ended so abruptly. She was above average looking. She was intelligent, cultured, and personable. So what was the problem?

Roger was sleeping in a small guest cabin next to her larger one. Her parents occupied a modern cabin fitted with built-in furniture. A small functional bathroom divided her cabin and theirs. It was agony laying under the same roof as Roger with Sleep, the elusive antidote to balm her wounds, out of reach.

Kara quietly edged out of the bunk and felt for the warm, comfortable robe she had left on the door hook. Slipping it on and tying the belt, she fumbled around for shoes. She picked them up and quietly opened her cabin door and, by the moon's light gleaming through the portholes, carefully picked her way through the main lounge and out of the door, closing it behind her softly. Outside the full moon was shedding its light over the harbor, displaying a shimmering silver mantle around its circumference; it was a sure sign of frost. Quickly Kara slipped on her moccasins and walking over to a beach chair, sat down. The canvas seat was clammy and cold. She quickly stood up and walked over to the port side of the boat's deck and looked out toward the bay, shoving her hands into the robe's deep pockets.

Throughout each day and each month the tide patterns became remarkably familiar to the tenants of Cormorant Bay. The low tides were the times for exploring the tide pools. Then during the months from September through April, when the seafood was in season, farming the tide pool areas took place. Picking the mussels and winkles clinging to the temporarily exposed craggy rocks, draped profusely with coarse thick brown seaweed, provided many occasions for impromptu group parties to cook their bounty on the beach.

Pulling the mussels away from their accessible anchorage did not bother Kara very much. She had become accustomed to doing this kind of thing from being a small child. What she disliked was pushing aside the long, thick brown seaweed with 'blisters' dotted over it to free them from the rocks. The long strands of seaweed, when found drying on the sand were a little sticky to the touch. They reminded her of a squid's tentacles. Jon used to scare her by stepping on a "blister" that made a loud popping sound as it burst. Sometimes it squirted water up to a distance of several feet. Often, to her horror, on herself.

She much preferred swimming in the few feet of seawater left in a shallow channel, which stretched for a few hundred yards along the exposed beach when the tide went out. It was a curiosity. In summer the children especially appreciated what they called their "swimming pool." The sun's rays warmed the salt water sufficiently to afford a couple of hours of water splashing fun, without feeling the full effect of the chilly ocean water, until it returned to its high tide level. Once again it covered the "swimming pool" and drove the young swimmers back to the sand dunes to play.

An entirely different environment presented itself during the later months of fall. Often the sun's radiance was hazily veiled by menacing black clouds, or partially hidden by gusting sands frolicking with a mischievous breeze. The nights grew longer and became quite nippy. This was the time of year when the short daylight hours were maximized. Invigorating walks along the beach, or scouring the area for 'sea glass' and unusual shells became favorite pastimes. Habitually, at this time of year, the turbulent outer seas would toss into the small bay's mouth extraordinary pieces of driftwood and, like a petulant baby, they would be disgorged on a carpet of sand waiting to be claimed.

Kara sighed. She was not aware of how long she had been gazing out at the moonlit dappled ocean, but the night air felt as if it were penetrating her body through to the bones.

Drifting smoke caught Kara's nostrils. Turning she saw two figures drawing nearer. Upon closer inspection she recognized Jon and his father, who was puffing on a pipe.

"Isn't it a little late to be out walking?"

They swung around in surprise. "What are you doing out here so late? You must be cold. Come and have a hot drink with us."

Kara welcomed the diversion. Jon assisted her down the steps from the houseboat and gave a concerned glance when he felt the frostiness of her hand.

James Williams was an Architect of noted distinction, but his avocation was boat building. The houseboat Kara was thawing out in was the second one he had owned and occupied on this beach. The first houseboat was christened "Much Ado about Nothing" and it had been the earliest to sit in the center of tents dotted around it. From the start it was used by all the "Ne'er-do-wells"—almost like a clubhouse. It said much for James and Renata Williams' generosity that they could accept this burden in their stride. It was at this juncture that James Williams began assuming the unofficial leadership of The Colony. James was eight years older than his wife, whom he married as his business affairs prospered and so they were in the enviable position of being able to afford the first houseboat. The "christening ceremony," which started a tradition, was held in an effort to unite the beach dwelling community. It was intended to motivate them toward ownership of their own vessels and to secure the intent of The Colony and its future.

The Williams' first vessel, "Much Ado about Nothing," had been named with tongue-in-cheek to downplay the obvious resentment and dissention that a couple of families were endeavoring to promote. This was the first boat to grace the beach and the Murphy and Secord families watched its emergence as it took shape under the skilled and loving hands of Jim Williams and other enthusiastic volunteers.

The Murphy and Secord families were having second thoughts about the group's land investment deal. Part of the conditions of ownership was to place a vessel, capable of weathering the storms and high tides, on the beach as permanent part-time accommodation within five years from the date of purchase. Each vessel would need the seal of approval from the Beach Owners' Committee to meet their high standards, as well as that of County Land Inspectors.

Everyone had agreed to this and signed contracts to that effect. The Murphy and Secord families no longer wanted to commit themselves to this pledge. They were attempting to change the conditions, pressing to build cabins with wood burning fireplaces and locating them into the hills. This would have ruined the magnificent uninterrupted view of dunes, craggy hills, and the wide blue sky seen from the beach level where the houseboats rested. Not only that, it would bring in an element of civilization that the community had agreed would be totally out-of-place in this tranquil lagoon setting.

The Beach Owners' Committee called for a special meeting. All viewpoints were aired. Jim Williams suggested a solution. The Colony could offer to buy back both the Murphy's and the Secord's land contracts, plus acquired interest on the amount of money paid for the land, for the length of time the contracts had been held. It was a face saving situation and an equitable one. The Murphy's and Secord's surrendered their piece of peace without hesitation. It was The Colony's pleasure to retain both pieces. Harmony was restored.

They were the only dissidents over the twenty-five years that this colony of beachcombers had been in existence. In the early days, if rain solidly quashed outside activities or a fierce gale tore along the stretch of beach, tossing sand recklessly in its path, impromptu meals and entertainment took place inside one of the completed houseboats. They were noisy, cramped times, which established a camaraderie that continued and strengthened over the years.

The second much larger vessel owned by Jim Williams joined the growing number of houseboats spreading over the beach area. It was contracted and built by a renowned Boatwright working out of the Gateshead shipping yards. It was a thing of beauty and the "Ne'er-do-wells" orchestrated a huge celebration for its christening. It had been a happy day. Old memories were resurrected and laughter was much in evidence; it was a time to renew their commitment to this community.

Only the finest materials were used in the construction of the new vessel "Angulus Terrarum" its name so appropriate in this "quiet corner of the world." Finite attention had been given to both interior and exterior design. Incorporating the latest equipment and technology into the vessel were for the comfort and convenience of its inhabitants. Kara snuggled into the mohair afghan as she sat with her legs tucked underneath her on the comfortable white, teal blue, and mocha colored canvas settee built into one of the teak walls. She sipped appreciatively from the mug of cocoa held for warmth in both hands. Too bad Roger had not participated in the communal activities. He would have seen the interior of this, and other vessels for himself with the realization that people who could afford crafts of such obvious quality did not do so by good luck.

Jon had been giving her strange looks from the time they entered his parent's boat, but Kara ignored his silent questioning. The hot liquid and tranquil surrounds eased Kara's troubled state of mind. Looking with amazement at her watch she expressed surprise and took the empty mug into the galley.

Kissing Uncle Jim on the cheek, she apologized.

"I'm sorry if I kept you up. I hadn't realized it was so late. I promised to take Roger into the village this morning and I can pick up any supplies you need at that time, if you let me know."

Turning to Jon she asked, "May I borrow your Jeep? Daddy's estate wagon is filled with loose stuff to be put into storage and it will bounce around if I take it over the dirt road."

Jon immediately responded.

"Of course. I'll go and get the keys and leave them in the usual place on your deck."

Informing his father they were leaving, Jon climbed down the steps, assisting Kara to the beach floor. Knowing how far hc had to walk to get to his boat and return again, Kara overruled him and said she would go along too.

They started walking in that direction.

When Jon was first going through the destructive period in his life, when the absorption and acceptance of his permanent disability hit home, but the physical and mental pain still persisted, his parents, in their usual generous way signed "Much Ado" over to him. It provided a private place where he could withdraw from the publicity and news media that hounded him unmercifully. When "Angulus Terrarum" was in the final stage of completion, Jon's parents had wondered what to do about the disposition of their first boat "Much Ado" as all the families belonging to The Colony possessed their own vessels. They did not wish to advertise it publicly and bring strangers into this haven that they had all protected fiercely and so this action resolved their quandary and provided the solution to Jon's dilemma.

Jackie, Jon's older sister who was married, visited her parents whenever the opportunity presented itself. They were a close-knit family, supportive and devoted to each other. The major dissention that came up with any regularity was that Jackie disliked staying at the beach—intensely. She had protested going there from the time of becoming a teenager, opting to stay at friends' homes in town rather than spending time with her family at Cormorant Bay. The odd times she did stay at the beach became quite harrowing for everyone around her. She complained about the sand insidiously getting into everything. She was fanatically scrupulous in cleaning everything that sand could have touched.

At first Jackie's parents considered this a silly tactic, a way to dodge spending time with the family at the beach. As time passed, it became a fetish. Renata Williams took her daughter to doctors and psychologists. They mostly agreed that it was a phase she would outgrow. It was her way of rebelling. After she moved to London and came back for visits, she would almost invariably make some excuse for staying in the family's city home rather than accompanying them to Wisherly, even for a day. It was the rare occasion when she consented to spend some time at The Colony. Even then she constantly complained—the sand ruined the fiber of the expensive clothing she insisted upon wearing at the beach; the sand infiltrated her food and spoiled her appetite; the sand scuffed the expensive London manicures. When Jon teased her about her idiosyncrasies, she became quite haughty. She much preferred the sophisticated city life that she and her older husband, D'Arcy, shared.

D'Arcy Frazier Fitzhugh owned the huge fashion house "Frazier's of Bond Street" in London, left to him by his grandfather, on his mother's side. Jackie had started work there, right out of college as a Consultant Trainee, doing all the menial work, which was an accepted part of the apprenticeship process. With her tall, willowy figure and classical facial structure, she was a natural substitute when the store's models were out on assignments or taken ill. Customarily wealthy patrons required several garments to be modeled before making a decision to purchase a custom design of the original. Jackie's increasing knowledge of the garments she modeled led her to deferentially inform potential clients about the creativity of the Designer, the quality of the workmanship and the fabric spun in their own factories. She elegantly moved around the Showcase disclosing these facts. Her slim long arms and legs, her trim waist and swan-like neck were the perfect attributes to display the exclusive garments. This was a departure from the silent presentation given by the in-house models and the clients loved this intimate disclosure. It was at one of these impromptu showings that D'Arcy first noticed Jackie. He was at first alarmed by the personal contact made with the clientele, but they assured him that her knowledge and beauty influenced their purchasing decisions and brought them back time-after-time. He considered training her to be part of his haute couture team, which traveled around the country showing the latest international fashions. After observing the flair with which she outfitted herself, looking chic and au courant using intriguing inventive touches, which reflected an ingenuity and perceptive judgment, he decided to introduce her to the buying world of designer fashions. She could become a Buyer.

Jackie adored apparel whether shopping, wearing, or designing and making it. Unable to afford to purchase the Couturier clothing she yearned for when going through college, she made a lasting impression on campus by wearing with élan her own unique creations.

Under D'Arcy's tutelage she learned quickly, readily soaking up as much information as he provided. Traveling in England to the famous woolen and fabric mills, flying to shows in Paris and talking to designers in their fashion houses were part of the training involved. D'Arcy also arranged to introduce her to some of the superior shoemakers of Italy and they spent a week picking their brains. She studied clothing construction, read books on every related subject and visited art museums for historical insight. D'Arcy placed her under the direct instruction of the Head Designer for one year, who rigorously added to and tested her knowledge.

Until she met D'Arcy for the first time and was introduced to him a month after joining Frazier's staff, Jackie was not aware that D'Arcy owned the business. Despite the difference in their ages, an easy camaraderie sprang up between them. The more they learned about each other, the more intrigued they became. They fell in love as a natural progression.

When Jon was in hospital undergoing surgery for the soccer injury, Jackie rushed to her parent's city home to be near him to show her love and support, but she had a hectic schedule and could only manage to be with him for a few days. When Jon moved into "Much Ado" she kept a steady stream of postcards, correspondence, and magazines addressed to Jon from where ever she traveled to be picked up at the small post office in Wisherly. This was her way of letting him know she cared about him, even though she shuddered at the choice of his geographic residence. So gauche! How could he live like that?

"Much Ado" was berthed farthest away from the rest of the houseboats. During the first winter of Jon's ownership, after discovering the futility of the surgery and ineffectuality of therapy, he had a desperate need to be alone. He needed to get away from the constant news media harassment and the cloying attention of well-meaning people. In addition, he did not wish to be observed, even by longtime beach friends, when trying to deal with the pain, anger, and hopelessness that often overcame him. He used a small motorboat for getting back and forth around the bay and visiting his parents. That was all he did until Kara coerced him into walking the sands with her.

On the way walking to his boat to pick up the keys for his Jeep, Jon put an arm around Kara's shoulders, turning her toward him.

"What's the problem, Kara? Why were you standing out on the deck turning into a popsicle?"

Kara turned her head away. She was still too hurt to open her feelings for examination by anyone, least of all herself.

"No problem, you're imagining things."

Jon shrugged his shoulders and they walked on, continuing to chat in the light, easy way they were accustomed to doing, until they reached "Much Ado." The keys to the Jeep were handed over to Kara.

Protesting the lateness of the hour Jon said, "If it wasn't for the blasted noise the engine would make at this time of morning, we could have used the boat to save time. We really should have our heads examined, meandering around at this ungodly hour."

Opening a small closet, Jon brought out a navy wool pea overcoat and handed it to Kara.

"Put this on—it's much more functional than that thing you're wearing trailing around the sand, as if you were the Queen of Sheba. You must have moved part of the beach over to this side of the bay the way it was dragging."

Tears filled Kara's eyes and Jon was concerned.

"You okay, Scooter? You know I'm just teasing." Contritely Jon thinks, *something is definitely wrong here.*

Attempting to smile Kara replied, "It's all right. I'm just tired."

Slipping out of the robe she was wearing, Kara put her arms through the sleeves of the short coat that Jon was holding open. She slipped the Jeep's keys into one of the pockets and picked up her robe. The silk elegantly colorfully patterned legs of her pajamas were in direct contrast to the plain wool coat.

Jon winked, "Now that's what I call classy coordination."

Kara smiled painfully. It was hard to acknowledge Jon's humorous attempt when she was still agonizing over Roger's cruel rejection.

Yawning, with a hand over his mouth, he mumbled, "I'll catch some sleep at 'Angulus Terrarum.' I'll walk you back."

"No need, Jon." Kara insisted, but he could be as awkward as she. They set out.

By the time they reached her parent's boat, Kara was exhausted. She was sure that Jon's foot must be causing him a lot of pain and she was remorseful.

"I'm sorry, Jon, for putting you to all this trouble. It was thoughtless of me having you traipse all over the beach on my account. I apologize for being insensitive."

Jon grabbed Kara by the shoulders before she started climbing the steps to the houseboat.

"What on earth are you talking about?" His tone was angry.

Kara pushed his hands away, snapping, "Nothing that concerns you."

She scampered up to safe ground, but not before Jon had seen the tears that impulsively filled her eyes.

Walking over to "Angulus Terrarum" Jon is deep in thought. *Considering how happy Kara has seemed to be with this new love in her life, she certainly was not projecting the starry eyed symptoms associated with the disease.* Sighing, Jon continues his reflections. *Love certainly must be blind. He would hardly have credited Kara with deliberately choosing Roger what's-his-name as the man of her dreams—or any other female's dreams, come to think about it.*

CHAPTER TWO

During breakfast the next morning Kara made the announcement.

"Roger wants to go into Wisherly to contact his parents." Her mouth pursed slightly as she added, "Since the amenities here are non-existent."

Silvia Olavssen quickly looked up from spreading marmalade on her toast to signal a quizzical glance at her daughter, who deliberately ignored it. *Hmm, trouble in Paradise*, she speculated.

Kara continued, "I'll be taking Jon's Jeep, so if you need any grocery items I can pick them up at the same time."

Shortly afterwards, Kara and Roger set off.

During the drive to the village the only conversation between them was regarding the telephone call he was about to make to his parents.

"If I can get a flight out today, I'll arrange to be picked up at Gatwick." He did not look at Kara as he added, "I'll simply tell them there has been a change in plans."

Kara felt miserable sitting in the Jeep parked a short distance away from the telephone kiosk, imagining the gist of the conversation as she observed Roger's animated face and gestures. *That's right*, fumed Kara, *get away as fast as you can.*

Reaching the general store, Kara parked outside and, with nothing further to say to each other, Roger went in one direction to look around the quaint old coastal community of Wisherly while Kara went into the store with the shopping list.

Unexpectedly, upon their return to The Colony, they found Jon lying in the coarse grass at the top of the steps leading down to the beach from the cliff parking lot. He was holding "The Wall Street Journal" in his hands and Kara saw Roger's mouth fall open in surprise when he recognized which newspaper Jon was reading.

Astonished he asked, "Is that a recent copy?"

"It's today's. Picked it up this morning," Jon crisply retorted, eying Kara closely as he spoke.

"Do you mean one can actually purchase such items in that rustic backwater place we just came from?"

A frown crossed Jon's handsome, tanned face. Standing up, he folded the paper carefully before replying.

"I doubt that *you* could purchase a copy there, but my subscription is handled by the newsagents of our fine village, who often come out to deliver it personally. Since I was awake very early this morning, I decided to save them a trip."

At this he handed the newspaper to Roger and turning to Kara asked, "Do you need help getting provisions down the steps?" Kara's smile of thanks seemed to convey her approval of the way he had handled Roger.

"Yes, please. Did you manage to get any sleep this morning?" she asked quietly.

"Enough," he answered shortly.

Kara looked at Jon suspiciously.

"How did you travel into the village?"

"Took dad's car," he replied. "I went in early just as the newspapers were arriving. I didn't want to interfere with your plans, waiting for the Jeep to be returned."

Kara looked carefully at Jon. His remark had sounded unusually cautious. Did he have suspicions?

They were in the process of carrying boxes of food down to the beach when Kara spoke somewhat reluctantly.

"Do me one more favor, Jon. I need to drive home to pick up my car hopefully to get Roger to the airport as quickly as possible and if I could take the Jeep, I'd really appreciate it."

Kara ran the words back through her head when she saw Jon's raised eyebrows and quickly added ". . . since Roger's mother is ill and he needs to return to his home as soon as possible."

Jon did not comment he simply handed back the keys.

There was a meditative expression on his face.

Quietly he reminded, "You do realize tonight is New Year's Eve? The Colony always puts on a splendid bash. Do you intend missing it?"

Kara hesitated slightly before responding. "Only if Roger can't get on a flight—in which case we will have to stay in town."

She involuntarily shivered at the thought.

Pausing, Jon said casually.

"There are a couple of things I have to do in the city, so it would kill two birds with one stone if we all drove in together. That is, providing you have no objection."

He looked at Kara intently, but she bent down to deposit the box of groceries on a step, so that her expressive eyes would not betray her. They knew each other too well to fib. She was more than willing to have Jon accompany them. In fact it would be a relief to have his company.

Kara felt a little ashamed contriving the reason for Roger's hurried departure, but her parents seemed quite relieved at the news and expressed concern for Roger's mother's health. Kara's parents, had she known, were still numb from the startling announcement that without much advance preparation she had invited this special person, who was a stranger to them, home for the holidays. They were equally troubled to learn that special person was abruptly leaving, still a stranger.

Kara's mother was concerned. Kara had not looked well for the last couple of days and she resolved to have a private chat with her daughter.

It started raining heavily as they were about to leave and Kara knew from experience that the rough private road back to the main artery would be difficult to negotiate in such weather. Jon volunteered to drive, which relieved Kara from that task. As they were exchanging goodbyes, Jon walked over to her mother and spoke for a few minutes. Whatever he said made her mother smile and she nodded her head. Kara felt quite guilty drowning in this conspiracy conceived for the convenience of this man whom she had thought to be so unique just a short time ago. Her emotions were raw and ragged. She questioned the capacity to make such a wrong assessment of a person, and oh, how it hurt.

Scrutinizing Roger as he effused his deepest regrets at leaving the warm and welcoming hospitality of his hosts, Kara saw him in a new light. What a hypocrite he was. How superficial and shallow and to think that she had allowed herself to be fooled by him. It dawned on her that she was mainly to blame for this predicament. She had been the one to elevate him in her estimation. Was love truly blind or could she be so easily fooled?

Of his own volition, Roger climbed into the back seat of the Jeep, leaving Jon to stow his luggage. Kara quickly put her own tote bag in the back of the vehicle and jumped into the front seat. Jon hurriedly claimed the driver's seat, getting out of the pelting rain as quickly as possible.

Until the smooth tarmac of the main road had been reached, conversation was limited. It took Jon's expert driving ability and concentration to keep out of deep ruts and potholes worn into the original dirt road over the years. Kara was not inclined to speak to Roger. *Maybe never again, she thinks grimly.* Jon, noticing the tight lines around Kara's mouth and the serious expression on her face, drew her into conversation. She was giving herself away by the telltale clues. Before long they were talking easily and naturally, completely oblivious to the passenger in the back seat.

The swish, swish lullaby of the windshield wipers was most insidious and Kara had to keep shaking her head to remain awake. Her self-appointed responsibility was to keep an eye on Jon, to make sure he did not fall asleep at the wheel. As little sleep as she had, she was sure that he had less.

It was late afternoon when they arrived at Kara's home. The rain was still hurtling down and Kara and Jon's conversation had come to a standstill. Roger had fallen asleep and the drive back had been quiet and uneventful.

The vehicle pulled into the protective portico of Kara's home.

Roger was snoring softly.

"Wake up, old chap, we're here."

Jon pursed his mouth at Kara.

Roger started moving, shifting uncomfortably in the confined space.

Jon raised his voice.

"Bring your bag, Roger, we are ready to dash into the house. The wind is blowing the rain in, so we'll have to hurry."

Roger opened his eyes with reluctance, sluggishly reaching out for his gear.

They scrambled up the wide stairs to the entrance where the door was being inched open by Hilda, looking trim and efficient in her black and white maid's uniform.

"Terrible weather for both man and beast," she said, handing out towels she held over her arm in readiness for them.

"Janet saw you arriving from the upstairs Sitting Room and dashed downstairs. That child's training is starting to pay off." Janet was Hilda's niece. The pride was apparent in her voice.

Kara, Jon, and Roger divested themselves of their damp coats.

Roger stood beside his luggage, blinking his eyes and looking around the impressive foyer. He watched as Kara immediately walked to the telephone sitting on an ornate gold stand in the dramatic entry way. The Middleton Airport Reservation Desk confirmed with her that early evening flights were available to Gatwick. Without a word Kara handed the receiver to Roger and left him to deal with the travel arrangements.

What a relief—Roger would be leaving soon. Kara walked into the lounge where Jon was already waiting. He stood with his back to the roaring fire.

Kara rang for Hilda.

"Please have cook prepare lots of café-au-lait for the three of us— we are very tired and cold."

The chill was as much in her heart as in her physical discomfort.

"The word has already been passed on to Mrs. Taylor, Miss Kara. It shouldn't take long at all."

Sipping the steaming cups of coffee while Jon completed the telephone calls he had to make, Kara and Roger sat silent. When Kara had met Roger at the airport they drove directly to the beach where her parents were already waiting. That, he realized with a shock, was all the knowledge he had of Kara and her lifestyle.

Still slightly groggy from the sudden awakening, Roger started sneaking glances around the huge impressive room.

The cream Aubusson carpeting stretched luxuriously across the length of the room. It was a perfect foil for the pale blue silk settee upon which he sat, absently stroking. Kara, opposite him, stocking feet tucked beneath her, looked comfortable relaxing on a loveseat of the same color and fabric.

Two Waterford crystal chandeliers hung from the high ceiling and deflected prisms of light on to the several stained-glass windows hung with billowing cream silk Bischoff lace-edged draperies. Thoughtfully chosen antiques and priceless objet d'art softened the overall opulence of the room, providing an aura of quiet elegance.

Roger was incredulous. He had made a massive mistake.

Regrouping his thoughts he made the instant decision to pursue Kara again. She had been terribly upset at their break-up and she adored him unashamedly. As she was relatively inexperienced and impressionable, it should not be an insurmountable task to win her back.

Re-entering the room Jon helped himself to the hot beverage, which had been left on an exquisitely carved serving cart, pouring equal portions of the strong coffee and hot milk into a delicate porcelain cup. Balancing the cup on its matching saucer he sat down beside Kara.

"My appointment for dinner has fallen through and so, if you are agreeable and time permits, I could drive you out to the airport. It is a nasty day for driving and if you are willing we can stop off for a bite to eat. I know just the place."

Speaking only to Kara, he waited for her reply.

Jon's thoughtfulness was very touching and Kara immediately agreed to his offer. Even taking into account the need for cautious travel, there would still be time to fit in a meal.

★ ★ ★

The Black Bull Inn in Malton was a tad out of the way and, knowing this, Kara did not comment upon it when they were shown into a private dining room with a glass domed roof. Under more normal weather conditions the dome would be open to display the evening stars. As they were being seated, a fire was lit in the mosaic tiled fireplace. The small area was tastefully furnished and the fire created pleasant warmth.

The damask tablecloth and napkins, silver cutlery, Spode china, and engraved crystal goblets spoke for themselves. They seemed to include Roger in their conversation. The overall trappings of affluence visibly affected him.

Each of the three courses served were perfect. When dessert was offered from a lace covered serving salver, Roger was in a state of euphoria. Noting Roger's behavior with distaste, Kara was pleased that she was able to keep her emotions under control. Lingering over coffee, the young, attentive water boy returned and shyly held out the day's menu toward Jon.

"Please, may I have your autograph?"

Jon looked at Kara and smiled. Obliging, he saw a delighted grin emerge as the young man read out aloud.

"It's all in the game. Best regards, Jonathan Williams."

He thanked Jon profusely before rushing off with his prize.

They could hear his excited voice calling out. "I've got Jon Williams' autograph. Look at this!"

Carefully setting his coffee cup upon the saucer Roger asked incredulously, "THE Jon Williams, the Manchester United center forward?"

Jon nodded his head adding tersely, "Former."

Roger was awed. Looking away Kara felt a sense of relief in admitting what a snob he was proving to be. Roger was an opportunist and she was a nitwit. Jon, for all the fame and idolization he had received during his soccer victories still remained easygoing and unaffected. Kara felt fortunate to call him her friend.

Studying Jon's face from across the table Kara smiled inwardly. If she told Jon how good-looking he was and how his athletic physique attracted admiring glances, he would no doubt chuckle at the compliment—and ignore it. Flattery was like water on a duck's back to him. Recognizing insincere and phony accolades had been part of shaking off the bogus soccer fans and Kara's admiration had increased watching Jon deal courteously with them. Jon's deep blue eyes appeared to be scrutinizing and assessing Roger with the same objectivity.

They were almost ready to leave when the maitre d' came over and stood beside Kara.

"Lady Bassenthorpe is on the phone and would like to speak with you, madam. Do you wish to take the call here or in private?"

Jon's grin was from ear to ear. Oh, the wretch, he had set all this up with the intent of teaching Roger a lesson. Lady Bassenthorpe, who was Jon's godmother, was devoted to him. She remembered every special occasion he had to celebrate with a card and expensive gift. She also visited him whenever possible. In addition, she was also willing to do almost anything he asked.

Kara said she would take the call in private.

Returning to the table, Kara saw a look on Roger's face that was difficult to fathom, but she could see he was hanging on to Jon's every word. It appeared that Jon had difficulty hiding his distaste. Looking over at Kara as she was seated once again Jon stated.

"While you were gone I filled Roger in with some chit-chat—mainly about the people at The Colony who he has been rubbing shoulders with for the past couple of days. I'm sure he found it very boring stuff."

He moved his shoulders in an almost apologetic manner.

Kara lowered her eyelids. He really was rubbing it in.

Roger's face had turned quite sickly as he once again realized that he had made another enormous error of judgment. He had just written off some of the most influential families in England. He immediately resolved to intensify his efforts to win Kara back.

It was still raining heavily when they returned to the Jeep. Roger, intent on repairing his relationship with Kara, feverishly sought her opinion on a variety of subjects. He referred to the good times they had spent together in an effort to revive fond memories and emotions. Roger's questions were answered briefly and to the point. Kara sat in the front seat, with the back of her head to Roger for the remainder of the journey to the airport. She would burst if she had to tolerate his presence any longer. Kara gave a sigh of relief to finally make out the airport tower. Rain was playing a staccato on the windshield, distorting the view and reducing visibility. Stopping the Jeep at the entrance to the Check-in section of the terminal allowed Kara, and Roger with his luggage, to hurry inside and get out of the rain.

By the time Jon joined them in the small waiting area Roger was in a spirited conversation with Kara.

"Please excuse us for a few minutes, Jonathan. The plane will be leaving very soon and I have some personal matters to discuss with Kara."

Jon said looking intently at Kara, "I'll be in the cocktail lounge, unless you would prefer that I stay?"

Kara shook her head.

"I'll join you shortly. Thanks."

Jon briefly shook hands with Roger and with a slight frown on his face, walked away.

Left alone, Roger pulled Kara into a corner behind a large decorative plant. He took both her hands into his own, holding them very firmly.

"You know I'm going to miss you enormously, darling, in the next two weeks before school resumes, but I will call you every night. I can't imagine how I thought I could survive without you. It was very foolish of me to act so hastily."

He bent forward to kiss Kara, but she hurriedly took a step backward and calmly disengaged her hands from his.

In a quiet, trembling voice she said.

"If you were the last person on earth I could not bring myself to speak to you again and I'm filled with revulsion and loathing at the thought of your touch. I gave you my love unconditionally, Roger, and you turned it into a mockery, a cheap ambiguous commodity. You have hurt me terribly and I won't ever forget the lesson you have taught me."

Without waiting for his response or reaction, Kara hurried away, showing straight shoulders in the swinging fur collared coat. Tears streamed down her cheeks. It was the first time she had been deliberately honest to the point of insult. She wept as she buried the false illusions that brought to an end an episode in her life she vowed would not be repeated. Ever again!

Jon was leaning against the outside wall of the cocktail lounge that bore the hanging sign "One for the Road" watching as Kara walked quickly in his direction, blowing her nose and wiping her eyes. It took Kara by surprise to see Jon waiting outside the bar. She had hoped to have her emotions under control.

"You okay?" Jon asked.

Kara affirmed with a nod.

"Sure you wouldn't care for a brandy before we set off, you seem a little shaken?"

Kara turned down Jon's offer, sniffing.

"If we make good time, we can be back at The Colony before midnight. I'd like to try to do that."

Conversation lagged as they began the return journey. The rain had turned into hail while they were in the terminal and driving had become even more hazardous. Directional road signs were almost impossible to decipher and visibility forced a reduction in speed to

15 kilometers. Getting back to The Colony tonight just might not be possible. Jon quickly glanced at his watch.

"It's almost ten o' clock and we seem to be stuck with this rotten weather. In fact it seems to be worsening; the defroster is barely functioning. What are your thoughts?"

Kara's home was not far from where they were. Optimistically she suggested, "Let's go back to the house and wait for an improvement. Given better conditions we might be able to make it to The Colony before midnight."

They opened the windows a little to try to clear the fogged windshield and sleet came through, settling on their hair and clothing. Kara used her scarf to wipe the condensation from the car's windows as they traveled. The sleet had changed to rain by the time they reached Kara's home and once there they again transferred their damp coats to Hilda who was waiting for them.

"Do you expect to be leaving again soon, Miss Kara?" she asked, raising her eyes in despair.

"It depends on the weather. By the way, aren't you spending the evening with your family, Hilda?"

Kara and Jon were rubbing their damp hair with the towels supplied by Hilda.

"They are on their way, Miss Kara. In fact they should be here any time now. Janet will be leaving with me. It's the weather that's delaying them. Is there anything I can do for you? Millie will be here if you need her. The rest of the staff have been given two days off."

Kara shook her head.

"Jon and I are waiting for a break in the weather. If that happens we will go out to Wisherly to celebrate New Year with the crowd there. If not, I'll give him a lively game of Chess."

Scathingly Jon retorted, "You really like to heckle me, don't you?"

Jon quit college when offered the soccer contract and admitted that the thought of further academic study was abhorrent to him. He was not cut out for it. His father had made his fortune in the building industry and fortunately recognized his son's aversion to 'being held captive by a desk.'

Kara, on the other hand, had been brought up in a more cerebral household. She enjoyed the lively discussions, the challenge of the debate and the opportunity to question and air her points of view.

From an early age she had the privilege of listening to the widely conflicting arguments and ideas expressed by people from all walks of life. It had been an interesting learning experience—exciting and thought provoking. She had become accustomed to participating, listening hard, and speaking confidently and quietly.

Kara's father taught her the game of Chess as a child and she continued to play whenever an opportunity presented itself. It had become a teasing point to challenge Jon, who loathed sitting still for more than a few minutes. Sitting quietly, planning strategies and moves in one's head for no sensible purpose, for hours at a stretch, was something he considered a waste of time.

Jon shook his head as he followed Kara into the large rumpus room, where she turned on the automatic gas jet to light the oak logs in the large fireplace. She prowled around twitchily moving items from one place to another, closing drapes and demonstrating a restlessness that Jon found quite unnerving. He could watch no longer. He stood up from the chair and walking into the library took two crystal goblets from the tall stained-glass Edwardian cabinet and poured a healthy amount of brandy into each. Without a word he handed a glass to Kara and sat on the floor beside the fireplace, with his back against the variegated plaid settee, watching her. Kara, balancing on the arm of a large burgundy leather reclining chair, was swishing the amber liquid around with a preoccupied expression on her face.

Jon's subdued voice interrupted Kara's thoughts.

"Would you rather I left? We obviously can't get back to Wisherly tonight. It would be foolhardy to try. I can come back again in the morning to take you there, if you wish, but in any case I'll phone to check what you want to do. You are obviously not in the mood for company right now."

Standing up and putting the brandy snifter on the fireplace mantle, he walked along a hallway into the foyer searching for his leather jacket that Hilda had taken from him. Quickly Kara joined him there and without a word took his hand and led him back into the room from which they had just left with its cheery fire, comfortable furnishings, and incandescent lighting.

Thinking, *my dearest friend, my confidante, my defender,* Kara faced Jon with an apologetic expression on her face.

"I'm sorry, Jon, it was not my intention to so rudely shut you out. Much has happened during the last few months, with the most demoralizing part taking place within the last couple of days. It is just beginning to sink in."

A frown crossed Jon's face, leaving troubled blue eyes examining Kara.

In retrospect, while waiting for Kara to return from Wisherly with Roger, Jon had mentally reviewed the clues he had been picking up over the past two days indicating that things were not going well between Kara and Roger. At this exciting stage in her life, Kara should be glowing with happiness, but she was not, and this greatly bothered him. Roger, in Jon's estimation, did not appear to be the right match for Kara. He had an air of bored condescension that Jon found irritating, but, more importantly, Roger's blasé attitude toward Kara was uncalled-for and unacceptable.

Jon shifted his gaze past Kara.

Still, the problem was not his—Kara would seek his advice if needed.

Cutting through his thoughts Kara asked impatiently, "Are you listening to me, Jon? You seem to be off into a world of your own."

Shaking his head Jon took hold of Kara's hand saying, "Can you bring yourself to talk about what is worrying you? It sometimes helps."

Before long they were laughing at their misinterpretation of the whole situation.

Kara thanked Jon for the astute way he had taken revenge on Roger by putting him in his place in such a gratifying method by revealing just how elite The Colony inhabitants were. They needed to be exonerated if just for Kara's peace of mind. She had not realized Jon had it in him.

Jon laughed in response.

"I'm pleased you feel that way because I started to have guilt pangs. When we tramped the beach back and forth last night, gosh, no it was this morning—it seems so long ago—I intuitively felt that Roger had been a cad and decided on my own method of reprimand, devious as it was. I recognized him as a snob, but held my tongue for your sake until I could do so no longer. I decided that the punishment should fit the crime, so to speak, and that it be one that would leave a lasting impression. The only problem was that when I saw you crying after saying goodbye to the Boy-o, I wondered if I had done the right thing."

He glanced warily at Kara.

She smiled slightly.

"I too finally came to the conclusion that Roger was a social climber, but it took a while to grasp. I wanted to believe he loved me for who I am. It was devastating to discover I could be written off so easily. When, thanks to your tactics, he realized his faux pas, I was so hurt and angry that I let him have it at the airport."

Jon raised his eyes toward the high ceiling.

"You let him have WHAT Kara? In public?"

She burst out laughing.

"Oh, what a nasty mind you have. I should have said that in no uncertain language I informed Roger how loathsome and contemptible I found him. I was crying because I really didn't think I had the courage to tell him that face-to-face."

Jon roared with laughter. They continued to compare their impressions, sipping the brandy and relaxing comfortably until the clock in the foyer began striking midnight.

Pulling Jon to his feet, Kara rushed him along the hall to the foyer where a piece of anthracite and a slice of bread were waiting on a small brass tray. Pushing the tray into his hands, she gently shoved him out of the front door.

Performing this had occurred with such speed that the Westminster chimes of the grandfather clock had not completed bonging. Feeling a little foolish Kara opened the door a few minutes later and looked outside, eying a disbelieving Jon. Shivering from his unexpected foray outdoors, dressed as he was in light clothing, he handed the tray back to Kara as he stepped across the threshold.

"Sorry! For whatever I did—am I forgiven?"

He rubbed his hands together and mused in a puzzled tone.

"Next time a love affair ends I'm going to make sure I'm nowhere near you. You do very strange things."

Kara smiled ruefully. They were on familiar ground—they could badger each other without fear of retribution. They were almost like brother and sister.

She put the tray down on a shelf of the gold leaf étagère and grabbed Jon in an emotional hug.

"Happy New Year and thanks."

Tenderly Jon kissed Kara on the mouth, a soft non-threatening gesture.

"Happy New Year to you too. No thanks are necessary, it was a pleasure."

They grinned in unison.

"I thought you knew this was a Norwegian custom. It's traditional. The coal and bread assures another year of shelter and food."

Jon shook his head in disbelief.

Kara's father, Gustav Olavssen, was born in Norway of parents related to Norwegian royalty. He was independently wealthy and had amassed an immense fortune by the age of thirty through his own efforts after using the initial stake from a trust fund. In his younger days, his blond hair and strikingly good looks caught the attention of Silvia LaBarbera. The seeds of love were planted at their first meeting, even though the balance of wealth at that time tipped the scales entirely in Silvia's direction. As the only child of parents who came from a long line of prosperous Italian shipping magnates, Silvia was accustomed to getting what she wanted. Suitors courted her not only because of her incomparable beauty, but also for the considerable wealth that would one day be hers. Gus Olavssen was drawn to her by the serene and charming manner she projected. From her first smile he was captivated and from the discreet look of admiration she paid him, her ocean green eyes ensnared and claimed him forever.

For years Jon's father had been involved in lucrative ventures with Gus Olavssen. Growing up Jon had become very familiar with Kara's background and heritage. Wealth she would never need to strive for. It was already hers.

Kara sighed.

"I wish we could contact The Colony. This is the first time I've missed celebrating New Year there. It feels so strange. I hope they aren't worrying about us."

Jon smiled.

"I warned your mother that if we had a problem getting Roger on a flight that we would stay in town and get back to Wisherly as soon as we could."

"Smart Ass!" Kara said affectionately.

Settling down in front of the fire once more with a glass of chilled champagne, Jon started bringing Kara up-to-date on a couple of ventures he was contemplating. He had to start doing something with his life, he had wasted enough time.

Kara was thrilled. This was the old Jon talking and her shining eyes concentrated on his face as he spoke.

Apparently when Jon reached his 21ˢᵗ year, the property from his grandmother's estate became legally his. At the time he learned of this bequest he was riding on the crest of his career. He was the acknowledged "Golden Boy" of soccer and he was doing what he loved most. The formal notification from the solicitors meant little to him; so much so that he had almost forgotten about it. It was during his worst days after the accident, when he believed that life held little hope for the future, that he started thinking about putting Grandma Sophia's property to use.

He went out to look at it a few months earlier.

Kara felt a surge of excitement and expectation. She could hardly wait to learn more. Jon had so much potential, she would back him to the hilt in whatever he decided to tackle; she had so much confidence in him.

Knowing he had Kara's full attention, Jon shifted his position, leaning over to refill their champagne flutes. He yawned and covered his mouth.

"I'm exhausted and you really don't want to know all this."

An impish twinkle was in his eyes.

Kara raised the full glass of wine menacingly.

"Don't dare, Jon Williams."

Smiling broadly, Jon continued.

"I've decided to breed Welsh ponies. I've always loved the animals. They are of rugged stock with an independent nature and I plan on crossing some breeds with them to elevate the line. I might also branch out into raising quarter horses or Arabians. Grandma Sophia's farmland is the perfect spot to start."

The more he talked, the more enthusiastic he became and Kara was swept into the fervor. She knew nothing about horses, but believing that if Jon thought he could be successful in this area, she was convinced he would.

Kara and Jon talked well into the early morning hours. It always came as a surprise to find how swiftly the time passed when she was with Jon and tonight, having so much to share, was no exception. The time had flown.

Tired and stiff they decided to call it a night. Jon accepted Kara's invitation to stay in a guestroom. Kara, in a surprisingly contented frame of mind, fell fast asleep almost as soon as her head touched the pillow.

The next day they returned to the beach and spent a couple of days assisting in closing up the houseboats. Winter had made its entrance and the seals and cormorants were commandeering the bay area again. They made their presence known at this time of year. Once the spring weather was established the houseboats would be opened up again.

✳ ✳ ✳

"I brought you a cup of coffee—we all seem to be pooped out."

Kara's startled eyes flew open.

Kenneth's father stood before her holding a Styrofoam cup. She struggled into a sitting position and haltingly took the cup from his hand.

For a disoriented moment she wondered who this man was.

"Oh, thank you. I need this—I must have dozed off for a few minutes."

Sluggish, as if she were two different people, living in two different worlds, Kara sipped the coffee. She ached all over. She truly despised Roger. She had never admitted this before and the hurt that she had suffered and the loathing she could conjure up at the thought of him, rushed back incredibly easily.

Kara recalled with satisfaction that during the final semester before graduation arrived, when Roger pursued her relentlessly, she avoided his overtures determinedly. Her resistance to his charms finally paid off.

It was a welcomed relief when Graduation Day arrived at the University of Durham. Kara's parents, and Jon with his, were the only guests invited by Kara to the ceremony at the prestigious college, which had been the county seat of learning since the late sixteenth century. The baccalaureate service was held in the famous Norman-built

Cathedral next door and the moving sermon given by the Most Reverend John Billings struck a chord in Kara's heart.

During the next few months, Kara remembered, she saw very little of Jon as he threw himself into activating the breeding farm. She understood how intriguing and compelling it was for him and envied his dedication and zealousness.

A general announcement came over the Public Address system in the airport lounge and Kara listened to it half-heartedly. Get me on the plane, please, she reproved. I am more than ready to leave.

Kara was starting to feel feverish. She could handle adversity and challenge, but she seemed to be stuck with her memories, which refused to be ignored. They crowded her thoughts. How did one turn off one's brain?

Kara put her hands up to her forehead. She had never experienced migraine, but the throbbing that persisted in her head seemed suspiciously close to the real thing. She was reluctant to close her eyes; it encouraged the return to the past.

Despite her attempts, the return was inevitable.

CHAPTER THREE

Kara was graduated from the University of Durham with a master's degree in business administration. With the degree in hand she realized, after working in various sections of her father's offices, that she did not want to spend the rest of her life dedicated to that type of work. Had those four accelerated college years been wasted? She was like flotsam on Cormorant Bay, drifting back and forth hoping to find a secure anchorage. Her only reprieve was in knowing there was no urgent need to rush into making other decisions. In voicing her reservations and concerns to her parents, they informed her they were confident that she was resourceful enough to find where her niche in life was. Until then she could rely upon them for their full support and assistance. Kara wished she had their confidence.

She could identify with Jon, remembering how depressed he had been when going through his "down" period. She had no aspirations or ambitions and with her wheels spinning could find no solution to the quandary she was in.

She had to go out to the farm and talk to him.

Kara realized that Jon was not giving her his full attention. They were sitting on a fence that surrounded a field of mares with their new offspring.

"Daddy offered me a permanent position as assistant to his Chief Executive Officer, but—."

In the middle of the sentence Jon climbed down from the fence. Walking over to a foal he lifted a back hoof and ran his fingers around it, gently probing.

With a look of satisfaction on his face, he returned to Kara and placed a tiny pebble onto her palm.

She had lost her train of thought and was finding it impossible to maintain a conversation at all in this venue. It seemed to Kara that she had never seen Jon appear so cheerful and contented. She felt happy for him, but it also brought a depressing sense of isolation. She should not have come. Jon was not a magician and he could not be expected to solve all her problems.

Sighing wistfully Kara jumped down from the fence.

She said in a tone reflecting more confidence than she felt.

"By the way, I am thinking of looking for a job down south somewhere, probably London."

Why did she say that? She had not even considered it until the statement popped out.

Jon looked at her lopsidedly and as if just realizing that she was his guest, squeezed her arm.

"Let's have lunch at 'The Five Sheaves' and you can tell me all about it."

Kara's face brightened and before they had reached the cozy little pub they were chatting normally once more.

The visit to Jon did make Kara aware that she had to resolve her problems without his help; he was much too busy with the farm. It would be selfish of her to distract him unnecessarily. It was not as if she could offer to work alongside him—she was completely useless around the animals; she would need directions for performing even the simplest of tasks.

It was a source of admiration to Kara that Jon had found the courage and conviction to make the commitment to an enterprise that took most of his time, money, and effort. There were no guaranteed results, yet he knew that raising horses and farming were exactly what he wanted to do.

Kara wished fervently that she too could reach a decision about her future.

Dedicated she could be, if there was a cause.

A month later Kara was still in a restless, uncertain frame of mind when she saw Jon's sister, Jackie, at a party to celebrate James and Renata Williams' 32nd wedding anniversary. Friends had offered their country estate, 'Foxton Hall,' for the occasion.

Jackie had recently returned from another of her frequent visits to America and Kara was anxious to talk to her. D'Arcy had accompanied Jackie for this special family celebration. It was not until after the lengthy five course meal had finished that Kara saw Jackie going into the conservatory, where after-dinner drinks were being served.

She noticed D'Arcy talking to Jon in the library and took advantage of the opportunity to get Jackie alone for a short time. D'Arcy usually stayed very close to Jackie when he visited the north of England—the hinterlands as he referred to her part of the country. It was probably because he was not familiar with many of the people he met and had little in common with them or their way of life, which was more rural than urban. He was always dressed fashionably and impeccably and Kara could see how well Jackie and he were paired. It was obvious that he was very proud of his beautiful younger wife and lavished her with attention.

Kara sighed. It must be satisfying to know that the person one is in love with returns that love unconditionally. Immediately quashing the thought, Kara's mouth tightened. There was no one in the world who could penetrate her defenses. She would not allow it!

Kara and Jackie had never been very close, there was almost eight years difference in their ages and their interests were quite disparate, but even so they genuinely liked each other.

Kara sat down beside Jackie and said without preamble.

"Jackie, now that I've graduated from the U. of D. I am seriously considering a move. I really want to get away for a while and I wondered if there was a position open with Frazier's."

Jackie looked at Kara in astonishment.

"You surprise me, Kara. This is none of my business, but do you have an ulterior motive for wanting to get away? You have always seemed so content with your life here."

Kara looked down at her fingers clasped together.

"I really need to get away for a while and I hope my parents will understand. They know I don't intend remaining in daddy's business for the rest of my life, but they are probably not prepared for a sudden move on my part."

She smiled rather sorrowfully.

"I haven't been able to settle down since that fiasco with Roger ended. I think a change of scenery will help me get over the affair more quickly."

Jackie studied Kara's unhappy face closely and held back a smile.

"Kara, stop trying to play on my sympathy. I am concerned about how your parents will take news of this nature."

Kara paused.

"They probably will have a fit at first, but if there's a position available at Frazier's, they most likely could accept that and feel more secure knowing that you were there to turn to in case of emergencies."

She stressed the last word.

"Besides, for providing this opportunity, I would be eternally grateful to you."

Jackie eyed Kara nonplussed before asking.

"Is there a particular area in which you are interested? I need help on this."

Registering a doubtful look on her face Kara responded, "I graduated with an MBA, so I suppose it's logical to stay within this discipline, but I'd be indebted for anything you found suitable and available."

Jackie looked at Kara curiously.

"No promises, but I'll do my best. D'Arcy and I have a full schedule for a couple of weeks, so it could be a while before I can get back to you. In the meantime, if you are serious, you should start preparing your parents for a possible change in your work plans."

This was a good enough start and pleased Kara. Jackie could be counted on. She did not make idle promises. Kara decided not to say anything to her parents at this point; it was a little too early.

In a happier frame of mind, Kara, went into the billiards room, temporarily transformed into a disco. The music was bouncing off the walls and even great-grandma Williams was tapping her foot, watching as the adults happily mixed with youngsters old enough to join in the festivities. Young danced with old, accomplished dancers united with toe stompers until a change of music separated them into age groups again. It was like looking through a human kaleidoscope. An ever-changing picture.

It was a carefree, happy occasion.

Kara joined a group shrugging their way through a popular hit number and suddenly realized how much she had missed dancing. Roger had shunned it. Jon had avoided it after his accident and spontaneously Kara allowed herself to become a part of the rhythm. She was naturally graceful and a lifetime of ballet, tap, and social dancing had given Kara what "Miss Tessie," the professional dancing instructor, called "a natural stage presence." It lent an uninhibited intensity to her movements. The floor area, as if by widespread acceptance, cleared for the remainder of Kara's solo performance. Spontaneous applause greeted Kara at the close of the number.

A trifle embarrassed Kara walked through the French doors, which led out to a lush lawn and a rose garden, decorated for the occasion with large Japanese globes of light. Her cheeks flamed as much from the exertion of the dancing display as from the feeling of mortification, which overcame her afterwards. Over the years this type of display should have become second nature to Kara. It was a compulsion she was powerless to resist. Dancing, it seemed, was in her blood. So why did she feel like a crass exhibitionist, vowing not to place herself in a similar situation again. Knowing full well, she would.

A quiet voice, coming from behind, startled her.

"I would applaud that as poetry in motion."

She immediately recognized the voice. Remorse was written over Kara's face as she turned to look at Jon.

"Why do I do this kind of thing?" she asked ruefully.

"If it means anything, I thought you were brilliant."

With a woeful moan, Kara threw herself into Jon's arms.

"Hey, hey, aren't we being a little dramatic about this?" he responded, patting her quivering shoulders. She stood motionless, allowing him to pat her back reassuringly.

"I must have looked such an idiot," she whispered, a sob in her voice.

"Not at all! You looked just as you did when you danced for us after performing in the Christmas Pantomime. You must remember entertaining relatives and friends at the parties held at your grandparents' home? Everyone had to do something, even if it was something simple like singing a carol or reciting a poem. I always detested that part," Jon confessed.

Kara laughed at the remembrance as they reminisced.

Without a word Jon took Kara's hand and led her back into the disco. To a slow dance number Jon automatically took Kara into his arms and proceeded to move around the floor. His gait was uneven, but Kara expertly masked his steps. Knowing how diligently Jon had avoided any kind of public attention, Kara was astonished by this display, even though they were among friends and relatives. Who could ask for a better friend? He had rescued her so many times.

At the end of the dance, Kara thanked Jon and squeezed his hand. He reciprocated in the same way, saying, "I really must dash, I hadn't intended staying for so long. Two of my horses are being shown at the 'Great Yorkshire' agricultural show in Harrogate in about seven hours," he wryly noted, looking at his watch.

"There's a lot to be done, in little time. Three of the college students who help with the chores will already have started the preparations, but they need supervision and that is where I come in," he grinned at Kara, "and a good place to go out."

Kara made a face.

"Sorry for delaying you, Jon. Now I feel guilty."

Reverting to their childhood format Jon said, "Golly, Kara, I wouldn't have missed seeing you making a spectacle of yourself for anything."

With a twinkle in his eyes, caused by the indignant expression on Kara's face, Jon walked away to say goodbye to his parents before leaving.

After chatting and dancing with a few friends and relatives for about an hour, it seemed to Kara that the effervescent sizzle of the evening had suddenly popped, like a balloon. For her, the celebration had ended.

After saying goodbye to Aunt Renata and Uncle James, Kara kissed her parents goodnight and set off for home in her own car. She planned on getting home and settled down in bed before her parents, who were using the chauffeured Rolls Royce, returned. The conversation with Jackie was fresh in her mind and she was eager to mull it over before going to sleep. Already she was both anxious and eager for Jackie's response.

✳ ✳ ✳

CHAPTER FOUR

Kara had not realized how much she was depending upon a favorable response from Jackie. Working four days a week for her father kept her busy most of the time, but at home she jumped whenever the telephone rang.

Three weeks to the day, Jackie phoned.

Attempting to be optimistic she informed Kara, "There's nothing in the financial field we can offer right now, but there are still a couple of possibilities which I'm having checked out."

Kara tried to avoid a feeling of despondency at this news and aswered.

"I am serious about making a change in my life and I was thinking of getting in touch with Uncle Peter in Toronto. He has a brokerage house there and he just may have some suggestions and connections."

This announcement took Jackie by surprise. Kara certainly was attacking this situation with a determination she had not hitherto credited her with. It was not a lengthy conversation.

Kara was disappointed that Jackie's response was not more optimistic and Jackie tried to refrain from projecting pessimism.

Returning from the library a couple of days later, Kara found a note left by Hilda asking her to check the message from Jackie on the answering machine. It must be good news. Kara was excited. She immediately returned the call. Jackie was in a meeting and so Kara left a return message. Kara's imagination took off. It did not seem likely that a position would be available in the financial area and Kara crossed her fingers hoping that the reason for Jackie's phone call proved to be favorable.

Jackie was in a hurry when she called again and in an unusually abrupt manner stated, "I have to return to a meeting right away, but would you be interested in taking a job as Office Manager with an agency in Southern California? They work on behalf of people with disabilities?"

She paused for a moment before continuing. "Think about it. I must rush. I'll call you after dinner tonight."

Before Kara could reply, Jackie hung up.

Kara was stunned. The USA? She knew no one there. Why on earth would Jackie think she would be interested? It was just after three o' clock in the afternoon. Unable to approach her parents with such radical and unexpected information, which as yet was too vague, Kara decided to drive out to Wisherly.

She changed into running shoes and a zipper-front camel and white Valencia warm-up suit. She informed Millie, who was dusting the lounge, where she would be and picked up the flask of freshly made coffee from the kitchen. Kara left with her troubled thoughts.

Kara had not been to The Colony for several weeks. She had not kept track of the tide table, but as soon as she reached The Esplanade that ran for a couple of miles along the coastline, she could see immediately how far the water had advanced. It was starting to climb the ribbed skeletal frame of the large shipwrecked sloop, caught in a freak storm years earlier. It was also approaching the huge craggy rock formations, which provided the impetus for children's playground fantasies—including hers when she and Jon played there so long ago.

Pulling the car over to the curb, Kara sat and watched the incoming waves contentedly. The water, inky black, moving powerfully and sensuously in its liquidity, gathered momentum urging the waves to reach out to the shore. Already the boat's outline was submerged and the water was swirling around the rocks on the inward journey, rushing to their foaming resting place on the waiting sand. She decided there was no point in traveling the remaining few miles to Cormorant Bay as much of its beach would be inaccessible. It was November and the tides and chilly weather conditions would both be making their presence felt in the little harbor.

Wisherly, at this time of year, was predictably deserted and when Kara pulled into the main parking area, usually occupied by summer tourists, she was not surprised to find herself alone. Locking the car she set off along the sidewalk, which followed the seawall, shoving her hands into the pockets of her jacket. Already she could feel the nip in the air. The other side of the main street was deserted. Amusement arcades, gift stores, and small cafes that catered to the seasonal visitors were closed. This was the extent to which Wisherly accommodated its unsolicited tourists. The remainder of the village went on with its activities uninterruptedly, summer and winter.

Even when summer was at its height, Wisherly remained fairly secluded. There was not much for young day-trippers to do here, and they soon became bored. There was a pub that served bar meals and had four guest rooms for summer rental. The only other accommodation available was a small family-owned hotel. Like the public house, it was an inconvenient distance from the beach and this deterred potential guests to a large extent.

When Kara was growing up it had been a treat for the young people of the beach colony to make the expedition into town. Sometimes they begged a ride, but often they set off early in the day and walked along the beach perimeter and around the rocky promontory. The promontory divided Cormorant Bay from the wide expanse of public beach known to The Colony residents as "Wisherly Side."

Ice cream was usually the group's favorite reward but occasionally, if they arrived there around lunchtime, they would buy fish and chips wrapped in layers of newspaper. Mingling with the tourists they contentedly munched their meal walking along the promenade, fortifying their inner needs in readiness for the long walk back. Occasionally someone from The Colony would arrange to pick up the group of children at a certain time, but usually it was an excursion that took most of the day. This was particularly true if distractions sidetracked them. Climbing and playing around the rock formations, watching the 'Punch and Judy' show on the beach, or playing games in the Arcades were favorites. The ultimate detour was the trip to the Italian Gardens where they tried to catch frisky minnows darting in and out of the water lilies that surrounded the lake.

Their parents did not usually object to these forays; they stayed in a group and usually behaved sensibly. Besides, after one of these trips they remained close to the houseboats "recharging their batteries" for at least a few days. Model, though somewhat lethargic children for a short time.

Walking briskly along "the front" as it was known by the local residents Kara smiled to herself at the memories. The bracing aroma of the salt air, wafted by the flirtatious breeze, rushed to caress her face. She could feel her skin beginning to tingle. Arriving at the bus depot, which signaled the end of the pavement, Kara crossed the road and started walking back to her car. She could see the ocean, but the sight of the beach was obscured by the seawall.

It was not until the parking lot was reached that Kara realized not once had she thought about Jackie's news, or the kindest way to approach her parents. Perhaps that was just as well. Until she learned more, there was no point in worrying or jumping to conclusions. Settling into her car, Kara poured a cup of coffee. It was hot and the mug served to warm her hands comfortingly as she sat on the front seat admiring the view.

Lowering her side of the window slightly, she could hear the waves gently slapping at the seawall. Kara appreciatively took in the panoramic scene, noting a couple of tankers out on the horizon and seagulls coming further inland to forage for food. Coming here had provided the tranquility she sought. She was ready to hear whatever Jackie had to say.

CHAPTER FIVE

Jackie phoned Kara a little after nine that evening. She took the call in her bedroom. Protesting Kara's barrage of questions, Jackie made a halt.

"Please bear with me for a while until I explain the events that have led up to the suggestion made earlier in the day. Sorry I was so abrupt, but I wanted to have you consider another possibility and give you thinking space. Did it shock you?"

"Yes, of course. I was quite unprepared. California is not exactly the neighboring county." Kara responded.

A lengthy explanation followed and Kara saw a side of Jackie that she had not observed before:

For several years Jackie had traveled the western route of the United States, doing business in Seattle, San Francisco, Los Angeles and the San Diego areas which had become surprisingly cosmopolitan. The inhabitants wanted, in fact demanded, access to fashions at least at the same time that New York and the east coast had them introduced. She had found the people less urbane than their counterparts on the east coast, but they had a zest for living and an exuberance that she found appealing. New Yorkers, on the other hand, were quite a different breed—more like Londoners.

Three months earlier Jackie had been carefully sunning herself on the loggia of The Beverley Hills Hotel, where she usually stayed when in the Los Angeles area, and noticed a young woman sketching. She had seen her the previous morning doing the same thing and wondered what she was doing. She was not using any subjects and Jackie was interested. She walked over to her and stood behind the easel, looking directly at the artist rather than her work.

"Forgive me for being rude, but you have been concentrating so seriously on what you are doing that I am overcome with curiosity. What is it you are drawing?"

Pausing, the young woman in the shorts and T-shirt passed a hand over her forehead and smoothed a lock of auburn hair back into place before responding.

Looking at Jackie, her suspicious expression changed to curiosity.

"Are you one of the models here for the show?"

"No. I'm here on business." Jackie answered.

After chatting for a few minutes, the girl whose name was Angela, decided to offer some information.

"My parents own a vineyard in Temecula, which is just starting to become recognized throughout California for the terrific wines we produce. We pleaded with the hotel's general manager to allow us to provide our wines at the fashion show as a promotional venture. I'm here to promote."

She grinned and handed over a couple of sketches of clothing she had been working on to Jackie. Jackie looked them over with a professional eye. She was impressed.

"Do you have a design portfolio?"

Angela looked surprised.

"I don't think you'd call it a portfolio. There are hundreds stuffed into a storage box under my bed."

They both laughed. A rising surge of expectancy grew in Jackie.

"Is there a chance I can see them?"

"Why?" A suspicious look crossed Angela's face.

"We may be able to come to a mutually beneficial arrangement."

Angela stood up abruptly.

"I have to go and change. I'll be serving refreshments soon."

She quickly gathered her equipment together, giving Jackie a quizzical look as she left the area.

Already possibilities were pulsing through Jackie's mind. She mentally scolded herself for not presenting herself professionally. That would be rectified at the next opportunity.

After the fashion show Jackie sought Angela.

"Would it be possible to visit you in Temecula to examine more of your sketches?"

Angela's glance was distrustful.

Jackie continued, "The business, for which I am head buyer, is also owned by my husband. We trade internationally. We are considering starting a tropical line of clothing, for use in winter by our clientele who gravitate to the sunspots on the map. Their complaints are that they can seldom purchase quality off-season clothing, which they demand."

Jackie handed over a white linen-like business card elaborately embossed in black and gold with the words "Frazier's of Bond Street, London." Angela glanced at the card and pushed it into a pocket. "Why don't the people buy the clothing in the places where they are vacationing, surely it would be available there? It should be a source of revenue."

Jackie liked this investigative questioning. She explained.

"When one is as rich and famous as the people for whom we design, it is a crime, in their eyes, to be seen at a social function wearing off-the-rack clothing. Heaven forbid that someone else is seen wearing the same ensemble. It would be a cause célèbre and it is a situation they endeavor to avoid at all costs."

Angela smiled. It sounded very snobby, but—for the jet set—logical. Angela dug into another pocket and brought out a pack of business cards fastened together by a rubber band. She handed one to Jackie. It listed the vineyard's address.

Angela's voice was somber.

"Let me phone you about this. I need to talk it over with my parents first."

She hoped the eagerness had been eliminated from her voice. She didn't want to build things up, only to be disappointed

Two days later Jackie arrived at the "Fruitful Harvest" winery located in Temecula in a hired stretch limousine. It was a long silver gray and black Mercedes, the embodiment of luxury. Jackie was impressed. There was nothing to compare with it in England. Thinking *Americans are so imaginative,* Jackie added, *and Southern California with its avant-garde society is particularly so.*

There could be much at stake here and Jackie was determined to pursue a hunch representing her company. She had telephoned D'Arcy after first seeing Angela's designs to get his impressions and advice. Clad in a Frazier's original ensemble, a white filament silk gown with delicate flowered inserts, which emphasized her slim figure and elegant posture, Jackie gracefully emerged through the chauffeur-held door.

Angela was sitting on a stool, with a floor easel in front of her, under the long porch of a building similar to haciendas Jackie had stayed at in Spain. She quickly stood up, wiping her hands on a piece of cloth taken from the pocket of a large paint splattered apron.

With a pleasant smile she approached Jackie.

"Welcome to 'Fruitful Harvest'." She walked all the way around Jackie and exclaimed, "I love your outfit—no doubt one of your company's designs?"

Jackie laughed and agreed.

"I 'm the only one here right now," Angela explained, "but that will give us time to go over the sketches I have ready, without interruption."

Angela led the way into the cool interior of the house, taking off and depositing the voluminous apron on a wicker chair at the porch entrance in the process.

Going through what appeared to be the reception area of the building, they walked along a corridor passing closed doors, until a large airy kitchen was reached. Apart from a small grassy area with what looked like an herbaceous border, the view was indisputably that of a vineyard, with acres and acres of grapevines planted for as far as the eye could see.

Accepting a large glass of ice-cold lemonade from Angela, Jackie commented on the view.

"What a beautiful sight. It looks like a still-life painting of mammoth size."

The endless rows of green, twisting, heavily leafed vines, decked with bunches of almost chameleon Sauvignon Blanc grapes, propelled the eye toward the muted tan, black, and purple foothills that seemed to stand sentinel on the horizon. The sky was a perfectly clear blue, cloudless, with not even the movement of a bird to distract from the serenity of the vista.

Jackie breathed in deeply.

"It's easy to see what an ideal environment this is in which to sketch."

She was not prepared for the loud guffaw that issued from Angela upon hearing this statement. It seemed so out of place in such an outwardly composed person.

Angela, looking a bit uncomfortable, apologized for the outburst and explained.

"No pun intended, but this may sound like sour grapes. Ever since graduation from 'The Los Angeles Academy of Fashion and Fine Arts' my first love, which is designing, has been pushed into the background. My parents needed me to manage their office since they spend so much time out of it. For one reason or another, the office managers before me just didn't work out. So I was stuck."

A frown clouded her face.

"I know how important "'Working it Out" is to my parents and so I have not complained, but now they can afford to employ someone with the proper qualifications. I guess I'm frustrated by it all."

She made a face and smiled apologetically.

"Why are they operating a vineyard with a time consuming business to pursue as well?" Jackie asked curiously.

Angela sighed.

"Dad's father, Grandpa Pip, died and left the property to him. It was still in its early years, with the land being of most value, but the vines were established and doing well, so they decided to keep it. Since most of grandfather's life savings were invested in these acres, dad felt it would be a living testament to him if we could make it a success. We have all worked very hard trying to make it so. It's been a struggle to keep on a full-time oenologist to monitor the grape production, but things have started picking up. Dad is talking of employing a part-time manager and this should cut back on the frequent trips we have had to make from Riverside to Temecula. It has been very tiring."

"Does this mean you will have more time to sketch?" Jackie asked eagerly.

"Not really. I'm not an accountant and it takes me longer to understand and learn new state regulations and requirements. Because "Working it Out" is federal and state funded, we can't make mistakes, otherwise our checks are held up until the matter is settled. At the beginning of each year federal and state manuals are issued providing important guidelines for the new policies coming into effect. These changes specifically apply to our client population and must be carried out to the letter. Penalties are made when strayed from."

Angela sighed heavily. "There's a lot of hard work in grasping and carrying out what's in the manuals. A CPA or MBA wouldn't have the problems I face in tackling this responsibility."

Angela's eyes filled with tears. Too seldom did she have time to devote to the ideas that were spinning around in her head. Sometimes she felt she would go crazy not being able to express the urge that was so dominant within her. Worse, her parents didn't seem to understand.

"My parents promised to get someone in to replace me, so that I could attempt to break into the world of fashion, but so far nothing's happened."

She shrugged her shoulders forlornly and vainly tried to change the subject before she broke down completely in front of this stranger.

"Sorry, I seem to be stuck in a rut and I don't see an escape route right now."

Remembering her resentment at being coerced into a family oriented venture, over which she had no control, Jackie patted Angela's arm in sympathy.

"To some extent I can identify with your sense of dejection. I grew up in an environment which I found wretched. My parents chose to spend much of their leisure time in a remote beach area and from being a young girl I hated it. The sand worked its way into my clothing, my hair and my nails, and even the food. When the wind blew it felt like sandpaper on my skin. Even now it gives me goose-bumps thinking about it."

She shuddered and crossed her arms over her chest, rubbing her upper arms as if an icy blast had entered the room.

Angela asked with interest, "How did you manage to get out of that situation?"

Jackie smiled, remembering.

"I took a job a long way from home and then married the owner of the business."

They grinned at each other.

"Do your parents still spend time there?"

"Oh, indeed. They love it. They have named it "The Colony" and it really is—very clannish and upper-class. My brother has a houseboat there and he wallows like a pig in a mud pond when he goes there."

Angela giggled.

"That's an unusual expression. Does it fit?"

"Pig in a mud pond?"

Angela nodded.

"Not really, I just made it up. Jon is usually appropriately dressed, but he does tend to be scruffy at the beach. Actually, so is everyone else. It seems to be a type of private rebellion in the safety of peers versus the normal lifestyle they are decreed to lead."

The observation went over Angela's head. At that moment she sensed a connection to Jackie that shook all other thoughts out of her mind.

Smiling self-consciously Angela quipped.

"Well, let's get on with the exhibition. I've never shown these sketches before, so I'm a little protective about them. Please try to be kind."

Several hours later they were still pouring over them. Some were roughly outlined; others had been completed in detail; many had been meticulously colored and several showed only sections of garments. Prodigious notes and comments were scattered over almost every page. The illustrations were spread out over the bedroom rug. They had become so engrossed in their project that time had flown.

Angela looked at her watch.

"Would you like to stay and have dinner with us? We usually try to eat around seven. It will be very casual, but it will give you a chance to meet my parents."

"As they don't expect a guest for dinner, won't that be an imposition?"

Angela stood up.

"No problem. I can remedy that with a phone call. I take it that means you will stay?"

Jackie nodded her head. "Thank you, I'd like to."

When Angela went off to make the phone call Jackie walked out to the driveway and directed the chauffeur to pick her up at nine o' clock.

Jackie and Angela, settling down once more to look over the sketches, waited for the rest of the family to arrive.

As they sifted through the designs, with Jackie sorting them into three separate piles, she asked a question that had piqued her interest earlier.

"How did your parents become involved in working with impaired people? That is a pretty specialized area, isn't it?"

Angela looked at Jackie thoughtfully.

"The proper name for them is 'developmentally disabled'. Sometimes 'handicapped people' is also used. It's quite condescending of us to categorize people with certain disabilities unfairly, don't you think?"

Jackie's face tinged pink.

"Sorry. I didn't realize. I haven't met any people like that."

Angela hurriedly continued.

"That's okay. We are especially conscious of how we couch our language, because this is something that has touched our family deeply."

She stopped speaking and looked at Jackie a little uncertainly before resuming.

"My parents met when they worked for the Department of Public Health for San Bernardino County. Mom was a social worker and dad became her supervisor when she transferred from an outreach clinic to the medical center in the city. In less than a year they were married.

They postponed having a family until after mom finished her master's degree and since she was working and going to school at night, it took three more years to attain. By that time they were ready to start a family. They wanted three children, but things didn't work out that way. Mom was thirty and dad thirty-four and nothing happened. They were ready to consider sperm banks, implantation and adoption, whatever it would take to have a child."

Angela took a sip of her warm lemonade and crinkled her nose in displeasure at the taste.

"They were so dejected that on impulse they decided to take a three weeks' vacation and go to Fiji. They needed to get away and apparently it was the perfect antidote."

She smiled and flapped her eyelids.

"Then around nine months later, I was born."

Jackie smiled, impressed.

"Fiji, huh? I must remember that."

"Well, they were so sparked up about having me that they kept trying for another baby, but again nothing happened. They were at the point of giving up trying and decided to return to Fiji for a vacation. I was eleven at the time. And guess what?"

Jackie nodded her head.

"Your mother became pregnant again?"

"Yes. They were thrilled. Actually, the way dad tells it mom said that because Fiji was such a potent elixir that it was off limits after that. It was a wonderful holiday and I still remember parts of it and of course we have lots of pictures. Mom was a bit worried because she was forty-three when Barbara was born, and she did have a difficult delivery, but she put it down to her age and the length of time between births."

Angela stared into space for a few moments before going on.

"Mom had expressed concern to her doctor about Barbara's reluctance to be cuddled and held close and other things which alarmed her. She was reassured that every baby was different and it wasn't until Barbara was almost two years old that she was considered to be autistic."

Shaking her head as if to remove the painful thought, Angela went on; "My parents were crushed by this turn of events, as you can imagine. In the process of researching and determining how to handle the best course for them to take, they became experts. They have amassed an impressive library of information on the subject. By the time Barbara was four my mother quit her job and started organizing support groups in southern California. Then it really took off. They contacted the state looking for a national organization to join and since there was none, they decided to start their own. Once that was established mom and dad decided that the next step was to start their own business, working with all people with disabilities on a full-time basis. That is how "Working it Out" came about. It is funded by both the state and the federal governments."

Jackie looked impressed.

"Jolly good! I really admire them. What a worthwhile occupation. By comparison mine seems quite meaningless."

"Then I'm in the same category, too. You have to be a certain breed to love the kind of work they do." Angela quietly responded.

Examining the sketch in her hand, Jackie asked.

"How did you get into clothing layout and design? It is quite a specific field."

Angie's face lost some of its tenseness.

"My grandmother gave me three almost life size cut-out cardboard dolls one Christmas. Since my parents were so involved with Barbara, I used to go to my bedroom and spend hours drawing and painting new outfits for my "three children." It was at grandmother's insistence that I went to an art college. She paid my tuition to make sure I did. She told me I could repay her when I became rich and famous."

Her voice dropped to a whisper.

"She died last year and I really miss her support. She always encouraged me to hang in until the right opportunity came along. It was her enthusiasm that got me over the rough spots when the office work was hard to handle."

Jackie leaned over and sympathetically patted Angela's hand.

They heard the front door open and without warning a large black Doberman Pinscher threw himself into the bedroom and into Angela's arms. Papers scattered in every direction and Angela wailed in dismay.

"Oh, Zeus, you're impossible."

She shook her head, sighing.

With one eye on the impressive animal, Jackie started carefully gathering up the scattered papers within easy reach. They were too valuable to see mutilated or destroyed. Her movements alerted the dog of her presence, but apart from a temporary stiffening of his neck and legs and a slight parting of his mouth to reveal strong white teeth, his aggression ended there. He gracefully walked over to her and Jackie automatically held out her hand, palm upwards, which he condescended to sniff. Then with the same suddenness with which he had entered the room, the swift moving dog bounded out, almost knocking over someone entering.

A little figure stood uncertainly in the doorway, looking at Jackie suspiciously.

Angela immediately stood up and walked over to her. Taking her hand she brought her to Jackie saying, "Hi, sweetie, this is Jackie, she is staying over for dinner—will you say hello to her?"

Barbara looked scared and moved behind Angela in an effort to separate herself. Jackie looked at her and smiled, but she didn't attempt to say anything—she really didn't know what to say. It didn't seem to be necessary to say anything. Barbara backed out of the room and her footsteps could be heard reverberating on the wooden floors.

Frowning, Angela quickly retrieved the remaining drawings strewn on the floor and put them back into the box.

"Let's go into the kitchen so you can meet the folks."

Feeling that perhaps she had made a mistake by staying, Jackie reluctantly followed her there.

Angela's parents were standing by the window with their backs to the room. Barbara had positioned herself behind her mother, squeezing between her stomach and the kitchen countertop.

Susan Warner turned her head to look appraisingly at Jackie as she entered.

"Jackie, these are my parents, Susan and Bart Warner. This is Jackie Frazier, a visitor from England."

Jackie automatically held out her hand and smiled when both parents turned around holding boxes in each of their hands. They had been in the process of transferring an assortment of the same white boxes from a large plastic bag to the kitchen countertop. They laughed, which broke the ice, and after putting the boxes down, shook hands.

Jackie smelled a tantalizing aroma and realized they must have brought home dinner. She was conscious of the unexpected casual invitation to stay and wondered if she was intruding. Perhaps she should have left earlier.

Angela's father looked at Jackie intently.

"So nice of you to come. Angie has been impatiently waiting for you to arrive. Bet she has been chattering your head off and we all know about what."

He had a twinkle in his steel gray eyes and when he smiled it altogether changed his rather stern features. He had a full head of brown hair that was tinged with streaks of gray at the temples that appeared to match his eyes perfectly. The particular shade of brown and steel gray made an impression on Jackie's color awareness. She made a mental note to use the unusual combination in some fabric designs.

Angela went over to a drawer and pulled out several placemats and gave them to Jackie.

"Do you mind?"

It sounded more like a statement than a question.

Jackie obliged. She had a housekeeper at home who did this sort of thing, but this was rather fun, like having a picnic.

Angela brought over a caddy filled with paper napkins and cutlery and Jackie smiled.

"I get the idea. I'm a fast learner."

The Chinese food was delicious and the ambience in which they ate was natural and friendly. Jackie used a fork, but expressed envy at the dexterity with which everyone handled the chopsticks and Barbara's awkward attempts were applauded. Even though they mainly discussed the vineyard and the office, the family included Jackie in their conversation, often digressing to explain something or tell an amusing story. They asked about Jackie's business—what did she do when she came to the United States? Their questions were couched in a friendly manner and smiling faces waited for her responses. Jackie obliged. They were going out of their way to welcome her and she was beginning to feel comfortable and at ease with them, especially Angela. Barbara watched and listened and sometimes seeing the others laugh, she would laugh too, but it was a rather strange noise, almost like a cackle. It unsettled Jackie.

Cleaning up was easy. Everything except the fork and placemats were tossed into the garbage can and Jackie thought this very inventive and convenient for these people who had little time to waste. Refilling their coffee mugs, Angela invited Jackie outside. A glass topped table and four chairs sat on a small patio. The sun was sinking behind the hills that looked black in the approaching night. A fruity scent hung in the air. Jackie breathed in the sweet, slightly musky aroma and a satisfied smile crossed her face.

"Thank you for a wonderful day, I have enjoyed every minute of it."

A puzzled frown creased Angela's face.

"Okay. I give up—what happened that I missed?"

Jackie laughed.

"I travel so much that having a meal with a family in their home is most unusual and very nice. My schedule seldom varies unless I can meet with friends for the odd get-together. Usually it is: the plane, hotel room and room service, fashion house or factory and a plane ride to the next point. All of which becomes quite routine and lonely after a while. So I do appreciate your hospitality."

Zeus was sitting beside Jackie, patting her with his big paw as a reminder to stroke his head.

Absently Jackie obliged, continuing in a low voice.

"I came here with the intention of making you a business offer, should the sketches be of merit. They are, but in learning about all the responsibilities you and your family have, I realize that my offer would probably be an added burden rather than a happy solution."

Angela gulped and quietly asked.

"Don't you think I might like to know what you had in mind?"

Jackie hesitated, looking at Angela speculatively.

"I was hoping, if details could be worked out, that you would consider an offer as a designer at our manufacturing plant in Barnsley, England. It is a newly created position, which D'Arcy and I have talked about recently. It would mean not only being responsible for starting up the complete collection of exclusive summer fashions for our wintering jet-set clientele, but also overseeing the pattern development department. In addition, it would mean working closely with Bill Thorpe, the marketing manager at the mill, to ensure that the fabric they will be turning out is exactly right for the specific designs."

Jackie sipped from the mug, a thoughtful expression on her face.

"This is, of course, a highly confidential position. Some of our competitors would give their eyeteeth to have access to our wastebaskets and so we have stringent policies, which everyone above a certain administrative level must adhere to. They are, in fact, very clearly defined in contracts. None of us is exempt."

Jackie paused and looked at Angela cautiously. She could see her shining eyes and expectant smile. She continued.

"The position, relative to the organizational chart, will be a junior one, but because of the potential importance of this new merchandise, it will come under my direct supervision. You should know that I am a perfectionist and can be a real pain at times. The salary is somewhat negotiable since, quite frankly, I hadn't anticipated finding someone of your caliber so unexpectedly and so much before we had planned on putting our plans into action."

Watching Angela's face, Jackie said with regret in her voice.

"Now I feel it would be irresponsible of me to be the cause for disruption in your lives."

With hands clenched together, Angela asked with a tremor in her voice.

"I'm really quite confused by all this, but the important thing I'd like to be clear on is if the job is being offered to me or not."

Jackie stood up and walked to the edge of the patio, looking out toward the black outline of the hills against the weak light of the new moon.

Standing for a few moments with her back toward Angela, she turned around slowly.

"If arrangements could possibly be worked out and with your family's consent, then the answer is 'yes', but it is a very big responsib . . . ."

Jackie froze as Angela, leaping out of her chair, jumped up and down excitedly. She rushed over to Jackie and gave her a warm hug, before dashing into the house calling to her parents.

Darn these Americans, Jackie thinks shakily. *They are so impulsive and unpredictable. I almost had a heart attack.* Then she smiled at the recollection of Angela's incredulous look as she listened to her proposal that had, to her surprise, become an official offer. Normally she did not work so impetuously, even though on this occasion she had already formed an opinion and had come to a tentative decision.

Jackie looked at her watch, barely making out the time from the meager light coming through the kitchen window. It was 8:45 p.m. The limousine should be arriving soon. She opened the patio door and walked into the house. Scratching on the screen door behind her indicated that Zeus also wanted to be inside.

He led her through the corridor to a large room she had noticed upon arrival. Angela and her parents were sitting there. It was a sparsely furnished room, but the dim lighting and pine paneled walls gave it a soft, well lived in look.

Conversation stopped when she walked in.

"Am I in the way? I just wanted to check if the limousine had arrived."

From the animated expression on Angela's face and the solemn expressions on those of her parents Jackie wondered how far the dialogue had progressed. She could feel a tension in the room.

Susan patted the cushion beside her on a sofa that had seen better days.

"Angela has just passed on some very heady news. It's come as quite a surprise and if you would put the information into your own words, perhaps we can get a better grasp on the situation."

Jackie willingly recounted what Angela already knew and answered their many questions before the headlights from a vehicle coming along the private driveway alerted them to the time.

They all rose to their feet.

Jackie's face registered remorse.

"If my intrusion has caused problems, I truly am very sorry and hope you will accept my sincere apology. Unfortunately there was no way of knowing your circumstances or, in fact, whether Angela was genuinely gifted. I had to discover this for myself."

Ruefully she smiled at them.

"As a specialist in the field I was compelled to make the offer to Angela and it is genuine. She has too much potential to ignore and she needs to know this, even if this is not the right time for another career to be activated."

Bart looked worried.

"Well, it's too late to continue this discussion right now and your limo is here. There's a lot to talk about and absorb. We'll get back to you in the next couple of days, if that's convenient. There's no point in dragging this out if it isn't feasible."

"Of course—you know where I can be reached."

Angela looked quite downcast. Jackie gave her an understanding glance.

As they walked over to the front door Jackie looked over her shoulder.

"Where is Barbara?"

Susan responded.

"She's in bed. All day at the clinic wears her out. It's very exhausting."

For all of you, Jackie compassionately thinks, noticing for the first time the dark shadows under Susan's eyes.

Pushing his nose into Jackie's hand as if to say goodbye, Zeus stood quietly waiting; rubbing his nose gently a few times, she responded.

The driver was waiting by the open back door of the impressive vehicle as Jackie said goodbye. Bart produced a bottle of wine on which was the "Fruitful Harvest" logo, pressing it into her hand with a smile.

"Something to perhaps celebrate with."

Susan shook hands warmly. "Please visit us again, even if things don't work out."

Jackie thought she sounded as if she meant it.

Angela, walking down the steps with Jackie, stood beside the chauffeur as he took the bottle of wine. Jackie held out her arms and Angela stepped in to be hugged.

"Thank you again for a wonderful day. I really do hope everything works out, but in any event I intend keeping in touch. I don't want to lose your friendship or the chance of recruiting you along the way."

Angela kissed Jackie's cheek and fitted a small roll of papers into her hand.

Jackie knew what they were. She was very touched

Jackie quickly moved into the luxurious interior of the vehicle and waved goodbye as it moved away. She really had enjoyed being with these new acquaintances.

She would be proud to call them friends. Traveling back to Los Angeles she closed her eyes and replayed the visit, wondering where it would lead.

The next afternoon Jackie received the anticipated call. Angela, Susan, and Bart took turns talking to her. They all had questions and after spending a long time discussing the issues decided that they would need to have another family conference. They would phone again soon. Jackie planned on flying out of LAX to London in two days, and gave them a private telephone number where she could be contacted.

During the time between calls Jackie mulled the situation over. Had she acted too frivolously in offering such a responsible position to someone as young and inexperienced as Angela? Had she knowingly been insensitive to this family already plagued by problems and what right did she have to cause additional strain? This was the first time a business commitment had been negotiated by Jackie in such a casual manner and she was a little disconcerted.

Three hours later Angela called again. If the position could be kept open for up to six months her parents would do their best to find an efficient office manager for the Riverside operation to replace her. They would also try to persuade a widowed aunt to live with them for a while to look after Barbara, until other options could be made.

Jackie approved. This arrangement would work out well for her—it would give more time to give birth to this newest concept.

Everything was agreed upon. They would keep in touch.

✱ ✱ ✱

Over an hour later Jackie's voice, sounding hoarse, finally petered out. She waited for a response from Kara.

There was only silence.

As if in a trance Kara heard Jackie exclaim, "Hey, are you still there, Kara . . . . ? Kara!"

"I'm here," she responded, "still recovering. That was quite a tale. You know I am going to have to discuss this with my parents and they are going to be shocked, but it sounds so fascinating. I already feel quite excited at the prospect of going out to California and starting an adventure of my own."

"You deduced that I was going to recommend you for the California position, didn't you?" Jackie accused.

Kara laughed. "That was a long circuitous route you took to get to the punch line."

They talked for a little longer. Jackie would be in Paris for a couple of days. This would give Kara time to broach the subject with her family and test the waters, so to speak. Jackie said she had not mentioned Kara to Angela or her family, because she was waiting for Kara's decision. The Warner's had indicated that they were still searching for a replacement for Angela. Perhaps nothing could be worked out with them—it was just an idea Jackie had. It certainly would solve Angela and her family's problem and perhaps also Kara's.

Audibly yawning and without further ado Jackie said goodnight and hung up.

Sitting staring at the elaborate ivory and gold French telephone, as if it were to blame for the conversation that had just taken place, Kara musingly replaced the receiver. She was both excited and anxious at the possibilities that this opportunity might activate.

How should she approach her parents with what would be a shock to them? By the time she left her bedroom and went down to the kitchen the house was darkened for the evening. Not needing to explain the unusually lengthy discussion with Jackie right away was a relief. Explaining the situation to her parents would need careful preparation Kara decided, as she warmed a cup of milk in the microwave and took it back upstairs.

CHAPTER SIX

The next day when Kara awoke, she heard rain rat-tat-tatting on the French doors at the end of her bedroom. Slipping on a warm plaid dressing gown, she looked out to see the rain pounding the tiled garden paths and splashing into the pond with such ferocity as if the raindrops were catapulted out of the water again. The grass was flattened by the constant rain and the bushes and trees, most of them deprived of their summer foliage, looked quite drab. The whole area looked bleak and forlorn. A mist obliterated the normal view of the gazebo and tennis court. It must have been raining for some time. Puddles were gathering inside the tree wells and the huge carved stone pots, holding a variety of hardy plants and sculptured bushes, which bordered the terrace, dribbled water over their rims in a constant flow. The continual gushing and swishing of water through the eaves troughs running along the roof above her head caused Kara to shiver.

She closed the heavy velvet drapes, switched on a hanging lamp and turned on and lit the gas logs in the Delft tiled fireplace.

Seventeenth century homes in the north of England, no matter how modernized they were allowed to become, could not compete with the unpredictable British climate.

The thought startled Kara.

She looked over her shoulder. It was as if someone else had spoken her thoughts. From where had they come? She loved her home, always had, and these intrusive thoughts were alien to her comfort level.

California was the culprit. Subconsciously the conversation with Jackie had stayed with her through the night. Getting out a notepad and pen Kara quickly started two columns: Pros and Cons. Kara sat back and reviewed the list—the entries were even.

She glanced at her wristwatch. It was just after eight and the rain continued to beat steadily against the roof. Her father was attending a conference today and did not require her services.

This was the time to find an ally in her mother, but first she had to be confident that her aspirations were, in fact, leading her in the direction she wished to pursue. Kara walked over to the floor-to-ceiling bookcases built into the walls on both sides of the French doors and removed the Rand McNally International Atlas, before returning to the fireplace,

Settling once more before the hearth, Kara opened the atlas and found California. Riverside was not easily located, but once she had identified its geographic position she started discovering interesting aspects. It was approximately two inches from everywhere—the beach, Disneyland, the mountains, the desert, Palm Springs, and just a bit further west was Los Angeles. Interesting place names popped out like neon signs: Morongo Basin, Cajon Pass, Rancho Cucamonga, Yucca Valley and Lake Arrowhead. A land for her to discover.

It did sound intriguing.

Turning back to the list, Kara proceeded. Pros: Travel opportunities; involvement in political, educational, and cultural aspects of the area (this was of special interest); study the Spanish language (adding to French, Norwegian, and Italian languages already spoken); and this is what it was all about—to experience a different lifestyle To heck with the Cons. Kara came to a decision. Go to California.

Half-an-hour later, sitting in the welcoming warmth of the breakfast room reading the morning's edition of "The Guardian" was Kara's mother. She turned as Kara resolutely made her entrance.

"Hello, darling, I wasn't sure whether you were working today or not. It is such a frightful day it will be lovely having you home to keep me company. I have postponed a beauty salon appointment and cancelled a luncheon with Jon's mother and, having done so, I already feel quite pleased with myself. I've given myself a clean slate for the day."

She smiled conspiratorially at Kara.

Dressed comfortably in a charcoal gray Harris-tweed skirt and matching pearl gray sweater and cardigan, Silvia Olavssen projected an unpretentious air of elegance. Her naturally wavy golden-brown hair was simply styled giving emphasis to the delicately silky complexion and clear green eyes that were replicated in her daughter.

The long carved oak sideboard still displayed the trappings of breakfast—leftover toast, a few pieces of bacon and some whole grilled mushrooms. Kara loaded the remains onto a plate and took it over to the microwave at the end of the sideboard. The pinging of the signal diverted Kara's mother's attention momentarily from the newspaper and she smiled at Kara. Looking at her mother's patrician features and lively, loving eyes, Kara wondered how she could possibly soften the news she had to divulge.

Hilda entered the breakfast room as Kara settled down to eat. She poured a cup of coffee from the carafe warming on a stand and placed it beside Kara with a big smile.

"Why we say 'Good morning' on a day like this, I'll never know."

She ran her practiced eyes over both the sideboard and the breakfast table. Noting the toast on Kara's side plate, she moved the crystal marmalade dish nearer.

"More toast, Miss Kara?"

Munching, Kara shook her head and Hilda left the room as quietly as she had entered.

Kara was beginning to feel adroit at deciphering the newspaper from a span of four feet. Folding it and placing it on the table a few minutes later, mother and daughter looked at each other.

"I talked to Jackie last night." Kara dabbed a linen table napkin across her mouth.

"Oh, really. Hilda relayed a message from her recently asking you to call her—anything important happening? We don't usually hear from her unless there is."

Kara took a sip of coffee before responding.

"I think so. I wanted to talk to you about it first because I know this is going to come as a shock, but it is something that is important to me and I hope you will think about it before expressing an opinion."

Kara was a little nervous after spilling this news.

Kara's mother raised her eyebrows in surprise, but waited for further comment.

Taking a deep breath Kara continued. Relaying the sequence of events starting with her initial hope for a position with The House of Frazier's fashion house, expanding to the unexpected offer from Jackie and finishing with the exciting prospect of working in California, Kara's voice trailed off.

Studying her mother's face as she was talking Kara was aware that her normally expressive face revealed little.

"Please talk to Jackie, mummy, she knows these people, they are friends." Kara locked her fingers together. "I have had an almost sleepless night going over the prospects and options, and I've decided to try it if the position is offered to me. It will be for a couple of years only and I'd like a change. Of course, they may not want me. Jackie hasn't approached them yet."

Silvia Olavssen looked intently at her daughter for a while.

"Did your interlude with Roger have any bearing on making this decision?"

Kara's lips trembled and her eyes filled quickly with tears.

With a soft sigh, Kara's mother whispered, "Oh, il mio tesoro, I wish you had confided in me." Hastening to Kara's side she dropped to her knees, taking her daughter into her comforting arms.

"So now you feel you must get away to heal, is that it?"

Kara nodded her head. They nestled together, cheek to cheek.

Giving Kara a quick squeeze, her mother returned to the opposite chair.

"Is this really what you want to do? It isn't an act of escapism, is it?"

Noting the look of concern on her mother's face, Kara explained,

"No, I've already considered that. I'm really quite excited at the thought of experiencing a new lifestyle and I am twenty-two, after all. The only countries I have visited are Norway, France and Italy and that was primarily to visit relatives. I'd like to see more of the world before I settle down."

"Your father is going to be shocked. Do you wish me to speak to him first?"

Kara looked a bit sheepish.

"Would you mind? Perhaps that way you can both talk it out. I know it must be disturbing news and I had to talk to you first. You handle my problems so much better than daddy. He shoots off into space before coming back down to earth again."

Kara's mother did not look forward to bringing up this surprising turn of events with her husband. Kara was their pride and joy, but to her father she still remained his little girl. She would have to plan her strategy carefully, if Kara expected to leave with his blessings.

Silvia Olavssen closed her eyes and Kara quickly left the room.

The next evening, after Kara left to see a movie with a friend, Silvia Olavssen broached the subject with her husband. After carefully explaining how the situation had come about, the extent of Kara's depression by Roger's cruel rejection and the decision to move temporarily to America to get her life together, she stopped.

"Poor Kara, for the first time in months she seemed excited and motivated and she will be so disappointed if it doesn't work out."

Her husband peered over his spectacles.

"And why shouldn't it work out, if Kara chooses to accept the position?"

"Well, dear, they haven't quite offered the job to her and they just may not want her."

Silvia Olavssen bent her head toward the needlepoint she was working on when she saw the flush of annoyance registered on her husband's face.

He rang the bell for Hilda.

"Get Jackie on the phone, please. I'll be in my office." As he walked toward the door he added, "We need to get some things sorted out here. If Kara wants that job, I doubt there are any better qualified applicants for it."

Impatiently he strode out of the room.

His wife hoped Kara was completely certain she wanted to make this move. Her father was about to make sure her wish was granted.

CHAPTER SEVEN

During the long plane flight to California Kara contemplated the series of events that had led to making the big decision to move so far away from her homeland. There must be a hidden purpose to it all because her boldness in taking on this challenge remained a mystery beyond her understanding. It had seemed like not only the next natural step to take, but also the only step.

Kara determined to start keeping a diary. The concept interested her. There would be much to absorb and it would be a good way to record her memoirs to look back on once she returned to England.

Feeling more satisfied than ever that she had made the right decision, Kara settled down to enjoy the remainder of the flight to her new, albeit temporary, home.

Upon arrival at Los Angeles International Airport, Kara located her luggage and checked through Customs. She immediately started looking for Susan and Bart Warner. She began smiling when she saw someone, looking exactly like the pictures she had received, holding up a sign that read 'Kara/Riverside.'

"Susan? Hello. I'm Kara Olavssen."

The placard was put down at her side.

"Gosh, welcome Kara. We were afraid we would miss you, weren't we honey?"

With her other hand Susan pulled a tall, well-built man over to stand beside her.

"Bart's been walking around looking for you, in case the sign didn't catch your attention."

Bart smiled a little self-consciously, showing Kara a recent photograph of herself that he was carrying in his hand.

Susan's voice had a slight accent, easily understood, one that Kara had become familiar with during their phone conversations, but it was startling to hear a very definite drawl in Bart's speech. He had a pleasant smile on his face and his voice was slow and vibrant, but she was really in trouble, she could not make out what he was saying. He held out his hand and recognizing this gesture, Kara swiftly offered hers.

Bart picked up both big pieces of luggage and strode toward the automatic doors leading to the sidewalk outside. Kara and Susan followed.

Bart said something and walked away, leaving the suitcases beside the two women.

Perplexed, Kara asked. "Excuse me, but what did your husband say?"

Susan laughed.

"I could see by your face that you didn't grasp what he said. He's gone to fetch the car. Bart is a Texan and sometimes he speaks a language all his own, but I don't think it will take you long to get onto his wavelength."

Kara said smiling, "That's a relief."

Kara observed the bright blue, clear sky, the tops of palm trees in the distance and the hum of activity around her. She felt as if she had just arrived for a vacation. Her skin tingled and her eyes sparkled. Already California's upbeat tempo was wooing her.

Kara sat in the backseat of the Cadillac watching the freeway scenery passing by. All the cars looked so big and the trucks moved so fast, far exceeding the speed the lorries in England were allowed to travel. The billboards and unfamiliar names of stores, shopping malls, and cities, kept Kara's head turning from side to side. It was both stimulating and tiring. Soon her head began nodding onto her chest.

"Would you like to stop for something to eat, Kara? In this traffic we won't be home for another hour."

Her head snapped into an upright position.

"Oh. No thank you. A light meal was served just a short time before the plane landed."

Kara settled back into her observation post. On the map Riverside had seemed fairly close to Los Angeles. Thinking this over, Kara decided that some of the other pre-conceived ideas she had might have to be revised.

The air travel had been tiring and the long car trip added to the sense of exhaustion that Kara experienced. She had not traveled so far before or felt so alone. Arriving at 2236 Via San Dimas in Riverside, Kara was more than ready to go to bed, even though it was still daylight outside. She had not slept much on the plane and her metabolism was protesting.

Shown to Angela's bedroom, which would be for her use, Kara succumbed.

The next morning, which was Saturday, Kara awoke to the smell of coffee. Susan had put a mug of coffee on a bedside table, and she was adjusting the mini-blinds when Kara opened her eyes.

Sitting up, Kara rubbed her eyes.

"I'm sorry. Is it very late?"

Susan turned to face her.

"Not really, but you have slept so soundly I thought you might want to get up and get on our California timetable. You can always take a nap in the afternoon, if it's needed."

Kara looked at her watch. She had adjusted it on the plane before landing and saw that it was just after nine o' clock.

"I've slept thirteen hours? I can't believe that."

Slipping out of bed she pulled on the robe hanging from the bedpost.

"We are about to have breakfast, if you're ready to join us. Bart's finishing things off," Susan said, adding as an afterthought, "Unless you would prefer to bring a tray back here."

Kara shook her head and picking up the mug of coffee followed Susan downstairs.

Bart was making toast and added a couple of slices to a plate as they entered the kitchen. Kara and Bart smiled at each other.

Barbara was sitting at the table, a cushion beneath her. She immediately attempted to climb down upon seeing Kara, a stranger. She was very petite and according to Jackie's assumption she was older than she first appeared. Barbara's face registered astonishment. Kara eyed the young person with interest, but she just smiled at her as she took a seat opposite.

Susan and Bart sat down at the same time.

"Good—you made the juice." Susan smiled her thanks to Bart.

"This is made from our own oranges," she said, pouring the golden liquid into glasses set out on the table. "It tastes so much better freshly squeezed."

She watched Kara take a sip.

"You're absolutely right. It's delicious. How lovely to be able to collect one's breakfast, literally right out of the garden."

At the unfamiliar accent she had been listening to, Barbara glanced at Kara, who winked at her. Her shocked eyes opened wide. She stared at Kara, who repeated the wink, this time with the other eye. Barbara giggled and her arms shook and her head bobbed back and forth. This in turn startled Kara, but Susan and Bart just started smiling. She had amused Barbara.

Kara's breath slowly returned as Barbara looked downward again.

Susan offered, "We can take you for a drive around the area this afternoon. You might find it helpful."

Kara quickly accepted.

It took all weekend to become even slightly oriented. Crossing streets with traffic driving the wrong way, hearing strangers address her as "honey" in various unaccountable accents and seeing so many billboards and advertising signs on almost every street corner was confusing. It was all so different.

Watching television was another revelation. There were so many stations to choose from. She could spend the entire evening just flipping through channels, previewing a little of this or that without making a decision to watch anything in its entirety. Unlike the only four channel options in England.

Susan and Bart were very informal "laid back" Californians. They were pleasantly surprised with Kara's enthusiasm and curiosity. Even though she spoke with the same precise, cultured tones they were accustomed to hearing in Jackie, Kara could in no way be compared to her. Jackie, being several years older than Kara and in the fashion business, always looked very poised and perfectly turned out. She had a veneer of sophistication that Kara did not display. Kara, on the other hand, was naturally beautiful, with a small turned-up nose, decorated with freckles and clear wide spaced eyes the color of jade agates found on rocky coastlines. Her hair, three shades of weather-beaten blonde, gave the overall appearance of tousled chic; they noticed how she ran her fingers through her hair when she was tired. Bart suggested to Susan that she try to determine how experienced Kara was in the "dating arena" as, with her stunning figure, he anticipated wolves around their doorstep. At 22 she appeared to be so much more vulnerable and innocent than her American counterpart—a problem they had not anticipated.

Spending the weekend together had given Susan and Bart an opportunity to notice that Kara favored the informal, as they did. Discovering Kara's droll sense of humor caught Susan and Bart off-guard—she was much more down-to-earth and likeable than they had expected.

Yes—Kara would fit in very nicely.

Work was not discussed until Monday after the three of them arrived at the office. The suite was on the ground floor of a complex consisting of seven red tile roofed, white stucco single-story buildings. They were arranged in a staggered oval shape around a man-made stream, which wended its way through a central courtyard area, with outdoor tables and chairs scattered around.

They entered through a frosted glass door that led into a hallway. The first door on the left opened into a reception area with a secretarial desk and chairs along one wall, with a table between. Prominently displayed on the small table was a large floral arrangement, beside which stood a decorative potted tree. A vase of flowers was positioned on top of a gray filing cabinet. A basket with white, teal, and plum colored blooms sat on the corner of the desk.

This was not at all the way Kara had expected a not-for-profit agency to look.

Susan looked at her watch.

"We have time for a quick tour around, before the others arrive, if you like."

Kara nodded her head. "Yes, I'd like that."

Five doors led off the reception area: a conference room, a lunchroom, an office shared by Susan and Bart, and an office to be shared by Kara and the job developer. The large room in which the inspection ended was the job coaches' room. As in every room they had entered, plants, trees, and flower arrangements proliferated. In the job coaches' room they were everywhere, even hanging from hooks in the ceiling.

Unable to contain herself any longer, Kara asked, perplexed.

"Excuse me for sounding rude, but is there a reason for all these plants being here?"

Susan chuckled, picking up a small flower arrangement from the nearest file cabinet and handing it to Kara. She touched the petals of a rose, feeling the soft silky fabric. A price tag was also visible.

"Later on in the week I will take you over to Building "G" where some of our clients work with job coaches on such projects as this."

She returned the basket to its place, saying, "It's not only a source of income, but also part of a skills training program."

Susan glanced at the large clock on the wall as the front door opened. It was 7:50 a.m. Ramona Guiterrez, the receptionist and "Jack-of-all-trades" entered. She was small in stature, a little on the plump side, with lively dark eyes and the creamy olive complexion associated with her Hispanic heritage. A grin accompanied her "Good morning" to Susan and Bart and she flashed a shy smile at Kara as she stowed her purse and a small brown paper bag into a desk drawer. Susan introduced them.

Susan warned.

"It will take a while to recognize everyone. Job coaches and Marcie, our job developer and Julie, her assistant, come and go with regularity, but you will meet most of them at the weekly staff meeting."

Kara presumed everyone in the lunchroom were job coaches. A few people were eating snacks there when Kara returned for a cup of coffee from the percolator she had observed Ramona setting up earlier.

Theresa, who was about to pour a cup of coffee, held up the carafe asking,

"Would you like some?"

"Please. It smells wonderful."

Pouring the steaming liquid into a plain white mug with a blue rim, taken from a cabinet above the sink, Theresa put the hot mug down on the countertop.

"The mugs in this cupboard are provided by the company, but most of us prefer to bring our own, it makes it more personal and there are no mix-ups."

"Good idea, I'll do the same thing."

Kara smiled her thanks.

Taking the mug back to her office, she placed it on the desk by the bay window, which looked out onto the patio. This had been Angela's desk and in Kara's mind it commanded the best area of the room.

Almost on cue, precisely at eight, the phones started ringing. It seemed to be the signal for everyone to snap into action and get started on their workday.

Kara opened the desk drawers, checking the contents. All the usual office supplies were neatly arranged. On her desk was the same gray telephone that appeared strategically around the various offices. There were also a Panasonic adding machine and a burgundy, pink, and pale blue floral arrangement. A comfortable chair on rollers stood on the plastic mat used in conjunction with the computer station nearby. Kara slid the gray cover from the IBM computer and picked up the IBM computer manual lying on the desk. Browsing through it helped her feel more comfortable with the system, which was familiar to her. She settled back to drink the coffee, admire the view and wait for Susan and Bart's forthcoming orientation.

Kara realized her indoctrination had already started—"Computer Station" and "win-win situation." She filed the new terminology away for entry into her diary. Suddenly the realization hit her. She really was in a new land, a huge progressive country. She hoped she would fit in.

Kara heard the door swing open and, turning around, saw her new office occupant.

"Ta, rah, ta, rah!"

Marcie Michaelson, standing poised in the doorway, had a big grin on her face as she precariously balanced in both hands an oblong cake decorated with a picture of Mickey Mouse who was holding an American flag. The words "Welcome, Kara" were etched into the frosting.

Walking over to Kara's desk, Marcie ceremoniously deposited the large cake there.

Kara smiled and facetiously commented, "Is this lunch? I can't eat it all."

Marcie burst out laughing. "Very funny." Lowering her voice she added conspiritorily, "We can share."

They studied each other, starting to speak at the same time. They stopped and laughed. Kara felt a sense of relief; the signs were there, she would enjoy getting to know Marcie Michaelson, Job Developer.

Upon first sight she already liked the lithe, tanned and attractive young woman with the stylishly short burnished black hair; she also approved of the way she dressed in a slim white dress, worn with a royal blue striped jacket, navy pumps and a large white purse.

Hearing the laughter, Bart came into the room. Placing a hand on each of their shoulders, he properly introduced them.

Marcie turned to Bart, seemingly unable to suppress her elation, saying,

"I have some exciting news for you and Susan that can't wait." She bubbled with jubilation as she unceremoniously led the way out of the office.

Bart followed, casting a quizzical look at Kara over his shoulder.

"Sorry for the delay, I'll phone for a client to come and take you over to the Workshop. That will give you an insight into part of our program and should keep you occupied until Sue and I have a chance to sit down with you."

Kara heard a door close firmly.

This seemed to be quite an unusual way to start off her first day, but this did not appear to be the usual run-of-the-mill type company. Kara stood near the window looking out into a small landscaped area. A petite curly haired pixie of an undeterminable age jumped out in front of her, waving her hands and bouncing up and down, saying something Kara could not understand.

Kara took an involuntary step backward and shot a startled glance in Ramona's direction. Taking in the situation immediately, Ramona headed for the entrance door and opened it to find the same little person waiting there, almost falling into the room in nervous excitement.

Holding her by the shoulders to restrain the Jack-in-the-box movements, Ramona said in a calm voice.

"Just a minute, Effie. Settle down."

She looked over in Kara's direction.

"This is Kara who's started working here and once you've calmed down you can take her back to your building."

Noticing Kara's look of alarm, Ramona spoke in a conversational tone.

"Effie has been with us for almost a year and has just returned to Phase I for a while. She will take you over to the Workshop—won't you Effie?"

Effie nodded her head vehemently.

Ramona went back to her desk and picking up a large manila envelope handed it to Effie.

"Give this to Norma, please."

Effie once again nodded her head.

Kara and Effie set out together. They eyed each other warily. Kara's longer legs took one step to Effie's dancing two or three.

They walked for a few minutes in silence.

"Do you like being in Workshop?" Kara asked, for something better to say.

She was not prepared for the response.

"I hate it, I hate it, and I hate you."

So saying the whirlwind named Effie ran along the paved path and over a bridge straddling the narrow strip of water and disappeared. Kara picked up speed walking quickly in the direction Effie had taken. Troubled, Kara crossed over the bridge and looked around. There was no one in sight.

"Effie," she called hesitantly.

A little stronger, "Effie, come out, I can see you."

I wish, Kara thinks in desperation, *if I could see through buildings and trees.* Just as she was deciding which of two paths to take, a lively chuckle came from behind her.

"Why do you talk so funny?"

Kara was taken aback. Taking hold of Effie's hand firmly, feeling it squirming for release, Kara mentally willed Effie not to take off again. Trying to keep Effie occupied she started telling Effie trivial things about her life in England. Effie stopped pulling away from her.

Effie gave Kara's hand a squeeze and with a quizzical look on her face said.

"You funny!"

She let her hand stay in Kara's.

"We here!"

It was abruptly announced and Kara felt as drained as if she had just run a marathon.

After knocking on the glass door bearing only the suite number "G-5," Norma, one of the job coaches Kara had met earlier, unlocked and then locked the door after they entered. Cheerfully Effie handed over the envelope and scuttled off past Norma.

"Did she behave herself?" Norma inquired.

For a moment Kara and the workshop manager stood silently looking at each other.

"Oh, you poor thing."

Norma put the key into her jacket pocket.

"How about a cup of coffee?"

Kara gladly agreed.

There was a very small reception area, which led into a large room with four trestle tables surrounded by chairs, each table piled with work in progress. Around the room were boxes and shelves filled with florists' supplies of every description. Glue, wire clippers, and various colored tapes were in use. It was a very organized scene. A small desk and wooden chair, occupied by a job coach, was at the far end of the room. Kara was acutely aware of the silence that her entrance had produced and the 19 pairs of eyes that viewed her in surprise.

Norma introduced Kara as the new office manager taking over from Angela. At the mention of Angela's name there was a sudden outburst.

"I want Angie back," said one.

"Who are you?" said another in a belligerent tone.

A third looking angrily at Kara shouted, "Go away."

A few started crying.

Norma looked at Kara apologetically and softly whispered, "Sorry." Kara was stumped she had never been in this kind of a situation before. Norma stepped slightly in front of Kara, as if to shield her, and sternly addressed the clients.

"Your behavior is very rude and I'm ashamed of the way you are acting. Angela asked you to help welcome Kara and I know she would be disappointed with this display of bad manners."

Kara cleared her throat.

"I can imagine how you feel. It is very hard to say goodbye to someone you care for. I have just done it myself, but I hope that Angela will find friends in my country, just as I hope to find friends here in yours. I'd like you to give me a chance to do that."

Sullen stares and an atmosphere of hostility met Kara's plea.

Norma took Kara's elbow and moved her toward an alcove at the end of the room. There was a cupboard, with a small refrigerator built underneath on one side and a sink set in the countertop at the other side.

"Don't let that upset you. Change is a big obstacle for them to overcome and you handled it just right." She patted Kara on the arm,

Pulling a Styrofoam cup from a plastic tube fastened to the wall, she continued.

"We make coffee for the staff and anyone else who wants it, but this area is basically for the clients use. They store their lunches in the fridge and there is a water cooler in each of the two work rooms." She poured steaming liquid into a Styrofoam cup.

"They bring their lunch and snacks and usually eat outside, unless it's raining."

The second room, which was the same size as the previous one, had two oversize trestle tables that had glue guns, staplers, and order pads scattered over them. The walls had shelves stacked with finished floral arrangements and also a chalkboard. A telephone was on the wall near a door that led outside to a patio. Another job coach Kara had not met before and three more clients were busily working in this room. Norma introduced Betty Martin and each of the clients by name.

"Bring your coffee," Norma said.

They went outside to the patio. It was a space just large enough to hold two picnic tables, benches, and two covered trash bins.

Norma looked at Kara with a sympathetic expression on her face.

"Try not to take this incident personally. You handled the situation extremely well. What you saw was their initial reaction to change. At present they are mad because Angela, who they knew so well has gone away and you, the stranger, the unknown, has replaced her and that is upsetting to them. Gaining their trust is usually the first obstacle to overcome and with every new client it seems we more often than not have to go through this preliminary stage. The good news is that most of the people we have referred to us are classified "trainable." We are not a baby-sitting agency and so we have expectations of each person enrolled here. The clients you have just met are in Phase I, or Workshop as we usually refer to it, and at that level they still have a way to go before they can graduate into Phase II. Using a simile, they might be likened to clay in its basic form. Our mission will be explained to you by Bart and Susan, so I'll stop at this point, but I'll be pleased to try to answer any questions you have."

Shifting to a more comfortable position on the bench and unconsciously grasping the cup tightly, Kara asked.

"What can you tell me about Effie? Is she a typical client; how old is she; what is her history? Suddenly I am very confused, wondering what I am doing here, so completely out of my depth."

Norma leaned over and patted Kara's hand sympathetically.

"Effie came to us from another agency because they could not handle her. The Regional Center, who in many respects is her guardian, decided that she needed to be in a different program, within a more structured framework. She is quite bright, even though she cannot read or write. She is surprisingly street-wise."

Kara interrupted.

"What is street-wise?"

Norma looked at Kara intently.

"You really don't know?"

Like a little girl in disgrace, Kara hung her head.

"I'm sorry, I feel as if I am learning a new language."

As if to justify her statement she added.

"Having been here for three days I am adding constantly to my vocabulary such things as a win-win situation; my computer station; gas not petrol; service station not garage; drug store not pharmacy; and even in this conversation with you there are more phrases, such as street-wise, our mission—what are we Crusaders?"

Norma cut off further conversation with a smile.

"I get the picture. Okay, street-wise usually means being able to look after yourself under adverse conditions. Let's say if you were visiting a big city from a country village you might give the immediate impression that you were a naive visitor and an easy prey for crooks on the lookout for such victims. If you were to carelessly carry valuables such as cameras and binoculars, wear lots of gold and expensive jewelry, carry a purse that could be snatched from you easily, you would probably be a target. Anyone street-wise would be very conscious of the need to protect these items and do so."

Kara nodded her head in agreement.

"Yes, I can see that."

Norma laughed and whooped.

"Gosh, guys, I think we have a classified "Trainable" here."

They laughed together.

Kara looked at her watch.

"I must leave. Thanks for explaining some things to me. It really helped."

As Norma walked Kara back to the front door a little voice pierced the hum of productivity.

"I like you Kara."

Waiting for the door to be unlocked, Kara looked into the Workroom. Every head was lowered attending to the task at hand.

Walking back to the office, Kara pondered her day so far. She recalled the little voice saying, "I like you Kara" and for a fleeting moment hoped that something important had just happened.

Bart and Susan were ready to see Kara, in fact they looked as if they had been waiting for her.

"Cup of coffee?" Bart asked, as he brought two cups into the room and handed one to Susan.

"No, thanks, I've already had my quota."

Bart closed the door and waved Kara to a seat. There was a pause. They looked at each other expectantly.

Susan was sitting behind the desk and after a quick glance at Bart directed her gaze to Kara.

"Before going any further, Bart and I wish to apologize for introducing you so abruptly and without preparation to our Workshop clients. If you are in a state of shock, we can understand that and take full responsibility for our insensitivity. In this business, we often must defer to immediate needs. As an example, this is exactly what happened earlier when Marcie brought up an issue that needed to be resolved right away. But it does not absolve our responsibility to you."

Taking a sip of coffee and leaning back slightly in the chair Susan smiled ruefully at Kara.

"Please forgive this lapse in awareness; we really are not as inconsiderate as we seem bent on proving to you. Can we start off on the right foot now?"

Noticing something moving out of the corner of her eye, Kara glanced past Susan and Bart out of the window to see Effie jumping up and down waving wildly to her through the glass.

"Oh. No." Kara said in exasperation, pushing back her chair. "How often does this kind of thing happen?"

She rushed out of the room, leaving Susan and Bart staring at each other in surprise. By the time Kara crossed the floor, Effie was already inside the foyer, hopping from one foot to another.

"Are you supposed to be here?" Kara asked suspiciously.

"'Course," was the answer. She continued her little dance, not missing a step.

Ramona came out of the job coaches' room and handed a large envelope to Effie, who snatched it and poised in the doorway said over her shoulder.

"You still talk funny," and with a delighted laugh, opened the door and skipped away.

Kara observing Susan and Bart standing in their office doorway walked between them and resumed her place in the room. They returned also, closing the door.

Bart looked at Kara rather cautiously.

"Well, we are pleased you decided to stay with us. We wondered if you'd have time to say 'goodbye' before you shot off into space."

Assessing what had impetuously taken place, Kara blushed.

"How awful of me—I must be getting neurotic. Ever since Effie led me on a wild goose chase this morning, she has been on my mind and then when she started contorting herself in front of your window, I began to think she must have been placed on this earth to test me."

Smiles were spreading over the Warners' faces and they asked what had happened earlier. Kara relayed the episode, saying it probably was not out of the ordinary for them, but it had been quite devastating for her, believing she could have lost a small, defenseless handicapped child.

Bert slapped his knee in mirth and looked to see Susan wiping her eyes with a tissue.

"Imagine how we felt, having just apologized for sending you over there and rationalizing that we would understand if you were in shock, to see you shoot out of the door like a bat out of Hell when Susan asked if we could start all over again."

Kara found amusement in this explanation and joined in the laughter.

"Oh, Kara, I haven't laughed like this since Angela was here."

A sad expression momentarily clouded Susan's attractive face.

"It's going to work out well, I can feel it."

Bart squeezed his wife's hand. Turning to Kara, he advised,

"What you should remember is that Ellie may be many things, but completely defenseless she is not. She is amazingly street-wise."

Again that expression. Kara felt a little smug recognizing it, without needing an explanation.

Settling down to business, Susan became the spokesperson.

"You already know the reasons why we started this business and the nature of it, but now that you are probably thoroughly confused let me give you a walk-through of the program itself. You may wish to make notes, but the information I am going to give is essentially to provide you with an overall picture. Things will fall into place, like a jigsaw puzzle, as they come up."

She continued.

"We are funded by both the State of California and the Federal Government and you will become very involved in this aspect as you assume your position here. We are contracted to teach each client who is enrolled with us how to become sufficiently autonomous to successfully hold a permanent job in the community.

To get them to this point we have four phases:

Phase I is the Workshop where the newly enrolled clients start out. Most of them have not had any kind of interfacing with the community at large. In order to be eligible for enrollment, a client must be between an IQ of 52-80 and be at least eighteen years of age."

Kara was starting to make notes on a yellow lined pad. So Effie was at least eighteen.

"With few exceptions they are invariably referred to us by the Inland Regional Center, who is the controlling and monitoring agency. Most clients come to us because they can no longer be kept in special education classes after a certain age. Those in this category usually have a disability from an early age and some are transferred from other districts if they move their residences. Others have disabilities caused by accidents or the effects of drugs and then there are those who come to us from other facilities. All have one or more disabilities whether physical or mental."

Susan took a sip of coffee and remarked, "There's much to learn and I don't want to over-burden you at this point, but you need to have an overall picture."

She returned the mug to a coaster.

"We teach our clients how to travel on public transportation. You probably don't realize that most of the people you saw were either dropped off at the Workshop by special vans used for specifically transporting them, or brought by parents or providers. They are unable to ride independently at this point on local buses, etc. and this is one of the things we must teach them."

Kara quickly voiced a question.

"Who or what are providers?"

"They are the people who own or manage a licensed facility, usually a large boarding-type house, where they feed and keep a certain number of people with disabilities. They too are state funded and must agree to be responsible for the people in their charge."

Kara nodded reflectively.

"Anyway, getting back to the Workshop topic," Susan continued, "we teach many subjects, such as, health and hygiene, safety signs and regulations, as well as socially acceptable behavior. In essence very basic rules to live by, with which most of these people are not familiar. They have had a tough enough time just getting through each day but now, to lead a productive life, they must start to conform to society's rules in order to gain acceptance."

Susan took another sip of coffee, looking ahead in thought.

"Once they graduate into Phase II their real training commences. They start on the piecework, counting a simple number of items and bagging them into lots. They receive a small stipend for doing this once the assignment is completed. In addition, they work on such things as the flower arrangements—remember what took place in the workshop you saw earlier? They also start going out on fieldtrips, traveling by public transportation. They are taken to look around factories, libraries, and museums, etcetera. On special occasions they are taken to one of the fast food restaurants for lunch, or perhaps a Baskin Robbins for an ice cream treat. These are all learning experiences, to discover what their comfort level is and how each reacts in various situations. Lunch breaks become a learning tool also. A high percentage of the clients consume their food in a quite unacceptable manner and have deplorable tendencies. We work on refining these before they reach Phase IV where they start working independently and mixing with a population who could easily be turned off by their poor habits."

Kara's eyes widened at this insight.

"Phase III is an important step for each client. We see the emergence of a person ready to test his or her own resources and become involved in a role more challenging than he or she has ever faced before. Marcie, or Julie our part-time assistant job developer, sets up a worksite with an employer. Next a job coach and up to five of the most appropriate clients are assigned to this job. At no cost to the employer we send our job coach to the worksite to learn all the steps involved in carrying out the work to be done. The job coach divides the work between the clients he or she has in their work group. It is the responsibility of the job coach to teach each client the work expected of him or her. It is also during this time that the clients are taught how to get to and from work daily, using the public transit system. Three times a week each client's workload of tasks is timed by stopwatch for three consecutive times to come up with each client's hourly pay rate. As their speed and proficiency increases, so does the amount they earn. It is a good motivator. It also indicates their readiness to go on to the next stage."

Susan looked at Bart.

"Do you want to finish off?"

"No. You are almost through and I'm enjoying listening to you. You know, Sue, I think you should attend the next Chamber of Commerce meeting and make a pitch."

She tossed a paperclip at him.

"Okay. Phase IV. As clients become more confident in handling a variety of tasks in Phase III and traveling to and from work, without many absences, the job coach at one of the staff meetings recommends graduation to the final level. This is contingent upon when the job developer is able to locate the type of position the client has professed interest and proficiency in doing. This step must be agreed to by the team of people involved in administering the affairs of the client.

Once again the job coach learns every aspect of this position and then works with the client on a 1:1 ratio teaching by hand demonstration, if necessary. Sorry, Kara. That means if the client doesn't understand the spoken instruction, the job coach places their hands over those of the client to demonstrate the procedure. This is the method used throughout our training. It works very well."

Susan took a deep breath.

"This then, is essentially, the nuts and bolts of our program."

Referring to her notepad, Kara said she had a few questions to ask. Waving her hand in Bart's direction, Susan sank back into the chair.

Kara started off.

"There are four phases to the program and each one seems packed with a lot of learning for clients who have never worked before and have problems of one kind or another. First of all—how long does this whole process take? Second, how can they all keep up with the curriculum if they can't read or write and have difficulty in mastering travel on public transportation?"

Bart was looking down at his hands, placed together at the tips, as if meditating. He looked over at Kara.

"Good questions. To answer the first part: Supposing we enroll a client with an IQ of 80, which is the highest we can expect, most are somewhat lower than this, providing they progress at a median level through each phase, they could go from Phase I through Phase IV in fifteen months. But this would be exceptional. Next: They learn by rote, being gradually introduced to things like traveling around the city. They commit this to memory by repetition and familiarity. It really does work."

Bart moved his big frame into a more comfortable position.

"This then, is only an overview," he reminded.

Bart stretched out his legs, yawned, and looked at Susan.

"Kara seems to have more questions, so why don't we wrap them up on the way home in the car?"

Susan looked at her watch and agreed. "It's a good time to stop, I'm ready for lunch."

Reaching into a drawer for her purse, Susan added, "There's a little restaurant across the street, Kara, or we can take you out to a fast food place for a pick-up meal, if you wish, but there's some business which Bart and I have to attend to afterwards."

"I'd like to take a walk. I'll go to the restaurant."

Bart directed the way to the "Inner Court," which was just a couple of blocks north.

✳ ✳ ✳

CHAPTER EIGHT

Kara walked to the restaurant that was part of an art museum. Consisting of one dining room for indoor eating and an open courtyard which held eight round glass-topped tables, it was a popular place with downtown workers.

It was 11:45 a.m. and it seemed very hot.

The courtyard was shaded and while Kara waited to be seated, the welcome coolness of the atrium-like setting enveloped her.

Already diners had occupied several tables and Kara, looking across the patio area, noted a small table near a flowing fountain. She was shown over to it. It was perfect.

Trailing plants cascading from ledges jutted out from the walls and small palm trees standing in pots were placed strategically to add privacy to the crowded area. Flowers in pots were at the base of the fountain. Tentatively Kara touched a petal and sighed with relief upon finding it real.

The menu was written in calligraphy with "Daily specials" such as a grilled tuna and cheese sandwich with a green salad that was a 'Vincent Van Gogh;' 'A Rueben' consisted of corned beef, sauerkraut, and cheese, with potato salad. The menu appealed to Kara's sense of humor. From a Disneyland special she chose a 'Popeye Salad' of spinach, goat cheese, and hard-boiled egg. The Olive Oyl dressing was delicious and the warm sheepherder bread was a tasty accompaniment. Sipping the iced tea, she trailed her fingers in the lower portion of the fountain. It felt very refreshing.

Looking upward between the green foliage Kara noticed carvings, half erased formations, in the stone parapet, which ran around the courtyard section. She could not make out what was written. On her way out, she asked what it said, but the young hostess said she had no idea. She started working there just two weeks earlier.

Stepping out of the museum's front door, Kara felt a blast of heat meet her. Already she could see it was going to take a while to become acclimatized. It was the beginning of February. At home she would have been muffled up in warm clothing. Everyone else was saying how lovely and pleasant the weather was and she, even in her lightest weight summer dress, still found the weather to be extremely hot. Walking back to the office for the two short blocks Kara felt as if she were burning up. It was a relief to get back to the cool interior of the office, where the air-conditioning was immediately felt. Now she understood the need for the water cooler conveniently standing in the foyer. Standing beside it she quickly drank the contents of the small disposable paper cup, and refilling it drank the second cup just as quickly.

Ramona came out of the lunchroom as Kara was pouring a third cup.

"Just sip," she advised, "you'll cool down soon now that you are out of the sun. You look very flushed. Your delicate skin will need to be protected and you might want to wear a skin barrier."

They smiled at each other.

Taking the water into her office Kara sat at her desk. Bart and Susan had not returned to the office from lunch. Turning on the computer Kara began refreshing the knowledge she had by skimming through the computer manual. That done, she turned to the required reading pertaining to the Rules and Regulations of "Working it Out."

Various other job coaches came in to the office and Ramona made a point of introducing them to Kara. Looking at her watch Kara saw it was 3:10 p.m. Ramona was standing at a file cabinet with papers in her hand when Kara approached her.

"Did Susan and Bart say they would be late getting back?"

"No, I thought they would be back by now—just a minute."

Picking up the phone Ramona entered several numbers. She spoke for a moment and silently handed the receiver to Kara.

"Hi Kara."

She recognized Susan's voice.

"We are on our way back to the office. We are passing through Colton and should be there in about fifteen minutes."

Kara thought they must have been standing beside the freeway—the background noise as they were talking was very loud.

"Can you keep yourself occupied until we get back?"

"Yes, I'm going over a file you asked me to review."

Replacing the phone Kara asked.

"Where is Colton and how were they communicating with us? Susan seemed to be speaking from a telephone booth by the side of a highway."

Amused Ramona responded.

"They have a cellular phone installed in the car, which makes it possible to place calls as they travel in the vehicle. It's a fairly new concept."

Kara's eyes opened wide. She must tell her father about this. It meant that he could make or receive calls while traveling in his car, providing the phone was connected. What a boon this piece of equipment would be in taking care of business, there would be little lost time or money. Wow! Jackie had told her how progressive Americans were and already she was discovering this for herself.

She shook her head admiringly as she followed Ramona into the job coaches' room where a huge map covering a 50 miles radius hung. It included parts of Riverside, San Bernardino, and Orange Counties.

"There's Colton."

Ramona pointed a finger. It looked relatively close to Riverside. Colored tacks and flags dotted the whole area.

"All those symbols indicate either where a client works or lives. It simplifies things in emergencies and in job developing," she explained.

Kara became so engrossed in studying the map that she was still there when Susan and Bart returned.

They both looked very pleased with themselves and beckoned Kara into their office. Watching Bart taking a large plastic tumbler to the water cooler was a reassuring sign to Kara. No one, no matter how long they lived in this particular area, was immune to the powerful rays of the sun.

They had barely taken the same seats when a glowing Marcie skipped into the room.

"Isn't it wonderful," she enthused looking at Susan and Bart who sat with delighted expressions on their faces. She also smiled at Kara, sitting waiting expectantly. Closing the door Marcie walked over to the low built-in window seat, pushing aside a silk floral display, before sitting down.

Without preamble she rushed in.

"As I explained to you on the phone very briefly earlier, they have never done this kind of thing before, but when I took Charlie with me and they were able to observe how well he behaved and responded to them, they actually signed the contract—right there and then. I couldn't believe it. They kept talking about having the general manager look it over, but then when the contract had been signed I saw that Jim Petrie, the guy I have been in contact with all this time, is the general manager. He later said they were somewhat apprehensive about employing our people and he apologized for being a little underhanded about handling the situation. As if to make up for this, he said if this crew works out well in the next two months, he will definitely employ another crew, with the possibility of a third."

Jumping up at this news, Susan, Bart, and Marcie started hugging each other.

Uncomfortable, thinking, *how can business be carried out in this way?* Kara, sneaked out of the room. Her exit did not seem to be noticed.

Almost a day had gone by and she had no clue as to what was expected of her. Everyone else seemed to be treating it like a normal day. What had she let herself in for? It was after 4:00 p.m. before Marcie returned to her desk and still in a visibly excited state, asked Kara to go and see Susan and Bart.

They were thrilled at Marcie's news, it was written all over their faces.

Kara automatically closed the door and took a seat near Susan's desk.

"You must think we are crazy, Kara, behaving like children, but Marcie has doggedly been pursuing this work lead for several months—yes, that's how long it can take to secure a worksite—and now, not only has a contract been signed for five or six of our clients with their job coach, but the potential is there for two more worksites to come out of it. Just imagine, eighteen clients almost guaranteed employment. It's wonderful news."

The news was too exciting to hide the big smiles it brought.

Looking at his watch Bart said he had an appointment in half-an-hour and had to leave.

Susan patted Kara on the shoulder and suggested that they start going over some of Kara's duties, as they were starting to pile up. Kara eagerly concurred.

On their way into Kara's office, Ramona popped her head out of the job coaches' room and waved them in.

A trestle table had been set up for a celebration, with the welcoming cake taking the pivotal position. Ten smiling job coaches, plus Ramona, and Marcie were waiting.

Susan turned to Kara.

"Well, Kara, this is not one of our more normal days, not that you have been in a position to determine this for yourself. Please believe me, we usually are a little more organized and calm going about our business. First of all we all wanted to welcome you to "Working it Out" and to let you know that you can count on each one of us for any assistance you may need."

Addressing the group, Susan stated, "If you have not yet met Kara, who is replacing Angela as our new office manager, please introduce yourself and tell her a bit about what you do." She quickly added, "Just the facts, ladies, no dramatics."

Turning to Marcie who was standing beside her, Susan said, "Another quite unexpected reason to celebrate is the excellent news from Marcie."

Patting Marcie's shoulder, she continued, "This is your baby, why don't you tell us about it."

Marcie, having settled down somewhat, informed the staff of the various stages that led to being offered the worksite commitment with a medium-sized factory.

Spontaneous applause broke out, with more hugs ensuing.

Marcie waved her hands to subdue the ruckus, and added,

"There will be two more worksites if we make a success of the first one."

Whoops and hollers followed and even Kara as unaccustomed as she was to such impetuous behavior, coming from her father's more decorous and controlled work environment, was impressed. The enthusiasm generated was contagious; she almost went over and hugged Marcie. Realizing what a short time she had known most of these people, she was aghast at her own reflexive response.

The cake was cut and passed around, and soft drinks were served. Kara was introduced to two more job coaches when they arrived later.

Driving back to the Warner's home, Kara had more of her queries answered. She was beginning to feel a little more comfortable especially as Susan had assured her that time would make sense of things.

After watching a special National Geographic program on television later that night Susan promised that, first thing the next morning, time would be taken to start Kara off in her position as office manager.

Getting ready to turn in for the evening, Kara took her diary out of the top drawer of a small desk much used by Angela. It had been emptied for her use and beside it stood a low padded bedroom chair in the same fabric as the drapes. Occupying the chair, Kara sat thoughtfully looking out of the window, admiring part of the row of palm trees that ran the length of the avenue like a stand of sentinels. In the darkness, silhouetted by the moon's ascendancy, the scenery looked quite romantic. For a fleeting moment she thought of her and Roger sharing this view. The insidious thought horrified her. Recalling his face with repugnance, Kara shuddered. She supposed it was because she was feeling a little lonely and homesick that her only brush with any kind of courtship unconsciously had promoted a romantic feeling. Brought on by the view from her window. Well, she had better get those kind of thoughts out of her head. She was going to be looking at this view for some time, so any amorous illusions should be dispelled immediately.

She sighed. Time for a quick shower and the diary entries.

Kara condensed the day's events, with the final entry "Bed 11:10 p.m." She tucked her diary back into the desk drawer.

With the travel clock's alarm set, her pink satin robe thrown over the bedroom chair, and the ceiling light switched off, Kara slipped into bed in the citrus yellow, apple green, and white bedroom, content to let her thoughts retrace the day. It had been interesting, even though she had yet to be introduced to her workload. She smiled to herself using the new word picked up today. *In no time at all I'll be speaking American*, she speculated, drifting off to sleep.

Kara's mother phoned at the end of the week. Susan took the call and spoke briefly with her, saying that Kara seemed to be settling in very well. She and Bart had no complaints, but she should check that out with Kara who was standing impatiently beside her.

Kara bit her lip and blinked back sudden tears upon hearing her mother's warm and loving voice.

"How are you, darling? We've missed you very much."

She sounded quite bereft and Kara determinedly sought to reassure her.

"I'm fine and things are going really well. Susan and Bart have been very helpful and the people at work seem nice, so try not to worry about me. We have just returned from the beach and I was thinking about you. Are you and daddy all right?"

She could visualize her mother referring to a list of questions and was not surprised when the expected cross-examination commenced.

Susan smiled at Bart and nodded toward the living room where they could hear Kara talking and occasionally laugh, in the infectious way she had, which seemed to affect those around her. They were cleaning vegetables at the kitchen sink for the evening meal and Susan laid her head against Bart's shoulders.

"I hope Angie is settling in, honey, I look at Kara and my maternal instinct rears its head. They are both so young and vulnerable and suddenly I feel like a split personality, worrying about our daughter and protecting our new one."

Bart dried his hands on a dishcloth, and lovingly took his wife into his arms for a quick embrace.

Kara surprised them.

"Oh, how nice. It makes me feel as if I'm at home. My parents are very romantic. I used to be a little embarrassed when my father swatted my mother's behind as he passed her, or she took hold of his hands as they were talking."

A hurt look momentarily clouded the clear green eyes.

"I now realize how elusive that special kind of love is."

She put on a bright smile.

"It is terrific to see you are still sweethearts, too."

This was more personal information than Kara had divulged during her entire stay and Susan and Bart were taken aback. Susan immediately drew Kara into their arms and they all hugged. Dinner was a turning-point in their relationship. They talked and laughed constantly. Even Barbara was affected by their good humor and banged her spoon noisily and laughed spontaneously in her shrill, high voice.

From that time on Kara became an active family participant. She consulted them as she would her own parents and they discussed decisions relating to their personal and business life that they would have deliberated with their eldest daughter. When Kara spoke to her parents on the phone, Susan and Bart did too. When Angela called or calls were made to her, Kara always added her own news.

Kara became very comfortable with life in California. She had visited most of the attractions touted in the area. Sharing the office with the outspoken and gregarious Marcie Michaelson was leading to the growth of a unique friendship between them.

It was the beginning of August and the weather was hot. After six months Kara began to wonder if she would ever become acclimatized to the heat. Unexpectedly Kara's father phoned. She was alarmed. He never initiated a phone call.

"Is everything all right? I'm taken aback to hear your voice. Mummy usually calls, so you have taken me by surprise."

Her father chuckled.

"I overruled her this time. With something exciting to suggest I couldn't resist being the bearer of good news. Your mother is listening on another telephone."

At this, Kara's mother interrupted with her own greetings.

"Darling, we are in the process of discussing our upcoming vacation and . . . ."

"Silvia!" said a threateningly deep voice. "I won the toss."

Kara giggled.

"Before your mother reneges on our pact, we want to let you know that we are planning on flying out to California for your birthday in September and staying for a couple of weeks."

Kara cried out in pleasure.

"Oh, that's terrific."

Then panic ensued.

"I don't think I am eligible to take a vacation yet and it would be unfair to ask Susan and Bart to compromise their work ethics on my account. After all I've been in the position for just six months."

She could hear her father snorting with annoyance in the background as the persuasive voice of her mother entreated, "Would you like us to speak with Susan and Bart?"

That would never do.

"Let me discuss it with them and get back to you. Perhaps a solution can be found. On the other hand, it may not be possible, so don't hold your breath."

She could hear the gasp at the other end.

"Don't hold your breath? What kind of language is that?" Kara smiled inwardly. It was time they were re-educated, too.

The next night, seated around the kitchen table with dinner cooking, Bart, Susan and Kara discussed the possibilities. Kara ran upstairs to pick up her diary and find a map of California, leaving Bart and Susan in conversation. They had a calendar, taken from the refrigerator, laid on the table in front of them.

A phone call from Marcie came in and Kara spoke with her for a few minutes. The two of them would be visiting her parents in Santa Barbara at the weekend.

When she returned they were smiling.

"It could work out. We are in the preliminary stages of exploration," Bart announced.

"If your parents wouldn't object to having their time split up into sections, it perhaps could be arranged. What do you think about these tentative suggestions? Unfortunately the first week of your parent's visit is an extremely busy one for you. Getting all the fiscal information ready and sent to the state and federal offices for payment is a mandatory and prime responsibility for "Working it Out" to exist and remain solvent. I am suggesting during that time that, with Barbara, I could take your parents up to our cabin at Lake Arrowhead for a few days."

Kara's display of disappointment led Bart to hurry on.

"You and Susan would naturally join us each day after work. It's less than an hour's drive from Riverside. In fact, you probably could start work earlier in the day and leave mid-afternoon. This would certainly give more time to spend together and the sleeping accommodation is quite adequate for all of us."

Bart paused, looking intently at Kara.

"At over 5,000 feet in elevation, the climate there is much more pleasant than it is here in Riverside through the summer and should be a welcome relief to your parents."

Warming to the subject he added.

"The air is clear and the mountain views are magnificent. If your father is a fisherman, the lake is right at the doorstep and there is a boat for tooling around in."

Kara laughed.

"You've just described Paradise for both of them. My mother is quite a well-known artist in Europe."

Joining in the conversation Susan said, "I hope this means that when I take the remainder of the week off work that they won't object too much to leaving the San Bernardino Mountains for the beach. We have a time-share arrangement on a condominium in San Diego and it is a very interesting area in which to browse around, to stroll the beach and to eat marvelous food at some of the restaurants there."

Kara's eyes shone.

"San Diego is just about two hour's drive away, isn't it? Is there room for all of us there?"

"No problem," Susan answered.

Bart placed his hand over Kara's.

"You and your parents probably won't feel that you are seeing as much of each other as you would like and you really are entitled by law to one week's vacation, so the second week is yours to spend with them. How does this sound to you?"

Kara was ecstatic. Leaping up from the kitchen chair she rushed around to them, hugging and kissing them spontaneously. Susan and Bart beamed at each other in delight.

"Do you mind if I phone them right away? I'm so excited—I can hardly wait to tell them."

Leaving her half-eaten meal Kara dashed to the telephone and dialed their private number.

A frown creased Kara's forehead as she listened to the phone ringing at the other end. Hearing her father's lethargic voice she looked at her watch. Oh, heavens, it was just after four in the morning. No wonder he sounded tired.

"Sorry, daddy, I forgot the time difference. I was so excited about the news we have to discuss that I picked up the phone without thinking. I'll call back during the day. All right?"

By this time a more alert voice responded.

"Oh, no you don't, young lady. Now that you have piqued our interest, you had better continue the conversation. Your mother has gone to another telephone to join in."

Kara heard the click, followed by a yawn.

"I'm here, darling, but don't expect much from me at this intolerable hour."

The next fifteen minutes passed swiftly with the vacation planned to everyone's satisfaction.

That night sitting at the desk before the bedroom window, filling out her diary for the day, Kara found it difficult to suppress the exciting prospect of seeing her parents again. How would she ever sleep tonight? She felt more like jumping over the new moon, which hung over the palm trees. She had so much to tell them, so much to show them. No, she definitely was not going to get much sleep tonight; she was far too elated. Somewhat reluctantly she climbed into bed and prepared herself for watching the dawn come in.

Staring out of the window into the darkened heavens, Kara imagined the silver slivered moon threading its way across the inky sky. It would glide across the hemisphere to a special little harbor where, looking down on its own reflection, Cormorant Bay lying quiet and peaceful could be observed. Lights from some of the houseboats would be twinkling and further over, toward the promontory, a bonfire would become evident. Nestling into the pillow Kara smiled contentedly, a "clambake" must be in progress. Uncle Jim would be in charge. Everyone would be sitting out on beach chairs or rugs, snuggled into warm sweaters or blankets, toasting marshmallows and making them into "S'Mores." Just as they always did.

Lulled by the beloved landscape and comforted by the occurrence of a familiar, happy scene, Kara was blissfully unaware how speedily sleep overtook her.

★ ★ ★

CHAPTER NINE

Keeping busy with her work helped the time pass more quickly for Kara, until the day before her parents were expected to arrive and at that time she became unglued.

It was Wednesday and a general meeting was to be held at 4:00 p.m. after the job coaches had finished their daily projects with the clients. Kara was noticeably fidgety, glancing at her watch or the clock on the conference room wall constantly. Clasping and unclasping her hands, doodling on her notebook and restlessly changing positions on the chair upon which she was sitting were nervous signals noticed by everyone in the room. When Bart asked Kara to present the office report, she visibly jumped in surprise.

Collectively the staff smiled. Kara's abstraction, becoming progressively more evident, had become a source of amusement. Consulting the prepared information, Kara blushed upon seeing fancy curlicues decoratively obscuring the carefully prepared material.

Too embarrassed to reply, Kara held the top page up for inspection and was greeted with howls of laughter.

Susan shook her head, smiling faintly.

"Without reconstructing the scene of the crime, can you salvage any information from it to bring us, more-or-less, up-to-date?"

Kara could do so and the meeting continued without further disruption.

Susan and Kara worked until late that evening so that they could take time the next day to meet Kara's parents at the airport. Marcie would be in charge once they left. Bart decided to stay at home catching up on paperwork the next day, with Barbara keeping him company.

Taking Bart's large and comfortable Cadillac, Susan and Kara left the office at three-o'-clock. The plane was due in just after five. Providing traffic was light they would have plenty of time to travel to the Los Angeles International Airport and be waiting to welcome Kara's parents after they passed through Customs.

As excited as she was, Kara managed to contain herself well. They exited from the freeway briefly to pick up hamburgers and cold drinks at a Jack-in-the-Box near Garden Grove and arrived at the airport with almost half-an-hour to spare. They visited the gift shop in the International Terminal and Kara purchased postcards of some of the places she hoped her parents would want to visit. In any case, they would come in handy for them to mail.

The plane had landed and the time had almost arrived. Kara felt like jumping up and down like a little girl. Impetuously she grabbed hold of Susan's hand. Susan had tears in her eyes and, for the first time, Kara realized how self-centered she had been in speaking of reuniting with her parents, when Susan must be wishing it were her own daughter who was coming. Kissing her cheek, Kara gave Susan a quick hug.

Kara saw her father first, pushing a cart filled with luggage, looking around into the crowd. Shoving her way through to the front of the waiting throng of people Kara called eagerly, "Daddy, oh, daddy," waving her arms to attract his attention.

Right behind him was her mother, who saw her first and hurried toward her. They were hugging and kissing when Kara's father joined them. Susan was standing further back, a whimsical smile on her face. They made their way to her laughing and talking at the same time. Recognizing that phone contact had been their main source of communication, Kara introduced them face-to-face.

After an inordinate period exchanging post-flight conversation took place, Susan said tiredly, "Let's talk in the car as we travel, otherwise at this time of day we may get caught in the tail-end of the commute traffic."

Kara's mother seemed to be a little distracted, glancing anxiously around her. When two figures approached them, Kara understood why. Angela left Jackie pushing a loaded buggy and flew toward her mother, with arms outstretched. Susan was completely taken aback and Kara saw with relief that Angela had her arms securely around her mother, sagging against her. Kara hurried over to hug Jackie.

"Oh, goodness," Susan said, holding her daughter firmly around the waist, "what a fantastic surprise. I can't believe this is happening."

Looking at her watch she repeated, "Please everyone we should be getting on our way—Los Angeles traffic can be very bad at this time of day."

There was a hint of anxiety in her voice.

Jackie responded

"Just a minute, Susan. Angela and I are here to work."

Noting the look of disappointment on Susan's face, she added, "But she has ten days to spend with you beforehand. There are several things I must attend to without her. Whenever there is free time I will phone and perhaps we can arrange an outing or two, but basically my time will be occupied and that was why it was a golden opportunity for Angela to come with me."

Susan went over and kissed Jackie warmly.

"Thank you for whatever part you played in this. Bart will be as thrilled as I am to have Angela home and you know you are welcome to join us whenever you can. You promise?"

"You can count on it. I want to spend some time with Kara anyway."

With that, Jackie summoned a Redcap over, pointing to her pieces of luggage.

"I think that may be my taxi to my second home at The Beverly Hills Hotel."

She nodded at the white stretch limousine pulling up at the curb.

Kara's mother teased fondly.

"Trust Jackie to go in style."

Drawing herself up to her full height Jackie postured in her best runway manner.

"Dahling, it's the only way to go."

Her naughty smile belied the haughty stance and she winked as she strutted after the Redcap.

"She's fantastic, mom, I couldn't have a better tutor and I can hardly wait to tell you and dad all that's happened. I have lots of pictures and things for you."

Angela hugged her mother again, reluctant to let her go. She looked over at Kara, who had an arm clutched around her own mother's waist.

"I guess we have to introduce ourselves, since everyone thinks we know each other."

Kara stepped forward with an outstretched hand and Angela, ignoring it, gave her a hug instead.

"I really do feel that I know you very well and I hope we'll have time to spend together."

Kara's friendly smile left no doubt that she was in agreement.

Susan and Angela went to get the car, leaving the luggage with Kara and her parents. There was a very jovial atmosphere and Kara stood between her parents holding their hands and participating in a lively conversation until the Cadillac appeared. The drive back to Riverside seemed so much shorter than it had when she first arrived in America some months earlier.

The Cadillac turned into the driveway of 2236 Via San Dimas and the front door opened almost immediately. Bart, with a hand on Barbara's shoulder, stood in the doorway waiting to welcome the visitors. Angela tore out of the car, almost before it had stopped, sweeping up Barbara who could not be restrained from rushing toward her. Almost as if in slow motion, Kara saw the look of astonishment that came across Bart's face when he recognized Angela and the crumpling of his features as tears rolled down his cheeks. It had been a shock.

Unloading the luggage, parking the car in the garage, and ushering everyone into the house gave Bart time to regain his composure. A grin, reflecting the pleasure at having his daughter home again, emerged.

Ten minutes later, with the luggage stacked in the hallway and introductions made again, drinks were served in the comfortable living room. In an effort to be heard over the various conversations taking place at the same time, Kara's father, in his usual dignified manner, rose to his feet and raised his hand for silence.

Looking at Susan and then Bart he addressed both.

"Please allow me to first of all thank you for your generous hospitality in providing our daughter with a second home and a family to whom she has become greatly attached. Kara's mother and I appreciate this deeply and are immensely indebted to you. It was with heavy hearts that we reluctantly parted from her. Silvia and I have already had the privilege of getting to know Angela, and we have found her to be a lovely young woman—a daughter of whom you can be very proud."

Gus Olavssen sat down beside his wife, who gently took his hand and squeezed it.

Getting to his feet also Bart responded to his guest's formal oration.

"Now I'd like to say a few words. Thank you for bringing Angie for this awesome surprise visit, I'm still in a daze, waiting to wake up. If one wish could have been granted to Susan and me, this would have been it, and so we thank you from our hearts, no matter whose idea it was. As we are not able to have our daughter with us, then Kara is at the top of our list, she is a delight and we thank you for letting us temporarily adopt her."

Everyone laughed as Angela playfully swatted her father's arm and moved closer to him on the sofa.

The dialogue commenced in earnest until most of the questions had been answered and hands began to cover surreptitious yawns.

Kara's parents rose to their feet. Silvia looked at Susan.

"We really should leave. Our journey is catching up with us and we are very tired. Arrangements have been made to stay at The Mission Inn in downtown Riverside and if a taxi can be called, we will bid you goodnight and look forward to seeing you again soon."

Bart immediately offered to drive them there and Kara jumped up to accompany them. Angela was almost asleep on the couch and Kara, leaning over her murmured,

"There's a cot being set up for you in Barbara's bedroom. I just want to finish putting on the sheets. It will only take a few minutes."

Angela smiled, sleepily contented.

From Seventh Street, the view of The Mission Inn appeared unexpectedly. At night, bathed in a luminescent glow, the magnificent building surfaced like an oasis in the desert.

Covering one city block it was sheltered in stunning gardens, partially allowing brief glimpses of its unusual century-old architecture to passers-by. Considered to be the Jewel of Riverside, the historic landmark lived up to the accolades heaped upon it. The senior Olavssens' sat up straight in their car seats, all the better to observe their approach to it.

"How lovely," Silvia remarked softly upon being assisted from the vehicle. The Campanile with its hanging bells was subtly outlined and the famous Anton clock, illuminated in its imposing tower, chimed a welcome.

Their luggage, placed on a gold colored trolley by a uniformed bellboy, followed them along the pathway through the Court of the Birds. Magnificent plant specimens were strategically illuminated and the Pergola running around the perimeter of this older section of the building was heavy with red bougainvillea.

Silvia and Gus Olavssen were equally charmed with the Carey Jacobs Bond suite on Author's Row, to which they were shown. Kara hugged her parents several times before reluctantly parting from them. Handing over a business card with her work phone number listed she beseeched, "Please call me early. We have so much to discuss and plan." She ran back to hug and kiss them one more time.

Kara and Bart rode the elevator down to the ground floor, chatting as they did so. Remembering when the Inn had to be closed-down because of fiscal difficulties Bart hastened to add that this happened years before Kara's arrival in Riverside.

"For almost eight years, we thought we had a white elephant on our hands. Deals fell through after millions of dollars had been poured into upgrading and earthquake proofing the various sections. The City tried to keep it going by leasing part of it as apartments and accommodation for students at the university. Eventually, Duane Roberts, a local entrepreneur and wealthy businessman stepped in and purchased it. We gratefully applauded him and gave a big sigh of relief."

Crossing from the elevator to the double doors leading outside, they walked over the breadth of a long hand-woven cream carpet, which stretched endlessly to the front door. "Isn't this an amazing project—the twenty-one California Missions are all shown in the chronological order in which they were founded."

Bart chuckled as he looked back at the wide floor runner.

"It was woven in Thailand, with French interpreters of the Spanish wording. I was told there are only two spelling errors in the whole thing—that seems pretty amazing to me."

In following Bart's conversation, Kara glanced along the length of the intriguing cream colored carpet and became aware of the soft, melodic strains that emanated from a Steinway grand piano. Dreamily caressing the ivory keys the pianist, in evening dress, serenaded guests sitting at nearby small tables

"Whenever I come here, I intend staying longer to browse around. It is so interesting. Now that my parents are here, I'll have that opportunity."

Kara yawned and Bart followed suit.

"Let's get back. If Angela and Susan have any sense they'll be in bed. It's been a long day for all of us."

Traveling back to Via San Dimas Kara lay back against the headrest and closed her eyes. Ahead were two full weeks of being with her parents, seeing them for at least part of each day. She mentally reviewed the arrangements made so far.

Opening her eyes she smiled at Bart.

"Isn't it silly, I feel like a little girl anticipating Christmas."

Bart returned her smile.

"Not silly at all. I know exactly how you feel. Susan and I have just been given an unexpected gift ourselves."

CHAPTER TEN

The visit of Kara's parents sped past and Kara was reluctant to part from them. During the time spent with Kara they came to the conclusion that their daughter was in no hurry to leave her adopted country. They also realized that without transportation Kara was very restricted in her movements.

Their decision to surprise Kara with a jaunty red Mustang automobile for her birthday was a difficult one to make. The pleasure and appreciation shown by Kara was counterbalanced by her parents sorrow at leaving her. They had hoped she would indicate her desire to return to England within the near future.

She had not done so.

Saying goodbye in the Bradley Terminal 4 of the Los Angeles International Airport had been hard for each of them. Kara's parents consoled her with the reminder that they had initiated the first visit to her and having accomplished this, they would return regularly. She could count on that.

Kara was beginning to feel very comfortable with her lifestyle in California. Becoming interested in Barbara's condition, she had long talks with Susan and Bart. They referred her to their own extensive library on the subject and also recommended people they knew who could feed more information to her.

It was through her developing knowledge and interest in the subject and the underserved needs of the disabled population with whom she worked that Kara decided to branch out into another field. With this in mind, she challenged her University of Durham degree against that of its equivalent in the U.S. It was her objective to transfer into social work.

After what seemed like an unusually lengthy process, covering inter-country verification and collaboration, by correspondence and telephone calls, Kara was eventually informed of the reciprocity arrangement decided upon and offered to her.

Included in the comprehensive list to become eligible for the Master's Social Work (MSW) degree, Kara would need to add higher level courses to those already achieved in sociology, advanced biology, statistics, and psychology in the Bachelor's degree stage. Reaching the Bachelor's degree level, with the successful completion of the courses outlined, Kara would be eligible to apply to enter a MSW program. The MSW program would take two years to complete and would require both classroom education and an internship—usually two days a week for the first year and three days a week for the second year. A Master's Thesis, which would be in the form of a long research 'Dissertation' would be required to graduate. After the two years of working under supervision in the field, an examination must be taken to become licensed by the State of California to become a qualified Licensed Clinical Social Worker (LCSW).

After some soul-searching, Kara decides that this is the route she wants to follow and under the sponsorship and supervision of Bart, who is a State LCSW, she begins the procedure. In the process of achieving her goal Kara, in collaboration with and the approval of Bart, changes her office hours to a flexible schedule. Accomplishing additional office work for "Working it Out" on weekends and staying late at the office were necessary revisions agreed to by Kara.

When the Phase I, workshop program manager's position became vacant, Kara applied for it. It was the lowest managerial post at "Working it Out." The job announcement was advertised and there were many applicants, including two job coaches from "Working it Out."

In fairness to all, Bart and Susan brought in a three-member team of experts to interview those who appeared qualified for the job.

After all the interviews had taken place and several candidates were called back for a second interview, the final decision by the interviewing team was made. They highly recommended Kara for the position.

There was some dissention among the job coaches when they heard that Kara had accepted the post when it was offered to her.

Susan and Bart called a meeting.

In his usual direct manner Bart addressed the staff.

"I think we all know why we are here."

Bart looked around the crowded conference room. There was a severe expression on his face.

"Susan and I are aware of the discord and rumors circulating around the office and we want to get this undercurrent out into the open for discussion. We won't mince words and I expect you to be honest in expressing your opinions, so that this matter can be resolved as quickly as possible."

He looked over at Susan as if for support. She nodded her head. Bart continued.

"Lola, you said you wanted to speak on behalf of Katie and yourself because you both applied for the workshop manager's position and Katie is out sick right now."

Lola, a buxom dark haired woman in her mid-twenties, looked at Bart defiantly.

"We felt it was unfair to promote Kara over us. We know more about the job than she does."

"How did you reach that conclusion?" Susan interjected.

"I've worked with the clients directly for over a year and Katie for almost two." Lola responded.

"Have you ever applied for a supervisory position with us before?" Susan asked.

"No. This is the first time I've been interested."

"So what qualifications do you bring that would give you the edge over Kara when you were interviewed?" Susan questioned.

Lola looked at Susan with a quizzical expression before replying.

"The experience. Working with the clients every day."

Susan smiled kindly.

"We all do that and Kara as office manager does more of that than you are probably aware."

She glanced around the room.

"How many here can identify Kara's involvement with clients?"

There was silence. Blank expressions were registered on most faces.

Ramona spoke quietly.

"Kara mixes with the clients a lot. They come to the office frequently and she goes over their SSI benefits with them as well as visiting their homes or board-and-care places to discuss any irregularities with their parents or guardians. She also sits in on the Inter Disciplinary Team meetings with the State and the Department of Rehabilitation that each client has twice a year."

She hesitated before adding.

"As far as I know, most of the clients really like Kara. When they come to the office they usually want to go to her for a hug or just to say Hi."

She smiled.

"They sometimes bring her a wilted flower or a drawing they have done and she loves it. Always makes them feel good."

Ramona looked at Kara, admiration plainly visible.

"I think she'll make a great workshop manager."

Looks of disbelief were showered at Ramona.

Bart stepped in.

"Thanks Ramona. Any other comments? Anyone?"

Jane, a new job coach, nervously responded.

"I thought you were supposed to promote from the ranks."

Bart nodded his head in agreement. "That's true, if staff is qualified. Otherwise we choose from the most suitable person who replies to our ad."

Susan addressed the group.

"Let me tell you why Kara was offered the job and remember that neither Bart nor I were involved in this decision. She was recommended by the interviewing team, which consisted of Amanda Smith, who is Director of a similar facility to ours in Los Angeles; also Hal Robinson, who is a State Facilitator for people with disabilities in Sacramento and lastly Dr. Bruce Jergens, who is Executive Director of the County of Riverside School for the Handicapped. All are very capable and eminently qualified people to determine the potential of applicants."

She paused and picked up a sheet of paper from the top of a nearby file cabinet.

"Kara has full knowledge of the fiscal management of this office. She validates the monthly time reports which each supervisor turns in and she also checks the timesheets of each job coach for accuracy. Remember how intricate they can become and the times they are returned to you for corrections? So, without going into more details, Kara is more familiar than anyone else with the office work that each manager is required to do."

Nodding heads followed this information. The light was suddenly dawning.

"As far as Kara's skill and expertise with clients goes, you have already heard Ramona give an insight into the interfacing she does, but what you may not know is that Kara is working her way through the social worker degree at San Bernardino State."

Susan's face tightened as she continued.

"Job coaches! Not one of you is currently enrolled in a college course, which might indicate your interest in qualifying for any promotions that come up. Bart and I have encouraged this and, in fact, have paid for the successful completion of relevant subjects taken by others. As far as I am concerned, it is up to each one of you to further your education if you are serious about getting ahead with "Working it Out"."

Exasperated, she looked at Bart.

He stepped in.

"I think you can see that Kara is more than qualified for the position she has accepted. She will need your support and assistance and Susan and I will be extremely disappointed if you fail her, because in doing so you also fail "Working it Out." We are a team here and every one of you is top notch at what you do and we appreciate your dedication and hard work. I'm sorry this situation came up."

He quickly looked at Susan. "Anything else?"

Susan's gaze went from face to face. Speaking clearly and distinctly she queried,

"Any further questions? This subject will not be brought up again."

No one responded and Susan and Bart left the room.

Marcie went over to Kara and hugged her.

"I'm glad that's over. I believe congratulations are in order."

All the managers and several job coaches found their way to Kara and offered their support. The rest left quietly.

Once the rumblings had settled down, Kara demonstrated steadily the strength and appropriateness of the decisions she made. As she progressed through the established organizational pecking order, her recommendations and solutions were received appreciatively. Kara already carried the trust earned through the interfacing with the State and Federal agencies in her role as office manager. Her honesty and real concern for the clients were apparent and when she aired her concerns and suggestions at state and federal seminars, there was no question with whom her allegiance lay. She became a formidable advocate for the disabled community.

It was with great relief that Kara received notification that she had passed the examination taken to become licensed by the State. As a qualified Licensed Clinical Social Worker she could add the initials LCSW after her name.

It was over four years since she had arrived in her new land and Kara felt a need to pay a visit to her parents. When they visited a couple of times a year, they seldom asked when she would be returning, but having committed herself to the work she was doing she decided to tell them of her intent to remain in California for a while.

The two weeks that Kara spent in England with her parents were relatively quiet. After the chaotic schedule she had pursued rigorously for the past few years, she was content to relax and simply enjoy their company. They had surmised that Kara's plans were long-term. During their regular visits to California they could see how dedicated Kara had become to the clients she worked with. Alerting her parents to her intent to become certified in that field was not the surprise Kara had expected. It followed, they reasoned, that Ms. Kara Olavssen, LCSW would expect to put her ideas into practice and test her own resources. Again they refused to be surprised when Kara brought up the subject during her vacation with them. They gave her so much support and confidence. How blessed she was to have such amazingly understanding parents.

Kara saw little of Jon during this time. She phoned a couple of times, leaving messages on his Telephone Answering Machine at the farm, which he did not return. Kara thought this was rather odd, but as they had parted on indifferent terms, she left it up to him to contact her.

The only time she saw him occurred when impetuously she decided to stay overnight at The Colony. He had decided to spend the day there with Tasha, his Retriever puppy. They surprised each other. Kara had gone for a swim in the "swimming pool" and in lying in the sun to dry off she had fallen asleep reading a deadly dull book.

Tasha loped over to Kara and started licking her salty shoulder with enthusiasm. Kara woke up startled to find Jon holding Tasha by the collar.

They stared at each other almost like strangers and Kara was very conscious of the brevity of her bikini. Jon surveyed Kara's tanned body.

"California seems to suit you in more ways than one. It appears congratulations are in order on your latest academic achievement. You always had a lot going for you, Kara."

Kara sat up, reaching for the oversized T shirt with the "Working it Out" logo imprinted on the front.

"Hello to you too, Jon," she replied, slipping the piece of clothing over her head. Her voice was cool and detached. She was a little annoyed that he had found her like this, particularly as he appeared to have ignored her earlier conciliatory attempts and now they suddenly were confronting each other.

Kara felt she was at a disadvantage.

Yes. Her gut reactions had been reliable. They had definitely grown apart.

Standing, Kara pulled the long, baggy shirt down past her thighs.

"I understand congratulations may be due to you soon, too. I've heard you and Angela are probably getting engaged."

She scrutinized Jon with curiosity reflected in her eyes.

He looked away before bringing his eyes back to meet Kara's.

"It's possible," he said brusquely.

He was not even going to answer her civilly. Kara looked at him in amazement.

"You really are a bastard. I thought we were friends, but now I wonder where the real Jon Williams has gone—if there ever was a real Jon Williams."

In frustration Kara thumped Jon's chest and Tasha, taken by surprise, started barking nervously. Jon grabbed Kara's fist with one hand as she attempted another jab while restraining Tasha with the other.

They looked into each other's face.

"I'm sorry, Kara, I've had a hard time confronting you, especially when I feel I'm deserting you. Angela has stipulated, in order to prove my commitment to our relationship, that the competition be eliminated and you are in that category."

Disbelief showed on Kara's face as she helplessly dropped her hands to her sides.

"I don't believe this. And you are going along with it?"

Jon looked embarrassed.

"I love Angela despite her whims and you can regard this as a cowardly gesture if you wish, but I don't want to lose her and to a certain degree I can see where she is coming from. I didn't realize how frequently you came into my conversation until she pulled me up about my "Kara fetish." She is hearing glowing reports from her parents now that you are working with them in California, which doesn't help."

He said as an afterthought.

"They are certainly right about how you have developed into a very beautiful woman; much too attractive for Angie's peace of mind."

Kara had a sinking feeling. Surely Jon would not cut her off like deadwood. Many of their life experiences had been shared. Surely he knew she considered him to be the brother she never had.

Tears came to her eyes and spilled over.

Jon took Kara's hand.

"Let's go for a walk. We can iron some things out, even though I can't make any promises."

Kara returned to California feeling worse than she did leaving it two weeks earlier. It took some time to settle down into her demanding and usually fulfilling routine. She just could not get Jon's rejection out of her thoughts.

It had become a pattern, over the last few years, for Kara to accompany Marcie to her parents' home in Santa Barbara about once a month and to spend the weekend there.

Usually they had a great time, but after a particularly lackluster game of tennis singles, Marcie said impatiently.

"Kara, ever since you came back from la-de-da land last month, you've been walking around like a Zombie. What happened there? And don't give me the brush-off again. I'll nag until you tell me."

Kara removed her drenched headband and threw it into the sports bag by her side. She hesitated slightly before responding.

"Jon told me he was most likely getting engaged to Angela and we could no longer be friends."

"Okay—then what happened?"

"Nothing," Kara said with a frown on her face, "I didn't see him again and I left England shortly afterward."

Marcie's face expressed astonishment.

"And that is it? Heaven's Kara, I thought you must have had a wild love affair with a married man with five kids, who discarded you in favor of his long suffering wife and you now find yourself pregnant."

She stopped for breath and Kara started laughing rather wearily. Marcie joined in.

"You certainly do put things into perspective."

Suddenly tears began to run unchecked down Kara's face and Marcie knelt in front of her, placing an arm around her shaking shoulders. She dried Kara's tears with the sleeve of the cotton jacket draped around her shoulders.

"Gosh, if he did this to you, he can't be much of a friend."

Marcie turned Kara's face toward her.

"How about a lover or a prospective husband! Did you think about him in that way?"

Kara sniffed and shook her head.

"No. I honestly didn't. We have been friends for so long I guess I'm just having a difficult time accepting his brush-off. It really hurts to believe he could drop me so easily. So much for the special relationship I thought we had."

Marcie's hazel eyes reflected sympathy.

"Well, he must be a weird guy and obviously not very smart, that's all I can say. Tonight at Duane's party we'll give Jon a real classy sendoff. We'll wish him and his future wife a good life and then forget about the foolish man. Okay?"

Kara smiled wanly.

"Considering that Jon and I see each other so seldom these days, I suppose I am being silly dwelling on something over which I have no control."

Kara shrugged her shoulders.

"Que sera, sera."

Seeing Marcia's puzzled expression, she translated.

"Whatever will be, will be."

In true cheerleader fashion Marcie leaped into the air, startling Kara with her athletic movements.

"Yahoo! We will start on your rehabilitation treatment tonight, and depending upon how receptive you are we'll continue until Dr. Marcie determines its success. Tomorrow's therapy will take place on the intrepid O' Rourke twins' yacht. Outfoxing them is always a challenge in such a restricted area and then later on, if there's time . . ."

Kara held up her hand and smiled. "I get the message."

Marcie was the craziest, most uninhibited friend she had ever had. She was also the most considerate and special. They understood each other very well and their friendship had blossomed from the time they first met, despite their disparate temperament and background.

CHAPTER ELEVEN

Kara had made it almost to the top of the ladder. Occupying the Phase IV program manager position brought the seniority that placed her directly under Susan and Bart's authority.

It came as a shock several months later, however, when Susan and Bart specifically invited Kara out to Sunday brunch at The Mission Inn and talked to her about their plans.

Susan patted Bart's knee and faced Kara across the table saying quietly, "We are seriously considering selling the business. We have accomplished what we intended doing, setting up a professional, well-run agency to serve this special segment of society and educate the population. After many hard, but successful years, we feel we can pass the goodwill on to someone else and retire to the vineyard without guilt."

Kara tried to sound enthusiastic about their plans, they certainly had earned the right, but the suddenness of their intent left her feeling miserable and unprepared. Her heart ached for the clients she had grown to understand and love. How would they react to the prospective tumultuous change that would throw their world into chaos?

Thinking along these lines Kara asked, "How will the clients adjust to this change? It is rather radical for them to accept, isn't it?"

Susan and Bart looked at each other with consternation in their eyes. Was Kara going to be difficult about this? They had their own doubts, but after a recent visit to Bart's doctor, his health had to be their prime concern.

Bart took Kara's hand into his own.

"The doctor says it's imperative that I take things easy for some time. This has not been an easy decision, Kara my dear. "Working it Out" is our brainchild and we have watched it develop with a lot of satisfaction and pride. We can only hope that the new owner will carry on our traditions and ethics."

Kara looked away. She bit her bottom lip and squeezed Bart's hand before replying.

"I'm so very, very sorry, Bart, to learn of your ill health. It has come as quite a shock to me, so I can imagine what a cruel blow this must be for you. Please let me know if there is anything I can do to be of assistance."

Kara's compassionate green eyes reflected sorrow.

Bart patted the hand still held in his own.

"The Lord works in wondrous ways. We feel sure He will come through on this. When adversity hits, humanity turns to Him. The believers believe."

Kara bowed her head. How fine the line between life and death.

Kara took a cup of tea out to her small patio and looked at the full moon overhead.

She pulled an afghan around her and snuggled into it as she sat down.

The thought of "Working it Out" being sold to strangers had upset her tremendously. How could new owners possibly understand the specific needs of all the special people she had worked with for five years?

How could they deal with Effie, when she was having one of her anxiety attacks at the job she had successfully held for a couple of years? Kara was so proud of her. What about Ricky? How would they know he was just showing off when he threatened to quit—that all he wanted was reassurance that they needed him?

The last few days had been very hard on Kara.

She lay back in the chaise lounge, cupping the hot liquid in her hands. She knew these clients so well. She had spent hundreds of hours figuring them out. Making decision with them and for them; arguing their cases with State representatives; canvassing for their rights and negotiating terms with the Department of Social Services.

Kara sat upright, spilling the scalding liquid over her slacks. Lack of sleep was affecting her.

Unzipping her slacks and climbing out of them as she hurried indoors, Kara threw the damp clothing into a hamper before she reached for the telephone. It would be early morning in England and her father should still be at home. She tried the private number in his den.

He answered.

With a hasty "Good morning," Kara rushed in.

"Daddy I want to run something by you quickly. Last Sunday, at brunch, Susan and Bart said they were about to put "Working it Out" on the market. Bart's heart has begun giving him problems and he's been advised to get out of the business."

Taking a deep breath, she continued. "I've been unable to get this out of my mind. Is there some way I can purchase the business? I want it so desperately. I haven't been able to sleep because of it."

Gus Olavssen sighed softly. He had almost expected something like this, ever since Kara became licensed.

There was a long silence and Kara felt a twinge of guilt at tossing what must be very disturbing news without warning. With a slight cough, her father proceeded.

"Your great-grandmother Stephenssohn's estate is being administered by Keith Carruthers, the Chartered Accountant who has been handling it for you for the past twelve years and I have every confidence in his business acumen. I'll call him this morning and ask him to get back to you. Is that all right?"

"Yes. Thank you daddy."

There was nothing further to say.

Before disengaging the line Gus Olavssen said quietly.

"The inheritance is yours, Kara. It was left to you very specifically by Nona Stephenssohn. She had every confidence in you, so let your heart and business propensity take you in the direction you must pursue. God bless you, my dearest. Your mother and I want only what is best for you."

Kara closed her eyes, the receiver still in her hand. What had she done to deserve such extraordinary parents? They gave their blessing knowing she was thinking of making a commitment that would isolate them from her life for an indefinite period of time.

A few hours later Kara received the expected call from Keith Carruthers having been given her office number.

After chatting for a few moments he got down to business.

"Lord Olavssen advised that you would require immediate liquidity from the estate of your grandmother. There is certain information that I need to have at my disposal. That is, Kara, if you would honor me with that information."

Kara smiled at the somewhat antiquated language used. It sounded quite quaint and very British, and very outdated, but he ranked highly with her father and apparently held in the highest esteem in his field.

When she quoted the purchase price she heard papers rustling.

"Of course we are talking American dollars. Is that correct?"

"Yes."

"There is more than an adequacy of funds."

This caused Kara to smile again.

Curious, she asked, "Just what are my assets?"

"They are quite extensive and I cannot give a comprehensive summary over the telephone, but the stocks, bonds and land investments are only part of your grandmother's bequest. Your grandmother's townhouse in Mayfair, which of course you now own, is being leased at an exceptionally good rate. It is let to a Member of the House of Lords, who is using it as his prime residence when Parliament is in session."

Keith Carruthers paused and the rustling commenced again.

"There are several other prime pieces of property which unfortunately momentarily escape my recollection. I remember though that there are several Norwegian and Italian ancestors who have willed estates and investments to you as the only living child of the Stephenssohn/LaBarbera branches. Would you care to wait until I access that information?"

"Not right now, but I would appreciate a summary mailed to me. What I need to know at this moment is if I can purchase the property I have in mind for an outright sum of money."

Kara could hear more crackling and once more the meticulously correct voice of Keith Carruthers came back on the line.

"Are you sure you wish to purchase the business lock, stock and barrel? Amortizing the cost over ten years has tax and other advantages."

Rather sharply Kara interjected.

"I want to purchase the company outright. Is there a problem getting the funds I mentioned earlier?"

"No, of course not."

"Then please transfer that amount, plus $100,000, to my market bank account as soon as possible. There will be operating expenses to cover until the business transactions are completed."

Rather reluctant that Kara was not willing to listen to his advice Keith Carruthers ended the conversation "by Kara's leave."

Kara sat at her desk, stunned. She had not thought much about her great-grandmother Stephenssohn's Will since hearing it when she was 17. She and her parents were so upset at the time that she had not absorbed the details. It was in Trust until reaching the age of 25 and mentally she had pushed its existence behind her since the reason for it greatly saddened her. Nona Stephenssohn was much loved and missed. Kara still remembered her favorite great-grandmother and the times they had spent together. She had listened thoughtfully as Kara had expressed her innermost thoughts and steered her gently in their discussions, prodding Kara to reason through her problems and dreams, separating reality from fantasy and recognizing both. The memory of a lifetime of affectionate hugs and kisses and the inevitable tears when Nona Stephenssohn had to return to her own home brought back the pain of parting like a stab to the heart. As if were only yesterday.

Laying her head on the desk over crossed arms, Kara wept. *Thank you, Nona. I'll really make you proud of me. Your money will be well invested, I promise you.*

Susan and Bart could not believe their business had been purchased for cash, outright. They looked with heightened interest at Kara. She was the epitome of English understatement. They had observed with interest her growth over the past few years and taking on the immense responsibility of running "Working it Out" with the eagerness and dedication she had shown had impressed the Warners' enormously.

Disadvantaged she was not.

Kara, guided by Jackie's professional know-how and impeccable fashion flair, had cultivated a flawless fashion sense. They both met a couple of times a year and invariably Kara's wardrobe had more sophisticated and exclusive items added. Kara's streaked hair, under professional care, had become a shade of golden blonde, strikingly complimentary to her lightly tanned complexion and lustrous green eyes.

Kara had taken out a membership in a health and exercise spa, which she used during the week. At weekends she swam regularly in the swimming pool at "Fruitful Harvest." Her curvaceous body was taut and firm and if her radiant smile did not gain first attention, her stunning figure most certainly did.

In her typically unassuming way, Kara did not seem to be aware of the impact she made. Susan and Bart had introduced her to the sons of friends and business colleagues, but after a short time she seemed to erect a barrier around herself. They had heard several ill-disguised remarks about "the Ice Queen." It troubled them more than it appeared to bother Kara and so they stopped playing matchmaker.

They were pleased when Kevin Scott stepped into the picture and started dominating Kara's time when she visited them at the vineyard. Again it led nowhere.

As program manager of Phase IV, Kara's work had taken place, to a large degree, out of the office conferring with employers, checking on clients, and trouble-shooting for job coaches. To add to her broad experience she had stepped in as job developer when Marcie had been ill for a couple of weeks, and did a commendable job. Kara presented herself in a highly professional manner and yet she had not lost the warmth and sense of humor that broke down barriers.

Yes, Kara would take "Working it Out" much further than the Warners' had. They could clearly see the probability.

Kara was spending the weekend at "Fruitful Harvest." The Warners' had their house in Riverside up for sale. They were in the process of having a ranch-style house built on a hilly section of the vineyard where the swimming pool was located, which was an area unsuitable for planting the vines. From this vantage point there was an impressive view of the valley and in summer it would catch the wayward canyon breezes.

After assisting with some chores around the main hacienda, Kara took Whinny out for a long ride. She returned in time to join Susan, Bart, and several of their visiting friends, by the pool.

Susan swam over to the pool edge and spoke to Kara, who had just lain down on a chaise lounge.

"Are you settling into your townhouse Kara? Do you need any assistance?"

Kara spoke without opening her eyes.

"Yes, and 'No thanks,' in that order. I'm doing fine. Only six more boxes to unpack. The contents of my storage unit were delivered a few weeks ago and I'd almost forgotten how much stuff had actually been collected over the last few years."

"What about that magnificent Regency mirror you bought at the Pasadena Auction Gallery. Is it going to fit in anywhere?"

Kara opened her eyes and smiled.

"Of course! Don't you think it was high on my list when I went looking for places to buy? It fits into the vaulted foyer perfectly."

With an impish grin she added.

"Since we both have ulterior motives, why don't you and Bart come out next week and have dinner with me, then you can see the place for yourselves. Unfinished as it is. Perhaps we can also schedule some dates when you both will be available to give me some of your "Consultation time," as you will be off on vacation soon."

Sitting up, Kara leaned over and took hold of Susan's damp hand. A serious expression replaced the playful one and her voice took on a husky quality.

"I really, truly do appreciate all the assistance you have given me since I took over the business at the end of June. You have both smoothed the way for me immeasurably."

Susan squeezed Kara's hand tightly.

"You know, Kara, starting out as office manager, as you did, and then going through each phase of the program has proven to be a well-rounded internship. The total experience will serve you well in the future."

She looked over at Bart idly swishing his hands in the water as he slowly traversed the pool lying on an inflated mattress.

"We were just telling Sam and Sally how innovative your ideas are and Bart said he fully expects, by this time next year, to find "Working it Out" to be one of the most progressive organizations in the State."

Kara's smile lit up her face.

"Did he really say that? That is very complimentary coming from someone with so much business knowledge and experience."

She stood up, adjusting the straps of her bikini top.

"Why is it that all the nicest fellows I know are married?"

As an afterthought she added, "Of course the ones I'm thinking about also have the nicest wives too."

Kara bent down and kissed Susan's moist cheek and dove into the pool.

CHAPTER TWELVE

For the next year Kara became obsessed with incorporating her own ideas and inventive concepts into "Working it Out." Having her business acumen and intellect tested on a daily basis served to strengthen her commitment to the success of the project and nudged her to even greater efforts.

Endorsement of the people she represented brought Kara into public view. She flourished and prospered during this time, becoming increasingly aware of the considerable influence she was beginning to exercise in her chosen field of endeavor.

For the first time in years, Kara felt completely happy with her life. Her business was becoming satisfyingly successful; she had time to become socially involved in the Riverside community; she was also making friends and selecting interesting men to date from time to time.

It was during this time that Kara received a newspaper clipping of Jon and Angela's intended wedding plans from her parents.

Despondently Kara handed the slip over to Marcie when they next met.

Marcie sniffed.

"They certainly took their time about this, didn't they? When my prince comes along he'd better be more aggressive than this," Marcie ridiculed. "Some Don Juan he is—their marriage will be almost anticlimactic."

It was disappointing news, even though Jon had prepared her for this some time ago, it signaled their friendship had been sacrificed in exchange.

The following February, sitting in front of the burning gas logs in her living room fireplace, a dinner tray on her knees watching the news on television, a fierce pattering on the sliding glass door indicated that a rainstorm had suddenly started. Setting the tray with the last remnants of the meal on a side table, Kara walked over to the French doors and opened the nubby white drapes. She switched on the outside patio light to view the welcome downpour. In Southern California rain comes as a blessing. Several years of drought had heightened public awareness for water economy and rainfall, when it occurred, was gratefully received.

Without warning this unexpected deluge brought back the unceasingly wet day in England, eight years earlier, when she made the decision to leave for her new land and Kara suddenly became overwhelmingly homesick. Finding the swiftness of the nostalgia mystifying, she wondered was the urgent need to see her homeland a premonition? With a sense of déjà vu she began planning a trip to England in mid-August, the slowest month in her business.

Approaching Susan or Marcia to run the operation during her absence was high on Kara's list. Rearranging their busy schedules would take time.

Learning of her intended visit should come as a surprise to her parents, Kara reflected. She has been so involved in effectively operating "Working it Out" that all else has taken a back seat, including them. Guilt pangs can become moral reminders, she noted wryly.

During the course of one of their telephone conversations, Kara's mother made the surprising statement, "Jon's mother informed me last week that Jackie had offered Angela the promotion to deputy design director. Apparently Jackie was astonished when Angela jumped at the opportunity to take it on. Jackie had presumed that since Angela and Jon had announced their intention to wed that Angela would no longer work for Frazier's and be retiring to the farm. Can you imagine Jon having a working, independent wife?"

Silvia Olavssen chortled. "Jon hasn't even heard of Women's Lib yet."

Kara listened in silence. This was not good.

Continuing the conversation Kara's mother went on, "Jackie thought it would be a mere formality offering the position to Angela, assuming she would automatically reject it. She didn't want Angela to feel slighted before the position was advertised in the trade papers."

Kara found her voice.

"What about Jon, didn't he have anything to say about this? Why would Jackie do such a dumb thing? She should at least have discussed it with the two of them beforehand."

Silvia Olavssen had no answer.

"How does one monitor the Williams' family? They are such a mixed bunch. I must admit though, it was a big surprise. We all expected the wedding to occupy first place with Angela and I believe this will change things. Jackie stipulated a probationary nine months training period and that of course will be in London."

Poor Jon, sympathized Kara, *he is such a traditionalist, and Angela with her California upbringing was a rebel in the making.*

Kara hung up the phone brooding over the situation. Despite all that had happened, she still cared for Jon. She hoped by the time she made the trip back in a few months that Angela and Jon had resolved this mess. She would discover for herself how the land lay.

Arriving at Newcastle Airport, Kara was astonished to find Jon waiting for her. She was alarmed.

"Is everything all right with my parents?"

His voice was reassuring.

"Yes. I volunteered to meet your flight instead of Arnold, the new chauffeur. He wouldn't recognize you and I wanted to be part of the "Welcome Home Committee.""

Kara raised her eyebrows as she handed over her flight bag. Quite a switch to the manner in which they had parted slightly over a year ago.

In the hour it took to reach Kara's home, they brought each other up-to-date on the general aspects of their lives, skirting sensitive areas. Kara was determined to remain at a distance. Jon had chosen to make the break between them and he should be the one to heal the breach.

Kara was waiting for Jon to mention Angela. He did not.

They were beginning to pass familiar scenery, when Jon exclaimed.

"Angela and I were on the point of marrying, but it didn't work out."

After making this bald announcement Jon took his eyes away from the road to watch Kara's reaction.

"I wondered about that. What happened, Jon?"

With a quizzical look he softly murmured.

"How far the grapevine travels."

A long silence ensued. Kara moved uncomfortably in the glove leather bucket seat of the Aston Martin. It seemed she had touched a raw nerve.

Observing her discomfort Jon continued with a sigh.

"It would appear that when the challenge was taken out of our relationship, Angela became either very complacent, or at the other end of the spectrum, quite jealous and demanding. She changed her mind constantly on the wedding date we had set and when Jackie offered Angie the position as her assistant, on a nine months trial basis, she leaped at the chance."

Jon frowned.

"Can you imagine what that did to our long-distance romance? I flew down to London a couple of times, but a farm is a full-time, seven days a week job and this is where I have to concentrate most of my efforts, in addition to—"

Jon stopped abruptly and quietly added "another venture which I'll tell you about later. Anyway, about six weeks ago, Angie flew up to the farm and I thought we were well on the way to working things out, when she blew up and told me to forget about getting married. Since then I have solved the problem."

Jon paused, looking ahead reflectively.

Kara allowed the silence to continue for a short time and somewhat impatiently snapped.

"Is this to be concluded, or should I take out a subscription?"

Jon turned to her, the familiar grin on his face.

"You know, I've missed you more than you will ever know, Kara, and you have just validated the reason."

With a warm expression on his face Jon said.

"Welcome home."

Kara stiffened in her seat. She did not know what kind of a game Jon was playing, but this was not the manner in which she had envisaged their next meeting, which as fate would have it was sooner than she had expected.

Jon hid a yawn.

"Sorry about that. I was up extra early so that I could finish some chores around the farm before coming to get you."

He continued.

"Where was I? Oh, yes, I wrote a letter to Angie freeing her of any and all obligations she felt she might have toward me. I did that a couple of weeks ago when I finally gave up on her mercurial antics. There has been no response from her since then and, as far as I am concerned, it is all over between us."

Kara searched Jon's face for clues regarding the depth of this disclosure. With one eyebrow raised he tapped his chest.

"The mighty heart still functions normally; I anticipate few affects."

There was a silence between them.

Jon glanced quickly at Kara and went on.

"I discovered that what could have been a win-win situation had become a no-win situation."

He was quite unprepared for the sudden burst of laughter coming from Kara.

"Are you okay? I wasn't aware my remark was amusing."

His voice held reproach.

"Sorry, Jon. It's been a long flight and hearing the phrase "win-win" coming so unexpectedly from you set off an involuntary reaction. It was one of the first phrases I heard when I first went to the USA which delineated the difference between my world and the new world I had entered into."

She attempted to describe her first encounters with American idioms and got hopelessly involved.

Jon looked hard at Kara.

"You know this conversation we are having makes very little sense and I propose we attribute it to your tiredness, unless you have returned to be admitted into an asylum."

Hearing Jon joshing her as in the old days filled Kara with a sense of pleasure. She impulsively reached over, squeezing his hand resting on the edge of the seat. She was surprised at the immediate response and the applied pressure of his hand in return.

This triggered a pang of guilt. Perhaps because she assumed Jon still belonged to Angela and any advances, even of the most innocent nature would be considered inappropriate, despite the length of their pristine acquaintance.

Kara folded her hands together on her lap.

"I'm sorry things haven't worked out well for you and Angela. I honestly mean that."

Jon glanced at her as if assessing her sincerity, but did not comment. They sat in comfortable silence.

Kara began to notice how close they were to her parent's home and eagerly started looking out of the window, commenting on new buildings erected and other changes made since her last visit. A short time later they were traveling up the long winding driveway. The trees and bushes were in blossom and the roses and hollyhocks put a swatch of color in the flower beds. The lawns were a vibrant healthy green in color, manicured meticulously. In California Kara had left the gardens in full bloom. The fruit on the dwarf peach and apricot trees in half-barrels on her patio were ready to be picked. Grassland and lawns were browning from the sun's powerful rays and the lack of rain.

Yesterday in California visualizing herself in England and now, in England, mentally not quite having left California, Kara seemed to be in limbo—living in two worlds.

Shaking herself out of her self-imposed trance, Kara watched as the huge oak doors opened. Kara's mother rushed out, closely followed by her father and Hilda and Millie, two of their long-time maids. How terrific it was to see her parents again, to feel their affectionate kisses and loving arms welcome her home. Jon stood by her side proudly smiling as if he had personally flown her back like Superman. Kara slipped her arm through his, including him in the age-old ceremony. Hilda and Millie, with ear-to-ear grins, were ready with hugs too. Martin, the latest addition to the Olavssen staff, stood nervously in the doorway ready to be of service

Carrying Kara's two pieces of luggage into the foyer, from where Martin, the new butler, would have someone convey them up to her suite, Jon joined the family in the lounge. They were all talking excitedly, happy to be together once more when he entered the room.

During a break in the conversation Jon stood up.

"I really should leave. A farmer's life is never his own. Will you come out and visit in a couple of days? I'd love to show you around, Kara."

Kara agreed and walked Jon to the front door. Thanking him for picking her up at the airport she impulsively aimed a kiss at Jon's cheek, only to find her mouth captured by his. It was not their usual sweet, friendly kiss. It seemed to Kara like something that could get out-of-hand. Her eyes opened wide as she pulled her mouth away in astonishment and, with her heart beating unevenly quickly, said goodbye and more rapidly closed the door.

How odd! They had never done that kind of thing before. What was the matter with Jon? If he were missing Angela he would have to look somewhere else for a romantic distraction. She was not about to balm his bruised ego. Bristling at the idea, Kara shook her head in perplexity and rejoined her parents who had moved to the easy comfort of the family room.

It was fabulous being home with her parents again. Her bedroom suite looked, as usual, very luxurious and enormous compared to the unpretentious bedroom in Riverside. But the comfortable townhouse had endeared itself to Kara—it had become her very own. Her home.

The house and the bedroom suite, where she had spent most of her life, surrounded by an accumulation of expensive furnishings and precious irreplaceable articles, had become her parents' home. She was merely their daughter, visiting. It was very beautiful and Kara felt pampered during her visits wondering how she had taken its splendor for granted as she was growing up. She recognized that indeed she had been indulged without realizing it.

A couple of days after her arrival Kara made a tour of the grounds with her father, who was eager to show the improvements and additions made after her last vacation with them. Rain had kept them indoors the day before, but the sun had appeared and her father was anxious to start the tour. There was a new 30 ft. greenhouse in which he was experimenting with vegetables and flowers, also an herbaceous border that her mother had planned, supervised, and cultivated diligently. Shown with pride was the final addition made. It was a trailing grapevine climbing over and through a specially designed fence.

"After touring the vineyards in Temecula, I became fascinated with the idea of trying to develop a compatible strain of the white Sauvignon grapes here in this alien soil. It was really a perverse experiment on my part."

Eagerly reaching through the green leafed vines, her father gently displayed a small bunch of pale green grapes in his palm.

"Look at these, Kara. They are a bit undersized, but I suspect that as they acclimatize to soil and weather, they will gradually improve. I find this so exciting. It opens up new possibilities."

Kara hugged her father at the look of satisfaction on his face.

"Quite an accomplishment, daddy. Are you thinking of getting into the wine business?"

"Could be," he added with a surprisingly obscure expression on his face. "I've given some thought to it." Kara looked at him with a sideways glance—she really should not be surprised by new experiments her father considered tackling. He invariably came up with remarkably profitable ideas, and this one seemed to be giving him a great deal of pleasure.

They walked back to the house for lunch.

The weather felt quite cool to Kara and before Jon arrived she changed into blue jeans and a white ribbed turtleneck sweater. As an afterthought she added a V-necked, cable-knit navy vest to ensure warmth.

California's heat must be thinning her blood.

Jon arrived immediately after lunch. Kara, sitting by the window of the upstairs sitting-room, watched a late model Jeep approach the front door and Jon climbed out, reaching back to pull out a bouquet of flowers. Kara's face tightened. She hoped he was not going to go through this type of ridiculous act with her and mentally prepared herself to handle the situation. She raced downstairs, arriving at the double front doors before Jon had a chance to ring the bell and Martin to respond to it.

He grinned at the sight of Kara and leaned against the door-jamb, confident in his own masculinity and appearance. He really was a good-looking man. For a moment Kara was caught off-guard, unaware of the length of time they stood looking at each other.

"Scooter, if you don't let me come in, mother's flowers will have wilted before I can present them to your mother and then I'll be in for it."

Kara laughed in relief. How stupidly oversensitive she was becoming. They walked into the lounge, where her mother was ending a telephone conversation. She acknowledged the flowers with delight and kissed Jon's cheek.

"Will you come back for dinner?" she invited, a sparkle in her eyes.

"No thanks. Actually I have a place in mind to take Kara, if she is agreeable."

"Looking like this?" Kara asked in astonishment.

"I don't know why I bother with you, Kara Olavssen. You're so vain!" he intoned, affecting the same type of whine Kara used to adopt when trying to persuade him to push himself further during their long therapeutic walks along the beach. Kara recognized herself in his words, and the memories of what they had been through together flooded back. How quickly he could bring them both into sync again.

She shrugged her shoulders.

"Oh, okay, I suppose."

Jon laughed.

"Your stay in the United States has really polished your graciousness, your Grace."

Kara smiled at Jon's facetious remark as she walked over to kiss her mother goodbye. She shook her head when she turned and saw the satisfied smirk on his face.

"You'll really have to do better than that to needle me, Jon. I can tell you haven't had much practice lately."

"I'll work on it," he said, winking at Kara's mother as they left.

They traveled out to Coppice Farm, chatting easily all the way. Despite her resolve, Jon was back in place in her life.

Getting closer to the farm Jon started pointing to barns, birthing stalls, and buildings scattered along the road they traveled.

"I had no idea the farm was so vast, Jon." Kara was impressed.

"Whenever acreage in the proximity of the farm becomes available, I snatch it up. It has almost become an obsession. There's over 65,000 acres at the last count," he revealed.

Continuing he added, "It's too bad you can't ride a horse, it's the best way to get around and see it all."

Kara smiled smugly to herself.

They drove for what seemed like a considerable distance through areas sectioned off by fences to retain mares with foals, paddocks, and grassland.

Looking over at the fields of tall grass Jon explained, "I specifically grow grass for hay. It feeds the animals year round, either fresh or dry. There are five barns around the farm providing supplies for the animals in winter and bad weather."

At last they arrived at a long low house, which Kara was hard put to describe.

She jumped out of the vehicle as Jon walked around the hood. He nodded his head in the direction of the building.

"It's a rather outlandish mishmash of architecture. The original cottage, which has been added to over the years, goes back to around the fifteenth century. My first intention was to build a modern farmhouse much more convenient to the main road. In the early days of living out here it was so time-consuming getting the land and buildings prepared for horse breeding that I had little time to think of other living quarters. This building, while not terribly attractive, was at least utilitarian and thankfully had been kept in good condition. Grandmother Sophia moved into a flat in York several years before her death, leaving the operation of the farm and occupation of the farmhouse to her old Manager. He was almost as eccentric in his ways as grandmother. He closed off most of the house, storing in that part antiques and furniture he believed were too ostentatious and valuable for the lifestyle of a farmer, such as himself. Before that the previous owners, being Squires or salt-of-the-earth farmers, had tacked on additions to fit their family needs as wealth and time allowed."

By this time they had reached the front door, although Kara found little to indicate its distinction. Jon stood there, keys in hand, not quite ready to enter.

"I lived here through the coldest winter the north of England has experienced in over one-hundred years, followed by the hottest summer in three decades and the interior of this building varied not one jot. It only has fireplaces in each room mind you—no central heating or air conditioning. It was amazing. I was so very impressed that I have not had the inclination to leave it. Except for certain modernization, such as in the kitchen and bathrooms and carpeting which were overdue, everything else has been left untouched."

With this explanation Jon unlocked and pushed open the heavy beamed door.

"If you were as tall as me, you would be cautioned to bend going through this doorway. It was made to accommodate the stature of citizens who were so much smaller centuries ago."

Jon's broad shoulders and height almost blocked the opening, confirming his statement.

Jon proudly took Kara on a tour, starting from the moment they set foot inside the original edifice.

"See how low the ceiling is in this room? The beams running across barely allow me to stand up and move around. That's another indication of our shorter forbearers."

Even so, the main room into which they had entered, despite its restrictive ceiling height, was surprisingly well supplied with natural daylight. There was a long, though narrow window on the same wall as the front door and another on the opposite wall. Both had window ledges two feet in width, depicting the solid granite construction throughout the original cottage. A huge stone fireplace ran almost the length of the third wall, with an old-fashioned metal grate to hold wood and a built-in black iron stove for heating and cooking purposes. Hooks, which displayed ancient cooking and heating utensils, hung over the fireplace. This had been an all-purpose room, but the fireplace section was the only indication of this. It had been converted into a living room and a feeling of coziness prevailed.

Expecting to see the creativity of a professional interior designer, it occurred to Kara that it was Angela's touches she saw—the green, lemon and white color scheme rang a bell. Strangely enough this thought did not agree with her. Kara conceded that it would have been the most natural thing for Angela, spending so much time here, to put her own stamp on her future home.

Jon led the way through the remainder of the disjointed house, pointing out its idiosyncrasies and shortcomings. Covering the huge kitchen, bathrooms and laundry room floors were well-worn tiles that had been made and installed centuries earlier by local craftsmen.

With interest piqued Kara asked, "How could a laundry room be part of a building built so long ago?"

Laughing Jon replied, "I took the liberty of converting what used to be a 'wood shed' attached to the house. A special permit was needed to go ahead with that project."

The carpeting throughout was a moss green, thick and soft; quite a luxury in a farmhouse. Kara liked it, again wondering whose choice it had been. As she traveled through, she became completely sure. Who else would choose a color scheme of green, yellow, and white? She had slept in such a room for over two years.

In a subdued frame of mind Kara walked outside with Jon when he suggested touring the rest of the property. They walked past a Dutch barn, which showed a depleted storage area—not much hay remained.

"This barn is closest to the stables and used constantly, so we replenish the hay weekly. There's much more stored elsewhere on the farm. In fact so much is produced that the excess is sold to neighboring farmers and riding schools in the area. It has become a bonus income."

Jon led Kara into a Tack room, in front of the horses' wing, after pushing aside a pair of muddy rubber boots. Covering two of the walls were 1st, 2nd, and 3rd place award ribbons, mainly in red, white, and blue. Kara read them with interest "Best of class," "Best of Show,"—so many of them.

She turned around and smiled at Jon, who was watching her with interest.

"I'm impressed—was that your intent?"

"Perhaps," he responded. "I thought you might like to see the results of many years of very hard work."

Immediately feeling chastised, Kara regretted her snide remark, which she attributed to the offending green, yellow, and white decorating scheme.

"Sorry, Jon. Great job."

Retracing their steps, Jon took Kara into the low covered main building, the stables, where most of the horses were kept. At their approach, a chorus of whinnies commenced. The protruding heads of a variety of horses appeared, manes tossing, leaning out of the top openings of the double-partitioned doorways. Jon patted each horse, saying a few words in passing.

They arrived at a doorway where a gentle faced mare was waiting. Jon smiled at Kara.

"This is 'Sleeping Beauty' a well-mannered, patient soul. The type of horse I would suggest for someone like you to learn to ride on."

"Are you suggesting I try?"

Jon asked eagerly.

"Do you think you could manage to ride her for an hour or two? I could show you much more that way."

Excitement glittered in Kara's eyes. Looking down at the ground she replied timidly, "I think so."

Going back to the entrance Jon picked up a telephone receiver from the installation on the wall and punched in three digits. Speaking to someone, he gave instructions to bring over two saddles—one for Black Jack and the other for Sleeping Beauty.

Jon led a large black bay out to the corridor between the two rows of stalls.

"This is my horse 'Black Jack'."

He was softly stroking and patting as he spoke. The horse lent his big head gently on Jon's shoulder in an apparently familiar gesture. Kara was quite touched. Jon was evidently very much at ease and in control in this venue.

Joining them a few minutes later was a young man who drove up to the entrance in a Land Rover and carried out two saddles. The two horses were quickly readied for riding.

Leading the horses outside Jon assisted Kara into the saddle. Mounting Black Jack he pointed the direction in which they would travel. They wandered "as the crow flies" no longer restricted to paths. Jon began indicating boundaries, new buildings erected, and fields planted with alfalfa and rape grass. Growing the rape grass was a new venture for him. He had plans for its further development into domestic cooking oil. Kara was fascinated as Jon described his daily activities as they rode. She had not realized so much action took place here. This was a huge enterprise that Jon ran.

They rode side by side. Eagerly intent on listening to Jon, Kara was unaware of the ease with which she was demonstrating handling Sleeping Beauty, and Jon was very conscious of it. Upon approaching a small brook running through a slightly hilly area, Jon dismounted and assisted Kara in doing so. They led the horses to the brook, where both animals drank. Looking into the water Jon pointed out the minnows darting around.

"Remember when we used to try to catch them in paper cups at the Italian Gardens?"

"Of course," responded Kara, smiling at the recollection of their less than successful attempts, "but it does seem such a long time ago, doesn't it? So much water has run under the bridge since then."

Jon looked at Kara intently and changed the subject.

"So when did you learn to ride a horse, Kara? You kept your secret very well and I'm impressed at how expert you have become. Do you have a horse of your own in California?"

"No. I ride Angela's horse 'Whinny' whenever I go to the vineyard. It is a personal dream of mine to own one someday, but that is in the future. I am far too busy for such luxuries right now."

Studying Kara thoughtfully Jon suggested resuming their ride.

Coming to a primitive wooden planked bridge, they led the horses over it. The old bridge wobbled slightly as it took the weight of the horses. Once across they mounted the horses and Jon looked at his watch and commented on it being almost time for dinner.

Kara expressed surprise. They were in the middle of a field, apparently miles away from civilization and here was Jon suggesting it was time to eat.

"I assume that is your stomach speaking to you, it's nowhere near dinner time," Kara drolly observed, fishing in her jean's pocket and handing over a peppermint candy wrapped in paper. "Under present circumstances this is the best I can offer. I need a little more notice to drum up a three course meal."

Jon accepted the candy with a grin, unrolled it from the paper and popped it into his mouth, scrunching the paper into a ball and stuffing it into the pocket of his jacket.

"With such a repast I probably won't need dinner after all."

So saying he quickly trotted off, with Kara following. Jon quickened his pace, looking over his shoulder to see if Kara was keeping up. She readily started playing his game. They rode around trees, sometimes with Kara following and sometimes taking the lead until Jon took over again. Kara felt exhilarated and thought wistfully *"This is so much more fun than the solitary rides I take around the vineyard and foothills."* She was settling into the steady rhythm of Sleeping Beauty's gait when Jon held up his hand to signify slowing their pace. As they did Kara noticed a road running alongside the fence they were approaching. Jon dismounted and walking over to the gate unlocked a padlock and shoved the gate open, indicating that Kara precede him. He followed afterward, leading Black Jack out of the field and replacing the lock.

Less than a hundred yards along the road Kara saw the hanging sign of "The Black Bull Inn," with its namesake depicted underneath. Kara was astounded. She was completely disoriented. She had no idea Jon's farm was so close to the Inn. Jon waved Kara into the courtyard of the hotel when he saw she was about to ride past.

Riding around to the back, Jon dismounted and tied Black Jack to a metal ring on the wall. He signaled Kara to do the same with Sleeping Beauty. He walked up several steps and motioned Kara to follow him. Kara did so with a puzzled frown on her face.

The door led into what seemed like a large storeroom, stocked with food supplies of every description. Another door on the opposite wall stood open and Kara could see part of a kitchen. Jon walked through it and obediently Kara trailed after him. A tall, rather plump man, who was in the process of tying a large burgundy and white striped apron around his ample middle, looked over at Jon and smiled.

"Hello, Jon. Do come in. Everything's under control."

He included Kara in the sweep of his arm as he took them through the spotlessly white kitchen from which tantalizing smells were emanating. Walking into another room, several waiters and busboys were busily stacking china, goblets, and cutlery onto large service trays. They looked very smart dressed in burgundy and white uniforms. Kara tried to recall if that had been the color scheme when Jon brought her and Roger here so long ago, but couldn't remember. Some things do fade with time, she conceded.

Leading the way, Leif took Kara and Jon around a large deserted dining room, through French doors and into an arbor of trailing rose vines. They walked through the powerful aroma of the cascading blossoms, which to Kara was like a perfumed cloud sitting like a veil of gossamer around her head. It was a lovely enveloping sensation and Kara shivered at the sensuousness it provoked.

"Are you cold?" Jon asked.

Kara shook her head replying, "The perfume out here stunned me, it is glorious—I was taken by surprise."

Jon turned to Kara and introduced owner, Leif Andersen, who shook hands with a smile and started walking toward the end of a cobbled stone walkway where three Pullman railway cars stood. They looked immaculate in what appeared to be a new coat of paint in a rich plum shade, with lettering and motifs decorating each coach in gold and white.

As they drew nearer Kara cried out in pleasure.

"As a little girl I traveled on the original Orient Express which was put into use for a special anniversary trip. It was an exciting journey for a seven years old child and it must have made quite an impression because I've never forgotten it."

Jon squeezed Kara's arm and, opening one of the doors in the middle car, assisted her up the two steps.

Inside it was warm and fragrant. The dining car they had entered had tables on both sides of a wide aisle, with white linen cloths on each. A small brass hurricane lamp stood in the center of each table and brass candelabras were interspersed along the walls. The carpeting was in the same rich plum tone as the exterior paint, as were the velvet chair seats and draperies at the windows. By contrast, the walls and ceiling were covered with white heavily embossed wallpaper providing a sense of space and openness. It was an elegant setting and Kara wished to capture it.

Kara's eyes sparkled.

"I'd like to take a picture."

She began taking the camera from its padded case around her neck.

"Just a minute, I can think of a better place to do that." Nodding to Leif they proceeded along the aisle, where Leif opened the tandem doors leading to the third coach and beckoned Kara to pass through.

She stopped immediately in her tracks, causing Jon to bump into her. The color scheme was the same as in the previous dining room, but at the far end an ornately carved bar ran its width. Two chandeliers shimmered from the ceiling and crystal hurricane lights decorated the tables. Fine white china, with a thin gold rim and crystal goblets were in place. Huge white baskets filled with trailing green plants stood on the carpet between each of the tables, separating them like screens.

"Oh, it's magnificent," she breathed, "So much more elegant than the Orient Express."

Leif smiled with pleasure at the spontaneous response.

A couple of busboys were busy laying sets of cutlery at each table. Leif went behind the bar.

"What can I get you? Test me. We have a very large inventory of which I am inordinately proud. It's kind of a fetish with me. You know, wine aficionado extraordinaire."

The big smile belied the teasingly boastful words.

Observing the activity around them Kara asked.

"Aren't we in the way here? It looks as if a meal is about to be served."

Looking at Jon first, Leif remarked, "There's no rush. We have closed off the main building for the evening and the three carriages will accommodate as many of our regular diners as we can squeeze in."

Kara noticed a couple of "Fruitful Harvest" labels among the great variety of bottles displayed on the bar shelves.

"I'd love a glass of 'Fruitful Harvest' Zinfandel. Did you know that it has taken gold medal awards in California for the past two years?"

"Yes." Leif again gave Kara a big grin. "I promote the product, too."

Jon said he would take a glass also.

Kara was captivated by her surroundings. She reached for her camera again. She took a picture of Jon sitting on one of the high barstools beside the exquisitely hand engraved mahogany bar with Leif grinning in the background.

Leif slipped away as Kara started questioning Jon.

"How long have these rail coaches been here and when did you discover the proximity of your farm to this Inn?"

"Whoa," Jon protested, "let's start at the beginning."

His eyes took on a tender light as they rested on Kara's eager face.

"At first I was reluctant to live on the farm, after all I have lived most of my life in a city, accustomed to all the modern conveniences. Even the months spent at Cormorant Bay with the fairly primitive, but workable facilities there didn't seem bad compared to the farm's antiquated bath and kitchen fixtures and their erratic mode of operation."

Kara smiled at the irritation brought to Jon's features at the remembrance.

"Anyway the realization finally hit me that if I was serious about making the business a success, I would have to get my act together and make a commitment. Fortunately latent soccer discipline came to my rescue as well as the local plumber."

Kara laughed out aloud.

"The first two years were very difficult. The outside pipes froze, due to a slow leak in the outdated system and there was only cold water available until it had been finally detected and remedied. Then my first foal was stillborn because the veterinarian lost his way one night, and I was too inexperienced to assist the mare with the birthing. Another tough time was when I was thrown from Black Jack as we were making our way back to the farmhouse after dusk. I broke an arm, but thankfully Black Jack's injuries due to stepping into a ditch were slight."

Jon shook his head in puzzlement.

"He really is in intrepid stallion. How he continues to have trust in me is beyond my comprehension."

There was silence for a while as if Jon had remained in that time era, and Kara sipped the familiar Zinfandel waiting in companionable silence until Jon was ready to continue.

A smile flitted across Jon's face.

"Fortunately the happier occasions compensated for the bleak times."

Jon took Kara's hand.

"I'll never forget the thrill of assisting in the first live birth of a foal. It still gives me goose-bumps. Several colts were born before the arrival of Lady Jane, who in essence is the founding brood mare of my stock. She is out to pasture now, having won many prestigious awards and in the process giving birth to several champions. You might like to take her out for a ride, Kara. She's still a great horse."

Jon patted the hand he held.

"You must be bored with all this dull stuff—tell me about your exciting life in America."

Kara laughed.

"Is this 'Show and Tell' day?"

Jon eyed Kara over his glass of wine.

"As you earlier pointed out, a lot of water has gone under the bridge. I'd consider it a privilege learning what you have done with your life since leaving England."

After staring at Jon for a few moments to ascertain if he were serious, Kara allowed her thoughts to drift back eight years.

"I've never admitted this to anyone before, but you started me on the path I now tread, Jon."

He looked shocked.

"Remember when I came out to the farm and told you that I was thinking of looking for a job in London?"

He nodded, with a puzzled expression on his face.

"That was precisely the time I decided to move away. The thought hadn't entered my head until then. You seemed so happy and fulfilled with your life on the farm and I felt so incomplete and unchallenged. As things worked out my move was to California not London, but it has been the right place for me to be. Do you know why?"

He was saved from guessing as Kara continued.

"Everything has come together. The MBA from the University of Durham laid a foundation, which has stood in good stead. I don't know how much news our parents have swapped, but I found my forte was in dealing with people with disabilities. They fed my need and my need fed them. Because of this obligation I became an MSW and then an LCSW—that was tough."

She glanced at Jon.

"I'm sure you are aware that I purchased "Working it Out" from Angela's parents."

Jon nodded, and Kara proceeded.

"Despite my initial reluctance, I found myself in an advocacy role. I used to be a bit embarrassed at first when friends, the staff, and professional cohorts informed me of newspaper articles written about my vehement defense of this special underserved population. That was a stroke of good luck. Catching the attention of the State Department of Rehabilitation, they suggested they come out and check my program. They were interested in some of the changes I had incorporated after taking over the business and apparently they conveyed my innovativeness to the federal government. Representatives from both agencies came out to assess for themselves just how efficient and productive the operation was."

Kara stopped and sipped her wine contemplatively.

With a playful expression on his face Jon spoke softly.

"Is this to be concluded, or should I take out a subscription?"

Kara's lips twitched in amusement and she reached over and patted his knee.

"The bottom line is that five months ago, they contacted me with a view to opening seven model facilities in the state, with the possibility of expanding throughout the U.S. As the most knowledgeable person, I was designated director of the whole project. It is quite an honor and I am thrilled at the prospect of advancing the concept."

Kara flashed an exultant look at Jon.

"Oh, Jon, I am so excited. Currently it is an agenda item before an ad hoc committee, which meets in Los Angeles to make a decision on it, shortly after I get back. Nothing has been finalized, but the process has been started and everything looks positive. After my parents, you are the first person I've told. I'm still pinching myself. It's almost too good to be true."

Jon looked at Kara with new respect.

"Quite the celebrity, aren't you?" he said, but his warm smile softened the words. "I'm very impressed, but what do you do for amusement, Kara? It sounds as if all you do is work."

She answered lightly.

"My personal life wouldn't interest you, it's very boring."

"Little about you is boring, so don't give me that crap."

The intensity of Jon's voice came as a surprise.

"Well, I'm on the Board of the Riverside County Philharmonic and a committee member of the Riverside Historic Society. How does that grab you? Doesn't that make my life more intriguing?"

Jon looked annoyed.

"Kara, I know you are not impervious to male attention and I know damned well you are far too attractive to escape pursuit by the male species. Between the two, there's a wide gap. Did Roger have anything to do with your apparent indifference? Since that happened so long ago, it would upset me to think such a nonentity could leave lasting scars."

Jon placed his hand over Kara's.

"I hope we are still friends, because that is where I'm coming from."

Pensively Kara stared at Jon as she absently stroked his hand.

"It's a long tale."

"We have time," he countered.

Kara sighed, looking sadly at Jon.

"After that fiasco with Roger, which hurt me dreadfully, I vowed never to make the same mistake again. Using this as the yardstick for almost every encounter I made with a prospective boy-friend, I found I was unable to make a commitment to any permanent relationship. I suppose by not facing my fear of rejection, it was easier to discourage further involvement than to examine the reason for my own phobia."

Kara closed her eyes as if to eliminate the distasteful thoughts.

Jon was looking at her with compassion when she opened her eyes.

"That is the problem I still face, though I have come close to overcoming it."

"Please go on." Jon entreated.

"A lot of weekends were spent at "Fruitful Harvest" when I first arrived in California. For several months I spent most of my time walking in the foothills, swimming in the pool, lazing around and reading or shopping in the quaint little town of Temecula. Generally goofing off. One Saturday afternoon in town I happened to bump into Kevin Scott, the vintner at the winery. Previously we had spoken very little and I was surprised when he asked me to join him for lunch. He had grown up in the Temecula area and I found his conversation very interesting. He had his own horse and he suggested that, if I could ride Angela's horse, he would take me to some of the places he had mentioned. I told him I couldn't ride and he immediately offered to teach me. Bart and Susan had no objection to my riding Whinny. He needed regular exercise after Angela left and Kevin was an accomplished equestrian to guide me."

Kara swallowed the remainder of the wine in her glass, and continued.

"We started riding further and further afield, eventually having picnics and staying out most of the day. In spite of my resolve not to get involved, it lay in the back of my mind that one day, perhaps when we were both ready, we would make things "permanent." I was in no hurry to make a serious commitment. Therefore, it came as quite a shock to find his fiancée waiting for us one evening when we arrived back at the vineyard, after a particularly pleasant day's outing. She was nasty and I can still recall her harsh language, almost at will."

Kara's shoulders shuddered remembering.

"That confrontation brought back hidden memories which I thought I had overcome. I didn't return to the vineyard again until I learned that Kevin had quit. It hurt a great deal and I have to thank my good friend, Marcie, for her assistance in recovering from that ill-fated episode."

Kara smiled at the memory of her ebullient friend's efforts to restore enthusiasm back into her life.

Jon waited.

"There was another man, a couple of years ago. He is a professor at San Bernardino State University. He did propose and I considered his offer seriously, but the very fact that I was taking so long to make up my mind, actually convinced me that I didn't need him in my life."

Kara toyed with the empty wineglass.

"I think you might have hit the nail on the head, Jon. It seems as soon as my emotions and feelings start to run away with me, I begin to panic. I can't believe love is strong enough to sustain me—and I'm even more convinced there is no man who can change my point of view. Sad state of affairs, isn't it?"

Kara sighed deeply.

"Now I stay with the older gents. They escort me to all the social functions I want to attend and they apparently get pleasure in showing me off at exclusive parties and elegant restaurants. If I have to tolerate some low-key smooching, so be it. I can handle that."

Seeing the hurt look in Jon's eyes Kara quickly retorted.

"Please don't feel sorry for me. I enjoy my life and wouldn't change any of it."

Jon walked around the bar returning with the bottle of Zinfandel, ready to replenish their wineglasses. Kara felt ill at ease watching Jon take this liberty. She was unaccustomed to flagrant bad manners and in Jon this was incomprehensible. Leif was nowhere in sight.

As she slid off the stool, Kara rather edgily volunteered to pay for the full bottle of wine, adding that it had been a very enjoyable break, but perhaps they should be returning to the farm. Jon's face registered astonishment and a dull flush spread beneath his tanned cheeks. For what seemed like an interminable period, they stared at each other. He really was behaving out of character, just when she believed they had regained their unique relationship.

Kara made to walk toward the door, but Jon's tall frame blocked her. He appeared to be uncomfortable and hesitant in commenting on the situation. *Good*, Kara grimly thought.

It was a relief to see Leif enter the coach and walk down to the bar. He picked up the bottle of "Fruitful Harvest" wine and wordlessly raised it toward them. *Surely he will notice how much has disappeared,*

Kara thinks guiltily, waiting for some indication of responsibility from Jon, but he merely shook his head and led Kara back to the door.

Silently they retraced their steps to the rose arbor. The seductive aroma remained, but for Kara the magic had disappeared. All because of a silly pre-judgment on her part. For all she knew Jon may have a standing charge account here. He certainly was on very good terms with Leif. Rather than allow this to ferment she would diplomatically find the answer as they rode back to the farmhouse.

Quietly Jon said, "Please sit down, Scooter, I want to tell you something."

Reluctantly Kara sat down on an old rustic bench in the arbor.

Clearing his throat, Jon paced back and forth with one hand in his jacket pocket and the other swatting the roses within his reach, sending out bursts of fragrance.

Kara sat motionless watching him.

It was such a beautiful setting, very romantic. She could envisage two sweethearts pledging their love in this idyllic spot. With a start she wondered if Jon had proposed to Angela here. Surprisingly the thought bothered her.

The air was cool on Kara's cheeks. She shivered, realizing that she must have been daydreaming.

Slightly irritated she acerbically snapped, "What's the reason for stopping here?"

Jon sat down beside her.

"Kara, I should have spoken to you about this earlier, but I wanted to surprise you and watch your expression—that way I could enjoy your incredulity. Your emotions are usually so transparent."

He looked intently into Kara's eyes and said in an apologetic tone, "Leif and I co-own this Inn."

It was such a completely unexpected announcement that Kara's mouth dropped open in amazement. Before she could respond, Jon hurriedly continued.

"I really am sorry for being so insensitive. It was something I thought you would take in your stride. You are usually so unflappable and in a stupid way I thought you would find it quite a joke."

He took hold of Kara's hands.

"As if that isn't enough, there is another surprise planned."

Jon had the grace to look ill-at-ease.

"Please forgive me, Kara, it was done as a welcome home gesture, not to shock you."

Drawing Kara to her feet and ignoring the bewilderment showing on her face, Jon hastily propelled Kara along the path and into the main building.

* * *

CHAPTER THIRTEEN

Lights flashed on everywhere causing Kara to shade her eyes with a hand to avert the brilliance. Rooted to the floor, she held on to Jon's arm. The deserted and previously barren dining room had been transformed into a lavish banqueting hall, crowded with well-wishers, all waving and smiling.

Kara eyed Jon out of the corner of her eyes. Gosh, he was crafty! He had kept her isolated from the Inn itself; they had sat and talked for almost two hours with no indication of all the activity taking place such a short distance away from them.

Kara and Jon's parents came forward hugging and kissing Kara, including Jon in their embraces. Kara was led to a table in the center of the room. She had the feeling she was floating, it seemed quite unreal—she was not sure she recognized the passing faces. Jon had an absurd grin on his face and looked extremely pleased now that Kara had started to smile again. A waiter pulled out Kara's chair and Jon immediately seated himself beside her. Everyone sat down.

A chilled fruit soup with a dollop of Crème Fraiche was already placed before each person. After a short statement of welcome and expression of delight at Kara's return to her roots by her cousin Barry, Uncle Henry, a Vicar, gave the Benediction.

It was only after she had consumed the tasty starter course that Kara realized upon looking around the room that everyone was dressed extremely casually—most of them in jeans, like herself.

"I'll never trust you again Jon Williams" Kara whispered, but the glow on her face belied the words.

One delectable course followed another until a trolley bearing a large rectangular cake was wheeled into the room. Decorated with pink and burgundy roses the words "Welcome home Kara" stood out on the white background.

Jon walked Kara over to the cake and brushed his lips against her cheek after the formal slice into the elegantly decorated cake was made. Pictures were taken of the two of them in various poses.

Melodic strains infiltrated the chatter as a pianist played throughout the meal. Kara was soothed to the point of wondering why she had left the land of her birth after all. It was so pleasant to be here with so many relatives, friends and acquaintances—and most especially basking in Jon's friendship.

As the meal came to an end, Jon stood up and waited for the murmuring of voices to still.

"Dearest Kara, dear family and friends, tonight The Black Bull Inn has been placed at your disposal. In a few minutes dancing will take place in the Camelot Court Ballroom and games will be available in the Jousting Hall. For anyone interested, tours of this ancient building will take place by request and it will be my pleasure to act as your guide. Please make yourselves at home."

He sat down to murmurs of approval.

Kara, having settled down after the excitement, whispered to Jon.

"How are we going to get the horses back to the farm?"

He spoke into her ear.

"Dennis has already picked them up in a horse trailer."

She swatted his knee—he was too smart for his own good.

Guests were leaving the tables and Jon took Kara's hand.

"I'm going to be busy for a while, so why don't you go off and have fun. The band is excellent. You'll have an opportunity to get in some of your exhibitionist type dancing."

He laughed and stepped back to avoid Kara's feigned punch.

Seeing some of her previous school friends waving to her Kara moved in their direction, making a face at Jon as she walked away.

When the beat of the four piece band lured dancers into the Camelot Court Ballroom, Kara, with most of the younger crowd, was immediately drawn there. Happily talking and dancing with friends and acquaintances for most of the evening, Kara realized that she had not seen Jon for a while. Announcing time for the final intermission, Kara decided to look for him.

Making her way to the foyer, she found him in the process of winding up a tour at the bottom of the wide curved staircase that led to the guestrooms on the second floor. As the group dispersed he sat on the bottom step and Kara joined him there.

"I'd hoped to be included in one of your tours, but I guess since it's getting to be so late you are going to tell me to buzz off."

"It would be difficult to say that to you, Scooter."

Jon stood up, pulling Kara to her feet.

He emitted a groan as he did so and Kara was immediately concerned, realizing the cause. She put her arms around his waist to hold him as he rocked back and forth unsteadily.

"Jon, you've been doing far too much and I feel rotten knowing I am the reason for putting you through so much pain. How can I make up for all the nice things you do for me?"

A twisted smile flickered over Jon's face.

"You could marry me and put an end to my misery."

"Always the joker, aren't you?" Kara replied. "Marry me and it would be the *start of your misery*."

As she released him from her grasp, Kara looked into Jon's face to observe his amusement at her pun. Instead his look of anguish alerted Kara that he was in far more pain than he was willing to admit.

Assisting Jon to a nearby straight-backed chair Kara warned, "I'll be right back, so don't attempt to move."

She hurried into the main dining room and immediately located Leif, who was unobtrusively supervising the clean-up process. Rushing up to him she blurted, "Jon is having problems with his foot. He's in an awful lot of pain."

Leif immediately responded.

"I'll go and get John's prescription from the farm."

Kara interrupted.

"Won't Jon have it on him? He usually is prepared for this type of emergency."

Leif eyed her thoughtfully.

"Yes. Quite right. I'll go and check. You obviously know Jon very well and it makes sense that he would carry the prescription on him. Especially recognizing the strain he has put upon himself lately."

Did he feel she had caused this? Turning around when he realized Kara was following him, Leif advised, "Kara, don't you think it would be better to rejoin your guests? They should be ready to leave within the hour and it would look strange if both you and Jon were absent at their departure."

Reluctantly Kara agreed. How discourteous it would be for her to disappear at this point and what a reflection that would be on Jon who had put so much effort into this event. Leif could attend to Jon.

She would rather have stayed with Jon. His agony, so reminiscent of earlier times, had resurrected emotions that had lain dormant. *Oh, Jon,* Kara thinks sadly, *you have gone through so much and shown such bravery. The pain and torment continues and I have been oblivious to the stress suffered, but I'll make up for it. I promise.*

Managing to stay pleasant and poised during the time it took to say goodbye to all the guests who had attended, Kara informed her parents that Jon's foot was giving him a problem and she and Leif would stay with him for a while. She would take a taxi home. Jon's parents had already left the Inn by the time she was aware of the dilemma and considering how late it was she decided to call them at a more reasonable hour.

The last hand had been shaken, the last hug and kiss exchanged, and Kara was free to go to Jon. She dashed back to the foyer, only to find it deserted. Catching sight of the night porter she asked if he knew where Jon was.

He directed her to the suite at the end of the corridor. Of course, she hadn't thought of that. Jon probably needed some privacy during the long hours spent here at night.

Facing her at the end of the corridor were double doors, one of which was slightly ajar. She cautiously peered inside and saw Leif sitting on a chair. He saw her and walked over to the door.

"You were right. Jon had some pills in his pocket and I administered a dose. He's not sleeping well, very restless and still in a lot of pain."

Kara nodded sympathetically and stated, "I'll stay with Jon. Give me your telephone number so that I can contact you if necessary."

Leif hastily wrote a telephone number on the back of a business card.

"You can dial me directly if you have any concerns. Please do, you won't disturb me any more than usual. Sometimes we seem to be on call all day."

He shrugged his shoulders. "Goes with the territory, I suppose."

Kara closed the door and occupied the chair that Leif had just vacated. She sat and scrutinized every move that Jon made. His moans and sighs grabbed her heart. Standing on the night table was the prescription bottle. Kara read the instructions. In three hours she could dole out another dose.

With a start Kara awoke.

The room was in semi-darkness and for an instant she had difficulty remembering where she was. Seeing Jon on the bed brought it all back. It was twenty minutes past the time to give Jon the pills and Kara wondered how she could have possibly overslept in an upright position on the uncomfortable chair. The awkwardness must have contributed to the crick in her neck and was probably the reason she awoke.

With two tablets resting in the prescription tube lid and a glass of water nearby, Kara was ready to wake Jon. He was groaning as he changed positions with difficulty on the bed. Kara expected to have some trouble arousing him, but as soon as she started rubbing his shoulder his eyes immediately opened. For a moment he lay quietly, closing his eyes with a sigh. Kara kissed Jon's temple as she slid an arm under his neck.

"It's time for your pills, love. Can you sit up just a little, so you can swallow them?"

He nodded and Kara popped a pill into his half-open mouth. Raising the glass to his lips, Jon took a sip of water and swallowed with a large gulp.

"Sit up just a little more, Jon," Kara urged. Struggling, he complied. After the second pill had been swallowed Kara felt she had just accomplished a major task. A Florence Nightingale she would never be.

For some time Kara sat and watched Jon slowly drifting into a deep sleep. Several times she dozed off, driven awake by moans from Jon or as her head fell against her chest. Kara went into the bathroom and washed her face and hands.

Feeling better, Kara looked at herself in the mirror. Without benefit of a purse she was hindered in making herself look more presentable. Innocently she had set off on this escapade unaware of Jon's plans for the party. Staring at her reflection, Kara contemplated the effort and cloak and dagger tactics used in the preparation of the surprise party for her. Jon certainly had her fooled. Imagine, jeans and denim outfits worn to an elegant banquet that must have cost a great deal, but the harm to his health was the greatest cost.

A flood of tenderness engulfed Kara as she looked over at Jon presently sleeping restfully.

Kara took the bedspread from the bench at the foot of the bed, wrapping herself into it firmly. Carefully she lay down beside Jon. There was plenty of room on the custom-made king-sized bed so she shouldn't disturb him. Oh, what bliss and comfort it was to stretch out and relax.

* * *

"Do you know you smile when you're asleep?"

Kara opened one eye warily to look at the speaker and tried to sit up.

"Jon, are you okay—is it time for your pills?"

She struggled to loosen her arms from the still snugly wrapped fabric and groaned upon looking at her watch.

"Some nurse I am, you have missed one dose of tablets with another coming up soon."

Keenly looking at Jon she was surprised to find him affable and relaxed. He was lying with an arm tucked under his head, looking at Kara from an oblique position.

"In answer to your question, my pet, I'm feeling fine—just sorry to have spoilt your evening."

"Don't be silly, at least you had the good taste to wait until it was practically over," she quipped.

Jon leaned over and rubbed the new growth of stubble on his chin against her cheek.

"Take that, and that, and that," he said as Kara squirmed to avoid the piercing whiskers.

"Stop it, Jon," she cautioned, "or you'll be sorry."

"Oh, really. Threaten me, girl."

"I'll jump all over you and make sure I incapacitate you."

Jon howled with laughter and threw his left arm and leg across Kara's body, holding her as if in steel bands.

"Do you submit?"

"Never," she responded trying to free herself.

He tightened his hold. "Changed your mind?"

"Jon, you're hurting me."

Immediately the pressure ceased and Jon gently took Kara into his arms upon seeing pain registered in her eyes.

"Oh, love, I would never intentionally hurt you. You are too important to me."

Jon delicately brushed his lips across Kara's closed eyelids, moving to her satin smooth cheeks and finding his way to her mouth. Tremulously Kara responded to the urgency of Jon's kisses. She could feel his growing assertiveness, and she was surprised. Even in the throes of this emotional tumult she questioned his loyalty to Angela, so recently recognized as his only love.

Unexpectedly and suddenly Jon pulled away from her.

In a husky voice he said "Kara I must go."

The torment reflected on his face indicated to Kara that he was ashamed of his actions, as if he were suffering guilt at betraying Angela. So he was not over her as he had strongly declared.

She turned her head away, trying to control the shaking that enveloped her body. She heard the bathroom door close.

Jon drove Kara home. Desultory conversation took place. For the first time in her life Kara was at a loss regarding how to relate to Jon. She wanted to reassure him that she thought no less of him for the momentary lapse in forgetting Angela. In fact if this were the reason for the apparent regret he had shown, she envied their relationship.

She had been quite shaken to discover that Jon could arouse in her a desire hitherto unconnected to their friendship. Closing her eyes and transporting her mind back to the occasion, it came back vividly overpowering. It was scary.

Jon looking at Kara as she lay back in the car seat with closed eyes saw a shudder pass through her frame. A pang of guilt hit him. He should not have taken advantage of the situation, even though the physical temptation had come as a surprise and thoroughly bowled him over.

After all these years he had not realized that Kara could hold a sensual attraction for him. He had watched her go through all the growing up stages and suddenly he was facing a new predicament—a dynamic, alluring, and intelligent woman had thrown all his preconceived notions of her to the wind.

Jon insisted on accompanying Kara into her home. She noticed he walked with a conspicuous limp. So he had not really recovered. Kara was angry. What a proud, insufferable man he had become. She had not realized how temperamental he could be. Strange that she had never noticed this trait in him before.

Seated in the breakfast room, Jon was on his best behavior.

"Well, Kara did her "Lady of the Lamp" stint and brought me back to the land of the living."

His tone was teasing and Kara looked at him sourly. What a good front he was putting on.

Kara said little.

"Are you feeling well, darling? You look a little fatigued."

Her mother's comments brought a rush of explanation from Jon.

"That doesn't surprise me at all. Kara spent most of the night being my ministering angel. Through her efforts I feel so much better."

Jon looked directly at Kara.

"I couldn't have asked for a more supportive friend."

Kara looked down at her hands and immediately back at Jon. Her intensely luminous eyes held him captive.

"I did only what I have always done. Maybe this is the first time you have noticed."

Soon afterwards Jon took his leave.

There was anxiety in the voice of Kara's mother. "Are you coming down with a virus, dear? You have appeared so listless for the past couple of days. Most unlike you."

She waited for her daughter's response.

Kara continued to sip from the cup of steaming tea. Making another attempt to communicate, Kara's mother asked, "Is there anything you are concerned about? Would you like to talk?"

The last thing Kara wanted to do was discuss Jon. She decided to go with the virus option. "I think I'm getting the flu."

"Will you feel up to visiting Aunt Clarice tomorrow? Skipton is a good two hours' drive away, but we don't have to go if you are not feeling well."

"Oh, the wonderful Ilkley Moor air will be an effective cure. I wouldn't want to miss out on that."

Silvia Olavssen completely missed the irony in Kara's voice.

CHAPTER FOURTEEN

Kara was filling in time before her return to California. It was a strange, unusual feeling, almost like a web insidiously spun around her that she was powerless to break.

A few days after the visit to Skipton, Kara and her mother traveled to the huge Metro Center in Gateshead to shop, with a visit to the theater afterward. These activities filled in more time, but not the ache that was in Kara's heart. Jon had entered her heart via the back door and had taken her by surprise.

She picked up a few mementoes at the Metro Center to take back to California as gifts and Kara's mother purchased special gourmet preserves and mustards that Jon's mother had asked her to get.

"Would you mind dropping these items off at the Williams' home tomorrow, Kara? Renata is having a party at the weekend and needs these things. Besides, it will give you an opportunity to visit. She will be so pleased to see you. I will be spending the day with your father, attending the Mayor's luncheon and then the ribbon cutting ceremony at the Town Hall with a reception afterwards."

The next day, without a reasonable excuse not to do so, Kara found herself reluctantly on the way to the Williams' residence with uneasiness accompanying her. Jon had a very busy daily schedule and so it was hardly likely that he would be at his parent's home. He was not a 'Mama's boy' popping in and out regularly, but Kara's anxiety level had reached such a pitch that the thought of being in Jon's presence affected her body temperature, turning her alternatively hot and cold.

Aunt Renata was waving goodbye to a few of her Bridge playing friends, who had visited her for lunch, as Kara drove up. She opened her arms to Kara and welcomed her with a hug.

"It is so good to see you again, my dear. I have been very remiss in not telephoning you to thank you for being a godsend when Jon was indisposed with his foot the night of your party. Jon has been full of your nursing aptitude." With a twinkle in her eyes she added, "Perhaps you missed your true vocation."

Kara denied it. "You know how Jon exaggerates."

The garden looked beautiful as they followed the crazy paving paths that meandered through the manicured lawns and topiary bushes.

"Remind me to have a bouquet gathered for your mother, please Kara, the roses are putting on an especially magnificent display this year."

Entering through the wide veranda of the eighteenth century home, Kara laid the package from her mother on a marble entry table. Renata smiled her thanks.

"You have a choice of coffee which is hot, but which was brewed half-an-hour ago, or fresh tea which will take only a short time for Jean to make whilst we chat."

"The coffee will be fine, thanks."

She intended leaving as soon as politely possible.

A plate of assorted petit fours was offered by Jean, the Williams' cook, who brought them in on a tray with the coffee. Kara declined the dainty confections.

"You're much too thin, Kara. You seem to have lost weight since you came home."

A sudden thought seemed to occur to Aunt Renata and in a cajoling tone asked.

"Is there someone special you are missing in California?"

Her eyes lit up at the prospect of hearing news of this nature.

"Sorry, Aunt. I'm becoming more and more convinced that the single life is for me."

A disappointed look passed over Mrs. Williams face.

"How old are you Kara?"

Funny how close friends and relatives believed they could ask any personal question they wished, with little thought to the appropriateness or sensitivity of the subject, Kara thinks pensively.

"I'm almost thirty-one."

"You look like a schoolgirl, but much better looking than you did at sixteen. To be honest, I'm surprised you haven't been snatched up before now. I understand Americans are not bashful when it comes to going after what they want. Angela certainly made a beeline for Jon and he took the bait. Sorry, Kara, I'm telling tales out of school—Jon doesn't confide in me, but I have a mother's intuition. Anyway, I was asking you about American men, James reminds me how I wander off the subject."

Kara managed to be non-committal and changed the subject to more general topics. When the phone rang, Kara almost leaped from the chair. Her nerves must be getting worse, she felt so tense.

When Clarence, the butler, announced a waiting telephone call, Renata Williams turned to Kara.

"I shouldn't be long. Please take the garden gloves and clippers from the back porch and put together a selection of flowers for your mother. Derek, one of the gardeners, should be out there and can help you."

Kara willingly obliged. It was a relief to get outside.

The variety of flowers to choose from was impressive. She wandered along the pathways, and around outstanding landscaped displays, eminently suitable to adorn the cover of "Home and Garden." *It really was a pity to sever the blossoms from their life system,* Kara reflects, *once cut they withered far too quickly.* Kara strolled around the garden longer than intended, enjoying the tranquility and finding pleasure in stopping to smell the flowers that attracted her. Thinking she heard a car turn into the driveway, Kara was immediately filled with alarm. Picking up the empty basket with the shears inside she panicked and rushed around a hedge, almost colliding with Jon who was standing beside a fountain, idly trailing his fingers through the water.

"Mother said you were out here picking flowers and you looked so peaceful I didn't have the heart to break into your reverie and disturb you."

He drew a handkerchief from his pocket and dried his hand.

"How are you, Kara?"

His tone was quiet and very formal.

"Just fine. I was getting ready to leave."

He took the basket from her hand.

"Well, let's get those flowers picked, because you will not be allowed to leave without them. How's that for a threat?"

A wan smile passed over Kara's face.

By the time the basket was partly filled, Jon had coaxed Kara into a more receptive frame of mind. By the time the basket was filled Kara had relaxed sufficiently to smile impulsively at Jon's intentionally and deliberately amusing remarks.

Turning to give the basket of flowers to Kara, Jon took hold of her hand. She tried to withdraw it, but Jon held fast.

"Can't we at least be friends, Kara? Please. We have known each other too long to allow misunderstandings and unfortunate incidents to come between us once again."

Kara hesitated.

Jon repeated. "Please, Kara."

She would be leaving in a week and it would be all over. She would not have to put herself through these excruciatingly harrowing mental gymnastics again—ever. Just tough it out, she urged herself.

"Okay," she said, smiling with some reservation, holding the basket firmly between them and waiting for Jon to move aside so that she could get back to the house.

His shoulders relaxed and a big smile appeared on his face.

"Great. Well now that has been established, how about coming out to the farm tomorrow? There will be a group of us. It really is a working day. We are going to plant a line of trees stretching about a quarter of a mile, to act as a windbreak, but we will take time to have a picnic and relax. You would really be doing me a favor by helping out."

She tried to come up with an excuse for getting out of the invitation, but no valid reason came immediately to mind.

Looking at Kara's expressive face registering reluctance, Jon quickly added.

"You did mention you would like to repay me for some of the things I have done for you." His eyes were like blazing neon signs signaling "Remember Party, Party, Party!"

Kara stared at Jon, wondering how he could be so patently coercive, giving her no alternative but to accept. How rude of him to force her in this manipulative manner.

Somewhat stiltedly Kara agreed to participate. There would be many people around and Jon would be kept very busy. They probably would see little of each other.

Jon made arrangements to pick Kara up, despite her protests that she could use her mother's car to drive over to the farm. Honestly, he was treating her like a child.

Jon arrived earlier than had been arranged and Kara was sitting talking to her father on a bench beside the Koi fish pond. She saw him through the family room French doors talking to her mother. Her heart skipped a beat, but she casually nodded and continued the conversation she was having, all the time being very conscious that Jon's eyes were upon her.

He joined them outside with a tray containing a pitcher of iced tea, glasses, spoons, and a dish of sugar. Kara's mother was followed by Millie, carrying a plate of assorted biscuits.

Addressing her husband and daughter, Silvia remarked, "Come and join us in the gazebo. You must feel uncomfortable sitting on that hard bench. You've been sitting there for ages."

Jon placed the tray on the wrought iron table and waited until Kara and her parents were seated before sitting also.

Kara listened to the conversation of the others as she sipped the beverage. They did not seem to notice she was not participating.

"I'm going to change, I won't be long."

She stood up and so did Jon.

"You look fine for the work to be done."

Kara looked Jon squarely in the eyes.

"I won't be long."

Jon observed the squared away shoulders as she walked into the house. It reminded him of the time she had put Roger in his place and the strut she had adopted on leaving him. A flutter of apprehension came over him. He had better not mess around any longer.

Kara changed into another pair of jeans and shirt. She combed her hair and brushed her teeth. She wished she did not have to go with Jon. He was really becoming quite dictatorial.

She sprayed her favorite Opium cologne behind her ears and picked up the container once more and added extra to her wrists. She would overpower him one way or another.

Jon was back in the house, making his way to the front door, talking to Silvia Olavssen when Kara walked down the stairs, checking her purse for keys.

"So I'm really going to wield the whip today. Your daughter will be a different person by the time she is returned."

Kara looked at Jon intently. His face was serious, but his tone was bantering. He could go either way.

With surprising alacrity they were out of the house, in the Jeep, and on their way to the farm. Kara sat looking out of the window. There did not seem to be anything relevant to chat about. Jon must have felt the same way; they sat in silence for several miles. When he spoke, she jumped. As her friend Marcie would have said facetiously, "You'd betta getta grip of yourself, honey."

When they arrived at the stables a number of people were already assembled, their horses saddled and waiting. Kara noticed Black Jack impatiently pawing the ground. Getting out of the vehicle they walked over to the group. Jon introduced each one, but the only one she recognized was Dennis, the groom who had saddled "Sleeping Beauty" on a previous visit. Everyone appeared to be in good spirits, joshing and laughing.

Jon held up a hand.

"The bushes are going to be planted from the south east boundary across to the barn beside the gate which exits to the Old Millbank Road."

He looked at his watch and continued, "Joe and some of his boys are probably setting things up right now. He knows what to do, so why don't you set off and we'll see you over there soon."

Taking Kara's arm he led her into the stables. Most of the stalls were deserted. Volunteers had commandeered the inhabitants.

Jon stopped at a doorway and Kara looked inside curiously.

She saw the back of a horse, feeding from a bale of hay on the back wall. At their approach it turned and trotted over to them, whinnying as it moved. Kara stood entranced. It was the most beautiful mare she had ever seen. It was smaller than most of the others housed in this area. It was a light tan color, with a shiny black mane and an elongated white triangle extending from its jibba to its muzzle. The animal came immediately to Kara and automatically she stretched out her hand and patted its neck, crooning nonsense. Turning her head to look at Jon she noticed how intently he was watching her. His face registered a look of satisfaction. For the first time he smiled.

"Love at first sight?"

Kara's shining eyes answered him.

"Oh, Jon, she's beautiful."

She turned back and gently stroked the horse's mane and the animal snorted in delight.

"You'd like to take her out then? Or maybe you'd prefer Sleeping Beauty," he teased.

Kara took a deep breath.

"I'd love to ride this one."

Awestruck she stood patting the object of her admiration, as Jon went off to get a saddle.

"Let's get going," Jon said, as he watched Kara eagerly swing into the saddle and bend down to pat the horse's flank. She flashed an excited smile at Jon, who swung himself up on to Black Jack.

They started moving off.

It was a lovely sunny day. The view of the Cleveland Hills was clear and unobstructed by the invariable collection of clouds or smog that usually surrounded them. Trotting comfortably behind Jon, Kara had an opportunity to savor the familiar countryside. The air was fresh, with short bursts of clover and eucalyptus buds intermingling with the grass and weeds that the horses' hooves crushed.

Rosebury Topping was easily visible and lagging a little behind Jon, Kara called out.

"The view from the 'top of the top' will be wonderful today. It's too bad we can't move the picnic up there."

Jon waited for Kara to catch up.

"What did you say, I couldn't hear?"

"It wasn't important," Kara responded, shrugging her shoulders, "but now that we have stopped, I'd like to take a photograph."

The scene was perfect. It would make a lovely picture. She turned her camera on Jon.

"Cheddar please."

He smiled almost grudgingly.

"Sorry, one more, I didn't get all of Black Jack in."

Stepping back, Kara clicked again and Jon dismounted, holding out his hand for the camera as he approached her.

"Let me take a picture of you and your horse."

A wistful expression came over Kara's face. She planted a kiss on the animal's neck.

"She's on my Wish List," she said, laying her cheek against the glossy hide.

She heard the click of the shutter and turned toward Jon.

"What's her name?"

"I thought you might like to choose it. She's quite a recent acquisition."

"Really? Then let me think about that. It has to be perfect."

Jon raised the camera again.

"Now you can give me the big smile edition," he said.

By the time they reached the rest of the group, they were at ease with each other as usual.

Jon brought the volunteers together and explained the process that would take place. He suggested that neophytes not familiar with this type of work should listen to the advice of their team leaders, and they especially should not try to keep up with the more experienced laborers.

From that time on Kara worked harder physically than she had ever done in her life. Even fighting the small fires at "Fruitful Harvest," while waiting for the fire engine to turn up, could not compare with this backbreaking job. They had been organized into groups of three, each unit with a certain section to plant. Trucks laden with Hawthorne bushes three to four feet in height toured the area, providing replacement supplies as needed. Holes were dug manually, except when rocky or hardened ground resisted human pressure and at that point an electronic post hole digger was utilized. As there were only three pieces of this equipment to work with, much of the labor was done by hand, each person on the team contributing to the effort. Struggling with the clumsy plants; lowering them in their biodegradable bags into the large holes; filling in the holes and tamping the ground around the bushes was very grueling work, Kara admitted tiredly. It seemed a never-ending project. Riding Black Jack back and forth or driving and unloading trees from trucks kept Jon very busy. His principal role was that of coordinator and supervisor, but there was no hesitation on his part in helping others.

The reverberating clanging of a metal rod against the old-fashioned triangular piece of steel signaled the call to lunch. Kara recognized it as a souvenir she had brought back for Jon a couple of years earlier. She had found it at the Pasadena Rose Bowl Flea Market. It was used regularly around the farm area to attract attention for a variety of purposes. Its summons was a welcome break for everyone.

Three picnic tables had been set up with a buffet meal attractively arranged on them, complete with heavy paper plates and plastic eating utensils. Bottled water and other drinks were available in ice chests. On the grass, around the tables, padded rugs similar to those used to protect furniture by moving companies, were arranged. Kara leaned against a tree trunk surveying the activity, peeling off her work gloves as she did so, trying to decide whether she was going to take a nap or eat.

Dennis, the stable boy, approached Kara carrying two plates filled with food.

"Jon asked me to give you this. He thought you might be hungry."

He passed over one of the plates.

"Thanks." The decision had been made for her.

Covering a yawn with her hand, Kara patted the blanket beside her.

"Please tell me about the mare I rode over here on this morning. It was an experience I won't soon forget, I loved every minute of it."

Dennis smiled shyly.

"Be glad to, she really is something, isn't she?"

He patted his pockets.

"Darn it. I've lost the knives and forks. I'll be right back."

Kara placed the plate of food on her lap and leaned back against the tree trunk in an effort to become more comfortable. If only she could keep her eyes open.

When Jon walked over with his plate of food, he stood and smiled at Kara's peaceful, dirt smudged face. She was fast asleep. She would give him hell for getting her involved in this strenuous, dirty project, and he relished the opportunity to interconnect with her. At least she would be very vocal. He was not accustomed to the silent punishing treatment from her that she had recently adopted. He removed her plate carefully and sat down to eat his own meal. In a quiet voice, so as not to disturb her, he started talking to Dennis and Pete, another of his friends who had volunteered to help with the tree planting project.

Sympathetically Jon tapped Kara on the shoulder.

"Wake up sleepyhead—it's time to get back to work."

There was no response. The others had begun disposing of their plates and plastic-ware and returning to their earlier work areas.

Jon shook Kara's shoulder a little more aggressively. She was out for a count. He knew how to waken her. Leaning over he kissed her slightly open lips, at first gently and after that more deeply, drawing back when he was tempted to take her into his arms in a more arousing embrace.

She opened her eyes and smiled at Jon, stretching her arms upward.

"I just had the most marvelous dream."

With wrinkled forehead she continued "but, darn-it, I can't remember what it was about."

"Probably me," he said waiting for the expected tirade, but Kara was obviously not in a fighting mood, she ignored his remark.

"Everyone else has gone back to work and I must get cracking, too."

With that, Jon offered his hand to assist Kara to her feet and with surprising meekness she took it. Black Jack stood waiting patiently nearby.

"Do you want to ride behind me back to your team?"

Kara shook her head.

"The walk will help waken me up properly."

Apart from a short break in the afternoon when cans of juice and sodas were passed out, everyone concentrated his or her efforts on getting the assignment completed by late afternoon. Kara was so tired. Her stomach was growling and she was beginning to feel quite nauseous. She could not remember whether she ate lunch or not.

Everyone was starting to leave. The last bush had been planted, the gardening equipment loaded onto the trucks that had brought in the plants and the whole area cleaned up. Kara waved goodbye to a few familiar faces and looked around to see where Black Jack and "little beauty" were. Jon was talking with a group of his friends, with his back to Kara, and she was unsure whether to join them or not. They seemed engrossed in their conversation.

Jon observed his friends looking beyond him with interest and turned to see Kara standing alone. He waved her over and conscious of her grubby shirt and jeans she slowly made her way to them. Putting an arm around her waist, Jon briefly introduced the friends she had not met. She recognized a few ex-soccer players and Leif was part of the group also. He had arranged the buffet to keep the hungry workers satisfied and had also taken care of the clean-up procedure.

They were talking of going over to "Joe's place" and helping him put up a barn at the end of the month and Kara was thankful that she would be back in California. She was so exhausted. Unconsciously leaning against Jon she did not pull away when his arm tightened, bringing her closer to his side. She was contemplating resting her head on his shoulder when she heard him say goodbye and with difficulty pulled herself away from him.

"Where are the horses, I couldn't find them?" Kara asked, looking around the wide open vista.

"You seemed so tired I asked Dennis and Pete to ride them back to the stables. I arranged to take the pickup with the picnic tables and gear back to the farm. That way you can have forty winks."

Kara looked away. She had been a real shrew and Jon did not deserve the unpleasant treatment she had been putting him through.

They walked over to the Ford truck and with difficulty Kara pulled herself into the high cab as Jon opened the door on his side.

"I think I'll spend the rest of my vacation in bed."

She yawned, making her jacket into a pillow.

"With whom?" Jon queried, leering at her as he put the key into the ignition.

For answer she threw the bundle in Jon's direction and immediately wailed.

"Ouch, that hurt—I ache all over and it's your fault, Jon Slater Williams," but she did not look angry and Jon smiled cheerfully.

"I don't think I ate lunch and I'm so hungry I could tackle anything, even your burnt offerings."

She looked at Jon with humor in her eyes and his heart took up a more rapid beat. He really would have to be careful with his emotions. He was becoming very conscious of Kara's charms and wanted to hold her in his arms and let her know how very important she was becoming to him. However she was so skittish he was on tenterhooks around her, afraid to speak in case she flared up.

He could not remember her being so temperamental.

He opened the glove compartment and tossed a roll of lifesavers.

"Have a feast."

She made a face, but accepted the packet without comment.

Kara admired the hills and the soft green patchwork fields as they traveled along the almost deserted lane. Jon pointed out the white horse engraved into the chalk hills.

"Please stop. That will make a terrific picture."

Dutifully Jon pulled over onto the side of the road.

"I can get the horse and you in the picture if you stand closer to the truck."

Jon shook his head as he looked down at his stained clothing.

"No way, Kara. Don't you think I have some pride left?"

He reached for the camera.

"I can certainly take a picture of you for your friends in California."

Kara looked down at her own soiled clothing and laughed.

"Touché! Can you imagine what my friends in California would say if they saw the impeccable Kara dressed like an abandoned ragamuffin?"

Jon, who had been leaning against the truck door, walked over to Kara.

"It depends upon one's value system, surely."

He took a large patterned kerchief from around his neck, saying

"Apart from a few well-earned dirt marks," that he proceeded to remove with the cloth, "what I see is a beautiful princess, in spite of the forced labor by the villainous and terrible ogre."

Kara's lips trembled.

"Oh, Jon," she said softly and quickly opened the truck door and climbed in.

Jon sighed. He felt as if he was on a see-saw—one minute wallowing in dejection and the next flying to the moon. For a grown man this was idiotic.

They reached the farm and dusk was beginning to settle. It gave a soft patina to the medieval setting. Kara, for a shocked moment, felt as if she were returning home. Rubbing her bottom, Kara stiffly climbed out of the cab.

"I don't think I'll ever be the same again" was her rueful comment as she waited for Jon to unlock the front door.

They could hear the telephone ringing and by the time they entered the living room, it had stopped. Jon shrugged his shoulders when he realized that he had not turned the new-fangled Telephone Answering Machine on before leaving for the day.

Kara stood beside the settee.

"You don't mind if I stand for a while?"

Jon pretended to swipe her buttocks and Kara yelped in protest. Lightly throwing an arm around her shoulders he said.

"Here's the plan. You go and have a nice long soak in the tub, while I throw our clothes into the washer and dryer. In the interim, I will prepare one of my special burnt offerings for your dining pleasure, madam."

Jon held his breath.

"Sounds wonderful, I only hope I don't fall asleep in the bath."

"I'll gladly come in and waken you."

"Is that part of the service around here?" Kara responded.

Jon could have bitten his tongue.

Somewhat subdued Kara drew the bathwater and added half a measure of Baddadas. Jon handed Kara a burgundy and gold paisley silk dressing gown and she closed the bathroom door and quickly disrobed, eager to get out of the caked and dirty clothing. Jon knocked on the door and she handed over her clothing that she had rather primly arranged into a neat package.

She relaxed in the comfortingly distinct smelling suds, allowing her hair to become saturated. She drifted in and out of shadowy serenity, until a soft knock on the door reminded her of where she was.

"Grub's up," Jon called, and as an afterthought, "five more minutes."

She looked in the mirror at her reflection. Clean she was—a beauty she was not. Slipping on Jon's robe and belting it around her waist, Kara went into the kitchen.

Jon was in the process of slipping a halved omelet onto each of two plates. He was in a terry cloth robe and his hair was still damp.

"Our clothes are in the dryer. They should be ready in half an hour. In the meantime, let's eat."

He placed a bowl of tossed salad on the table, and brought a chilled bottle of champagne from the refrigerator.

"Jon, this looks and smells terrific, you'd better control me or I'll eat your share too."

Jon grinned with delight. The barrier was down. They chatted and laughed and Kara felt as if indeed she had come home.

As they cleared off the table and loaded the dishwasher Kara turned to Jon with a tiny frown.

"I thought you had a full-time maid and cook?"

"Yes I do. I gave them the night off."

Noting Kara's suspicious glance, he quickly added.

"Because I originally thought we might eat in my suite at the Inn tonight, but I hadn't realized what a messy laborer you would turn out to be."

Jon refilled their wine glasses with the remainder of the wine and tweaked Kara's nose as he handed over her glass.

"Let's go and relax for a while."

They made their way to the living room.

"Would you care to listen to music, or watch T.V.?" Jon asked.

"I'll probably fall asleep whichever is chosen, so I really think I should be getting ready to leave." Kara suppressed a yawn.

Jon left the room returning to say that the jeans were still not dry enough to wear. Readily Kara settled down on the long settee, ruffling her still damp hair between her fingers.

Jon, in passing, also ran a hand through Kara's hair.

"It's much too wet to go out into the chilled night air. You're in England now, not California."

He disappeared momentarily. Returning with a towel over his arm, he said, "I don't use hair dryers they make my hair stand up on end. This is just as good."

He took hold of Kara's hands.

"Stand up," he commanded.

"No, I'm too comfortable—what are you thinking of doing?"

Without further ado, he pulled Kara to her feet and turned her to face him. Placing the towel over her hair he started rubbing back and forth with slow rhythmic movements, his big hands methodically covering her entire head.

It was hypnotic.

Closing her eyes Kara put her arms around Jon's waist to steady herself.

"Mmm," she murmured, "this is brilliant please don't stop."

"I know something that would be more than brilliant," Jon said inaudibly, feeling Kara's enticing body through the thin silk of the robe. Jon took the towel away, but Kara continued to stay with her hands firmly grasped around Jon's waist, her eyes closed and a seductive pout to her lips.

Jon lifted Kara's face to his.

"I've never seen you looking so beautiful. You are a very seductive woman."

Kara's vivid green eyes flashed open and Jon was enmeshed in them.

He drew Kara into his arms and, encouraged when she offered little resistance, started kissing her gently and sensitively, becoming more demanding as she responded to him.

"Oh, Kara, I love you so much, you must know that you have always been the only one for me."

Like a dash of icy water, the magic spell was broken. Kara pulled away and sat down on the settee.

"Please don't lie to me Jon. A couple of months ago you and Angela were embroiled in wedding plans and I can understand how upsetting it must be for you, but I will not be considered a convenient replacement."

Kara's face flushed in anger.

Jon sat down beside her and took her hand.

"In the past we have not resorted to lies between us. There has been no need. What I am telling you, Kara, is that you are a vitally important part of my life and I am becoming more and more aware of the driving force to hold on to you. I realize that this is a bit sudden, but please don't disregard what I have just said. I do love you. I suppose I always have and I want you to think about that."

Jon's 'Out-of-the-blue' declaration put Kara off-balance. She was not ready to cope with it right now. Puzzled at this swift turn of events, she spoke hurriedly, "I really must leave. It's been a long day and I'm too tired to become involved in a conversation of this nature."

They dressed and left for the drive to Kara's home. They were both quiet until Jon drew up under the portico.

He asked in a subdued voice. "Will you come and have lunch with me tomorrow? I do have a business to run and there are chores to attend to, but I really must see you soon."

Kara looked a little disturbed and she fidgeted in the vehicle's seat. Jon's voice held exasperation. "Since when did you have to be afraid of me, Kara?"

She sighed and patted his hand. "All right, how about eleven—is that too early?"

"Fine."

He smiled briefly as Kara closed the Jeep's door.

She walked up the wide stone steps without turning to wave goodbye.

CHAPTER FIFTEEN

The next day the first thing Kara noticed when she stood inside the front door of the farmhouse was the wicker picnic hamper. She was a little uneasy about that.

Jon had appeared cheerful upon her arrival and kissed her cautiously on the cheek.

"It's a lovely day for a picnic. Thought we should take advantage of it. You look nice. Ready to leave?"

His clipped sentences left Kara with the impression that she was not the only jittery person in the room.

Once they were on their way, Kara started relaxing. It was a beautiful day for a picnic outdoors. The sky was clear and the sun shone warmly. Jon put a cassette into the stereo and they started listening to the score from "The Phantom of the Opera" as they traveled along familiar country lanes.

"Are we going to the moor?"

Jon nodded his head.

"Any objections?"

"No. One of my favorite places."

Jon allowed himself to smile and again Kara discerned some nervousness in his manner. As they traveled higher on the narrowing roads, Kara noticed the appearance of the low growing heather bushes for the first time. By the time they had reached the top of the moor, the heather and gorse bushes appeared everywhere, covering the terrain in the familiar purple and yellow hues. Jon pulled over into a makeshift parking spot, quite close to the area known as Sheepwash. At one time in the past farmers had used the creek for shearing purposes, but environmental controls had put a stop to such unhygienic methods.

Kara bounced out of the Jeep and started sniffing the perfumed air.

"You look like a bloodhound." Jon remarked, glancing at Kara as he started unloading the picnic trappings.

Kara walked back to assist.

"I'd forgotten how lovely it is up here. We seem to have the place entirely to ourselves."

With a frown she turned to Jon.

"Why is it so deserted?"

"Remember this is a weekday. Most people can't take time out to do delightful things like this during the week and it is an isolated spot. At the weekend this place will be packed with people."

Kara walked around looking for a suitably flat spot to lay the blanket, which would also serve as their table. Finding a place nestled between the gorse and heather bushes she shook out the large gray cover and smoothed it onto the ground until it lay flat.

Jon brought over the picnic hamper and a cooler chest and laid them nearby.

"Let's walk down to the creek."

He held out his hand and Kara took hold.

They walked across the wooden bridge, stopping to watch the water gushing over the rocks below. Kara ran down the incline to the water's edge and pulled off her sandals.

The creek was as icy cold as she remembered it.

"There are so many memories here and they are all coming back. Do you remember the times I camped out here with my Girl Guide Troop?"

Jon lay back against the bank, a contented expression on his face.

Kara's feet were beginning to turn blue. She approached Jon and sat down beside him, placing her chilled wet feet on his warm bare legs.

He shuddered.

"Once a pest, always a pest. Yes, I recall your terrible teens. You are bringing it back vividly. You were very proud being Patrol Leader of the Kingfisher Patrol. I remember you in your short little navy blue uniform, with your knobby knees showing. I also recall my father watching as you practiced making knots, over and over again until you got them right."

He mimicked "Left over right and under, right over left and under."

Kara was astonished.

"What an amazing memory you have. How could you possibly remember all that from so long ago?"

"Oh, believe me, it didn't come easily."

Jon smiled and pulled Kara to her feet, once the sandals were replaced.

"I'm ravenous, let's eat."

They retraced their steps over the bridge to the blanket.

They enjoyed a simple Plowman's lunch of crusty farmhouse bread, fresh local cheeses and sliced ham, with huge ripe strawberries for dessert. All washed down with a chilled bottle of Chardonnay, drunk from clear crystal wineglasses.

Resting on the blanket, Kara and Jon drifted in and out of conversation as they tracked the progress of the cloud formations passing overhead. It was pleasantly relaxing and when Jon took Kara's hand into his own, rubbing the palm with his thumb as they talked, Kara felt a sense of serenity. Being with Jon brought very comfortable feelings.

Jon rolled over onto his side, balancing on an elbow as he looked into Kara's eyes. He took hold of a strand of hair, which had fallen over her face and smoothed it back, resting his hand on her cheek.

"You know, in retrospect, I think I must have been in love with you for a very long time, despite your knobby knees, and gave you a hard time just to disguise my adolescent emotions."

Kara's eyes closed and her mouth trembled.

"You're making it very difficult for me to resist you, Jon."

"Then let me make it easier for both of us."

At this he drew Kara into his arms and proceeded to show her both a tenderness and urgency in his caresses that overwhelmed her. It was a long time since Kara had experienced the infusion of desire and the sense of illicitness in finding delight in Jon, her almost brother, heightened the physical arousal. Her heart was thumping wildly as she clung to him, allowing his hands to wander over her upper body, unchecked.

Visibly shaking, Jon withdrew from Kara and sat up, putting his head into his hands.

Kara was intoxicated by the conflicting sensations that had overtaken her. Jon's ardor had taken her unawares and she was thoroughly shaken by its intensity.

Hesitantly she placed a hand on Jon's shoulder.

"Please don't blame yourself, unless you have regrets. If it makes sense, I wanted you to do whatever you wanted to do."

Jon raised his head, turning it to kiss the slender hand still resting on his shoulder. Kara leaned against Jon's back, sliding both of her arms around his neck and fastening them together on his chest.

"If this is love, I think I'm going to like it" she whispered, nibbling on his ear.

Jon groaned and pulled Kara into his arms once more.

"I didn't plan on this happening, Kara, please believe me."

Willingly she submitted to his kisses.

Two shots rang out and they both sat up in alarm. A loud plop was heard coming from the brook and a black Labrador leapt past them in search of the fallen trophy. A couple of men with rifles in their hands came over the hill and stopped when they saw Jon and Kara sitting looking at them.

Jon stood up as they approached.

The hunter in a deerstalker hat directed his comments to Jon.

"Gosh, sorry old boy, we hadn't realized there was anyone around. Hope we didn't scare the hell out of you? It's the first day of grouse hunting and we decided to have a go right away, what!"

In her nervousness Kara felt like giggling at the typically English twang. Jon pulled Kara to her feet.

"We were about to leave, so you will have the area to yourselves."

He was breathing deeply and his face was taut.

Gently carrying a still breathing bird, the dog sat down, waiting for his master's command. The man took the bird, patting the dog's head. The dog energetically shook his wet body, violently splattering water on them. They all smiled. It broke the awkwardness of the situation.

Nodding their heads the two men retraced their steps, with the dog obediently following.

"What will they do with the grouse? It was still alive." Kara's face registered concern.

"Before they put it in the sack, they will most likely break its neck, but it looked as if it was in its last throes."

Kara shuddered. She did not like to witness that kind of senseless killing.

Kara quickly packed the hamper and cooler and Jon folded the rug. They carried the items back to the Jeep. Jon broke the silence.

"They arrived just in time."

Kara glanced at Jon puzzled.

"Why do you say that?"

Resting against the back of the vehicle, Jon pulled Kara into his arms.

"Because if they hadn't disturbed us, I couldn't have resisted you any longer and I wouldn't want to be accountable for having put you in that sort of a predicament."

Kara's parted lips sought Jon's eager mouth. They stood entwined, savoring a rising need, which permeated Kara's responsive body with an engulfing glow. They heard another couple of gunshots.

In a rough voice Jon said.

"We don't need an audience. Let's drive back to the farm."

On the way there they held hands.

"Once again I gave the staff the night off. I mentioned to Leif that we probably would have dinner in the end dining car tonight, but when we get back I'll call him to cancel those arrangements. I don't feel like sharing you with anyone right now."

Kara squeezed Jon's hand, her shining eyes agreeing with his suggestion. Kara had never been as happy as she was right now. She had not realized such bewildering, overpowering feelings could exist within her, and she was eagerly anticipating the time she and Jon would spend alone together tonight. Was she really falling in love with him? Kara was stunned at the prospect—this certainly would change her life.

Jon opened the door to the farmhouse and a puzzled expression crossed his face.

"I'm sure I switched the lights off when we left this morning."

Advancing in front of Kara he walked through to the kitchen and she saw him freeze in the doorway. A delighted scream met his entrance and there was no doubt in Kara's mind who was there.

Angela threw herself into Jon's arms, kissing him passionately.

"Baby, it's wonderful to see you again. I could hardly wait to get here."

Seeing Jon's stunned face she said, "I phoned yesterday to let you know that I was on my way to see you, but there was no reply, so I decided to surprise you—and I did, didn't I, darling?"

For the first time she seemed to be aware that Kara was standing in the middle of the living room. Placing her arm possessively around Jon's waist she commented sweetly.

"Well, if I had to find Jon with anyone, I'm glad it's with you, Kara. Knowing what good friends you are could leave no room for distrust. Am I right?"

Her eyes hardened as she looked at Kara. When the Jeep drew up outside she had observed the infatuated look Jon gave Kara as he assisted her from the vehicle and the reciprocal glow reflected in Kara eyes. She was livid. She would soon put a stop to this.

Angela placed her left hand up to her throat and the huge diamond caught the light, glittering as coldly as its owner was staring at Kara.

Jon removed Angela's arm from around his waist.

"We really have nothing to discuss, Angela. If you had spoken to me before you made this hasty visit, you would have discovered that you were wasting your time."

"Sweetie, you have every right to be upset with me. I know I haven't been as attentive to you as I should have been, but I can explain everything just as soon as we are alone."

She glared at Kara, who was standing uncertainly in the same spot.

Feeling flustered and bewildered, Kara turned and left the room, making her way to the bathroom to regain her composure. Kara's thoughts wandered. *This is not the Angela I thought I knew. Evidently Angela still considered herself engaged to Jon—flaunting the ring had established that. Jon said he had broken off the engagement and perhaps that was the reason for Angela's vindictiveness in finding me here with him. Yet Angela knows that Jon and I have been friends all our lives— but not sweethearts—how could she possibly know this when it is still so new to me?*

She sighed. "Hell hath no fury like a woman scorned."

Walking past Jon's bedroom she noticed Angela's open luggage on a chair, with the bedspread turned back and a flimsy negligee carelessly thrown onto the pillows. Kara felt a wave of nausea sweep over her. Obviously Angela was very confident of her hold over Jon.

181

Closing the bathroom door behind her, Kara rested her head against the cool wall tiles. Was it just an hour ago she had been supremely happy, ready and willing to climb into that same bed herself?

Walking over to the mirror, she observed her appearance. Her reflection showed an unkempt image. Comparing the flawlessly coiffed Angela in the sensational couturier creation with the forlorn creature staring back at her, Kara dejectedly admitted defeat. At this point she must hold on to her dignity. In reality she had expected Angela walking back into Jon's life—an issue not yet faced up to by him and one she must also face.

Turning away from the mirror, Kara sighed. It was a disheartening issue. He couldn't have both of them. She left the bathroom, deliberately looking at the negligee on Jon's bed to make sure that her eyes had not deceived her earlier.

The door to the kitchen was closed. Standing in the living room once again Kara could hear Jon and Angela in conversation. Jon was speaking in a low tone and Kara could not make out his words. Angela's voice seemed deliberately loud and Kara heard her say quite clearly, "Oh, honey, I'm sure Kara's not interested in hearing the kind of things we have to say to each other. With the exciting news I have to tell you, I'm sure we can work things out."

Kara had heard enough. She picked up her purse from the hallstand and quickly and quietly left the house. Taking care not to turn on the car's headlights until she had traveled several hundred yards along the road, she shuddered at the turn of events. In her misery she tried to convince herself that she had had a lucky escape—Jon the predator, Jon the predator, Jon the predator. She could not get the words out of her head. By the time she arrived home, she had a headache of gigantic proportions.

All weekend Kara waited for some attempt by Jon to explain the situation. Her parents had guests over for a dinner party Saturday evening and Kara listened anxiously waiting for the phone to ring. By the time she could plead suitably of tiredness, a bout of nausea overcame her and legitimately released her from the social obligation to her parents. In a somber mood Kara speculated that as Jon had not contacted her the short-lived romance was over.

Sleep was elusive. Kara's mind fixated on the events of the day searching for an acceptable conclusion to puzzling questions. Was Jon's deceit intentional? Did Angela truly love Jon, or was jealousy the motivator? The most bewildering question was why she had so easily capitulated to Jon's advances?

A sleepless night ensued.

By dawn she was a wreck. The bedroom phone rang and Kara grabbed the receiver quickly. It was Lavinia, an old school friend calling.

"Sorry for phoning so early, "K", but Bert and I are planning a day's outing to York. Are you able to join us? Remember you said you would, if you could."

Kara thought for a split second. It did seem like a stroke of good luck. The outing would keep her outdoors all day and her inaccessibility might perturb Jon, if he phoned.

"Sounds terrific. I'll be ready by the time you get here."

Kara had not met Vinnie's fiancé, Bert, before. As the day progressed she was pleased and also a little envious of the exclusive relationship the two shared. They all toured the Minster, which had always been one of Kara's favorite architectural buildings, took pictures outside the church where Guy Faulkes had been baptized and had lunch in the charming "Three Tuns Inn." They insisted on Kara taking the Yorvik tour. It was the reconstruction of a Viking town discovered quite accidentally eight years earlier, dating back to the eleventh century. It had been exposed in a dig by archeologists shortly after Kara had immigrated to her new home in America. Kara learned much of the details from her father, who as nephew of the late King Olav V of Norway had opened the exhibition officially. Her parents had sent pictures of the event

Getting into a moving overhead "space capsule" Kara was transported back to this early time, complete with the authentic smells of burning fires and food cooking when passing over a village. Fishermen bringing their catch into the harbor and the salty smell of the sea brought back the invigorating aroma of Cormorant Bay and reminded Kara of the peace and tranquility it afforded. She resolved to go there as soon as possible, to get her thoughts in order and her life back on track again.

Kara invited Vinnie and Bert to join her for refreshments after returning from their outing to York. Kara's parents welcomed her friends and, as was their nature, extended their hospitality.

When Hilda entered the room with an assortment of petite sandwiches on a large tray Kara asked nonchalantly, "Any messages for me?"

"Not one, Miss Kara." Hilda replied, "The phones seem to have taken a well-earned rest today."

Noticing the disappointment on her daughter's face, Silvia surmised that this had not been a good vacation for her. It had appeared to start off so well.

Producing a selection of "Fruitful Harvest" wines Kara's father entertained Vinnie and Bert by recounting his excitement at having a shipment of the same wines they were drinking sent from California to stock his wine cellar. Noting the interest generated as the delectable wine was being sampled by his guests, Gus felt compelled to exaggerate the anecdote for their amusement.

Warming up to the subject, Gus continued.

"I felt quite smug being the sole beneficiary in England of this line of fine wines. No one else could claim this distinction. Quite an achievement for a wine aficionado I might add. Consequently in taking my wife to dine at The Black Bull Inn shortly afterward, you can imagine the astonishment when I specifically ordered a bottle of the Cabernet Sauvignon from the "Fruitful Harvest" selection to find that they actually had it in stock." He repeated, "In stock!"

Expectantly he waited for comments.

"You're joking." Bert exclaimed, taking a sip of the wine from the wineglass in his hand.

"Oh, what a shock for you, thinking only you had access to the wine in England." Vinnie said.

Leaning closer to them Gus expounded, "That was not all I discovered that night. I was bowled over in finding that they also have sole distribution rights in this area of England."

"Oh!" they both gasped.

Pushing his glasses on top of his head Gus took a swig of wine. Winking at his wife, he continued—"So now I don't have to import my favorite wine, I can get it anytime I wish right here in my home town."

Watching as Vinnie and Bert's expressions changed from sympathetic to fooled, Gus chortled, "I really got you going then, didn't I?"

Vinnie laughed delightedly. "I'd forgotten what a joker you are—you had my compassion for a minute of two, until I remembered being fooled by you in the past."

Kara shook her head, allowing her father's incomparable sense of humor to bring a smile. She was feeling tired and not in a very social mood. After a second glass of wine consumed quickly she became alternatively outspoken and broodingly introspective. Silvia Olavssen was disturbed by Kara's odd attitude—something was wrong. With record aplomb they managed to get Vinnie and Bart out of their home graciously. They asked Kara to explain the reason for her unbecoming behavior.

"I don't wish to talk about it. It's something I can handle and it really is not important. Besides, by returning to California, the whole situation will be automatically resolved."

Looking at the crestfallen face of her mother, Kara walked over and kissed her.

"Sorry if I've caused you concern. Sometimes things don't go the way we think they ought." She straightened her shoulders "And sometimes that works out to be the best in the long run."

Concentrating on placing her feet properly on each stair, she made her way to her bedroom suite.

This night proved to be no different to the previous one. Tormenting possibilities of how Jon and Angela were spending their time together led Kara's imagination into distressful situations. Unable to stand the despondency further, Kara hurried out of bed and started packing ready to leave for Wisherly at the crack of dawn. She needed some time to work out this new problem and Cormorant Bay, her heart's comfort zone, is the repository to nourish her spirit.

Leaving a note indicating where she is going, with instructions not to inform *anyone* because she needs a little time alone, Kara silently slipped out of one of the side doors to the row of garages. She encountered no one.

She stuffed her luggage into her father's old estate wagon and eased her way along the mist shrouded winding lane to the main road.

What a relief it was to be back in familiar surroundings, protected by its privacy. During the day Kara took long walks along the beach, mulling over her feelings and dissecting them mentally with the skill of a surgeon. Roger was a twerp, not even worthy of her tears and heartache, but he had generated the pattern to which she seemed destined. Kevin, the vintner, on the other hand had taken her unawares. She had been a willing participant, an eager companion, and ready for their future together. Kara derisively recalled that his fiancée also had the same idea.

Perhaps that was why when Ben Hughes, the gentle professor, came into her life she was ready to turn him down, on principle, before he could set the familiar pattern into motion once again. Kara shook her head. Poor Ben, poor Kara.

Kara sat on the deck of the houseboat looking out at the calm blue water.

Why Jon, Kara questioned? He who has had her full and complete trust; he who has been a subconscious part of her entire life; Jon is the unknown factor, surprising her with his unexpected ardor and declaration of love. Why has he withdrawn from her without explanation, or apparently any intent to do so? This was the greatest hardship to bear. It was difficult to admit that Jon had feet of clay and had let her down.

Tears trickled down Kara's cheeks.

In retrospect, she should have repulsed him, suspecting that he was on the rebound from Angela, but he had been so persistent and totally believable. The few tender and thrilling times spent in Jon's arms and the captivating stimulus of his kisses also brought a bitterness and hopelessness that cut to the core. Her head ached. Would she never arrive at a decision with which she could feel at peace?

How can she leave him feeling so uncertain? How can she stay knowing his deceit?

It is a bitter pill to swallow. At night time lying in her bunk listening to the gentle lapping of the waves as they come to rest on the beach, and the sound of the odd rat scurrying around looking for scraps of food, Kara sought to find an answer. Is there nothing sufficiently distracting to quell the ache in her heart? The sense of despondency that surrounded Kara deepened. The most heart-wrenching aspect was facing up to Jon and Angela's physical involvement, which apparently still continued.

Jon must have found her an easy conquest. Perhaps he was not the pillar of strength and decency she had believed him to be. Nothing made sense and her senses became numb.

Of one thing Kara is sure. She will overcome this experience, just as she did with Roger, and the vintner, and the professor. She will become less trusting and more wary. She has made a good life for herself in California and would not choose to make any changes there, especially if the project with the State is accepted.

At last a decision has been reached. Obviously she is not the marrying kind and she is not the type of person to become involved in affairs. Some people are smart enough to learn from their earlier mistakes, she most certainly has to learn from this one.

Having somewhat unwillingly come to this decision, Kara decides to leave Cormorant Bay and return to her parent's home. She will be leaving for California in two days and while packing her tapestry luggage she has a strange compelling hunch that she may never come back here again. Sadness and consternation hits her as she hurries out of the bedroom and onto the deck, as if afraid that in her crumbling world, this special place will vanish too. She has to reassure herself it has not.

Standing looking out at the azure water, cupped in its safe and peaceful harbor, Kara silently gives thanks for the privilege of finding so much peace and tranquility here and for once again drawing her back to find solace and composure, giving her strength to make the decision she has come to.

From her reverie Kara hears a voice calling to her from the steps that lead down to the beach. No need to turn around, she knows so well who it is.

She is ready for him!

Standing her luggage and handbag near the door, Kara commences closing and locking each window. She is almost finished securing the vessel when Jon climbs onto the deck.

"I was hoping to be here before now. There is a lot we need to discuss."

Raising surprised brows Kara looks at Jon standing in the doorway. She is pleased to have made the effort to change from her grubby warm-up suit into a white seersucker sundress; it complements the golden tan she has acquired over the past two days tramping the beach. Jon stares as if caught off-guard and with a purposeful look on his face moves toward Kara.

Recognizing the intent Kara walks behind a captain's chair, resting her hands on the smooth wood, which served as a barrier. Suddenly she was less sure of her emotions.

"You didn't have to go out of your way to rush down here, Jon. I don't return to California for another couple of days—you could have phoned before I left, if Angela had no objections."

The chill in the air was evident.

Jon attempted to walk closer to Kara, but her stance stopped him.

"This is ridiculous, Kara, you ought to know me better. At least sit down so that we can discuss this like sensible people."

Seeing Kara throw her head back in a familiarly mutinous gesture, Jon pleaded.

"Please, Kara."

It was the hurt expression on his face that forced Kara to comply. Jon sat on a chair across the table from Kara. He studied her face intently.

"Why did you run away, Kara?" He asked softly.

Indignation rose to the surface. Of all the insufferable, insensitive things to say.

"Oh, I guess I just didn't feel like hanging around, intruding upon the time you and Angela obviously wanted to spend together—alone."

Oh, darn! She had not intended blurting out such a childish statement. Quick tears sprang to her eyes and she turned her head away to hide them. In an instant Jon was there, kneeling beside her chair with her hands in his own.

"Kara, don't you believe I love you? This is something I have just discovered in the last few months, although intrinsically I've known it all my life. We were meant for each other."

Kara raised her moist eyes to Jon's.

"Why didn't you try to contact me? Why didn't you come to see me and why did you allow Angela to so completely claim you the moment we returned to the farmhouse? That's not love, Jon. If it is, I want no part of it."

So saying, Kara withdrew her hands, rose from her chair, and walked over to the portholes and continued fastening them. It was suddenly quite dim, except for the shaft of brilliant sunlight making its entrance through the open door.

Kara's eyes felt heavy with unshed tears.

This was not going at all the way she had envisaged. She had to get out of here. It was suddenly much too constrictive.

Jon was immediately behind her, not quite touching but heartbreakingly close. She could feel his warm breath on her hair.

"Angela has returned to London. She knows how I feel about you."

"Jon, I saw Angela's luggage in your bedroom, with her negligee on your bed. It looked like a well-established pattern, which was expected to continue. Angela was wearing your ring and the moment you saw her you were entranced. You certainly didn't appear to have distanced yourself from her then. Remember I was there, I saw it all and felt very much in the way."

Jon's face reflected exasperation.

"Kara, compared to you, she played a relatively small part in my life. We can discuss this for whatever length of time you wish, to clear up any doubts you have, but honestly, my love, she was a part of my life which is now over and she came back uninvited. I was quite shocked to find her waiting for us."

"Perhaps I, too, am a diversion." Kara said quietly.

Jon shook his head remorsefully.

"Angela enjoyed being around horses, which is how we first became attracted to each other, but there was little else of substance there. Foolishly, I didn't distinguish or recognize the symptoms of a passing infatuation. I have never had time before for such distractions. Really, Angela had little tangible influence in my life."

Kara objected to this.

"Jon, I saw Angela's touches everywhere I went. Even the horse you gave her served as a tie. It was a reason for her to return and a constant reminder to you."

Anger was becoming evident in Kara's voice. Looking at Jon directly she added, as if an afterthought, "and besides it was obvious you were recent lovers."

For the first time Jon hesitated.

Kara picked up the handbag from beside her luggage and walking back to the chair, searched for a packet of tissues, as she listened.

"Yes, that's true and we did become engaged and, as you know, we also had made marriage plans. That is why I feel a certain responsibility to Angela. She came into our circle and Jackie encouraged me to be kind to her. Angela made herself very agreeable. She is a free spirit and I liked that. At first it was a matter of mutual enjoyment in each other. I certainly had no long-term plans and the engagement followed more as the path of least resistance, since the farm took such a toll on most of my waking hours. Incidentally, Kara, Angela zeroed in on me, she can be quite aggressive and determined."

Jon moved closer to the doorway, leaning against the frame of the door, reflectively eyeing Kara.

Just realizing what had been said earlier he queried.

"Why did you say you saw so much evidence of Angela around— you mentioned the horse, which actually belongs to me. She rode it when staying at the farm. It was easier to allow it to be called "Angela's horse" at least everyone knew which one we meant. What else did you mean?"

A puzzled look was on his face.

Kara gritted her teeth. He really wanted to drag this out.

"From the color scheme in the farmhouse to the 'Fruitful Harvest' wine bottles at The Black Bull Inn. The yellow, green and white theme is the one she has in her bedroom in California and which I lived with for over two years. The wine is self-explanatory."

Kara looked at Jon triumphantly, as if expressing a fait accompli presented in court.

There was a small silence before Jon burst out laughing.

"You silly goose! The yellow, green and white scheme had nothing to do with Angela. When I moved into the farmhouse it had hideous patterned wallpaper in several rooms and dark brown carpeting throughout which made the rooms look smaller and quite dreary. Mother came out and declared the place uninhabitable and I left all refurbishing arrangements up to her. She was the person who chose the green carpeting to bring in the outdoors and at the same time had all the walls painted white. The yellow trim brought in a ray of sunshine, I was told."

With a nefarious grin Jon quipped.

"You didn't realize I was so knowledgeable on interior decorating, did you?"

Kara looked away rather shamefacedly.

"Now for your other concerns."

Jon paced around the room, quiet, with a pensive expression on his face. He sat down opposite Kara once again.

"The wine was actually your father's suggestion, having been to the California winery and being impressed with their products. He was instrumental in making arrangements for their import. I really have little to do with that aspect of the business. Leif is the expert, so apart from enjoying a glass of 'Fruitful Harvest' wine now and again that is my total involvement."

With a sinking feeling of acceptance Kara recalled the bottles of 'Fruitful Harvest' in her parents' home cellar. She could not argue with Jon on that score.

Kara sighed as she rose and walked over to the door. How easily explained, but why were the doubts and hurt still there?

Jon followed, placing the palms of his hands on the door at each side of Kara, holding her captive.

"You can't imagine how bewitching you look, in that seductive dress with the sun shining through it."

Kara's cheeks flushed at the implication. Jon bent and lightly kissed her lips.

"Now, where are we in the interrogation?"

Kara struggled to move away, but Jon's large hands held her shoulders firmly against the door.

"We have to get all this nuisance stuff out of the way before we can get on with our lives again and there's not much time to resolve a great many important issues. Please, Scooter, you are much too forthright to hold this against me without a fair hearing."

The earnestness on Jon's face touched Kara's heart. She instinctively turned her face up to his. Encouraged by the tenderness in her eyes, Jon gathered Kara into his arms and pulled her close, gently showering kisses over her face, until unable to contain himself further he sought her lips and coaxed the reaction from her that he desired.

Kara moved closer to Jon, feeling his body tremble as they came together.

Immersed in the developing excitement, Kara became aware of Jon's hands slowly exploring and caressing her, running his hands along her body.

Kara withdrew from Jon's embrace.

"Please stop, Jon. This won't resolve anything. It just complicates the issues and there's too much to discuss."

He remarked in a dry voice.

"I'm beginning to understand how you have become so successful in your work, Kara. You really are in control of your emotions. I salute you."

Thinking, *Not nice Jon,* Kara flinched at his cutting remark.

Returning to the coolness of the dim room, Kara sat on the edge of a chair near a small table, her back straight and her face inscrutable. In passing, Jon took Kara's hand and gently pulled her over to the settee, putting an arm around her shoulders after they were seated.

"Relax Kara, I've never forced myself on anyone and I'm too scared with you to try. Suddenly you have become an enigma. I thought I knew and understood you as well as myself, yet now I have so many doubts. You obviously distrust me and just to put your mind at rest Angela and I did not sleep together that 'fateful night,' or do anything else to incite your anxiety. In fact, we argued most of the time, but of course you were not around to take note of that."

He absentmindedly stroked Kara's bare shoulder.

"Incidentally, the reason why Angela returned so unexpectedly and at such an inappropriate time was because mother sent pictures to Jackie of the little get-together I held for you. Apparently Angela thought we had become totally enamored with each other. She apparently was not ready to relinquish me to you. I informed her in no uncertain terms that the decision was no longer hers to make."

Dubiously Kara looked at Jon.

His face was expressionless. Removing his hand from Kara's shoulder, he ran it through his hair, rumpling it, looking much like the small boy Kara remembered justifying why he had spent his allowance in the Arcade shooting gallery.

"Kara I tried my hardest to contact you and when I finally got over to your house, because no phone calls were being returned, Martin in coming to the door and seeing me, remembered that he had forgotten to pass on my messages to you. Ask him if there is any doubt—he and

I were very upset about this oversight. Anyway he twittered around, saying you had gone away for a few days and couldn't be reached. I immediately thought of Cormorant Bay and knew where to find you—a retreat as far away from the world as possible."

Pausing for breath Jon sighed and returning to the gist of the conversation added,

"To cut a long, long story short, this is the first opportunity I've had to come to you, but if it is of any consolation, you have been in my thoughts constantly and I've been impatient to see you. I was petrified that this whole situation would be blown out of proportion in your imagination and judging from the cool reception I've received, it seems as if that is the case."

Looking directly into Kara's darkened eyes Jon said quietly.

"I've told you I love you and at this point you will have to trust me. Once you settle your affairs in California and move back to England, we will have time to work everything else out. Right now the most important consideration is to establish whether in fact you love me and will marry me soon. There must be no doubt about that."

In an almost desperate voice he went on, "There is too much at stake."

Kara was shocked that Jon would expect her to immediately give up her lifestyle without discussing the options and the possibilities. It added a callous dimension to his character, a flaw that could not be overlooked.

Controlling her voice to suppress the panic that quickly had surfaced at this sudden, questionable declaration, she responded.

"I've always loved you Jon," She took a quick, jerky breath, "not in the way I have recently begun to feel about you, but in knowing that you are and have been a very important element in my life. In the past two weeks I have had to consider you in a different much more personal way and it has turned my world upside down. To be honest I really don't feel there has been sufficient time to take in all that has happened between us. I suppose I still consider you and Angie at the "almost married" stage.

Kara's voice trailed away and they both sat on the settee, silent. In a small voice she continued.

"I hadn't realized how deeply you could affect me, Jon, and that is where the problem lies. I must have time to come to a decision, away from you where your kisses and passion affect my judgment and resolutions. I swore, after Roger and the others, that I would never allow my emotions to rule my head. Against my will I felt myself becoming attracted to you in an almost unrealistic way. I'm not even sure that what I feel is love. Growing up together you were my hero and in later years, my trusted confidant. I was impetuously ready to trust you implicitly in the exciting dream we had started. There was even an element of illicitness that crept in."

Kara shook her head, a puzzled expression on her face.

"Perhaps you are asking for more than I can give, Jon, expecting my love unconditionally in such a sudden, insistent way. You are assuming, regardless of the successful and satisfying lifestyle I have established in California, that all I have worked so hard to achieve can be easily forfeited."

Speaking her thoughts out aloud she stated bluntly, "Would true love selfishly ask that of me—or are you playing games?"

Jon jumped up.

"Stop this Kara. I've told you that I love you. What else can I say to convince you? Angela has gone back to London knowing exactly the way I feel about you—and her."

He walked around the room, pacing restlessly, the limp noticeable.

"This isn't a good situation to be in. I want you to stay. I want you to be my wife, but most of all I want your trust otherwise we have no foundation for the kind of life I know we could have together. You have to make that commitment, I already have."

Jon's face had a strained, tight look. The intensity of his feelings had brought a sallow tinge to his skin, which made him look older than his thirty-three years.

Straightening his shoulders he said in a tense voice.

"The next move is yours, Kara. Three months should give you sufficient time to make a decision—away from 'my passion.' That is all the time you should need."

He smiled somewhat wryly, taking her hand, kissing the palm and closing her fingers over it.

"Goodbye, love, my life is in your hands."

Jon abruptly turned and walked to the door, stopping to salute her briefly before going down the houseboat steps. He disappeared from view.

Kara was appalled at the suddenness of it all. No pleading, no remonstrations—just goodbye. The enormity of this final step hit her. He was giving her exactly what she had asked for, but she did not feel victorious or reassured.

Kara instinctively turned to run after Jon, to say she needed him, she was being foolish—they could work it out, but her feet became glued to the floor while her heart raced to join him.

CHAPTER SIXTEEN

Kara was startled from her reverie by the announcement that British Airways Flight BA5945 was ready to commence loading passengers. Its destination was Los Angeles.

She shook away the cobwebs with an effort. How she longed for her familiar lifestyle once more and a feeling of normalcy.

Kenneth rushed over, pushing the pack of playing cards into her hand. "Thanks, Kara. Maybe you can read to me on the plane. Daddy said that game wore him out."

Not waiting for a reply, he skipped back to his father.

Kara sat back and rubbed her closed eyelids with the back of her hands, sighing softly as she mentally prepared herself for the long journey ahead.

Families with small children were to be accommodated first on board the plane. Kara waved to Kenneth who was clutching his mother's hand, while his father struggled with a sleeping child over his shoulder and various pieces of carry-on luggage.

Putting away her work planner, she retrieved her boarding pass and passport from her handbag. No hurry, the queue to embark was moving slowly. Depositing the half-empty cup of cold coffee into an overflowing trash receptacle, she moved into line. At last the headache had disappeared.

Upstairs on the jumbo jet, familiar with the layout, Kara searched for seat 64.A. She was pleased to have reserved this place. It is her favorite spot, beside a window, with plenty of leg room because of the location of an emergency door. The seat came with an added bonus—a lidded storage area under the window that was very convenient. She intended storing the valuable pieces she carried in it.

A steward, hovering around, offered to assist and directed Kara to the middle seat.

Kara demurred. "No. This can't be right, I reserved the window seat."

A look of consternation came over his face. "I'm so sorry, but your Boarding Pass shows 64.B."

He submitted the stub for Kara's inspection.

Kara was flabbergasted and her voice conveyed annoyance.

"I distinctly requested the window seat and had it confirmed. I can't believe this is happening. How can the situation be remedied?"

The steward looked ill-at-ease.

"If the window seat is not taken at the time of departure you are welcome to take it, but it appears the plane has been booked to capacity."

Uncomfortable with having a disgruntled passenger so early in the flight he tried to smooth the predicament, his voice suitably regretful.

"If that seat is not to your liking, I will do my utmost to see what can be done once we are airborne."

Taking Kara's wool coat he folded it precisely and carefully relegated it to the built-in overhead compartment.

Kara tried to hide her irritation. What a prima donna she was becoming. It was really her own fault for not checking the Boarding Pass earlier. She had assumed it was correct. It was time she returned to work, her brain was still on vacation. Rescued by her sense of humor and in a somewhat calmer frame of mind, she took a copy of Jean M. Auel's book "The Valley of Horses" from her purse in an effort to settle down until the plane took off. This was the third attempt she had made to finish the book since purchasing it at the time of publication.

The person in aisle seat 64.C. arrived.

A pleasant voice said "Hello," and Kara looked up and smiled vaguely. A short, bespectacled man divested himself of his jacket and put both it and his carryon into the overhead luggage holder. Taking off his shoes, he slipped on the socks supplied by the airline.

He turned to Kara with a smile.

"Hi, I'm Jeff Vanderhorn from Pretoria, South Africa. I'm on my way to Los Angeles to attend a computer conference."

Kara returned the smile. She nodded politely saying "Hello," without offering her own name.

Before donning the eye mask Jeff explained to Kara.

"I'm exhausted. I hope to get in forty winks before the meal is served. Would you wake me if I'm asleep? If the attendants are anything like the ones on my flight from South Africa they won't bother."

Kara again nodded. Some traveling companion he was going to be, but that was good, she needed time to herself.

Looking at her watch Kara observed how close the time was to take-off. The seat to her left was still unoccupied. She became optimistic.

The flight attendants started moving along the rows, checking that carry-on luggage and baggage were properly stored. Kara felt a surge of expectation. The pre-takeoff procedure had commenced.

A trim stewardess in the navy uniform with red and white accessories stopped at her aisle and flashed a radiant beam over her shoulder.

"Right here, sir. If there is anything I can do—"

Another effervescent smile was thrown in the direction of the first one. Noticing Kara's carry-on bag protruding by her side, she said in a slightly different tone of voice.

"Madam, you must put your luggage in the overhead compartment, since access to the emergency door must be kept clear at all times."

A figure passed in front of Kara and took possession of the window seat.

With a mutinous expression on her face and a distinctly cold edge to her voice Kara answered in her precise well-modulated diction.

"I really don't care to have it out of my sight. It contains heirlooms, which are delicate and irreplaceable. I deliberately chose to sit in this row to ensure their safety."

The attendant looked slightly ill at ease, confronted with this information.

"I will be responsible for it and there's plenty of room beneath this seat."

Gently pushing the offending bag securely under her chair, Kara raised her book to signal the conversation had ended.

She heard, rather than saw Mr. 64.A get to his feet and walk over to the aisle, opening and closing the overhead cargo door. He knocked a book off his chair in settling down again, which landed on Kara's foot.

"Terribly sorry," a vibrant voice intoned, coming from about her knee level in retrieving it. Kara ignored the apology, raising her book higher and moving her feet away. What an absolute klutz.

The "No Smoking, Fasten Seatbelts" signs flashed on. Attendants walked up and down to check that passengers had complied with these regulations and in the process waking Jeff to have him conform.

As the plane taxied along the runway, stewardesses standing in the aisles demonstrated the instructions being given on the screens for using the flotation devices, escape routes, and oxygen masks "In the remote possibility that such emergency measures need to be taken."

A man's clipped English voice came over the public address system.

"Cabin crew. Please take your seats in readiness for take-off."

The jumbo jet started gathering momentum as it sped along the runway, suddenly rising rapidly into the air, aiming toward the sky as it continued its mighty thrust upward.

Kara lay back against the headrest. What a relief. At last it was time to settle down and get her life back on its comfortable course. Jon's proposal would have to wait until it could be considered rationally.

The plane dipped its wings to the portside, circling in its flight pattern out of Heathrow International Airport and Kara looked to the window to watch the last vanishing vestiges of London. Blocking the receding panorama completely was the latest edition of "The Daily Telegraph." Kara was vexed. She hoped this was not an omen of how the trip was going to proceed.

The "No Smoking, Fasten Seatbelts" signs were turned off. People started moving, getting up and walking around, as if they had been sitting for a lengthy time.

Kara caught the attention of a passing attendant.

"Please check to see if there is either a window or aisle seat available."

"I'm sorry, miss, the flight is fully booked."

Kara's lips pursed. She heard the newspaper rustling and sensed being inspected. She deliberately ignored the scrutiny.

What a blasted nuisance. Taking three weeks away from her business had its drawbacks. Besides the pile of problems that doubtlessly would have accumulated during her absence, Kara was anxiously waiting for the verdict on whether or not the State was prepared to approve their contract with her for the model facilities they had proposed.

Kara shuffled in her seat, thinking about the importance of it. A State appointed committee would be meeting at the end of the month to make a final determination on her worthiness to receive funding, even though the State and Federal authorities had initiated the offer. True to style, they had to have outside endorsement of their own convictions.

Working uncomfortably on the wobbly tray, Kara threw an exasperated look at the head hidden behind the newspaper headlines. She attacked her workbook with a vengeance.

Immersed in her self-imposed assignment, she was startled when the voice of the flight attendant standing in the aisle asked, "Would you care to have wine or a cocktail before dinner?"

Before she could respond, the occupant in the seat to her left reacted immediately.

"Rather! I'd like a red, preferably French wine. What do you have?"

He decided a Bordeaux would be adequate. Adequate! Kara inwardly fumed. He was probably one of those pompous aficionados who would drink anything as long as it was bottled in France.

Remembering Bart and Susan's long struggle to bring "Fruitful Harvest" to the peak of its operation, was suddenly brought back to Kara. In her own small way she had trodden the hard road with them, working nights and weekends to keep the vines protected by using the antiquated "smudge pots" when sudden unexpected frosts hit the area. She also recalled the horror of battling two fires that had quickly spread out of hand a short time after she had arrived in California. The swimming pool had been used as a reservoir. Everyone who could be mustered to help passed buckets and dishes of water in "Sorcerer's Apprentice" fashion until both the Temecula and Fallbrook Fire Departments' fire equipment arrived to take over.

Certainly she was going to plug California wines.

"What do you have in California white wines?"

"There's a Chardonnay by Sterling Vineyards or a champagne Brut by Cuthbertsons."

She selected the champagne.

Packets of nuts were handed out with the wine. Kara continued writing. She was conscious of being observed. Turning she surveyed her space traveler. He was not looking at her he was eyeing the packet of nuts.

"They're yours, if you wish."

She pushed them to the edge of her tray.

"Thank you."

He accepted them readily.

"I'm ravenous. I barely made it to the airport in time to catch the plane. Not even time to pick up a candy bar."

Glancing at the long legs sprawled out beside her, Kara could hardly imagine a candy bar doing much to appease his appetite.

Kara blinked her eyes when as if reading her thoughts, he said, "Bad traffic jam in London this morning. Thought I would have had time to stop for breakfast, or at least grab lunch at the airport, but," he shook his head "there was insufficient time."

With a charming smile he shrugged apologetically.

"Please forgive my lack of good manners. I usually don't go around commandeering other people's food."

He had nice teeth, white and even. His lips were well defined and sensuous. Kara nodded, smiled coolly, and returned to her notebook.

She furtively noticed that the 'man next door' continued reading his paper, consuming the peanuts and Bordeaux with apparent enjoyment as he did so.

The meal was ready to be served and Kara had not opened her wine. The smell of food had roused Jeff and he was rubbing his neck and pulling over his tray in readiness for the meal. Jeff chose the beef tenderloin entrée and Kara, when approached, favored the salmon. So did "daddy longlegs."

With their meal before them, he leaned toward Kara.

"Why is it that your portion looks larger than mine? What did you do to deserve it?"

That did it!

"Compensation," she snapped.

With raised eyebrows he asked for an explanation. "Why is that?"

"You are sitting in my seat," Kara replied curtly.

He attempted to disguise a smile.

"That is a highly inflammatory remark. Quite unsubstantiated since the object under discussion is very obviously occupied—and not by you."

Kara's brilliant green eyes flashed darts. In a deliberately restrained voice she informed her traveling companion of the airline confirmation of 64.A. It was her favorite seat. She was annoyed to find that it had already been seized by someone else. In fact she was still a bit miffed that he was sitting there.

A roar of laughter ensued and against her will Kara found herself smiling.

"My secretary has a standing order to book this seat as soon in advance as possible, since I travel this route every six weeks or so. Therefore, I would say that I have first claim, not to mention receipt of the Boarding Pass."

His eyes challenged hers.

She really was being bitchy about this whole issue and, conceding that she was being irrational, Kara flashed an apologetic smile.

"I'm sorry. I shouldn't take my problems out on you."

This disclosure took her companion by surprise. He looked at Kara intently.

In a very reasonable, though slightly astonished tone he suggested, "Let's call a truce. For whatever legitimate purpose, you may use my "our" seat whenever required. I most certainly would not wish to antagonize you further."

A brief smile escaped Kara's lips. She really had been acting out of character. This man was not responsible for her misery.

Having committed himself he added.

"This of course has a condition attached."

Kara looked at him suspiciously through veiled lashes.

"In exchange for your salmon."

Shaking her head in disbelief, Kara handed over her food tray.

"I wish all my problems had such an easy solution."

Tucking enthusiastically into the salmon, Kara's neighbor turned his head.

"By the way my name is Nicholas Prendergast—what's yours?"

Without a moment's hesitation she answered, "Kara Stephenssohn."

They exchanged polite smiles.

Pushing a trolley, the wine steward came along again.

"A French Chardonnay, please, "Nicholas said.

"The Sterling Chardonnay," Kara immediately responded. Was she carrying this wine promotion a little past the bounds of propriety?

"Do you really prefer California wines?" Nicholas asked curiously, pouring half of the wine into his glass. "The industry is still in its infancy."

Kara reacted instantly.

"Yes, I really do. Part of this is due to a certain involvement I have had with an award winning Californian vineyard for several years. In the process I have become somewhat knowledgeable on most aspects of the industry. Although I am not a connoisseur, I do appreciate good wines, particularly white, since reds tend to give me a headache."

Impetuously she challenged.

"Would you care to swap half of your Chardonnay for mine?"

Nick agreed to this with a smile, passing over his half-empty bottle.

"Great. Let's have our own wine tasting."

They sipped their wine, glancing at each other from time to time.

Kara, listening to Nicholas, tried to determine which part of the United States he was from. He pronounced certain words with a British inflection. The more he spoke, the less sure she became of his accent. He told her he did a great deal of traveling around the world and it grew quite wearying. He considered himself an internationalist. His voice was mellifluous and polished, indicating to Kara that he was accustomed to addressing people and keeping their attention. He was probably from the east coast, Boston, perhaps.

Having had the chance to appraise his features as they talked, Kara was quite intrigued with Nick's eyes. They were of such a dark shade of brown, they looked almost black and together with the wide black brows that framed them and the enviable thick eyelashes, his face commanded attention. They certainly were his best facial distinction Kara decided. His skin was lightly tanned and Kara surmised he did not spend a great deal of time outdoors.

To some segments of the female population, Kara decided, he might be considered handsome.

Nick picked up the empty Sterling Chardonnay bottle and looked at the label.

"Not bad. In fact it is quite palatable."

Observing Kara's reaction, the look of a lioness protecting her young, Nick coughed and added.

"On a scale of 1-10, this probably would rate a 6."

The green eyes had narrowed.

"Or, come to think about it, most likely an 8. It really has a surprisingly mature bouquet."

Obliquely he looked at Kara with a jesting look on his face.

"Yes—I just may buy a case of it."

Kara started laughing and Nick joined in.

Apologizing Kara said, "I'm sorry. I'm not a very good traveling companion to have around right now and I certainly had no right to be so uppity."

She looked sideways at Nick and a roguish gleam appeared in her eyes. She added quickly, "Not on such short acquaintance, anyway. I reserve that right for my nearest and dearest friends."

Nick winked.

That was the kind of thing Jon did.

Kara looked away. She really had been quite open and friendly with this man. It came as a surprise that she had lowered her defenses so easily. How had that happened?

She turned her head to look at him again, as if to find the answer.

He was looking at her.

Nick cleared his throat and held up his glass toward Kara before taking a sip and turning away.

A wary look flitted across Kara's face.

At the end of the meal the trays were cleared away,

Kara slipped the small bottle of champagne into her purse. This could be the antidote to a sleepless flight. It was a problem that always presented itself.

Nicholas pulled out a book and Kara returned to organizing her paperwork. Jeff, in the next seat, slipped on the sleep-mask again and fell asleep almost immediately. When the movie started, Kara put on the earphones issued earlier and tuned into the proper channel to bring in the sound. It was a British comedy and Kara found it quite amusing, laughing spontaneously throughout.

At its conclusion, the main cabin lights were turned on. Passengers started moving around, eager to stretch after their confined inactivity.

Nicholas stood up, flexing his shoulders as he looked around the section. From Kara's vantage point he looked very tall and extremely masculine. He looked down at Kara.

"Since you mentioned returning from vacation, I assume you live in California. Have you lived there long?"

Kara nodded her head affirmatively. "Eight years."

"Well," he added, "you obviously have retained your English sense of humor."

Nick, looking over Kara's head, nodded to someone and moved over to the aisle before walking away.

To arrive at that conclusion, Kara mused, *he must have been observing me.*

She found that a little disconcerting.

Kara took her toilet bag out of her carry-on and carefully placed the two bags in bubble-wrap into the window storage area. It contained four of the Meissen and Delft figurines that had belonged to Nona Stephenssohn. She could not look at them without seeing her. They had been appraised and meticulously wrapped by Sotheby's and she carried their certification in her purse. They were part of the collection that she had inherited. Her great-grandmother had loved them and so did she. They brought back affectionate memories of the times Kara had visited Nona, listening with interest as the objets d'art were explained to her. Then there was the excitement of looking them up in the huge musty manuals that authenticated them.

Kara sighed. Traveling was not at all what it was cracked up to be. Fervently she hoped to sleep for the remainder of the flight. The visit to England had placed a burden on her heart. She was riddled with doubts about Jon. When she was with him she was vulnerable, captivated that he could be the love of her life. When apart, as now, she could clinically analyze him with detachment, aware of his flaws and seeing him in a different, less attractive light.

Getting to her feet Kara ran her hands through her hair and stretched her arms above her head. Gosh, she was tired. She had not slept well for the past week. It would be so good to get back into her own bed in her own townhouse. Kara was unaware of the sensuous tableaux she made. With long blonde hair and svelte tanned body, head thrown back and eyes closed, she made a strikingly alluring and graceful figure.

Talking with one of the stewards, Nick was acutely aware of the eroticism. He caught his breath. He had not thought about his traveling companion upon early inspection as being a beauty, but looking at her he could imagine a sculptor wanting to capture the essence of her. There was something about her that intrigued him.

He rubbed his eyes. He really would have to cut back on the rigorous routine he had established. He was cracking up.

Kara went along to the lavatory, feeling better after brushing her hair and teeth, washing her face and hands and applying a touch of perfume. Making her way down the aisle back to her seat a tall blond haired man about her own age barred her progress.

"Liza? Liza Benson?"

Kara stopped and looked at him puzzled.

"No. You are mistaken."

She attempted to pass. He placed a hand on her shoulder.

"Don't you live in Pasadena?"

Kara shook her head. He started asking questions and Kara looked at him with frosty eyes. He was not disguising his efforts to engage her in conversation and she was unmoved by this type of flirtation.

Kara was on the point of retracing her steps and returning to her seat via the opposite aisle, when an arm was placed around her waist and a deep voice murmured.

"Honey, I wondered what was keeping you—I've set up the chessboard so we can have that game you promised."

Turning, Kara looked up into Nick's amused black orbs, as he firmly steered her past the slightly flustered Lochinvar.

With flushed cheeks, Kara informed Nick when they reached their seats.

"I suppose I should thank you for being helpful, but I really am quite capable of handling this type of situation by myself. Believe it or not, these incidences have occurred before."

In a submissive gesture Nick held his hands up in the air.

"Guilty, M'Lady—it was no business of mine, but I thought I detected a look of consternation that a Knight of the First Order couldn't ignore."

Kara decided to slough off the incident, if he wanted to intervene on her behalf, so be it. It was a gallant gesture.

"Sir Galahad, I hereby dub you Knight of the Airways and Champion of all creatures great and small."

So saying she impetuously touched him on both shoulders to confer the honor and smiled at the absurd situation.

"Sorry, I'm being silly. In space and spaced out."

Nick smiled and took hold of her hand, gently kissing it as would a nobleman being honored with a knighthood by his Queen. There was an amused expression on his face.

"I like this game. What do we do next?"

His lips felt soft and warm on her hand and Kara felt a shock travel through her body. It made her feel quite weak, so great was the physical affect upon her.

She quickly removed her hand from his.

A steward came to the edge of the aisle and beckoned Nick to follow him.

Inwardly shaking, Kara switched her seat to the reclining position, lying back and closing her eyes. She lay there attempting to recover from this unexpected sensation, panicking at the perfidiousness of her emotions.

Two days ago she was being torn apart, unable to decide whether or not she wanted to marry Jon and here she was trembling at the touch of an absolute stranger. They were ships that pass in the night. She had not realized how messed up she was.

Unaware of the time lapse, Kara awoke with a cramped neck. Slowly turning her head she saw Nick engrossed over a magnetic chessboard. Watching his moves for some time she mentally played the game along with him.

In a low voice Kara murmured. "In that last move might it have been better to move Queen to Rook 5?"

An interested look came over Nick's face.

"Well, well, you really do play chess. You're not just another pretty face after all."

Kara brought her chair back to the sitting position.

"Using such provocative statements can get you into trouble. Are you always so opinionated?"

Nick pushed his chair back, rubbing his eyes and yawning.

"Sorry. I wasn't prepared. You are basically on masculine territory and you took me by surprise. Where did you learn to play?"

They looked steadily at each other for a few moments.

"I'd really like to know."

Seeing Kara hesitate, he pressed, "Please."

She shrugged her shoulders.

"My father taught me and he still plays quite often with friends and, actually, anyone who will humor him. His standing is that of an Expert in the Chess Federation and has been for years. He has little ambition to improve his rating. I played a couple of games with him while I was home, but I was so rusty, he defeated me easily."

With his eyes closed Nick asked quietly.

"What do you do to keep busy, Kara?"

She paused for an instance before sketching the type of work she did, without getting into specific details. He lay so motionless she thought he must have gone to sleep.

He opened his eyes.

"Very interesting."

Kara could not hide her smile.

"My work is not very glamorous, but I love it and in today's world it is very necessary. Somehow I thought you were the first man I'd bored to sleep."

Nick shook his head and sat up.

"I'm almost dead on my feet, yet I have the worst time sleeping on planes."

"So do I." Kara said sounding like an echo. "I kept the champagne, hoping it will knock me out for a few hours, but in difficult cases such as yours, perhaps it can be arranged for the little man with the rubber mallet to come along and perform his magic."

Nick smiled tiredly acknowledging Kara's offbeat sense of humor.

"I suppose you know him personally."

Stifling the reminder of the frequent sleepless nights encountered lately, Kara's face took on a vulnerability that struck Nick's heartstrings.

"It would have helped," she said quietly turning away from him.

Nick closed his eyes. Those green eyes, suddenly mistily soft had affected and disturbed him unbelievably. He wanted to reach out and console her. This woman, this stranger. He wanted to know her better.

He said looking at Kara through half-closed lids.

"I'm a good judge of character. It's part of my work. You are obviously a very attractive woman. That is quite apparent. I like your sense of humor and quick mind, but I think there is much more to Kara Stephenssohn than this. I find the discovery fascinating."

The seldom use of her disguised travel name and the unexpected compliment caused Kara to flush. The personal statements made candidly were without intimidation or innuendo. Neither his voice nor his glance insinuated a flirtatious attitude. He was quite an unusual man and they were having a very odd conversation.

An announcement was made over the public address system that the next movie would be commencing in ten minutes and passengers sitting beside a window were asked to pull down the shade. The plane was following the sun around the earth in its journey back to California and daylight flooded the cabin constantly. That, and lack of sleep, were hard on the eyes, not to mention the rest of one's body.

The same attractive stewardess who had led Nick to his seat came around and leaning toward him whispered in a breathy voice, "Nick, I'm free now, ready and willing if you are?"

Nick shot a quick look at Kara.

He stood up and followed the stewardess.

Well! It may not be her job to judge character, but she certainly could judge the lack of it. She had heard of hanky-panky in the skies and this appeared to be a noticeable illustration of it. Suddenly feeling cold Kara took the sterile gray blanket out of its plastic bag. The cabin lights were dimmed and the movie started. Jeff was snoring slightly with his head lolling onto his shoulder and his mouth open loosely. Completely relaxed. Kara felt envious that he could pass the time so beneficially and painlessly.

The movie was one Kara had already watched. She moved the small pillow around trying to find a comfortable spot, in the hope that sleep would overtake her. Sighing, she elevated her seat to the upright position. Perhaps she should turn on the overhead seat light and get back to the novel.

A figure stood in front of her. It was Nick. He crouched down, a drink in each hand.

"Here's a Tequila Sunrise. Funny name for the nightcap we are having at high noon, isn't it?"

He offered a plastic tumbler.

Kara seemed a little reluctant to take it and Nick looked at her closely.

"Did I disturb you?"

"No."

Her voice was subdued.

He settled into his seat, turned to Kara and raised his drink. "Cheers."

She nodded, holding the plastic glass in both hands.

Murmuring softly Nick leaned over.

"Sorry I had to dash off, just as we were getting into an interesting conversation, but I had placed a trans-Atlantic call and Gail came to tell me it could be processed. Bad timing, what!"

Again an English idiom.

Kara quickly looked at him as he said this. His face was clear of intrigue. Kara took a sip of the cocktail and said impetuously.

"Since you travel extensively, you must get some interesting propositions. I should imagine though that it would take ingenuity to find the right ambiance at 35,000 feet, in a crowded plane, to follow through."

Realizing how forward she had been Kara was quick to add.

"Please forgive my rudeness. I usually get myself into trouble for saying what I think, particularly when it's not my concern. Please accept my apology."

Nick looked at Kara in surprise.

"Do I understand you were questioning my motives?"

Kara looked uncomfortable.

"As I said, I spoke without thinking and as a perfect stranger I apologize for my lack of good manners. Will you please accept my apology?"

"I don't think so." Nick interjected, eyeing Kara speculatively.

"I feel quite devastated having my reputation impugned—by no less than someone who views herself as perfect. A stranger at that."

Kara looked indignant.

"I didn't say I was perfect, you are distorting the issue."

Nick looked serious.

"Did you, or did you not, say you were a perfect stranger?"

A peal of laughter escaped from Kara.

"I did say that, didn't I, but you took it out of context."

Naughty green eyes twinkled at him and Nick's heart skipped a beat.

He took a deep breath.

"I felt our previous conversation had potential, but this has even more—and it would be interesting to continue."

He was looking at Kara contemplatively.

"You could make a fascinating study, Kara. Beneath that veneer of civility and composure, I see indications that there actually is a core of molten lava, waiting to erupt—I'd like to be around when that happens. But, as you so aptly remarked, we are getting into each other's business. I like your frankness and if sleep evades us, I think we could have much to talk about. There is still a long journey ahead of us and "Miles to go before we sleep.""

He had just paraphrased from her favorite short poem by Robert Frost. A tingle went through Kara. She was having the kind of conversation she would never have dreamed possible with someone she had just met.

They talked for some time, ignoring the movie, keeping their heads close together to hear each other speak.

Kara was unaware of the point in time when she fell asleep. When she awoke, she found her head on Nick's shoulder. Blankets had been draped around her and pillows were used as padding, stuffed around Nick's shoulder so that Kara could rest more comfortably.

She was embarrassed.

Kara struggled to disengage herself, but found Nick's arm firmly across her shoulders. How could she have felt so relaxed with someone she had just met?

"Take your time waking up."

His voice was so close to her ear that she could feel his warm breath on her cheek.

The closeness of his presence and the expression of solicitude projected on his attractive face, forced Kara to close her eyes to gain control of her escalating heartbeats.

Nick removed his arm to massage his cramped shoulder.

Disembarkation forms were being passed around, and by way of conversation in allowing Kara to regain alertness, Nick remarked.

"Immediately after we land, I have to rush off. Stupidly I set up a dinner appointment in Los Angeles for this, my first evening. Something I don't normally do. A car will be waiting. Unfortunately I'll have to dash to get through the airport in time to make the appointment, so I am taking the opportunity to ask if I may contact you. I would very much like to see you again."

Kara declined and Nick looked at her solemnly, with a slightly baffled expression on his face.

"I've been away from the office for three weeks and the next few weeks will be terribly busy and crucial. I anticipate a back-log of work."

She smiled wearily before adding, "Besides, you obviously weren't listening when I told you I was over-my-head in a personal dilemma, which I have yet to work out."

Even though we've hit it off, we are just casual travelers, pushed together only because of the seating arrangements on a plane. It could get too complicated to take things further and I already have too many other concerns, Kara thinks ruefully.

No, it definitely would not work out.

Nick scrutinized Kara's face carefully before turning away.

Over the P.A. system, the pilot announced that the plane would be locking into its landing pattern very soon, with arrival at Los Angeles International Airport on time at 5:30 p.m.

In filling out a Customs Declaration form Kara needed clarification on one of the questions. She turned the form over and leaving it on her seat, walked back to the galley area where the crew had congregated.

It seemed there should be no problem getting the family possessions she was bringing back through Customs. Quickly she completed the form and put it with her passport.

The "Fasten Seat Belts, No Smoking" signs blinked on.

Kara glanced at Nick, who closed the book he was reading. He gave her a veiled look and a half-smile, which did not quite reach his eyes. Looking out of the window he surveyed the scenery below as the plane began its final descent.

Apart from muffled coughs and babies crying as their ears were affected by the drop in altitude, the landing itself was executed smoothly. Audible sighs of relief could be heard as the soft thud of the wheels met the landing strip.

"That bag looks heavy, allow me to carry it for you." Nick offered.

"I can handle it, thanks."

Walking quickly side by side they headed for the luggage carousels in the baggage area.

Without warning, reaching over, Nick took the carry-on bag.

"You look a little lop-sided and I need the exercise."

He really is rather sweet, Kara conceded, but determinedly refused his second attempt to get in touch with her.

Nick assisted Kara in getting her luggage loaded from the carousel onto a buggy and they separated to pass through Customs.

Observing Nick standing in line, with a hand casually resting in his jacket pocket and his valise snug between his feet, Kara thought what a remarkable presence he had. He looked sophisticated, slightly bored, and totally at ease. Unflappable! He would stand out anywhere. Why had she not noticed what a terribly attractive man he was?

As if sensing her gaze, Nick turned around smiling quizzically. For a moment Kara hesitated, there was still time to slip him her business card. Reaching into her purse and wildly fumbling around for her wallet and dropping items on the floor in the process, she brought out her passport instead. The opportunity had passed. She was next in line.

She did not see him again.

CHAPTER SEVENTEEN

During the next week Kara thought about her traveling companion several times, regretting to some extent that she had not taken him up on his invitation. She could at least have met him one more time, if only to determine whether he measured up to the image she has created in her mind. He had been considerate and intriguing and eradicating his face from her memory was challenging. Strange how she can bring his face to mind so much more quickly than that of Jon. Perhaps this is some psychological thing she is going through. A trick to gauge the affect Jon's unexpected proposal has had on her—or maybe to prove how fickle she is.

Toward the end of the week Kara took a phone call from "Mr. Seymour." Nick identified himself as soon as he heard Kara's voice. She was shocked to hear his. Her hand trembled as she held the receiver.

"Are you playing games?" A hint of annoyance was in her voice.

"But I am Nicholas Seymour Prendergast, if you want my complete moniker. They are at least my own names."

Reprovingly he asked, "Is Stephenssohn part of yours?"

Kara was taken aback. There was a short silence.

"I'm sorry, that was very cowardly of me. I don't usually take the path of least resistance, but in answer to your question, yes, that is part of my family's name. How did you locate me?"

"It's a long story," Nick volunteered, "But if you will have dinner with me Friday evening I'll be happy to tell you all about it. I'm traveling to the Palm Springs area for the weekend—almost on your doorstep."

Kara hesitated. She should not see this man again. A flashing neon sign jogged her memory: "If it looks too good to be true, it probably is."

It applied to him. She made up her mind.

"Mr. Prendergast, I really do not have the time or the inclination to become involved with anyone right now and I'm truly sorry that a cultured, attractive man like you would perceive me as a prospective notch on your gun."

Nick thought that was an interesting interpretation.

Kara continued.

"Actually, looking at my calendar," as she was frantically pushing papers out of the way on her desk, "I'll be busy that evening and in fact for the entire weekend."

Nick puckered his mouth. She made it sound like the rest of her life.

Nick's soft, entreating voice sent goose bumps along Kara's spine.

"Please don't turn me down, Kara. I really must see you again. I'd hoped you would see me because you wanted to, but now I'm afraid I'll have to resort to blackmail."

Kara drew an uneasy breath, waiting for Nick to continue.

"You dropped something on the floor as you pulled out your passport in the Customs lineup and I have it in my possession. It is a Florentine gold Waterman fountain pen with the initials KMS engraved on the shaft."

He waited for Kara's reaction. He heard her quick gasp.

"Just a minute."

Her voice was quite subdued when she came back on the line.

"You could 'Express' it to me, if you would."

She had discovered its absence.

"Certainly if that is your preference. What is your address?"

That would not do. Next she would find him outside her door—he seemed to be the persistent type.

A satisfied smile spread over Nick's face when Kara asked.

"Are you familiar with the restaurants on Hospitality Lane in San Bernardino?"

When Friday arrived Kara became a little nervous. She had no intention of getting involved with Nicholas Seymour Prendergast and it was up to her to discourage any inclination he may have to the contrary. With this nagging thought in the back of her mind, she determined that this dinner obligation would not be allowed to become more than that. She dressed in a jade green linen suit with a gold chain around her neck and small gold earrings. She would have dressed this way for any business meeting. She had conditioned herself to regard this rendezvous as such.

Hospitality Lane was usually called "Restaurant Row" by the area's diners. There was an abundance of fine eating establishments dotted along its one mile length. It was also conveniently situated immediately off the arterial #10 Freeway.

Kara was a few minutes late getting to The Lotus Garden Restaurant. Nick was in the cocktail lounge, nursing a drink, waiting for her.

He watched her enter the room looking chic and professional, and sexy. She exuded a vibrancy and vitality. It was one of the few times when words failed him.

She took his breath away. Again!

Kara smiled, acknowledging Nick sitting at the bar. He immediately walked over to her, taking her hand. He had almost forgotten what a dynamic smile she had.

"Would you care for a cocktail before dinner?"

Kara declined. "I really can't stay long. I have an early morning appointment."

Nick looked disappointed.

"But it's Saturday tomorrow. Surely you know 'All work and no play makes Jill a dull girl'."

"Unfortunately, yes—here's Ms. Jill Dull standing before you."

Nick was wearing a beige lightweight woolen suit, with a stark white shirt and modestly patterned tie. The outfit was the perfect foil for his immaculately groomed dark hair and refined features. He wore a suit extremely well Kara decided. She was pleased she had worn a suit also. Two could play the power game.

They were led to a booth and instead of Nick sitting across the table from her, he sat beside her. He was very near. His shoulder touched hers a couple of times when discussing the menu. He looked very handsome and Kara's throat tightened nervously. She would have to be careful.

With merriment in his eyes Nick looked up from the wine list.

"I'll order sake, it should be safer."

Kara smiled remembering their wine controversy on the plane.

"I'd like to stick with green tea, if that is all right with you."

"Fine with me, I drink almost as much of it as coffee," Nick confessed.

A large oriental teapot was placed on their table and Nick poured a measure into two small china cups.

Nick raised his hot drink toward Kara.

"The last wish I made came true, so here's hoping this one does."

They clinked china against china.

Kara pondered this remark, not sure she wanted to know what his wishes were. On the other hand she could better prepare herself if she removed the speculation.

"And what are they?" she asked, deciding to throw caution to the wind.

"The first was in seeing you again and I'll tell you the second by the time we leave."

There was a whimsical expression on his face.

Kara was betwixt a threat and a promise.

Maybe it was the ambiance or perhaps because Nick was so easy to be with that Kara found herself responding to his effortless conversation. Upon realizing how comfortable she was becoming with him, she mentally shook herself, blaming the exhausting fourteen-hour workdays for the lowering of her defenses. How was it he seemed to have this effect on her?

During a break in the dialogue Kara remembered her astonishment at Nick tracking her down.

"How on earth did you manage to locate me? I didn't think any clues were left."

The look she gave him was teasing rather than reprimanding.

He looked into her expectant face.

"If I didn't have a super sleuth secretary, I'm sure it couldn't have been done. I gave her the details—you worked with people with disabilities, probably funded by the State or Federal Government and that you worked and/or lived in either Riverside County or San Bernardino County. Oh, and that your name actually is Kara—Olavssen."

Kara took her eyes away from his face.

"It was due to her persistence and tenacity that I was able to contact you."

It had upset Nick, on the plane, when Kara point-blank refused to see him again. In fact it had aggravated him more than he had realized. Not because she did not want to see him, which was her prerogative, but because for once he had become the pursuer. He wanted desperately to see her again and he had no control over the situation.

He recalled how his heart felt as if it had plummeted when he discovered the name Kara had given him on the plane was not the one written on her Customs Declaration form. He had broken out in a sweat realizing how close he had come to having her vanish from his life.

". . . . and I thought you were sleeping when I blathered on about all that stuff. But how did you discover my last name taking into account my travel nom de plume? Did you get if from my Customs form?"

Nick smiled briefly.

"Yes, I was very sneaky—and desperate."

He looked at Kara reprovingly.

"Discovering that threw me somewhat and it also filled me with dismay, since there wasn't much else to work with, and made my secretary's work much more difficult. I hope she will forgive me—I made it a priority project for her and she went through telephone books covering a large section of southern California, placing dozens of phone calls before locating you."

He squeezed Kara's hand.

"Now I can inform her that her efforts were well worth it. She has earned her salary."

Nick reached into the inside pocket of his jacket and pulled out a slim cream velvet box and handed it to Kara.

"My first reaction is to hold on to this and use it as a bargaining tool again, but my conscience won't allow that."

Kara opened the lid and saw her grandmother's pen resting on the silk padding. She bit her lip and turned her shimmering jade eyes to Nick, saying softly.

"Thank you. This belonged to my great-grandmother Katella Margarethe Stephenssohn. Despite my apparent carelessness, this pen is irreplaceable to me. I just may leave it in the case you have provided, as a reminder."

She closed the lid and carefully slipped the box into her purse.

In a baiting tone Nick said, "A reminder of me?"

She smiled. "I'll take the 5th on that one. By the way how did you get the pen—we were in separate lines at the Customs check point when it obviously dropped to the floor?"

Nick smiled conspiratorially. "Sometimes I can be inventive. The young woman standing behind you in the queue picked up the pen and I walked over and told her that you were my girlfriend and offered to introduce her to you once we passed through Customs. She said she remembered seeing you sleeping on my shoulder in the plane and handed the pen over without further questions."

He waited for a response from Kara.

She barely smiled, saying dryly, "Very inventive."

Nick poured the last of the tea into their cups.

"Are you annoyed with me for being obstinate and disregarding your wishes not to see me again? You stipulated those terms. I had no intention of agreeing to them."

His candor brought a smile to Kara's face. He moved closer, staring. Her eyes widened, as she pressed her back against the wall—surely he was not going to try any funny business here.

Drawing back when he noticed Kara's retreat Nick said with amazement in his voice.

"I've been comparing how perfectly your clothing matches your eyes. You really have beautiful eyes, the prettiest I have ever seen. I could willingly lose myself in them."

Kara looked downwards to escape the appreciation shown on Nick's face.

"Not to mention the longest lashes, also. Kara you're too much!"

Kara blushed, feeling like a schoolgirl. His closeness was giving her a heat treatment. He really was overpoweringly charming. Whatever his work was, he must be good at it.

Kara looked at her watch. It was after ten o' clock and they were sitting with their second pot of green tea. With an effort Kara remembered her early morning appointment.

"I must go. I have some work to do before my meeting tomorrow."

Nick's face registered regret.

"Sure you wouldn't like to go dancing or to a nightclub, a coffee house, anything?"

Firmly Kara declined.

"I really do have a busy morning scheduled."

Having already taken care of the bill as they were finishing their meal, Nick moved out of the booth, offering his hand to assist Kara as she slid over. They walked outside and stopped at Kara's Lexus. Taking her keys, he opened the door, replacing them in her hand after swinging the door open for her.

"Where did the evening go?"

Leaning against the car, Nick looked pensively at Kara.

"You know I will be calling you, don't you?"

Kara delved into her purse and produced a small wallet. She handed Nick a business card.

"Now that you have found me, this is where I spend a great deal of my working hours. I wouldn't want to tie up more of your secretary's time."

A smile creased his face as he slipped the card into the top pocket of his jacket.

"Merci beaucoup. Claudia, my secretary, will be grateful for your thoughtfulness."

Placing his hand on Kara's elbow he helped her into the driver's seat and leaning down kissed her warmly on the lips. Standing back he closed the door and waited until Kara started the engine and adjusted her seatbelt. She rolled down the window.

There was a twinkle in her eyes.

"I had a very pleasant evening, contrary to my expectations."

Impetuously she put her hand over Nick's, which was resting on the open window frame.

"Thank you again for retrieving and returning my pen. I really am most appreciative and grateful to have it back."

Suddenly remembering she asked.

"You were going to tell me your second wish."

He bent down again, thrusting his head through the window and once more kissing her lips, this time lingering longer.

"You just made it come true. Ask me again."

Shaking her head as she raised the window, Kara backed out of the parking place. She waved briefly as she drove away and in the rear view mirror could see Nick still standing watching her leave.

An aura of anticipation and excitement envelopes Kara during the thirty minutes' drive back to her townhouse and the sensation stays with her that whatever happens from this point on is out of her control.

Chiding herself for dramatizing the situation, she thinks, *How ridiculous—I'm acting like a schoolgirl with a man I know very little about. He did not volunteer a business card, a telephone number, or even provide concrete information about himself or his background.*

What a twit she is becoming. Kara shook her head in disbelief.

She did not care for the disorienting affect Nick had on her.

Kara popped into the office early Saturday morning to pick up a client file that she needed for the meeting. The light on the answering machine indicated a message was waiting.

She switched the machine to the "play" mode.

"This is a missing person report. I am missing the most incredible woman in the world terribly and will do whatever is necessary to have her returned to me." Kara smiled, recognizing Nick's voice.

Reversing the tape and obliterating the message, Kara noticed that it had been recorded the previous night close to midnight— probably a short time after he reached Palm Springs, or wherever he was going. Nick certainly did not waste any time, but he probably had much practice. Kara sighed. Why did her natural level-headedness fly out of the window when her emotions became involved? She should be getting the hang of this "love me, love my ego" syndrome. Kara resolved that the next time she saw Nick would be the last. She would explain to him that she was in the process of deciding if she wanted to marry someone else. That should dampen any ardor he might have for her. It would also remove her from the emotional topsy-turvy ride she was on, because of their meeting by a fluke chance of fate.

Kara glanced at her watch. She would have to rush to make her appointment on time.

CHAPTER EIGHTEEN

After leaving Kara, Nick drove to Rancho Mirage where he was spending the weekend with his cousin Wendy and nephew Gerald. Several years earlier Gerald had been diagnosed as being severely autistic and Nick was following the steps used in the boy's treatment and in the process had become interested in pursuing alternative procedures.

He had brought work with him from the Beverly Hills office, which accumulated at an alarming rate during his absences. Claudia, his senior executive secretary, had set up three large pocket files for his attention: "Now," "Soon" and "Sometime." The casualness of her labeling belied her efficiency. She kept him precisely on track.

All weekend he was in a restless mood. Kara's intriguing green eyes and sensuous mouth disturbed his thoughts. He smiled recalling her off-beat sense of humor and infectious laugh. He also remembered her indifference to him, the man, and that bothered him more than he was willing to admit. She had been reluctant to discuss her personal life, but he had skirted that area also.

Sighing, Nick picked up his briefcase. He had procrastinated addressing the contents of the bulky files since his arrival. Now, a day later, he had no choice. Wendy and he passed in a hallway.

"Back to the grind for a few hours and then before I leave I'd like to talk to you about Gerald."

Wendy nodded in agreement, her expression serious.

Ensconced in the study, Nick started working his way through the "Now" file, making notations in his monthly and yearly calendars of appointments and writing reminders and notes on the yellow post-it notes. He recorded messages and letters on the handheld Dictaphone machine. He would be handing the completed audio cassettes to Claudia and her staff for transcription.

Nick yawned and stretched his tall frame, leaning back in the chair. Coffee time.

He went in to the kitchen and helped himself from the "Interminable Pot" as Wendy called the coffee machine. Looking out of the long wall-to-wall windows at the inviting patio and pool area Nick considered taking a break and swimming a few laps before returning to the endless paperwork. Tempting as the thought was, Nick resolutely returned to the study with the mug of coffee.

He methodically continued working through the correspondence and reports.

His eyes flickered over the words and he went back to reread them. He shook his head. He knew he was tired but not hallucinatory. He turned back several sheets.

"Let's try it again." he said aloud and went back to the beginning of the letter.

Dear Dr. Prendergast:

This letter will outline the confirmed meeting of the ad hoc committee, established to review the relevance and effectiveness of the seven model establishments currently under consideration by the State of California, under the Department of Rehabilitation umbrella.

In order to properly assess the performance and appropriateness in contracting "WORKING IT OUT' as the model agency, the following documents are enclosed for your perusal:

1. Background information: agency inception to present time.
2. Fiscal solvency.
3. Qualifications of principal/owner.
4. Contract coverage.
5. References.

Please become sufficiently familiar with the above information to make a decision on this at the scheduled meeting.

Thank you for your participation and the valuable time so generously donated in considering this important new venture.

Sincerely,

etc., etc.

Okay, Nick decides, *that's fine—nothing unusual there.* He turned to the second page and quickly skimmed through it. That was in order. Reference was made only to the unnamed past and present owners. Fiscal solvency was impeccable, it was owned outright by the present owner. Nick turned to the next page and drew a quick breath. It was the Resume of Kara Margarethe Olavssen, President and Chief Executive Officer of "Working it Out," Riverside, California. She had an MBA, MSW and LCSW—smart girl! He finished looking through the two remaining documents. It was a very generous contract. She must be good, the State did not overcompensate. The last page gave excellent references.

Nick went back to his bedroom and took the business card from his jacket pocket comparing it to the resume. Yes, there could be no doubt, it was his Kara. Nick closed his eyes and rested his head against the door frame. He smiled. She was intelligent, beautiful, resourceful, sexy, and amusing. No wonder he had been attracted to her immediately. They were made for each other. Convincing Kara of this would be a priority—right at the top of his "Now" list.

In the meantime thinking about Kara and her charms and other tangible wonders had quickened Nick's pulse and raised the pressure in other areas of his anatomy.

Getting rid of superfluous energy drew him to the pool.

On Monday, as usual, Kara was at the office early before the general staff arrived, getting a head start on the day. After attending a monthly meeting at the San Bernardino office of the Department of Rehabilitation, she arrived back at the office mid-morning to find an elegant bouquet of pink rosebuds, mauve orchids and white Baby's Breath displayed on her desk. A sealed envelope with a card inside stated: "Only you can make my third wish come true. Nick."

Kara caught her breath. He worked fast. He had very quickly made use of the business card she handed him Friday, she observed.

It was almost two weeks later when Kara received a phone call from Nick.

"I'll be passing the end of your street next Friday. May I take you out for dinner?"

Before giving her time to respond he pleaded.

"Please, Kara. I'll be devastated if you refuse. I have to leave Sunday for Europe."

Kara could hear the urgency in his voice.

She did not need to consult her daily planner. She wanted to see him again.

"Would you like to pick me up at the office around six?"

Her quick submission surprised him.

"That's terrific. Yes, that's great—the address on your business card?"

Kara smiled as she replaced the receiver. He had a very seductive voice. She closed her eyes and leaned against the back of the chair. The rest of him wasn't bad, either. Startled, Kara sat up. Where were these thoughts coming from?

With such sabotaging thoughts invading her protective armor, Kara was pleased to have agreed with Nick to be picked up at the office rather than her townhouse.

Considering the possible ramifications if Nick had collected her at her home, she would have been obliged to invite him in for a drink upon their return. Thinking this made her feel uncomfortable, as if the stage were being set for whatever might take place next. She would have to get rid of such thoughts. Nick had behaved very courteously on their last outing, the brief kisses indicating only that he had enjoyed spending the evening with her.

There had been others who expected more, for less.

Friday arrived with Kara feverishly working her way through the day, having little time to dwell on or anticipate the evening.

Apart from a couple of job coaches finishing off their weekly reports, everyone else had left on time. She was usually alone Friday evenings. It was the one night she could count on the office being deserted. Kara collected her toilet and garment bags from the back seat of her car passing Jennie and Tanya upon her return as they walked through the hallway getting ready to leave.

Jennie eyed Kara's containers.

"Looks as if there's something special coming up tonight. Have fun."

Tanya giggled. She had recently started working for Kara and was a little in awe of her.

Kara smiled.

"Thanks. Have a good weekend both of you. I'll get the door."

With this she followed them, locking the door after they were outside. She saw them with their heads together—she could imagine their speculations. Other than Marcie, who was tight-lipped when it came to Kara's private life, her staff usually did not get a glimpse of her personal lifestyle.

Kara had allowed plenty of time to freshen up and change in the bathroom. Her toilet was almost complete when she heard loud thumping on the glass front door. It was fifteen minutes before six. Surely Nick couldn't be here yet? Peering out of the bathroom door across the corridor from the office, she could see him waiting.

He could wait a few more minutes.

Kara had decided to wear a Couturier designed slim black linen sleeveless sheath from Frazier's, with deceptively expensive Italian black suede pumps and an opera length rope of pearls with matching earrings. The pearls had belonged to her great-great-grandmother and were especially treasured by her family. Upon her 21st birthday her mother had passed them on to her as she was dressing for her official birthday party. Slipping her fingers over the smooth surface of the beautifully preserved necklace, memories of her home flooded back. She would phone her parents at the weekend, her vacation was already receding and she missed hearing their voices. Guiltily she added Jon's name to the list.

Contemplating her full-length reflection, Kara decided she had made the right wardrobe choice; it was the perfect foil for her tanned skin and simply styled blonde hair. Très chic!

She sparingly sprayed the latest Elizabeth Taylor perfume around her neck and over her wrists. She was ready to greet him. Kara picked up her belongings in readiness to return to her office. Nick had his back to the front door and so did not observe her crossing the corridor.

Dumping her gear in the bottom drawer of her desk, Kara walked over to the front door, just as Nick turned around.

She smiled a welcome as she unlocked the door to admit him.

"You look very nice," he commented quietly as his eyes softly caressed her.

Kara felt her heart flutter. He had spoken very correctly, but the evident admiration in his eyes left her flustered. He stood gazing at Kara with an absorbed look on his face. Almost as if he was pressing her image indelibly into his memory. For a moment Kara felt as if a spell had been woven around them. His eyes so dark and persuasive seemed to be looking into the nucleus of her being.

She swallowed and turned away.

"I'd be interested in a tour, if you wouldn't mind showing me around. Someone I know needs treatment and rehabilitation and I'm anxious to secure the right services. It's something I'd like to discuss with you—at another time."

Kara conducted him on a brief tour of the office. He appeared to be genuinely interested in what he saw, asking questions and making intelligent comments that surprised Kara. It was not a superficial conversation.

A grin came over Nick's face when he spotted the fully blooming, but drooping, bouquet displayed in a prominent position on her desk.

With heightened color and as cool a tone as she could muster she responded.

"Thank you for the flowers. It was very kind of you, but totally unnecessary."

Another grin accepted her backhanded thanks.

Picking up a James Galanos black silk jacket and black linen clutch purse from a chair Kara proceeded to the door, unlocking it. Nick opened the door, taking the keys from her fingers as they stepped outside. He locked and tried the door, immediately handing the key chain back to Kara, who smiled her thanks and slipped it into her purse.

He did these things so well.

Nick took Kara's elbow and led her past her own car, across the parking lot to a black, with gold trim, Jaguar convertible.

Kara looked at Nick with a puzzled expression on her face as he opened the door and handed her into the front seat.

"It's a friend's."

Kara raised her eyebrows.

Wealthy friends he must have to borrow such an expensive vehicle, Kara surmised. When she recently purchased her Lexus SC400 coupe, she had idly looked at Jaguars. None she had seen were under $100,000.

After Nick slid into the driver's seat he buckled up his seat belt, as Kara had automatically done. When a law was put into effect, it paid to comply. Looking more closely at Nick, Kara thought he was dressed perhaps a little casually; but even in an open necked white silk shirt, with a heavy gold chain showing and black gabardine slacks, he was picture perfect. She could not fault him, but dressed like this where were they going? Was she overdressed?

Nick started the engine, which hummed effortlessly. After pulling on the emergency brake and pushing a button, the convertible roof began emerging like a butterfly from a chrysalis, coming down to envelop the two of them in a cozy mantle. Excusing himself, Nick leaned in front of Kara and pulled a lever on the enclosed roof, which clicked as the heavy canvas joined itself firmly to the rest of the sleek vehicle. The closeness involved in performing this rudimentary task left Kara unexplainably disturbed. The tantalizing aroma from Nick's hair was very provocative. When he brushed against her bare arm to lock the roof, she had an overwhelming urge to touch the wisp of hair that had fallen over his forehead.

Kara joined her hands together on her lap, as if to restrain them. This would never do, she hadn't counted on these strange reactions.

It was only after several minutes had passed that Kara became aware of the direction in which they were traveling. She had surmised Nick would frequent the Los Angeles area restaurants, which proliferated there, but saw they were on Highway #60 going east, rather than west, heading toward Palm Springs and Indio.

Looking over at Nick she asked, "Where are we going—Palm Springs?"

"Right! I apologize before the evening starts, because this is not the way I had planned things. I only learned today that it is necessary to go over some documents that need to be signed so that they can be taken to Paris by a colleague, who will be returning tomorrow."

Nick paused for breath and looked at Kara a little anxiously before continuing.

"François is staying with mutual friends in Rancho Mirage and will be attending a party that my cousin, Wendy, is giving. So it makes sense to meet him there. If you are interested we have been invited to stay for cocktails and dinner, but I defer to your decision."

They drove for half-an-hour, passing the Morongo Indian Reservation Casino, which already had a backup of cars waiting to be admitted into the parking lots; past the turbine generating system, with the look-alike propellers rotating in the warm evening breeze that roamed over the undulating hills. Kara had driven this way many times before, but for some reason she had not been fully cognizant of the surroundings. Tonight everything was etched clearly into her memory. A short time later they passed the outskirts of Cathedral City and finally reached the Rancho Mirage community.

They had not talked a great deal during the drive, content to relax and enjoy the scenery. Nick had mentioned that Wendy had been divorced for some time and had a son called Gerald, who was currently visiting friends. With a lopsided look at Kara, Nick told Kara that Wendy received a comfortable alimony settlement to keep her in the style to which she had become accustomed.

Reaching a spectacular waterfall entry they were admitted into the private walled community through a motorized security gate by an attendant who recognized Nick.

Traveling past an elaborate Club House and wending their way around a road with acres of green velvet turf embedded on both sides, Kara noticed a glow in the sky ahead of them.

Following her gaze, Nick commented wryly, "We are almost there," nodding his head in the direction of the bright light.

Shortly afterwards they drew up outside a palatial Mediterranean-style villa, a terra cotta roof and ornate wrought iron balconies running along its length.

The entire building and surrounding area was alight with every kind of equipment capable of producing a brilliant glow. Colored lanterns were slung from trees, hertz floodlights picked out beautifully landscaped areas. The scene rivaled the stage of a movie set, as showy as only Californians know how.

There were few automobiles parked in front of the house.

"Where is everyone? Are we early?" Bemused Kara looked at Nick.

"No. Most people leave their cars at the back of the Club House. Wendy has a shuttle limousine service running back and forth all night."

Kara looked at Nick with a gleam in her eyes.

"I love these exclusive little get-togethers."

Nick winked.

"Just say the word and once I've attended to this business, we can be out of here just as quickly as you wish. This is not my idea of a good time. That's why the car is here for a quick getaway."

Nick reached for a briefcase from behind the driver's seat and Kara, upon reflection, tossed her jacket and purse back into the car before it was locked. Nick had indicated this would be a short visit.

They walked toward a solid high gate, set in an equally tall patterned adobe wall, which looked as if it surrounded the entire estate. The heavy door swung open at their approach and a man walked toward them smiling broadly at Nick.

"Bon soir, mon ami—you made the good hour. Not long I wait."

He had a distinct French accent; Parisian, if her assessment was correct, Kara decided. Reaching Nick he embraced him enthusiastically. Nick turned to Kara.

"This is my good friend and business partner François de Veaux." They were formally introduced.

So this is the person they have traveled here so specifically to see. François eyed Kara appreciatively and kissed the back of her hand upon introduction. *Aha, is this where Nick acquired this custom, without being embarrassed in doing so,* Kara wondered.

François complimented Nick on having such a charming companion and Kara had the distinct impression that he had gone through this ritual with Nick before. Many times.

The two men walked ahead of Kara, speaking to each other in French. It was business talk and Kara smiled to herself listening to them, wishing it was more interesting. Serves them right for assuming she would not understand their conversation.

Nick fell back a pace and took hold of Kara's hand.

"Sorry, my French is not the best, but Franc's English is deplorable. We usually try to compromise. I do most of the talking."

They laughed.

They reached the covered patio, which was decorated with colored lanterns. People swarmed around the area and Nick, walking slightly ahead of Kara, still held her hand.

"With luck, we will be out of this madhouse inside of an hour—is that too long to wait?"

Kara shook her head. Nick was looking around for someone. Several people, who looked familiar, patted Nick on the back as they passed.

"Wendy." Nick called.

A short, slightly plump matron in a flowing tropically designed chiffon caftan turned around.

"Darling, how lovely to see you again."

She ran her eyes over Kara as she bussed Nick's cheek.

"This must be Kara, so nice of you to come."

She reached out a hand to squeeze the one that Kara extended.

"Franc and I have some business to attend to. I'd like to leave Kara in your capable hands until we are through."

Nick pronounced his friend's abbreviated name in the French patois. Kara had heard a couple of people address François as Frank. How quickly the translation disintegrated.

Wendy took Kara under her wing, introducing her to friends and neighbors. Among those she met were Gerry and Betty Ford, Sonny Bono, the recent Mayor and past entertainment star, and his wife, Mary.

As if inspirationally struck, Wendy declared.

"Oh, I know someone who will be very interested in meeting you. George and I are good friends."

They wove their way in and out of the crowd, stopping for a few words here and there until Wendy stood in front of a man, sitting alone in a chaise longue by the edge of the swimming pool.

Kara wondered if Wendy was matching up the "loners."

He sat up straighter, but did not attempt to move from his chair until Wendy gave Kara's name. Smiling, he swung his legs off the chaise and stood up to shake hands.

"What a pleasure. Miss Olavssen. You are making quite a name for yourself in the Inland Empire. I've learned much about your operation and I was planning on coming over to see it for myself. Any objection?"

Kara shook her head. "Not at all, I'd be delighted."

George Parkinson was a State Rehabilitation Director, with jurisdiction over San Bernardino, San Diego, and Riverside Counties. He had an office in the State of California's executive offices situated on Lime Street in Riverside. His remarks to Kara had been genuine. He had been one of the five members of the ad hoc committee who recently had reviewed the case for the State and its Proposal to one Kara Olavssen of "Working it Out."

Kara's face brightened. She had heard of him. He was the department chief responsible for many of the major decisions of critical importance in Southern California that affected her organization. He was a bigwig.

Wendy smiled at both of them, shaking a finger at George and admonishing him to take care of Kara, as she would hear about it if he did not.

"I'm about to get another drink, would you like something?"

"A glass of Chardonnay or Zinfandel would be nice, thanks."

She sat down to await his return.

The large pool had a fountain in the center, with cascading colored sprays issuing from it. There was a waterfall running into the pool at one end and Kara could see it overflowing at the other end, but could not distinguish where it was emptying itself. She giggled at the absurd thought that it was running down the hill, flooding the arroya below. George returned with two glasses of champagne.

"Hope this is okay."

He handed over a flute.

Kara spoke as she removed the glass from George's hand.

"Thank you. For an alarming moment I thought the pool was overflowing and no one was paying attention."

George laughed.

"I thought the same thing the first time I saw it. I guess it is a shock to the senses, though it no longer perturbs me."

He took a few sips of the wine.

"Would you like to clear up the mystery of the disappearing water?"

"Yes, please. Otherwise I may not sleep well tonight."

They smiled easily at each other.

Carrying their glasses of champagne, they walked across a cement bridge under which the flow from the waterfall swirled into the pool. Crossing over to a parapet that provided a 360 degree view of the mountains and the twinkling lights of Rancho Mirage and Palm Springs in the distance, Kara gasped.

"Oh, it's breathtaking—like fairyland."

Kara's eyes grew wide with delight.

George nodded in agreement.

"Let's get on with the tour. We have to walk down a couple of flights of stairs, so I hope you can manage in those high heels."

A wrought iron handrail, set on ornate railings, served as support in negotiating the stairs that curved downwards showing off the garden with each curve. A platform with a seat divided a set of stairs and at this point Kara could watch the overflow from the swimming pool cascade down into a pond, with colored underwater lights. Twisting and turning in the motion of the water were translucent mermaids. Kara stared in fascination.

"Those figures look so realistic, don't they?"

George grinned.

"Come and touch one, if we can catch it." They walked down the last set of stairs.

He took off his jacket to display brown arms under a short-sleeved shirt. Lying beside the pond, he trailed his arm in the water.

Kara crouched down beside him.

With a massive circular sweep he brought a strangely shaped object out of the water. Trickles of water ran down his arm.

"Quick, feel it."

Apprehensively Kara reached out a hand and touched a peculiarly glutinous substance.

"Why, it's shapeless and colorless."

George laughed and threw the jelly-like object back into the swirling water, where they observed it taking shape again.

"Quite a transformation wouldn't you say?"

He wiped his arm on the small handkerchief taken from the top pocket of his jacket.

Intrigued Kara stood up, watching the eddying forms writhing and whirling as they circled continuously in their endless marathon.

"How can they look so realistic and colorful in the water and so yukky out of it?"

George slung his jacket over his shoulder.

"The force of the water molds the elongated shape and the iridescent colors reflected on the bottom of the pond pass through the viscosity of the material. That is what we see."

Kara was impressed.

"I've never seen anything like this before."

"Nor will you for a while. This is a brainchild of Nick's and it's still in the experimental stage. I understand he has a patent on it and like most of the things he tackles, it doubtlessly will take off—big."

Kara looked thoughtful. So Nick was an entrepreneur?

George took Kara's elbow, guiding her past life-sized marble statues and a grotto set into the hillside.

It was truly overwhelming.

They walked to the edge of the terrace and looking back at the house could see only the top story, but the hum of voices from the patio level filtered down to them. Kara had spilled most of her champagne walking down the steps and George went over to a nearby bar for refills.

A group of large rocks were placed strategically and Kara sat down on one of them to take in the glorious view. She slipped off her shoes so they did not rub against the rock surface and tucked her legs underneath her skirt. George returned with the drinks.

"Have you ever been to the "Pageant of the Masters" held by Festival of the Arts every summer in Laguna Beach?"

He passed over a glass of champagne. Kara shook her head as she accepted it.

"Well, last year one of the many pictures they portrayed was the 'Mermaid on the rock in Copenhagen.' Seeing you sitting outlined against the night sky, compared very favorably with their interpretation."

Kara looked puzzled and George explained.

"It really is a remarkable duplicity. A huge stage forms the picture frame, in which people actually model motionless on the background of a famous painting. I've tried to catch the actors moving, but even with binoculars trained on them I've never seen even an eyelid flicker. It's an extraordinary production."

His enthusiasm captured Kara's interest.

This conversation had broken the ice and once they started discussing their work and how it interfaced, the time flew past. They discovered they knew several of the same people quite well and had a couple of mutual acquaintances. In addition, George had a subscription to the Riverside Philharmonic concert series, of which Kara was a committee member.

Kara and George, sitting on the rocks, with their backs to the house were unaware of Nick standing on the pathway behind them. He had heard them talking and laughing before he reached them. Kara turned her head to look at the cascading water and saw Nick.

"Oh, Nick. Good, you're through?"

"I have been for quite a while. I've been looking for you."

There was stiffness in his tone.

Kara slid off the rock, picking up her shoes and walking over to the path to put them on.

"Do you know George? George Parkinson."

"Yes, we know each other."

Nick nodded his head as George walked over to them with his hand outstretched.

"Long time, no see."

It was said in a light conversational tone, but Nick frowned slightly, as if he did not care for the choice of words.

Nick took Kara's elbow.

"A buffet supper is in the process of being served. The restaurant reservation I made was for eight-thirty. It is now after nine. Do you wish to stay or should we try to get in somewhere else?"

He looked slightly annoyed and Kara could not decide whether it was because the dinner reservation had fallen through or that he had found her with George.

He had put her on the spot.

"I suppose it will be more practical to stay here."

"Very well. Let's join the others, shall we?"

George trooped back after them. A damper had been put on the conversation. They walked back in silence. Reaching the top of the stairs, Kara looked back and smiled at George.

"It was nice talking to you—even if it was mainly shop talk."

George took hold of Kara's hand, holding it longer than was necessary, Nick thought. His jaw tightening at the familiarity.

Reaching into an inside pocket, George withdrew a wallet and handed Kara a business card.

"I'll look forward to seeing you next week."

So saying, he nodded and walked away. He was deep in thought.

It was not his place to inform Kara that the State contract for her services had been approved and endorsed by the ad hoc committee on which he had recently served. The voting was almost unanimous. What had surprised him was that Nick Prendergast, considering his interest in the project, had voted against it. It was particularly unconventional to find that he had brought Kara, who would be in charge of the project, to this party.

What was his game? He reflected on that.

Then it hit him. Of course. Nick had waited until he was sure a quorum would approve the contract and once that had been established he had gone on record as making the only dissenting vote, thereby removing himself from being in the 'conflict of interest' position."

Riveting!

Kara had mentioned that she and Nick had met only recently. Therefore, George deduced, she most likely would not have any idea of Nick's involvement in being an essential part of the decision-making team. In any case, if they had just met, the planning and outcome for this project were in the final stages and out of the hands of Kara.

Still pondering the situation, George found it interesting that Nick would distance himself from showing partiality, yet at the same time protect Kara so that the contract could not be challenged. Considering the brief timeframe of their acquaintance, it was not possible for them to have been in collusion on this deal.

George shook his head in disbelief. They must have met purely by a twist of fate.

Nick must have plans for the little lady. George had been surprised at Nick's reaction upon finding Kara and himself in seclusion. It was the first time he had seen Nick lose his cool. How about that.

George chuckled to himself, it could be fun watching Nick this evening.

"Just what did he mean by that?"

There was resentment in Nick's voice as he watched George walk away.

Kara looked up at Nick's face. He seemed upset, but who was he to question her?

"When George and I were talking, it seems that two new clients, recently enrolled at "Working it Out," are from George's district. They live in San Bernardino County and still come under the jurisdiction of George's Department, so we will be working together closely in this regard. George expressed interest in coming to the office to look over the program."

Nick's face was devoid of expression.

"So I suppose Good Old George will be acting as liaison?"

Kara had to block a smile.

"No. George is the department head. Apart from giving him a tour of the operation, I don't expect to be dealing with him directly, rather his subordinates. I'm just a little fish in a big pond."

This did not seem to appease Nick.

"Right, and he's a shark."

Kara laughed outright.

"Do I detect 'sour grapes' there, Nicholas Prendergast?"

She squeezed his hand.

"I'm sorry that our dinner plans didn't work out, but let's enjoy the rest of the evening."

It probably will be our last together Kara suspected, surprisingly somber at the idea.

A little of the tenseness seemed to leave Nick's frame as he smiled a little sheepishly and loosely put his arm around her shoulders.

Most of the guests were sitting down at tables or on benches that rimmed the patio, already eating. Kara felt a little contrite. She and George must have been talking for quite a long time. No wonder Nick was upset. They joined a short line of people waiting to reach the buffet tables and Kara's heart flip-flopped. Standing behind the tables were attendants in wine and lemon colored uniforms, so closely reminiscent to those worn by the staff at The Black Bull Inn. A lump came into Kara's throat. What would Jon think of her now, so quickly involved with someone else?

Nick, studying Kara's face, presumed the contrition so clearly expressed there was due to his behavior. He slipped an arm around her waist.

"Please forgive me for being so abrupt. I searched for you for at least fifteen minutes and by the time I found you, I was almost beside myself with worry, in case anything had happened to you. I don't know a fraction of the people here, some of whom are gate crashers and my concern was increasing the longer I explored the house and grounds."

He really did look upset, but it seemed a trivial reason to be so worked up, Kara reasoned.

"Thank you for being concerned, but I can look after myself. Nick. What do you think I did before you came into my life?"

Kara squeezed his arm.

"I'm sorry you were inconvenienced and that the restaurant reservation didn't work out, but I was just biding time, waiting for you to finish your business, which I was told was the reason for coming here in the first place. I did not feel my behavior was inappropriate, especially as your cousin Wendy made a point of introducing me to George."

Nick raised his eyebrows in surprise.

They had reached the buffet tables where hot and cold entrees were invitingly displayed, but suddenly Kara did not feel hungry. Nick looked at Kara's plate as they walked over to a table.

"Are you all right? You don't seem to have much to eat there. I really am sorry if I upset you."

Kara looked at Nick but did not respond.

They sat down at a table already occupied by four people. Casual introductions were made. Waiters came around filling champagne glasses and Kara accepted more.

Hearing her English accent, the man to her left turned.

"Belinda and I have just returned from a three weeks' European tour. It was great. We spent a week in London. Fabulous city. Do you get back often?"

"I was there last month."

Nick listened quietly until the conversation petered out.

Music commenced in the distance and Kara looked at Nick questioningly.

"Around the other side of the house is another patio, about the same size as this, but with a gazebo at the end. Wendy, in true modus operandi will have a band playing there for the remainder of the evening."

People had started strolling in the direction of the music and Nick turned to Kara.

"Would you care to dance? We can return for dessert afterwards, if you wish."

Kara agreed a little reluctantly. The thought of this man holding her in his arms brought mixed feelings. He evoked a response in her that was almost frightening after such a short acquaintance.

The patio to which they walked was enclosed, with four Casablanca fans moving the air around. An inlaid section of the floor was made from parquet blocks and a few tables and chairs were arranged around it. Certainly not enough to accommodate the eager crowd gathered in this section. The musicians were enthusiastically playing a popular fast number and the dancers were gyrating according to their ability.

Kara smiled. The universal method of communication was in progress.

Kara slipped easily into the rhythm and she was surprised seeing that Nick did too. They improvised together with Nick admiring Kara's style and groaning inwardly at the sensuality she projected.

A slow dance started and Nick immediately took Kara into his arms. He had waited all evening for this opportunity and it was his to claim legitimately. There was no objection from Kara as he pulled her closer and when she looked up into his face she saw a sensitivity and tenderness, which was unexpected.

Franc interrupted them, tapping Nick on the shoulder. Nick looked at his friend in astonishment. Surely he could not be cutting in to dance with Kara, when it must be apparent to any observer that he was spellbound by this beautiful woman in his arms.

Franc spoke rapidly in French saying, "The telephone call you were waiting for has come through. I put them on hold."

He smiled apologetically at Kara and walked away.

Nick sighed and shrugging his shoulders escorted Kara to the edge of the dance floor.

"I don't think this telephone call will take very long—please try to stay out of mischief."

Kara looked to see if she was being reprimanded, but Nick's glance was teasing.

Kara exchanged her empty flute for a bottle of chilled Lake Arrowhead water. Belinda and Barry joined her as she sat at a table drinking it. They sat chatting until Nick returned. He apologized for taking longer than expected.

Wendy, with her caftan billowing around her ample frame, floated over to their table with a few people in tow. She put her arms around Nick's neck.

"Are you familiar with the "Cat and Mouse" line dance?"

He nodded affirmatively and Wendy clapped her hands.

"Oh, super, I thought you would know, having just come back from Europe."

Pulling him to his feet she eagerly pushed him in the direction of the band.

Turning around Nick retorted.

"Just a minute, what is this all about?"

"Please demonstrate it, darling. The musicians are ready to play whenever you are and we are all dying to learn."

A look of horror came over Nick's face.

"Even if I could do it well enough, you know there's no way I would volunteer to demonstrate it."

Howls of disappointment met this statement.

"That's too bad," said Barry.

"Belinda and I tried to learn it one night in a Soho nightclub, but we didn't quite get the hang of it. It is a fun dance though."

In a quiet voice, as if being dragged out of her, Kara muttered.

"I'm familiar with the routine. If you are desperate I can try to show you."

"Brilliant." Wendy gave Kara a big hug and promptly ushered her over to the dance area.

"Silence everyone. We are in for a real treat. Kara is just back from Europe and has volunteered to coach us through the "Cat and Mouse" line dance.

Wendy patted Kara's arm encouragingly.

Kara had a sinking feeling—impetuously she has done it again.

She stood beside Wendy transfixed.

Looking nervously over the heads of the group in front of her she could see Nick, alone, lounging against the wall scrutinizing her.

A round of applause indicated that the announcement was met with approval. It was time to perform and walking down the gazebo steps, Kara made her way to the dance floor and waited for the introductory bars of music.

In perfect synchronization she moved to the music, her body effortlessly responding. Beckoning to those nearest to her to join in, she soon had willing participants around her. When she looked over at Nick, he shook his head.

The music ended with much laughter and applause. Chortling at the gaffs they made, the crowd insisted on practicing the dance a few more times, until they breathlessly agreed they had had enough.

Kara looked for Nick, but the wall space he had occupied was deserted.

George intercepted her passage. The sensuous strains of a tango had started.

"It would give me the greatest pleasure to dance this number with you."

She was tempted to refuse, to go and look for Nick, but as he had been the one to leave the area, she smiled her acceptance and she and George retraced their steps to the swarming dance floor.

George, a little on the portly side, was surprisingly light on his feet. He was an excellent dancer. They matched their steps precisely, dramatically twisting and turning in the exaggerated postures of the provocative Latin style.

This was one of Kara's favorite dances, but the form fitting dress did not lend itself well to the seductive movements. Once she became aware that she and George held the floor, she also became acutely aware of this. Thankfully the dance ended and applause greeted the finale.

George put his arms around Kara's waist and swung her around, planting a kiss on her cheek saying.

"Isn't she wonderful—I could dance the night away with her."

He bowed to Kara and more applause and laughter followed.

George claimed Wendy for a dance as the music started up again and ready for a break Kara walked out of the patio and back to the pool site.

She waved away the waiter offering more champagne and again walked over the little bridge to the promontory overlooking the twinkling city lights. From this vantage point she could see a figure silhouetted against the starry backdrop down by the large rocks. Carefully treading down the flights of steps, Kara found the path and headed in that direction. She stopped abruptly. There was no one there.

Where had Nick disappeared? She was sure it was he she had seen.

Suddenly she was swung off her feet and caught in a bear hug.
Startled jade eyes looked into stormy black ones.

"That was quite an exhibition I just observed."

He was breathing heavily and anger lurked.

Kara suppressed a scream.

Trembling, she found herself being released very slowly, sliding down the length of this paradoxical man.

How unfair he was being. A shiver shook Kara's body.

Immediately he hugged her contritely,

His face was on her cheek. She could feel his body, pressed against hers, shaking.

"Please forgive me, Kara. I can't believe how much has gone wrong with this evening. I desperately wanted it to be perfect. I have looked forward to it so much and then, wham, Murphy's Law suddenly came into effect. Every damned thing that could have gone wrong has."

Tenderly he took Kara's face between his hands and kissed the mouth that had tantalized him almost from the moment they had met.

Groaning, Nick pulled Kara closer, savoring the softness of her lips.

Kara pushed herself away from Nick, placing the palms of her hands on his chest.

"This is not going to work out. I'm confused and upset. I seem to have gone through quite an upheaval this evening and I barely know you. It is late and I would appreciate leaving here as soon as possible."

Ignoring the hurt expression on Nick's face, they walked back to the upper level patio in silence.

Wendy caught sight of them, and waved them over.

"Are you planning on staying overnight?"

"Definitely not."

Kara responded with such alacrity that Wendy looked at her in surprise. She shifted her gaze to Nick, who was wearing an unhappy expression on his face.

"Sorry for getting in on a lover's quarrel. Am I in the way?"

"Yes" said Nick. "No" said Kara. Simultaneously.

Holding Kara's elbow Nick looked at Wendy with an imploring expression on his face.

"Please excuse us for a few minutes, Wen."

He started leading Kara toward a darkened area, with some kind of a building in the background.

Kara stuck her heels into the springy turf and resisted. Having already gone through a couple of unnerving ordeals this evening, she was unable to cope with another.

Hesitantly, Nick gently took Kara's other hand, pulling her around so that they were facing each other in the semi-darkness.

Peering into Kara's troubled eyes Nick's face reflected an anxiety that was apparent in his words.

"Kara, I sincerely apologize for my behavior this evening. Please believe that I don't normally behave this way, but you have affected me like no other woman has."

He looked down at the ground, miserably caught off-guard by these new disturbing reactions.

"I totally accept the blame for the way things have turned out. When I went back I saw you and George dancing together and getting along so well I was overwhelmed by feelings which took me off-guard."

The look of unhappiness reflected on Nick's face caught Kara by surprise.

"For the first time in my life I was engulfed with jealousy."

His voice dropped to a whisper.

"I'm sorry. I didn't handle it well. I felt very threatened and vulnerable. I don't want to lose you, Kara."

Kara stood silent, a skeptical look on her face.

Nick sighed and turned away.

Bringing his gaze back to Kara he said.

"I could have told you on the plane that I was falling in love with you. I knew it almost right away." Nick watched Kara's face looking for her response, a sign of forgiveness.

"Please give me another chance, Kara."

Nick's voice trailed off and his pent-up misery was apparent both in his voice and in the dejection mirrored on his face.

Kara's eyes filled with tears.

"Nick, forgive me. Do you remember on the plane when you asked to see me again? I told you I had enough problems without adding to them. I really meant that. Tonight it was my intention to tell you that I couldn't see you again."

Nick gasped, looking at Kara in disbelief.

"Why would you say that? Granted my behavior tonight has been less than admirable and I sincerely regret the whole incidence, but I can't be mistaken in believing our paths crossed for a reason. Finding you has found me astonishingly unprepared and totally unnerved. I was beginning to believe you did not exist. Now, I can't let you go."

Tears coursed down Kara's cheeks.

"Last month, on vacation in England, someone I have known and loved all my life proposed to me. It was so unexpected and sudden—I can't go into the details, but I felt that the brief time we spent together was not long enough to make such an important decision. I was given three months to make up my mind."

Nick looked shocked.

"I don't understand. If you have known and loved this person all your life, how come it was suddenly sprung on you?"

Kara wiped away her tears with the back of her hand.

"Jon and I grew up together. We were kindred spirits. During my last vacation he expressed his love for me and I told him he was on the rebound from a recently broken engagement. He denied this, setting out to prove that he had always loved me."

Sniffing, as the tears continued to flow, Kara added

"And he did a pretty good job, I was almost convinced. But not quite. Not well enough to agree to give up everything I had established in California and return to England to become his wife."

Hope stirred in Nick's eyes.

"There is a chance for me?"

Impulsively Kara took Nick's hand.

"No. In all fairness I promised Jon an answer and I made the decision, to myself, that for three months there would be no encumbrances to interfere with that. Jon didn't place any restrictions or conditions. I must be free to keep that promise."

"I would be willing to accept your decision in three months if at that time you decide to marry . . . . Jon"

Nick spoke the name with some reluctance.

"I can't bear the thought of not seeing you again. Whatever your terms are, I will abide by them just as long as we can still see each other."

"You know it wouldn't work out, Nick. I would feel guilty, being with you, when in essence I have given Jon prior claim. How can I possibly be rational with you around, dominating my thoughts?"

Nick's eyes brightened.

"So I dominate your thoughts. That is the first crumb you have thrown me."

Hastily Kara retracted that statement.

"I didn't mean that. I scarcely know you. Jon has been in my life all my life."

Nick sighed and looked at his watch.

"We are getting nowhere and it's late. Since you are adamant about leaving, we should go. We can talk in the car."

Taking a handkerchief out of his trouser pocket, Nick held Kara's chin as he wiped her face, gently.

Kara's lips trembled at the unguarded display of ardor on Nick's face.

Moaning softly, Nick took Kara into his arms.

"You look so young and defenseless; I can't let you go. I adore you, need you, want you and I think, regardless of the words you are saying, that you feel the same way about me."

He had been kissing her eyes, her throat, and claimed her mouth, urging her to respond to him. Kara shuddered and with a soft murmur surrendered to his demanding mouth.

"Oh, my love, you must feel more for me than you are willing to admit."

His voice was rough with emotion and his eyes glittered, as if tears lay there.

They heard footsteps walking in their direction on the paved pathway and Kara attempted to move away from Nick, but he held on to her firmly, reluctant to let go.

"Please Nick, we must leave—I couldn't face anyone right now."

Slackening his grip he nodded mutely, taking her hand and tucking it through the crook of his elbow. A couple walked past them, immersed in conversation, not even looking in their direction.

"Did you bring anything from the car?" Nick asked.

Kara shook her head.

"No. I left my purse and jacket there. I didn't think we were going to be long."

Nick glanced at Kara sideways; he was not about to get into a discourse on this statement.

Producing a set of keys he removed one that had a small "panic button" accessory for his car alarm attached to it. He handed it to Kara.

"I'm going to need a couple of these for my briefcase so, if you wait for me in the car, I'll go and get it, say the necessary adieus and join you very soon."

A brief smile fled across Kara's face.

Nick walked to the large gate with Kara. A security guard was on duty. He opened the door for them.

"I can walk to the car myself, Nick, I can see it from here. Hurry and say your goodbyes."

With a roguish grin on his face he grabbed Kara and kissed her.

"Thanks for the invitation. We may never get back to Riverside, if I play this right."

Leaning against his shoulder Kara laughed weakly at Nick's absurd conduct. What a sweet, moody, multi-faceted individual he was. Patting her derriere as he gently shoved her in the direction of the car, Kara added to herself "and chauvinistic."

Looking back she saw the door close behind her.

Kara pressed the battery operated opener as she neared the car and heard the doorknobs unlatch.

The hairs on the back of her neck stiffened; she suspected danger.

She lifted her hand to her throat.

She was passing the trunk of the Jaguar when a hand clamped itself over her mouth and a sharp object was stuck in her side.

A hoarse voice whispered in her ear.

"Make a noise and you're gonna get it."

Another voice came from behind her.

"Did ya get the keys ya idyat." Struggling Kara attempted to twist and get away.

"You get 'em I have plenty to do keeping this broad under control."

Kara's pearls glinted softly in the moonlight.

A dame coming out of a fancy place like this did not wear cheap stuff. Kara could feel a hand exploring her body.

"Take them off, honey, in fact take everything off."

Kara resisted, feeling the pearls pulled over her head.

"For craps sake, where are the keys, she must have had 'em in her hand? Stop messing with the babe, ya idyat, find the keys and she's yours."

Kara's slim skirt was yanked up and pulled over her head and clamped shut, obliterating her view.

She started to scream and the next thing she felt was a severe pain in her temple.

The fireworks display began.

Kara falling against the trunk caused it to open—it was not locked.

"Hurry up, shove her inside, the car's open."

They picked Kara up, roughly throwing her inside, slamming the top of the trunk shut. They rushed around to the doors just in time to hear the doorknobs click shut. In astonishment they looked at each other. The doors had been open all the time. Furious at being outwitted, they banged and kicked the doors and the shrill wail of the alarm started, increasing in volume and tone.

The gate was thrown open and suspecting that they had been observed the two thieves split the scene, using the rope that got them over the high wall into this private compound to get them out again fast.

The only compensation for their evening's labor was a lousy string of pearls.

CHAPTER NINETEEN

Nick had just said goodnight to the guard when he recognized the rising protest of his car alarm. His immediate thought was of Kara and summoning the guard to follow him, he vigorously thrust open the gate and they both raced toward the Jaguar.

There was no one inside the car and it was locked.

"Kara," Nick shouted, panic rising in his voice.

What had happened? Where was she? His immediate thought was abduction. If that was the case why was the vehicle not taken? Kara had the key and the car itself was a valuable commodity. What had set off the alarm?

He searched the immediate area, and deduced that the key and the panic button must have been taken with Kara. None of his reasoning made sense. The guard, using a flashlight, was moving farther away looking for evidence.

Okay! Get your thoughts in order, Nick commanded himself. He was panicking and floundering. Snapping his thoughts together, he took a set of keys from his slack's pocket and he opened the briefcase. A duplicate set of car keys was inside. It was a precaution that had almost slipped his mind, in his first panic-ridden reaction.

Thankfully he retrieved the keys to the car.

He pressed the button and the alarm ceased and the doors clicked open. Intuitively he walked to the trunk and opened it. A half-naked figure confronted him.

Oh, dear Lord, what had happened?

Bending down he pulled the fabric of the garment down to expose Kara's face. He was alarmed. There was a large gash on her forehead with blood seeping from it. Her face looked waxen, as if dead. Easing the skirt down over the diminutive waist and curving hips, a lump rose in his throat. He saw something roll in the process of doing this and picked up what looked like a button and absently slipped it into his pocket. If anything happened to Kara, he would hold himself totally responsible. Methodically he felt for her pulse. Thankfully it was fairly strong. Kara started moaning as he quickly and professionally ran his hands from her head to her feet observing and assessing her condition.

The guard returned to the car.

Nick said in a tight voice, "You may be needed as a witness. Please note the gash on her head. I'm sure there are other injuries and so I am taking her to the Delano V. Roosevelt Hospital in Palm Springs for medical attention. Do you know Mrs. Wendy Rutherford?"

"Yes."

He handed over a business card.

"Inform her that there has been an accident and I will phone her from the hospital to explain. Write your name, telephone and company name on the back of this other card. Until you are questioned by the police this must go no further, you understand?"

"Yes." He scribbled his name and telephone number.

Together they observantly lifted Kara on to the passenger seat of the car to the accompaniment of her moans and whimpering. Fastening the seat belt carefully Nick gently laid Kara's left arm outside the restraints of the belt to avoid further pain.

In record time he reached the hospital.

Nick parked in front of the door to the emergency section. Kara lay with her eyes closed and labored gasps shook her shoulders.

"Hang in there, Kara. I'll be right back."

He dashed into the corridor, reaching for the wallet in his back pocket as he did so. Impatiently he showed his credentials at the check-in counter and in a tone that spoke of authority summoned assistance, saying he would be waiting outside by his car.

It was after 1:00 a.m. and apart from a man, who was sitting on a chair in the corridor reading, there was little activity that he could see.

Dr. Don Carmichael, Chief of Staff, who happened to stop off at the hospital after an evening out with friends, hurried toward Nick, eagerly shaking hands and introducing himself. He was followed by an aide with a wheelchair, who assisted Nick in getting Kara into it.

Nick walked at the side of the wheelchair, observing Kara as they moved along the corridor.

With Nick in attendance, Dr. Carmichael quickly examined Kara, who was moaning piteously. They talked after Kara was taken to the Radiation Department for x-rays, with Nick giving details of the manner in which he had discovered her and his own preliminary conclusions.

The surgeon asked if there were signs of rape.

Nick felt a shock go through his body. Where had all his training gone? He had been so relieved to find Kara alive that he had not thought of that aspect.

"Her undergarments were in place and I did not investigate further, nor could I do so ethically, as you know. I was primarily concerned about the physical trauma visible."

Without Kara's consent such an examination would not normally take place. A wave of nausea swept over Nick. The thought of Kara's possible violation filled him with remorse.

When Kara and the x-rays were brought into the examining room, Dr. Carmichael took the x-rays from the technician and both doctors looked them over, as they were clipped to the inspection panel.

There was a crack in the left Ulna, Nick was already aware of this, the slight swelling and Kara's pain upon touch had indicated that. The ribs were tolerable, no fractures as suspected, but they would bear bruises. A smile was on Nick's face as he pointed to one of the x-rays. In the center of the breastbone was a rectangular object, with the definite outline of a key sticking out each end obliquely. She was so gutsy and quick thinking. Nick leaned against the wall. He could not wait until he could tell her that and so much more.

Kara started stirring and moaning, trying to find a comfortable position. Quickly walking over to her, Nick took hold of her right hand, carefully avoiding the injured arm. He kissed her cheek and her eyes fluttered open. She looked at Nick with pain reflected on her face.

"Oh, Nick," she gasped "I hurt all over."

"Darling, hang on to my hand as hard as you can. It may help you a little. Medication is in your system and it should be taking effect very soon." Nick was relieved, at least she was clearheaded

Kara had been administered fentanyl and she appeared to be resting fairly comfortably. She would need to have her left arm put into a cast.

He leaned down and spoke into her ear.

"Try to relax, I'm not going to leave you Kara, I'll be right here taking care of you. I love you."

Nick had to swallow hard to stop his emotions from taking over. This woman had come into his life with such a swiftness and intensity that had overwhelmed him. One thing, of which he was sure, he had waited for her all his life and he would not willingly surrender her.

Kara's eyes closed in artificial slumber.

Nick nodded to Dr. Carmichael and they walked to a couple of chairs at the end of the room.

Summarizing his findings Dr. Carmichael offered them to Nick, in the manner of a student presenting an oral examination to a panel of experts, knowing their expertise far outweighs his own. As the attending doctor he must do this. Kara has a slight concussion caused by the blow to the head, which severed the skin and would need stitches. The fractured Ulna of the left arm will be put into a cast or soft shoulder splint. Contusion of the ribs will be remedied with time. Dr. Carmichael added that he will personally attend to the repair work on Kara's head.

Nick quietly adding "Of course, the sutures will be placed as close to the hairline as possible to avoid a permanent noticeable scar." The intense look he gave indicated that only the very best results were expected. Nick looked a little nervous, the surgeon noted. Love affects even the mighty, he reflected. This woman must be very special to him.

After the diagnosis had been made, Nick nodded and left the room. There was nothing more he could do for Kara right now.

While Kara was in the capable hands of the chief surgeon, Nick phoned the Palm Springs Police Station and made a report. He gave Wendy's telephone number and address and an office number where he could be contacted, plus other details he could furnish. He was asked to wait in the hospital foyer, someone would meet him there.

Next he phoned Wendy, giving her a synopsis of the events that had taken place. He said he was taking Kara to her home and would stay with her for a couple of days. Observing a police officer walking into the foyer he said he had to dash; he would phone her from Kara's place.

A forensic/fingerprint specialist had accompanied the officer and asked to be shown Nick's vehicle, so that fingerprint dusting could be done. It might help as there was so little information to work with. Nick finished the remainder of the report with the officer, giving him his business card so that he could call him to provide more information on Kara. He had realized he did not have her home telephone number or address. He was becoming addlebrained. He was not accustomed to becoming emotionally involved with a patient, particularly one close to his heart. It was very unprofessional of him.

Walking outside Nick and the officer met the forensic specialist, who was heading toward them. He held up a slim black object.

"This was wedged under the passenger seat—I thought the young lady would want to know it was safe."

It was Kara's purse.

Eagerly Nick opened it. There was a lipstick case, a twenty dollars bill, a Visa credit card, three keys on a keychain and a driving license.

"Thank you very much. You have just solved MY problem." Until then he had no idea where she lived.

He gave them Kara's office telephone number, which he had memorized, and her home address. His car keys were returned to him by the forensic specialist and it appeared that their business was complete. He accepted a business card from each of them, shook hands and retraced his steps to the Waiting Room, where Dr. Carmichael was standing.

With his head down and deep in thought Nick almost walked past him.

"Is there a female doctor in the hospital or on call tonight?" he asked.

"I'll check."

Nick sat down in the Waiting Room, tapping his foot impatiently.

Triumphantly Dr. Carmichael joined Nick in the empty room.

"Dr. Lisa Manning will be with us in a few minutes. She came on at midnight and is with a patient right now. What did you have in mind—the examination for possible rape?"

Tersely Nick agreed and added, "If you have any question about performing this procedure, I'll take responsibility for recommending it."

Don Carmichael looked at Nick with a studied expression on his face.

"What you are suggesting is normal procedure under the circumstances. It is completely in line with hospital policy when suspicious indications are evident. There is not a problem here. Our objective is to protect the young lady and unfortunately the medication she now has in her system will affect her normal decision making ability"

Nick nodded his head.

"Sorry if I snapped at you. It's been quite a traumatic evening, one way or another."

He continued in a brisk, professional voice.

"Which member of your nursing staff, who is on duty right now, can be relied upon for confidentiality?"

This seemed to pose a problem and Dr. Carmichael frowned.

"That is a question the Director of Nursing could have answered more ably than me. Let's ask Lisa when she gets here, she works more closely with the night staff than I do."

They both walked back to the examining room and Nick immediately went and checked Kara, holding her right hand as they continued to talk.

Dr. Carmichael smiled broadly and Nick smiled wearily back.

Nick nodded over at the x-rays.

"I'd like to have the C frame, if that's possible."

It was the one that displayed the key and "button" most dramatically.

Taking it down immediately it was slid into a large manila envelope and handed to Nick.

"My wedding present."

There was a twinkle in Don Carmichael's eyes.

"If that proves true, you will be one of the first to receive an invitation," Nick pronounced fervently.

He was looking at Kara and when her eyelids flew open, it took him by surprise. She should have been out for a count. In a fuzzy voice she whispered.

"You won't leave me, will you?"

Her agitation was apparent.

Nick's throat tightened.

"You have my word on it. I'll never leave you, my love. I'll be here."

Kara closed her eyes and Nick caressed the hand he held in his own. He should have asked her permission to do this routine test, but she was already as tight as a bow, in pain and shock. If blame was placed—he would accept it.

Dr. Manning arrived looking puzzled. It was a very quiet night, why the summons to report to the chief of staff?

Dr. Carmichael was quite brief in his instructions and Dr. Manning understood completely the sensitivity and confidentiality of the procedure which she was about to implement. He asked that she report back immediately after the examination had been completed.

Dr. Manning was immediately all business as she turned on her heel and left the room.

"Could you use a coffee, Dr. Prendergast?"

"Sounds great and please call me Nick."

A pleased expression surfaced on the surgeon's face.

"Just black, thanks."

After he left the room, Nick stood looking at Kara. He hoped she could cope with the mental shock as well as the physical affects. She probably would have at least one black eye and sore ribs, poor babe, and wait until she found her arm movements restricted. Stooping over he gently kissed her cheek.

He hoped she would not have to face a more distressing situation.

Dr. Manning returned with a mature, salt and pepper haired RN who looked with interest at Nick before wheeling the gurney out of the room.

"This won't take long; we'll be in the Examining Room at the end of the corridor."

She passed Dr. Carmichael entering through the doorway with two cups of coffee.

"Dr. Manning's and my report will not be available for a few days, but they can be mailed to your Beverly Hills address, if that is convenient."

He handed the coffee in a Styrofoam cup over to Nick whose face registered surprise.

"How is it you seem to know so much about me?"

The glance the doctor gave Nick was one of genuine astonishment.

"Who in the medical profession hasn't heard of you? I have attended a couple of your seminars and send my Interns as often as they can be spared, when they take place in close proximity to the hospital. They are worth every penny allocated to them from our tight budget. I highly recommend them."

There was a slightly awkward lull in the conversation. Nick was not accustomed to being both complimented and reprimanded in the same breath. Compliments could be taken lightly, but the criticism alluding to the cost of his lectures hit home. He was aware that his expertise and knowledge came at a stiff price. Franc set the fee for the seminars. It had not occurred to Nick that there were valid medical practitioners who could not afford to attend his Workshops, even with financial help. He would look into this.

Dr. Manning came into the room and beckoned to Dr. Carmichael. He left the room with her.

This was the toughest part—waiting for the results.

Dr. Carmichael returned with a big smile on his face and Nick's frame visibly relaxed.

"Good news, there was no evidence of semen or penetration. Dr. Manning also mentioned that in this day and age you will find yourself to be a lucky man."

Nick's relief was clearly reflected on his face.

"Miss Olavssen is ready to leave. A prescription is with her right now. She is healthy and in excellent physical shape and recuperation should follow naturally. The wound should heal nicely."

He peered at Nick and half-smiled.

"We know that she will be in the best possible hands."

A grin creased his face as he shook hands with Nick and handed over the car key and "panic button" found in Kara's bra.

Nick shook his head disbelievingly as he shoved the unit into the pocket of his slacks.

"Perhaps you could keep the hospital in mind next time you are down this way and honor us with a lecture."

Nick retrieved a business card from his wallet and handed it over.

"My secretary will expect a call from you with this in mind. She keeps on top of my schedule and I will ask her to fit it in."

There would be no charge. He owed Dr. Carmichael and the hospital a favor.

They shook hands in agreement.

They were part of the "old boys" networking system.

Following Kara's wheelchair back to the car, he pondered the doctor's remarks. Dr. Carmichael had obviously been speaking in a general way about Kara being in excellent shape, but it had touched a nerve and Nick was reminded that Kara was not his to defend or protect. Yet she possessed him as no drug could ever do.

Lifting Kara out of the wheelchair, two medics carefully, but awkwardly, due to the cast on her left arm maneuvered her onto the front passenger seat of the Jaguar. Nick carefully fastened the seatbelt around her with the cast lying incongruously over it. Picking up his blazer Nick tucked it around Kara's torso. Bunching up the black silk jacket to make a pillow he slipped it under Kara's head and closed the passenger door firmly. Thanking the medics for their help Nick walked around to the driver's side, opening the door and getting in. Looking intently at Kara, who was sleeping fitfully under sedation, he was astonished to think that she was thirty-one years of age. If he had not noticed the date on her driving license, he would not have believed it. She looked so young.

Nick had been a little concerned that Kara was much younger than he, but the six years difference in their ages changed that—they were perfect for each other. Leaning toward her, Nick lightly kissed Kara's mouth. Her lips were cool to his touch. Remembering how indignant Kara had become on the plane when he had referred facetiously to her comments about being "a perfect stranger," an amused expression came over his face.

She was perfect in his eyes and happily no longer a stranger.

Frequently glancing at Kara by his side, Nick drove in silence along the highway. As the sky started lightening with the advent of dawn, cars began joining him on the journey. They all travelled together, in the same direction, in isolated modules, each with a different course mapped out. He wondered where his and Kara's journey eventually would take them.

Running the previous evening's events through his head, Dr. Carmichael's comment came back to him. "Dr. Manning also mentioned that in this day and age you will find yourself to be a lucky man."

Of course. During the examination they had found Kara to be a virgin. Nick looked tenderly at Kara beside him. The impact was physical. A warm glow spread through his body and a happy smile surfaced on his lips.

Suddenly Jon did not seem to be such a big threat after all—besides he was not in California, or even the USA, unlike Nick who was. Perhaps, after all, they were worthy adversaries.

Approaching the Box Springs exit, Nick quietly pulled the car over onto the shoulder of the highway. He took Kara's laminated driving license from his shirt pocket. "Crestwood Garden Townhomes, 6684 St. Christopher Drive, No. 22." Extracting a map from the door pocket, he switched on the interior light and looked at Kara, who was restlessly moving her head and moaning softly.

Consulting the index he quickly found the location. It was not far away, which was a lucky break. Quietly returning the map to its place and turning off the interior light, he glanced over at Kara. Her head had drooped over on to her shoulder against the window. She looked awkward and Nick smoothly put the car into motion, anxious to get Kara settled more comfortably as quickly as possible. It was too bad the back seat of this model was simply a jump seat, not suitable for an adult to lay or even sit on with ease. He should trade the vehicle in.

Exiting at the next off-ramp, he made his way along a long, darkened lane until he saw lights in the distance. He wondered how often Kara used this exit at night. It was a lonely lane several miles from civilization. Stop lights indicated Canyon Crest Drive, which meant he was almost there. After several more stop lights he saw the sign on the right hand side "Crestwood Garden Townhomes."

Urbanization confronted him.

It was not a large complex and number twenty-two was easily located. He parked his car in the driveway. It was after 6:00 a.m. and Nick's adrenaline level, after the uneventful drive, had settled down. Taking Kara's purse from under his seat, he removed the keys from it, and switched off the car's lights and engine, leaving the alarm system on.

The path to the front door led through small bushes and flowers, with rocks interspersed between them. By process of elimination, the correct key was found and the door opened. Nick walked in switching lights on in the dim interior, looking for a bedroom. The first door he opened along a short hallway proved to be it. He pushed the door open and walked outside, leaving the front door slightly ajar. It was unwieldy getting Kara out of the car without assistance. He was very conscious of Kara's limb sticking out so oddly. Deciding the easiest way to carry her was over his shoulder, he awkwardly manipulated her body into place, steadying the cast with the other hand. Kara was moaning increasingly by the time he managed to place her on the bed and his conscience was nagging. Maybe he should not have been so anxious to remove her from the hospital, but if she had stayed so must he.

Nick stood watching, allowing Kara time to gain some semblance of calmness. She had sufficient medication in her system to combat the pain, once his handling effects had dissipated.

Satisfied that she had slipped into a sluggish sleep, he went outside. He hoped neighbors had not witnessed him carrying Kara over his shoulder. That could be embarrassing. Retrieving Kara's purse and jacket, as well as his own blazer and briefcase from the car, he also picked up the manila x-ray envelope. Once on the pathway he pressed the automatic car lock monitor and heard the knobs click closed. Retracing his steps, he noticed mail in the box by the front door and removed it on his way inside. He locked and bolted the front door.

Putting everything on the settee Nick unlocked and opened his briefcase, placing the manila envelope inside. Fishing in his pockets he produced the duplicate set of keys and replaced them into an inside pocket, where they were kept in the briefcase. Fingering the object that had slipped from Kara, he discovered it was not a button, but an earring. Absently he placed it into the briefcase, which he locked and placed on a chair. He put the purse and mail on top.

Seeing a refrigerator in another room Nick carried the two coats into the kitchen and placed each around the back of a chair. He looked inside the refrigerator for something to drink. There were sodas, milk, and a bottle of Sterling Vineyards Chardonnay, which brought a smile to his lips. There was also a bottle of "Fruitful Harvest" Zinfandel. He had not come across that brand before. He helped himself to a soft drink. Popping the tab, Nick looked around the kitchen. It was small, but nice. It had a greenhouse window with a selection of herbs and small plants growing there. The color scheme was blue and white and it was very neatly organized.

He liked it.

Taking the soda into the living room, he sat down, leaning against the cushions decorating the settee. This was an exceptionally pleasant room. He sat up more interested than he had given his tired body credit for. The carpeting was a deep mauve, with white walls, and the furniture was upholstered in varying shades of blue from soft duck-egg blue to almost lavender. It was an interesting combination.

A small table held a large vase of fresh flowers, just starting to wilt, and a group of pictures was dotted around it. It led him to stand up and walk over to it. There was a picture of Kara with two people, obviously her parents from the way they were snuggling together. The mother's arm was around her waist and her father's arm around her shoulders. She had to be an only child Nick surmised, and realized he did not know nearly as much about her as he would like. They had much to discuss.

Another picture showed Kara sitting on a palomino horse, in what looked like a vineyard setting, looking away from the camera with a shy smile on her face. He wondered who had taken the picture. It was a good one. The picture in the next frame he picked up alarmed him. A younger Kara, in a slim fitting long black gown with a long string of pearls around her neck, was looking up and laughing at a young man in evening dress, who held Kara around the waist. He had a big grin on his face and Nick felt as if his heart had dropped into his shoes. This was Jon, he knew immediately—he was a very handsome man.

Quickly Nick replaced the picture. He should not have been so curious.

As if to bring reassurance, Nick walked into the bedroom to check on Kara. She had settled down and was sleeping peacefully. Even with the padding around her head, she looked adorable. An urgent desire to cradle her in his arms invaded his senses. The stark white cast resting on her waist, served as a deterrent, but did not avert the longing.

A beige colored damask Victorian slipper chair stood nearby and Nick pulled it over and straddled it, leaning his chin on top of the carved back. He sat for a while caressing her with his eyes. If she only knew where his thoughts were leading him.

Carefully Nick removed Kara's scuffed shoes, feeling her bare silken skin in doing so. He was aware that she was not wearing stockings when he found her stuffed in the trunk with her dress over her head, but that information had not registered. His professional training had taken over. Touching her had awakened his senses. It was a big bed, if he could just lie next to her, monitoring her, he would feel infinitely much better. Perhaps! On the other hand, being so close to her and unable to express his love and desire would be like being in a straightjacket of his own design.

Stretching his arms above his head, Nick yawned and stood up. Better not dwell on thoughts like this—he needed to get some sleep. Quietly he swung the chair back into its place.

Searching through a built-in closet outside the main bathroom, he found two blankets, one of which he carefully laid over Kara; he would not attempt to move her inside the sheets.

It was just after 6:30 a.m., a full day from the time he last slept. It was daylight outside and the inside lights were still on. He went around turning them off. Going into a second bedroom, he pulled the mauve satin bedspread back from one of the twin beds and sat down on the bed to remove his shoes. A thought occurred to him could this be someone else's room? Did Kara share this apartment? He was too darned weary to think about this right now. His eyes felt as if sand was ingrained in them.

Kara should sleep soundly for some time. The blow to her head and the medication in her system should help block out the trauma of the stressful situation for a while. A couple of times he had spoken her name and she had responded reluctantly, as if being disturbed against her will. She would be fine.

Nick attempted to settle down but could not. He needed to be within sight of Kara.

Grabbing the pillow and blanket from the bed, he went into Kara's room and lay on the rug beside her bed.

The shriek of the telephone brought him back to awareness. Nick rushed into the living room in the direction of the noisy apparatus and firmly seized the telephone receiver.

The sun was shining brightly through the window.

"Hello."

"Can I speak to Betty?"

"Wrong number" Nick said shortly, hanging up.

In reflection he wondered if Kara did have a roommate.

Rubbing his eyes, he looked around the living room and then took a tour of the townhouse. First he went into the bedroom with the twin beds and slid open the mirrored closet. Seeing that the space was used as a storage area, his sleuthing efforts were satisfied. This bedroom was en suite, which would make it convenient for taking a shower later. He was pleased that Kara did not share her living accommodation and decided that he was becoming much too proprietary in his thinking.

A separate airy bathroom, living room, dining room, and kitchen completed the tour. It was a large apartment, tastefully furnished, and reflected a flair for color and design. The enormous antique mirror in the foyer was the initial indication of entering into the quiet luxury within.

The telephone had not awakened Kara and Nick took advantage of this to make several telephone calls. Opening his briefcase on the guest bedroom desk, he produced a business card holder in black leather with gold engraved initials in the corner. Using his telephone calling card he phoned Claudia, his recently promoted Senior Executive Secretary, who supervised the typing pool. He left a message on her home answering machine, saying there was some urgency in returning his call and to note it was not one of the usual numbers he was calling from. It was Saturday and he hoped she would not be gone for long.

The next call was to British Airways canceling his flight the next day. Producing his international calling card, Nick dialed a transatlantic number directly.

Deciding to investigate the kitchen for food, Nick grimaced at his own lack of culinary expertise. He walked back into the guest bedroom and pulled the local phone directory from a bookshelf. Heading for the yellow pages, he let his fingers do the walking in finding the delivery service he was looking for.

"Battaglio's" was the fastest pizza service around, guaranteeing delivery within half an hour or no charge. They certainly did live up to that claim, Nick decided, looking at his watch as he left the window to open the door, when the familiar waving pennant-decked car turned into the driveway. No need to interrupt Kara's rest at this point.

Helping himself to a couple of pieces from the box placed on the kitchen table, Nick put them on a plate and took them into the bedroom to sit with Kara as he ate them.

She was motionless, breathing very lightly, the rise and fall of the blanket being almost imperceptible. He put the plate on the bed clothes, reaching over to check her pulse. Her eyelids fluttered, but she did not open them. He resumed eating, monitoring Kara as he finished his meal. Patience was not one of Nick's strong points. Picking up the empty plate and taking it into the kitchen, he made a list of items he could accomplish while Kara slept.

He phoned Wendy.

"Hi Wen, Nick. Have the police contacted you yet?"

Wendy answered quickly, "Yes, early this morning. Apparently they had already talked to Neville, the security guard, using the information you gave them. I wasn't able to offer much information, but the police did find a pearl earring, which was assumed to be Kara's. Do you know if she lost one?"

Remembering the earring he had casually slipped into his briefcase, thinking it was a button, Nick replied, "Could very well be— if so, I have the match."

"How is Kara, is she going to be all right?"

An anxious tone had crept into Wendy's voice.

She heard a long sigh, before the response came quietly in the cool, detached manner he used when speaking from a professional standpoint about a patient. As brief as the summary had been, Wendy could hear Nick's voice slowly crumbling as the conversation trailed to a close.

Surprised at the emotion displayed, Wendy spoke impetuously.

"Kara sure must be very special. A couple of people attending the party offered assistance immediately, when they discovered what had happened last night."

"Who for instance?" Nick shot back.

"Well, George for one. I surmised he was interested from the way he was drooling over her at the party, but he seemed reluctant to step on your territory."

"Who told him?" Nick asked sharply.

"He talked to Neville, the security guard, when he brought the message from you. There is no need to worry, George is a close one; he won't let it go any further."

Nick asked in a resigned voice, "Who else?"

"Franc. He left for the airport a couple of hours ago. He said he would see you in London on Monday. I didn't have Kara's home number and the hospital said Kara had already been checked out under your care when we tried to reach you there."

Nick's voice sounded tired.

"Wen, I think I'm in love with Kara. In fact I know I am. She considers herself committed to someone else and does not want to see me again. It's a hell of a mess and I'm going crazy hoping to change her mind. There is so much to iron out and the thought of going away and leaving Kara without resolving the problem is extremely troubling."

He admitted this with a wry expression on his face.

"Strange comments coming from me, eh? Sorry to burden you with this Wen, but you are one of the few I feel safe confiding in."

Wendy cleared her throat. This was heavy stuff and she was shocked by Nick's dejected attitude. It had taken so long to build up his facade. Suddenly she was nervous.

"Good luck, my dear. I hope it works out for you and Kara. Heavens only knows, you deserve it."

They were starting to tread on sacred ground.

Ready to end the conversation, Nick asked Wendy to give Gerald his love and then quickly said goodbye and hung up.

Wow, Wendy thought round-eyed. *How quickly he had succumbed. Nick had known Kara for such a short time and already he had declared his love. For so long he had presented a sophisticated, man-about-town image, charming and in total control, hiding an emotional wound she had doubted would ever heal. Please, Kara, be sensitive to him.*

In hindsight Wendy wished she had had the opportunity to talk to Kara for more than the odd times they had occasion to do so at the party. Nick's affairs were well known both internationally as well as in Rancho Mirage. He was a first-class flirt a, "Love-em and leave-em" type, never failing to attract the most beautiful, successful, and wealthy women—he could have his choice, including many married women who batted their eyelashes. It embarrassed Wendy to see the flagrant displays attempted by women who should have known better, in their efforts to entice Nick when he attended her parties. What they were not privy to was that Nick was not at all interested in them.

Oh, well, there was nothing she could do, except worry, now that her dearest cousin had confided in her.

Nick hung up the phone feeling better having divulged this information to Wendy and getting it off his chest. She was the sibling he never had. He had not intended exposing his feelings about Kara, but he was so apprehensive and unaccustomed to the emotions that had invaded and captured his heart that his concerns had just spilled out.

He would have to mask his feelings better than this, otherwise he would be confessing his plight to every stranger who took pity on him. Smiling at the unlikely simile, Nick poured a glass of milk for himself and took it into the living room.

Before the phone had completed its second peal, he grabbed it. Claudia was at the other end.

"Great, thanks for getting back so quickly. Sorry to impinge on your weekend once again, but there are several things I would like you to do."

He summarized that he had cancelled his British Airways reservation for Sunday and instead would like a reservation made for the Monday morning Concorde flight out of J. F. Kennedy International Airport, plus the usual stuff, but leave the return date open. Also put things right with The Claridge Hotel in London and make the necessary changes. It was very important that his next request be attended to very quickly. He had left a message with Franc's answering service, alerting him that he would not be able to get to London on time for the beginning of the seminar. He would, in fact, be missing most of the first day's agenda. Franc would need his notes and reference material to go over beforehand; he asked Claudia to fax it to him immediately. Nick informed Claudia where to find it in his desk. The next request was by far the most unusual and Claudia was surprised, but not completely disconcerted by it. She had learned to be flexible and prepared for any assignment her enigmatic boss lobbed at her.

"Righteo, Nick. I'll start on this list immediately and get back as soon as pos."

Claudia had worked five years for Nick, starting as his private secretary, until now she supervised three others. She had quickly realized that 'confidentiality' was included in her work ethics. He was a very private man. His demands often bordered on perfection. The fact that he recognized this trait and apologized for his lack of sensitivity and then made up for it ten-fold was sufficient justification for her total loyalty and support. She had a great job and a boss she admired and respected completely.

Nick heard soft moans and shuffling coming from the bedroom and he rapidly strode into that room.

Taking her right hand into both of his, Nick watched Kara striving to come around. He observed every nuance of expression passing over her features. She completely possessed him and he was willing to be enslaved. Dominated by these strong emotions, Nick was shaken when Kara opened her eyes and looked at him without recognition.

They stared at each other for several seconds.

"Kara it's me, Nick," he said anxiously.

She closed her eyes.

"Please don't do this to me, darling, speak to me."

Once again the lids lifted with an effort, but this time a spark of recognition glimmered in the vivid eyes and a weak voice said.

"Hi, Nick."

The couple of words were like music to his ears. Kara closed her eyes again and Nick understood.

"Much pain?"

"Mmm. Arm and head," she mumbled.

Nick stood up, patting her hand.

"I'll be right back."

He returned with a glass of water and two pink and two white pills to find Kara awake and struggling to get into a sitting position, giving agonizing little gasps with each attempt.

"Stop! What do you think you're doing?"

The abrupt tone of his voice, immediately arrested Kara's movements.

Putting the glass and pills down, he stepped over to the bed and shifting her into a more comfortable sitting position, smoothly slid a pillow behind her.

"That better?"

There was a gentler inflection in his tone.

Kara nodded. She had been taken aback by his commanding voice.

"Were you in the military?" she querulously asked.

Nick burst out laughing.

"No, but it has been suggested at various times that I would make a good sergeant major."

A smile lurked around his eyes. He took the glass of water and the pills on the spoon and handed them to Kara.

"They're perfectly germ-free, I washed my hands."

"Thank you. That was my first thought," Kara murmured, concentrating on swallowing them.

She didn't notice the grin raised by her droll comment.

Kara lay back against the pillows and Nick removed the glass from her slender fingers.

"Are you hungry?"

"Not really. Just terribly thirsty."

He returned to the kitchen and set up a tray comprising of a glass of orange juice, a large glass of milk and a cup of black coffee barely warm that he would drink. He placed a couple of pieces of pizza, which he had stored in the refrigerator, on a plate and heated them in a microwave oven. The heated plate went on the tray together with a couple of paper napkins.

Kara looked at the tray and then at Nick.

"Truly a feast fit for the Gods."

Shaking his head he deposited the tray on the bed beside her.

"You know, considering how worried I've been for the past twelve hours or so, you are providing a levity that amazes me."

Kara looked down at the glass of orange juice held in her hand.

"I suppose I am being flippant, but I'm quite scared and not sure that I remember what happened. What can you tell me?"

"Let us start off by telling me what you remember and I will try to fill in the gaps."

The juice in the glass was shaking perilously and Nick gently removed the glass from Kara's trembling hand. He sighed and wished he hadn't to put her through this. If only it hadn't happened.

With a quiver going through her body, Kara looked at Nick in panic.

Damn. This was going to be worse than he had suspected.

"Nick, I've got to get to the bathroom right away and I suddenly seem immobile."

He smiled in relief. This woman took him from the sublime to the ridiculous in a heartbeat.

"I can handle that."

So saying he threw back the blanket and cupping her in his arms, carefully avoiding the injured limb, he carried Kara into the bathroom, depositing her carefully onto her feet.

"I can manage," she whispered.

He dutifully closed the door, standing outside, waiting for the expected summons. The form fitting skirt which he had pulled over her slim hips was molded to her shape. One handedly she couldn't possibly accomplish the necessary functions.

Shuffling and sounds of frustration came to him through the door and then he heard the resignation in her voice.

"Nick, I need help."

The simple declaration turned his heart over. Pushing open the door he looked into troubled eyes.

"Kara, I am going to close my eyes in assisting you and then I will turn around and walk out. You have nothing to fear from me. All right?"

She nodded her head dubiously.

"The agony and the ecstasy" had been simply a well-worn phrase, but now he experienced it first-hand. Good to his pledge, he left Kara to complete her ablutions and stood resting against the bedroom wall shaking.

The toilet flushed and after another scuffle, he heard Kara's voice.

"Nick, it is not going to work the same way in reverse. I am almost naked."

He couldn't help smiling at her predicament and the importance which she placed upon it.

"So! Would you like to stay there until your arm has healed, or can we come to a compromise?"

"Like what?" There was an edge of suspicion in her voice.

"First, you will have to get out of that dress eventually," he was trying to be amusing to get her to relax, "Second, I am very trustworthy and would not dream of placing you in an uncomfortable or embarrassing position and you do need assistance."

Hesitantly Kara asked, "So what do you suggest?"

There was no window in the bathroom.

"Put out the light and see how dark it is in there."

He heard a click.

"It's fairly dark."

"Do you have a robe or something loose to wear, because your arm will have to stay in that contraption for several days before it should be moved in any way?"

Kara instructed Nick where to look and a short time later he knocked on the bathroom door.

"Get ready I am coming in. Stand near the shower."

Light coming from the room behind him cast a brief beam, which was extinguished as he went in and quickly closed the door behind him.

This was like playing "Blind Man's Bluff."

"Kara, I am standing by the door. Reach out your good arm and find me. I don't want to knock your arm."

He was going to add "Or accidentally grab you," but decided not to bring that possibility up. He was on venerated ground as it was.

Kara's hand touched his shoulder and he took hold of it, running his hand up her arm to her shoulder.

"Turn around a little I am going to unzip the back of your dress."

Surprisingly, without objecting, she turned.

"I have to take your arm very briefly out of the sling. You will feel some pain, I can't do anything about that, but as soon as I slip your arms out of the armholes, and your clothing is removed, it will be replaced immediately."

Breathing heavily Kara did not protest.

Nick moved around Kara, feeling for the three Velcro fasteners and the belt around her waist, which were part of the protective device.

"Hold the cast with your other hand for a minute while I put this gadget down."

Kara cried out in pain.

"I'm sorry, darling. I'll be as fast as I can."

He slid the dress over her shoulders and it automatically slipped down until Kara's hand, which was supporting the cast taken out of the sling, stopped it.

"I'm going to hold your injured arm and if you put your other arm down by your side, the dress should fall easily."

He felt the garment slip down and he briefly released Kara's hand to allow it to pass and fall on the floor.

Kara moaned and swayed slightly. He placed his arm around her slim, bare waist to steady her, and felt a flood of desire overtake him as his hand contacted the satiny smooth skin.

Shakily picking up the protective mold, he slipped it carefully under Kara's arm, passing the Velcro straps around her waist, conscious of dryness in his throat at the touch of her again.

He groaned. If this wasn't masochistic, he didn't know what was.

Quickly he lightly passed his hands down her hips and slid the panties, nestled around her knees, to the floor.

Kara involuntarily shivered.

"Step out of everything." His voice was husky.

Where did the dratted robe go?

Feeling around the rug, he located a soft, satiny object.

Turning it around and around in his hands he said in desperation.

"I don't know how the hell to put this on you, I don't even know what I'm doing."

Kara laughed nervously.

"I think I can manage. It is very loose. Just help me put my head through the opening."

Nick opened the door and walked out.

Perspiration stood out on his forehead. He had never been affected this way before. Little did Kara know how intensely he had to control himself from caressing and letting her know how desirable he found her.

When Kara joined him in the bedroom, he lay with his eyes closed on the bed, as if in pain.

"Are you all right Nick?"

He rolled over and stood up without answering directly.

"If you feel up to it, let's go into the kitchen where we can talk. Fresh coffee is brewing."

"That's nice. Thank you." Kara's eyes had a shine in them when she looked at Nick.

If this had turned the tide in his favor, he would be eternally grateful for his self-control.

He brought the tray back into the kitchen where he busied himself setting up the cups for coffee, while Kara munched on a piece of pizza.

"When did we get the pizza?" she asked curiously.

"Shortly after I looked in your refrigerator and inventoried the supplies and decided my cooking ability was sadly lacking. I'm really hopeless in a kitchen."

Turning around he looked at Kara.

"I hope this slight defect doesn't lower me greatly in your estimation."

Kara laughed spontaneously. She was beginning to enjoy his quirky sense of humor.

Nick's eyes crinkled as he joined in.

When the coffee was ready they sat at the kitchen table sipping it, silent and comfortable.

Nick broke the silence.

"Kara I've just arranged something which I did not consult you about. I did this to assuage my own conscience and I really would appreciate it if you accepted it in that spirit."

Kara looked confused and sighed.

"Please tell me. You go off on a tangent, just when I think I am getting to know you."

He reached over and laid his hand over hers.

"There should be a phone call soon, letting us know when to expect two or three females for you to interview. This will be for the live-in position as nurse, housekeeper, personal dresser, and cook—you name it, until you are well enough to do those things for yourself."

Before Kara could put words to the indignation reflected on her face Nick squeezed her hand and rushed on.

"I will have to leave on Monday to attend to business and I can't go off and leave you to manage alone. If you object, Kara, I shall have to cancel my trip and stay with you and do all those things for you myself. I will not leave until I know you are being properly cared for. Of course it will be my responsibility to pay all expenses involved."

Kara's lips had compressed tightly.

"I am not accustomed to anyone living with me."

Nick smiled pleasantly.

"Yes, I had surmised that and I think it's wonderful. I wish I could stay and be the first."

Against her will she smiled and her face softened.

"Oh, Nick, what can I say? You are doing so much, but I can't become indebted to you. Forgive me for sounding so churlish, because I really do appreciate all that you have done, but I feel as if I am being punished because I reneged on my promise to Jon."

Looking at Kara thoughtfully Nick asked, "Does he have so much hold over you?"

Before Kara could answer, the telephone rang and immediately Nick walked over and picked up the receiver. Kara found that amusing. He did it as if it were his normal practice, as if he did live with her.

"Would six-thirty and seven o' clock tonight be okay for two interviews?"

Kara nodded her head. Who was she to argue?

Nick looked relieved as he hung up the phone.

"That was my secretary, in case you were wondering—she can be relied upon completely. She is very discreet."

Kara was leaning back in the chair with her eyes closed. He brushed his lips against hers and her eyes immediately flew open.

"You're tired, darling. Do you want to nap until the interviews start?"

How easily the endearments fell from his lips. Kara was becoming accustomed to hearing them and more frighteningly liking the familiarity. Was she such an easy conquest?

She stood up.

"Yes, I think I'm ready to take a nap."

The soft fabric swished around her feet.

"You didn't answer my earlier question, but it can wait until later," he reminded. She chose not to answer.

Nick offered to assist Kara back to her bedroom, but she smilingly refused.

"My legs are not affected, so you must not 'baby' me."

Lying down on the bed was a little awkward, but she managed, with Nick watching her. She looked a little flushed. Nick sat on the edge of the bed and took hold of her wrist, making a discreet check of her pulse rate.

"I'll waken you in about an hour. Sleep well."

Her pulse was normal. He covered her with the light blanket, kissing her cheek as he did so.

"You have some mail. I'll leave it on your nightstand."

In retrieving the mail and Kara's purse, Nick noticed an airmail letter and curiously he pulled it out. Turning it over, he saw a gold return label with a crest of arms and an English address emblazoned on it. The sender was Lady Glorene Bassenthorpe. Kara moved in illustrious circles. She had told him that she was getting out of her depth by becoming involved with him, but he was beginning to realize that he was in the same quandary, but whereas she was fighting it, he could not.

He deposited the purse and mail on the carved night table.

Opening his briefcase in the second bedroom, Nick made space on the desk to work and started going over some contracts. He glanced at his watch and set the alarm. He usually became so engrossed in what he was doing that time slipped past unnoticed.

CHAPTER TWENTY

Nick looked at his watch. The alarm's chime alerted him to the time. He gathered up the papers he had been working with and placed them in the briefcase, locking it automatically out of habit.

Kara was lying with her right arm under her head, staring at the ceiling when he walked into her bedroom.

"Haven't you slept?"

Kara did not answer and he noticed the mail scattered over the bed as he walked out.

Nick returned with a tumbler of water and more pills. Wordlessly assisting her into a sitting position, he handed the medication and water to her.

They were both silent. Nick asked, "Would you like to freshen up? The agency person should be here very soon."

Somberly Kara started sliding toward the edge of the bed, ignoring Nick's outstretched hand. She made her way to the bathroom and closed the door. The airmail letter had been opened and Nick dismally recognized that Kara's attitude must have been affected by the contents.

He cleared off the kitchen table and wiped the surface. He was not sure where Kara would want to conduct the interviews, but if the expression on her face was any indication she probably would not care.

Five minutes after the appointed time the doorbell rang. Kara was sitting at the kitchen table tucking the voluminous garment around her, as if to make it appear less noticeable.

Nick opened the door and Kara could hear an indistinct conversation taking place. She heard the door close and Nick led a tall, well-built redhead into the kitchen. Kara asked her to be seated and Nick pulled out another chair and sat down. He had a notepad and pen in his hand. Kara looked at him, but he did not speak.

Eyeing the agency employee dubiously, Kara introduced herself and looked over at Nick.

"I'm Nick, a friend of Kara's and I'd like to sit in on the discussion."

Responding to Kara's request, Gina provided a run-down of the work she could be expected to do as a private Registered Nurse and mentioned the type of duties she was willing to perform. Yes, she was quite a good cook, nothing fancy. She was a good driver, no traffic violations or tickets. She had no objection to light housework, but she did not do the heavy stuff and windows, though she would do laundry, but no ironing. Gina kept looking at Nick, who made notes from time to time.

Kara looked unhappy and tired.

Nick decided to step in.

There were a few things he would like to know. Did she smoke, take prescription drugs on a regular basis and did she consider herself to be a social drinker? She said she smoked and had an occasional drink, no drugs. Yes, she had a boyfriend—he lived in Chino. What time off would she require? They usually saw each other one or two times through the week and at weekends. This is the time off she would need. Would there be a problem in washing and drying Kara's hair, helping her in and out of the bathtub. He deliberately did not look at Kara as he asked these questions, but heard her intake of breath.

Gina said she guessed this would be okay.

Was she comfortable with this type of arrangement? There probably would also be grocery shopping to attend to and accountability of funds spent.

Gina handed copies of references she had brought with her to Kara. Nick said he understood she was bonded through the agency and Gina agreed. In winding up the interview Nick asked if there was anything else they should know or she wished to say. No. Where could they reach her tonight, if necessary and could she commence Monday if required? Yes.

Nick set the pen on top of the pad and smiled at Kara.

"Anything you wish to add?"

"No, I think you have covered everything."

Kara thanked Gina for coming and Nick showed her to the door.

Nick returned and stood in the doorway of the kitchen looking at Kara.

"Did we overlook anything?"

"Only my weight, date of birth and bank account number."

He looked at her sharply. Was she being cynical?

Her face showed only amusement.

"Nick, I would have been offended if those questions had been asked of me in an interview. In my business I would be sued or accused of prejudice, racism or personal infringement for even bordering on that type of cross examination. Are you sure you can ask those things?"

"I can justify them in that they were asked with your safety and welfare in mind. The answer is yes. They were questions I wanted answers to and I couldn't imagine you getting around to asking them."

His protectiveness and astuteness invaded her senses and made her feel more miserable than she had thought possible.

The doorbell rang again. Nick looked at his watch. This one was eager. It was five minutes to seven.

He showed a middle-aged lady, with graying hair into the kitchen.

Kara asked her to sit down and Nick leaned against the refrigerator.

"I'm going to have a drink, anyone else care for one?" he said.

"Yes, please, a diet soda would be nice," Kara responded as she looked enquiringly over at the occupant of the chair beside her.

"Not for me, dear, I've just finished dinner."

Nick took two cans out of the refrigerator and put one down in front of Kara and popped the top of the other one. As he was doing this, Kara's can of soda was picked up and opened.

"Do you have a glass handy?" the gray haired lady asked.

Nick smiled as he took two from the cupboard and handed one to her.

She was going to do nicely.

Once again Kara asked for background information and Emma, as she was called, supplied it. She was a widow, with two grown daughters. Emma said she loved to cook, do laundry, and housework. What about grocery shopping? Yes, of course. She was a good driver she drove to Portland, Oregon, twice a year for a couple of weeks, to visit her daughter and family and spent time with her other daughter in Pomona a couple of times a month. She played bridge with friends once a month and that just about summed up her lifestyle.

As an afterthought Emma added, "I love reading good books and knitting sweaters for the homeless in my spare time. I don't smoke, never have. Of course I am a Registered Nurse."

Nick asked, "How do you feel about taking care of Kara—washing her hair, helping her in and out of the shower or bathtub?"

"Oh, my dear, that is what I would expect to do."

She reached over and patted Kara's good hand.

It was such an unexpected kindly gesture that Kara's eyes became moist.

Nick asked a few more penetrating questions.

Turning to Kara he asked.

"Do you need any more information?"

"No, that's sufficient. Thank you Emma."

With a charming smile Nick turned to Emma.

"Please excuse us for a few minutes. Allow me to show you into the living room."

He took Emma's elbow and propelled her out of the kitchen.

"What do you think?" he asked upon his return.

"I like her, but don't you think we are asking her to do too much? It sounds like a 24 hour "On-call" job and she is not young. Besides I thought you preferred the other one."

Kara's glance was veiled.

"You don't give me much credence, do you?" Nick retorted, eyeing Kara shrewdly.

"Why would I entrust a woman, younger than you, who will continue to smoke in a non-smoking home and has stipulated quite strongly what she will and will not do. She has a boyfriend whom she expects to see regularly and to whom she will give preference should a choice need to be made."

He stopped for breath.

"Not for a moment would I feel comfortable with her under your roof."

Nick contemplated his glass of soda.

"She does not get my vote."

Suddenly feeling lighthearted, Kara responded.

"I agree, I really feel very satisfied with Emma. I just wanted your impression."

Nick kissed the tip of Kara's nose.

"I'll go and fetch her."

Emma left. Everything was arranged. She would be back by lunchtime Monday.

"I think we should celebrate," Nick said jubilantly. "How about a small glass of wine?"

Kara agreed, but her smile was a watered down version of the real thing. Nick frowned. Ever since she had become aware of that damned letter, she seemed to have distanced herself from him.

Instinctively he felt threatened.

That must not affect his judgment or allow his suspicions to take over. The discussion they must have would be a difficult one—not so much for him as for Kara. It was of such importance that it should not be postponed much longer.

In fact, the sooner the better.

Pouring a good measure of the "Fruitful Harvest" Zinfandel into a crystal glass, and partially filling another, he carried them into the bedroom and nodded for Kara to climb on to the bed. He placed both glasses on the night table.

There was no time like the present. Regretfully Nick admitted, "This is not going to be a pleasant or easy discussion, but it must be addressed."

He sat down on the edge of the bed.

"We have to talk about the events of last night, both for your enlightenment and recovery and for the sake of my guilty conscience. I am here for you, dearest, remember that."

He held out his hand, and instinctively Kara placed hers into it. Hot tears instantly hit her lids. His touch was very comforting and the welcomed intimacy left her feeling very vulnerable. She closed her eyes.

Sipping the wine Nick waited until Kara had composed herself.

"Try the wine, Kara. I didn't pour very much for you, but a little will help you relax. It's very good."

He passed the goblet to her.

"Let's try again and I will contribute what I can."

A lengthy silence ensued.

She took a couple of sips of wine. Coughing nervously she ventured, "Here goes."

She coughed again and spoke in a voice that trembled slightly.

"After walking out of the compound, I went towards the car. I remember the gate closing when you went back inside. I pressed the opener button just as I was approaching the car and I had a strange feeling that someone was watching me. I think I had reached the back of the car when I felt a hand over my mouth."

Kara's eyes opened wide and she started shaking.

Nick removed the glass of wine from Kara and placed both glasses back on the nightstand. He took her hand, stroking it soothingly.

"Go on, my love."

Struggling to keep her poise Kara continued.

"I didn't see anyone—I just heard voices."

Her voice drifted off.

Nick had known this would be difficult. He was suffering with her.

"What happened next?"

He was trying to handle this in a calm, professional fashion, but his ire was up and the ferocity of his feelings surprised him.

"I automatically shoved the key into my bra.—I didn't want to hand it over."

She sounded apologetic.

Nick was amazed that in the face of danger her thoughts would be on something like this.

"I heard two men's voices. One person grabbed me and the other was looking for the keys to the car. They were behind me, so I couldn't see them."

Kara shuddered.

"And then—" Nick encouraged.

Kara looked down at the bedspread and put her hand up to her face, spreading her fingers to cover her eyes.

"He had his hands all over me and tried to take my clothes off."

Nick caught his breath sharply. The bastard! It was difficult to acknowledge the helplessness that overcame him. Slipping off his shoes, he climbed on to the bed.

Taking Kara into his arms, he carefully arranged the cast.

"Lean against me, sweetheart, I need to hold you."

Kara sank back against him.

There was silence.

"Oh, Nick, they took my pearls."

Kara turned slightly to look at Nick. There was anguish in her eyes.

Immediately he responded.

"I'll replace them."

Tears ran down Kara's cheeks.

"No, you can't—they were family heirlooms."

"Were they valuable?"

A gulp and a nod followed.

"They were given to me on my 21st birthday, expressly from my Great-grandmother's estate. I shouldn't have worn them, but I couldn't resist showing them off. I've never done that before, but I was a little nervous about going out with you and they bolstered my confidence."

Looking at Nick, she whispered.

"Ten years ago they were appraised at over a million pounds."

Nick gasped.

He was accustomed to dealing in exorbitant paper money transactions, exchanging a fortune with a signature, but Kara's confession completely threw him.

Who was she?

Nick rocked Kara back and forth in his arms, endeavoring to comfort her while confronting this new serious robbery issue. He remembered the earring, which he had absently put into his briefcase.

"I did find one earring."

"Where was it?"

"In the trunk."

"In the trunk? I was in the trunk?"

She started shaking.

"Did you find me there?"

"Hush, sweet. I'm going to tell you what I know and I will try to be as accurate as possible. The fact that you were in the trunk could possibly have saved you from a situation I hate to think might have taken place."

"For instance?" she pressed.

"They could have searched you and found the car opener and then driven off with you somewhere. There are very serious implications here since you could have been raped, killed, held hostage for ransom, so many awful possibilities."

Impulsively he hugged her closer, not noticing Kara wince from the pressure on her sore ribs.

"The Jaguar's alarm system is such that when the doors are unlocked using the "panic button" as it is called, all the doors including the trunk are opened. The police conjectured that when you were hit on the temple, that you fell slantwise, hitting and sliding off the trunk and fracturing your arm in the process. This action prompted the trunk lid to open up, instead of locking as it normally would have done. This must have been the time when you were put into the trunk. By the time the robbers reached the front of the car, the alarm device had been re-activated, automatically locking all the doors, including the trunk. With the key hidden on your person, you were in the safest place."

Softly caressing her ribcage, he continued.

"I heard the car alarm and by that time it had grown in intensity, as it does. Apparently unknown to the thieves the doors and trunk lid had opened when you fell against it, and in an effort to find the key on you, they missed finding the car doors open. They realized this when they heard the car doors automatically lock again. Upon making this discovery and kicking the car doors, the alarm was activated."

He placed a soft kiss on Kara's collarbone. She shivered.

"Who found the keys?"

Her face was flushed.

The gentle sweep of Nick's thumb along her aching ribs was bitter-sweet. Kara was powerless to stop him.

"Dr. Carmichael's assistant at the hospital returned them to me and this is probably a very appropriate time to thank you for their safekeeping."

Nuzzling the back of her neck he whispered.

"Given a choice they were kept in exactly the place I would have wanted to find them."

His lips played around Kara's ear, nibbling the lobe. When she turned her rosy face around in protest, Nick claimed her lips, savoring their fullness.

She was caught. Her traitorous emotions succumbed.

The ringing of the telephone interrupted their rising desire.

"Damn." Nick muttered under his breath as he leaned over to the bedside phone to answer it.

Breathing deeply he turned to Kara and asked if she had a sewing machine.

Looking puzzled, she shook her head.

"Would you mind if Emma brings hers? She used to be a dressmaker at one time and has ideas for making you some outfits to wear until your arm gets back to normal again."

Kara nodded her head in confirmation. Nick's comments were brief before he hung up.

"From the sound of Emma's voice, she is absolutely ecstatic about coming to live with you for a while. Hope you are prepared for some mothering."

Kara's lips curved into a smile; the whole situation was becoming ridiculous.

Nick sat on the chair beside the bed.

Without a word he handed Kara her glass of wine again and took a couple of generous swigs from his own before speaking.

"You should receive a copy of the police report in a few days and I am going to phone them as soon as we have covered this nerve wracking stuff and inform them about the pearls and anything else they need to know."

As an afterthought he added.

"By the way, Kara, I was the one who found you and this will be mentioned in the report. When I summoned the guard over to look at the gash on your face I had already covered you again, so you have nothing to worry about."

Kara flinched at this revelation and looked at Nick in alarm.

"What are you trying to tell me?"

"Your dress had been pulled over your head when I found you and when I pulled it down, the earring dropped into my hand and I automatically shoved it into my pocket. I hadn't observed precisely what jewelry you wore, although I believe I did state you were wearing some."

Kara continued looking at Nick silently.

"At first I thought you had been abducted and then when I found you in the trunk, I was so relieved to find you alive and breathing, even with the nasty blow to your head, that I automatically arranged your clothing to protect you from prying eyes. Please believe that."

Agony was mirrored in Nick's eyes, allowing Kara a brief look into his innermost feelings.

The odd look was disappearing from Kara's face and a little smile surfaced.

"Yes, I do. If I accused you of sex at 35,000 feet, I would never dream of mentioning the possibility of it happening in a car trunk."

A relieved smile appeared on Nick's face.

"You really are a trooper, Kara. You are so easy to love."

Kara's smile disappeared and a hauntingly pensive look replaced it.

Nick spoke hurriedly, taking Kara's hand into his own. She was as skittish as a filly in heat.

"Because of your distress and the injuries sustained, it was felt that giving an accurate account of the incident might not be something you could deal with at the time of admittance to the Emergency Room. For your own protection it was advised that an examination take place to determine if a rape had occurred."

Kara's eyes opened wide in shock.

"Thankfully there was nothing to worry about in that regard, but it was something that had to be established. A woman doctor and nurse made a very discreet assessment. The need for confidentiality was emphasized."

Kara sank back on the pillows and tears escaped from her eyes. Her shoulders were shaking.

"I just can't seem to stop these tears. I'm really not a crybaby, but all that's happened is so difficult to handle right now." She turned her head away from Nick.

Nick stood up, and paced around. If feelings could be graded 'A' through 'Z' Kara and he had just experienced the whole 26. He kissed Kara's cheek, tasting the salty tears and rubbed his cheek against hers, drawing away when his scratchy whiskers brought a protest.

"I'm sorry for putting you through this, Kara. I'll get your pills. This has been very tough on you and sleep is the best rejuvenator right now."

He returned their glasses to the kitchen countertop. Kara had scarcely touched her wine. The medication would help settle her down for the night,

By the end of the questioning Kara had looked tired. Nick sympathetically had traveled with Kara through her ordeal, and like her, he was emotionally drained. A good night's sleep would be beneficial to both of them.

Kara was able to perform some of the basic toiletries herself and while she was doing this, Nick phoned the Palm Springs Sheriff's

Department giving what information he could on Kara's pearls and offering a substantial reward for their return.

Kara entered the living room and Nick motioned her over.

"The police are asking for more precise details about the pearls."

She took the receiver from his hand and continued the conversation.

He and Kara would have to discuss this further tomorrow.

Apart from the pizza, they had eaten some fruit, but very little else.

"Would you like anything to eat? I can have something delivered."

She walked toward her bedroom.

"No thanks. I'm ready for bed. I'm tired."

He kissed her gently on the mouth as he tucked her into bed.

Kara closed her eyes and Nick stood for a while observing her, wishing fervently that he had the right to climb into bed with her.

Being close to her, to hold her, to let her know that he would always be there for her was all he wanted. His secret feelings would have to remain so.

The mail had slid from the blanket. Nick collected each piece.

A scented page with flowing writing in purple ink caught his attention. He saw the name 'Jon' and took the bundle into the living room and sat down on the settee. He was compelled to read it; his anxiety was too great to pass up such an opportunity.

He read:

Darling Kara:

Greetings from the Olde World.

I was going to phone you, but decided to write instead. I talked to your parents this morning. They are very proud of you, delighted that you have become so successful in your chosen field in America. In this enlightened day and age all I can say is "good for you."

I hope you know that you have always been special to me, dear child. I saw your beauty, strength of character and potential a long time ago. It took Jon a longer time to discover these attributes for himself. But discover them he has.

I am writing because I know that Jon will not. You are constantly on his lips. He misses you desperately, my dear, and it hurts me dreadfully to see him in so much agony. He is far too proud to contact you since, in essence, he left the next move up to you and I cannot believe you are so insensitive to his needs that you would choose to ignore them. Kara, he placed his life in your hands.

Please contact him. He needs to hear from you and if you could reassure him of your love, you would both make me the happiest Godmother ever,

Affectionately,

Nick sat as if frozen to the piece of furniture. How could he compete with Jon when an influential member of the British peerage was behind him, ready to back him to the hilt in his quest?

He shuddered at the thought.

Who else of influence was willing to go to bat on Jon's behalf?

Troubled, Nick put his face into his hands.

Kara had come into his life by accident, but almost immediately he had known that she was meant to fill the void in his heart. He had waited so long for her. Jon, on the other hand, had been given a lifetime to come to that decision and even with the odds in his favor he had to have someone else lobby for him. What kind of a man was Jon to recognize so late Kara's uniqueness and all that she had to offer?

Nick smacked the arm of the settee in frustration.

Given Jon's opportunities, he would have found a way to pledge Kara to a life together. He could not have accepted "no" for an answer. He would have involved her in his life so completely that she would be intricately involved, caught in a web woven by love.

A thought struck Nick and for a moment hope was kindled. Could he do it; could it happen? He quickly stood up and started pacing the room, looking in on Kara as she slept as if to corroborate his ideas.

Thoughts galloped through his brain. He would need more time to explore the possibilities. At present he was overly tired, but these new circumstances had heightened his alertness and triggered powerful thoughts, bringing for the first time a degree of promise.

Kara and he still had much to discuss and without sleep he would be useless. Was it only 24 hours since this whole unbelievable incident had been triggered?

Nick sighed. His reluctance to go away and leave Kara lay heavily on his heart. In such a short time she had become an integral part of his life—he could not envisage living without her.

Dragging the same blanket and pillow back into Kara's bedroom he decided once more to sleep on the rug beside her. If he could not comfort her, at least being beside her would comfort him.

CHAPTER TWENTY ONE

Nick awoke to the smell of coffee. He was lying uncomfortably on the floor beside Kara's bed and when he raised himself on his elbow he could see that the bed was deserted.

He looked at his Rolex—it was 7:40 a.m. What day was it? He had to look closer at the watch face to see the date. Good, Sunday, at least there was another day to resolve a few more things. Lying back with his eyes closed, getting his thoughts together, Nick felt a soft kiss on his lips. Opening his eyes immediately he found Kara in front of him on her knees. He must be dreaming. So far she had not willingly become instrumental in initiating advances.

Looking steadily into Nick's eyes Kara said, "Good morning, I wanted to surprise you with breakfast. I couldn't have you passing out on me for lack of food."

Her tone was jesting.

How he wished he could take her into his arms and convince her that the only thing he needed was her love and that she in return would offer it unconditionally to him. Coming to him in a moment of affection as Kara just did had completely confused and unnerved him. Was it a realistic possibility that she was starting to care for him?

Resisting the impulse to return her kiss he smiled answering,

"It's about time, you lazy wench, lead me to the banquet."

Standing up, he assisted Kara to her feet.

They walked into the kitchen and he was pleased with the efforts she had gone to. The table was set with blue and white placemats, blue cloth napkins and fine patterned china. A serving plate arranged with scrambled eggs, sausage and grilled mushrooms took center place with a rack of toast beside it. The remains of the orange juice had been divided between two glasses.

Pulling out a chair for Kara, Nick observed the careful way she held her left arm. She was in pain.

"This looks wonderful, but I'm concerned that you have gone to too much trouble."

She smiled forlornly.

"I guess I did get a little carried away, but I couldn't have you passing out on me, and I can only take "Battaglio's" now and then."

Nick left the table and brought back the two vials of pills and a glass of water, admonishing her to take three tablets of each.

She did not question the instructions.

They ate breakfast quietly, Nick watching Kara carefully to offer assistance should she need it.

Some color had begun returning to Kara's face and discomforted though she obviously was, her face was serenely beautiful.

He would never tire of looking at her.

Kara became aware of Nick's intense scrutiny, and before she could comment, Nick quickly stepped in to block any retorts.

"Would you like tea or coffee?"

She let the moment pass.

"I'd like to have tea out on the patio. It's usually so pleasant at this time of day."

Looking past Kara to the end of the kitchen Nick saw sliding French doors and through the sheer curtains he could just make out a fenced enclosure with bushes outlined. They stood up at the same time and Nick pressed Kara back into the chair.

"I owe you." He picked up the plates as he spoke.

When Kara objected, he laughed, saying "You should allow me to get experience in areas like this. I am the worlds' worst at domestic affairs."

"Okay, but will you pay for breakages—you are handling 18th Century Limoges china?"

Her tone was serious, but there was a glimmer in Kara's eyes as she said this.

Nick set aside the dishes. He could recognize a red flag when he saw one.

Still, he felt good.

Waiting for the electric kettle to boil, he set up a tray. A few more days of this and he would become quite familiar with this little kitchen.

Kara was finishing her orange juice when the phone rang.

Nick was stacking odds and ends in the dishwasher rather haphazardly, much to Kara's consternation, and he looked over at her.

"I'll get it," she said quietly.

It was her mother.

Kara gave a sigh of relief that she had taken the call and not Nick. Otherwise there would have been some explaining to do.

Although not intentionally listening, Nick guessed from Kara's easy conversation and the tone of her voice that she was talking to her family.

Her face was hidden and he was surprised when she came back into the kitchen to notice how glassy-eyed she looked.

"You okay?"

She nodded.

Carrying the tray out to the patio and placing it on a small white iron table between two outdoor recliners Nick helped Kara sit down comfortably. He poured a cup of tea for Kara, holding up the jug of milk. She shook her head. He placed the cup and saucer before her and poured a cup for himself.

They sat in silence for a few minutes, breathing in the fresh morning air.

Nick stood up and walked around the small perimeter, admiring the dwarf fruit trees and plants.

Turning to Kara he said abruptly.

"Did you tell your parents about this weekend and all that has happened?"

Reluctantly she answered.

"No, I just couldn't do it. It would be too much for them to comprehend at this point and I just couldn't spring that kind of news on them."

"So when will you do it?"

She looked ill-at-ease and set her cup down.

"I don't know. It will be so upsetting to tell mother about the pearls and daddy will want to come out here and look for the assailants himself, or at least get started on a search."

She smiled dejectedly.

Nick walked behind Kara's chair and ran his hands along her shoulders.

Kara's back was stiff and the muscles taut.

"Well, how are we going to resolve this?"

His hands were moving concentrically, gently easing the tense body tissue. After a while Kara's head sank back and her eyes closed, and a long sigh escaped. She moaned softly as Nick's practiced fingers worked deftly into the muscles.

"Does that help?"

"Very much. This would be a good time to go to bed and relax."

"I'll second that," Nick responded in an unsteady voice.

He felt Kara's shoulders shaking beneath his hands and looking down saw she was laughing silently.

"Just testing," he replied, pleased that she had not taken offense for once.

He continued massaging for a few more minutes. It was as therapeutic for him as it was for her.

Returning to the chaise, he refilled his teacup.

"Kara, the police and insurance people are going to need proof of the value of the jewelry. I've been thinking. I will be on business in England this week and since I feel responsible for what has taken place, I would like to meet with your parents and discuss what has happened, answering their questions, calming their fears, and bringing back copies of the documents needed. What do you think?"

He held his breath waiting for her response. It would be better to have Kara's permission, but regardless he would find a way to see them.

She sipped her tea.

"It would be putting quite a burden on you and how would you explain our connection since my parents have not even heard of you?"

A stricken look crossed Kara's face.

"If Jon happened to meet you, he may misconstrue our relationship and I would not want to cause him more pain. I already feel guilty about breaking my promise."

If it did not hurt so much Nick would have been amused. He was accustomed to avoiding and surviving female pursuit and here was the love of his life trying to widen the distance between them, as if he had a fatal disease.

"Come on, Kara. Who would believe we were having an affair, given the short time we have known each other?"

"Yes, that's true," she mused, "but what about my parents?"

"We'll decide on something, okay?"

Hesitantly she agreed and Nick was secretly relieved. This was the greatest hurdle to overcome. He would need to be prepared before meeting them. Kara's input was vital to giving credence to his visit and she could fill in the blanks before he left. Nick changed the subject. Kara had given the approval he needed.

"Will your car be safe outside the office?"

"I've already taken care of it. I left a message for the Security Guards. They are on duty nights and weekends and they are familiar with my car. Tomorrow morning I will ask Marcie to drive the Lexus here. There's a spare set of keys in my desk. It will give me an opportunity to talk to her about how to proceed during my short absence. In the meantime, I think I had better look over my wardrobe to see what I can possibly wear without looking too much like a bat in distress."

Nick threw his hands upwards—she was on her own.

"The most use I would be is if you need anything lifting or moving."

Nick placed the cups and saucers on the tray and carried it into the kitchen, feeling very pleased with himself. Kara followed him in and Nick returned and pulled the sliding door shut and locked it.

Looking at himself in the bathroom mirror, Nick grimaced at his reflection. Stubble was beginning to appear on his face and his clothing was ready to be changed.

"Kara, I took a shower earlier and it was then I realized how ill-equipped I am to do even the simplest things. I'll have to leave."

The look of dismay on her face was gratifying.

"I'll probably be gone for only an hour or so. I have to get some toilet articles," he rubbed his facial stubble, "and some clothing before these fall off."

He looked down at his rumpled shirt and slacks with something akin to disgust.

Kara's nose crinkled at his expression and he burst out laughing, throwing his arm loosely around her waist and kissing her impetuously. He adored her and the sooner she realized his intentions, the better.

Kara's smile was shy as she looked back at him through incredibly long lashes, and she backed away a little nervously.

Take it easy, Nick, he cautioned himself.

He turned to the yellow pages of the phone book and made a few notations.

"I should be back around two. Can you bear being without me for so long?"

His humor was pronounced, but he was not about to push his luck. He left before Kara could reply.

His car had been standing in the driveway for most of the day and a couple of neighbors eyed him curiously as he hurriedly climbed into it.

It had taken Nick a little longer than anticipated to work his way through the list, but he was satisfied with his outing.

He rang the doorbell, suddenly anxious and unsure of himself.

Kara answered instantly, a welcoming smile on her lovely face. She had changed into a jade green and white patterned caftan, which brought out the intensity of her eyes. Even the odd shape she presented did not deter from her attractiveness in Nick's eyes. He looked at Kara with affection and shoved a Victorian bouquet into her hand. Her lips twitched as she accepted the offering. Nick was clean shaven and his hair had been groomed. He wore a Hardy Amies white track suit, with sky blue trim, and a silk tank top in the same azure shade exposed underneath. White running shoes completed his outfit.

Kara could hardly take her eyes off him. He looked like a modern day Greek god, on an outing, having sprinted down from Mount Vesuvius. She saw him for the first time not wearing a suit. Nick was waiting to be invited inside. Kara did so by waving the flowers in her hand like a wand. She was afraid to speak; her voice would have betrayed her. Seeing Nick standing before her had awakened the realization that this man was not only incredibly handsome, but also had the ability to quicken her heartbeats and leave her breathless and defenseless. She was lightheaded and her tongue stuck to the roof of her mouth.

Taking the floral arrangement into the kitchen, she brought out a vase to fill with water. Nick set a couple of packages on the console near the door and went out to the car again. The doorbell rang and Kara answered it, finding Nick outside smiling ruefully.

"I guess I locked myself out."

Kara nodded understandingly.

"I used to do that all the time and then I hid a key outside."

As Nick brought in more packages, she went to a small Davenport desk and brought out a key.

"This is a spare, which you may use while you are here."

Pocketing the key, Nick carried a large flat box into the kitchen and placed it on the table. He leaned against the wall waiting for Kara to notice it. She looked questioningly at the package.

"Please open it."

There was an eager look on his face as he waited.

She attempted to do so using one hand without success and Nick walked over to assist, impatient for her to see the contents. He removed the lid.

Kara started withdrawing an object from the layers of tissue, which became too awkward to handle with just one hand. Nick stepped in to help. He held up a full length cape in white wool with intricate cream and beige embroidery flowing down the front and along the hemline.

Kara averted her eyes, but not before Nick had seen the interest shown.

He carefully placed it around Kara's shoulders and she ran her hand over the fabric. It felt soft and lightweight. It was elegant—just what she would have chosen had she to make the choice.

"I thought it would be easy to wear over your clothing, during the time you had to attend to business. It will also partially disguise the cast and later on the protective splint."

Kara had a closed expression on her face.

"I hope you don't think it was too presumptuous of me to do this." Nick spoke and there was a trace of anxiety in his voice.

Kara sat down on a chair.

"Nick, I'm overwhelmed and embarrassed. I didn't want you to do anything like this and go to such expense. You have put me in a difficult position."

Nick sat down on a chair across the table from Kara, looking at her cautiously.

"This was not done with the intent to embarrass you or have you indebted to me. It was actually done to help me feel that I was being of some use to you."

In a mollified tone he asked.

"Don't you like it?"

Kara looked at the gold and silver identification embossed on the box top and struggled with her reply.

"Maison Mirielle" is an exclusive boutique. I shop there occasionally. I also know how expensive their lines are."

A flush rose to Kara's face as she answered somewhat defensively.

"This wrap is gorgeous, but I cannot accept it. The only thing I can do is thank you for being so thoughtful."

Nick looked thunderstruck.

No one had ever refused his gifts before.

They looked at each other across the table, with Kara clearly defying him, waiting for an argument.

"Whatever you say," he snapped, exasperated.

He walked out of the room obviously upset and Kara shivered, despite the warmth of the cape, which she absentmindedly stroked. The luxuriously soft fabric served to remind her of her refusal and she slipped the garment off, laying it over the back of a chair. It was impeccably designed. A sigh escaped her lips.

Kara sat for a while after hearing the front door slam. She was sure her rejection had just ended their association. He was so authoritative and domineering. She could still feel the anger generated by Nick and the brusque manner in which he had surrendered against his will, demonstrating that he was not accustomed to being opposed.

She sat for a long time immersed in her thoughts.

What an unusual man he was. She smiled hesitantly. How many men could go into an exclusive women's establishment and take the time to choose an elegant piece of clothing with taste and expert judgment, and be comfortable in that milieu. He certainly had not appeared to be out of his element. Kara felt a stab of regret at her automatic refusal of the gift when Nick's intent had been to please her.

Why had she been so quick to reject his attempt to rectify the situation? She should have handled it more appropriately, but recognizing the exclusive salon's labels had shaken her. He must have spent a great deal of money on the couturier clothing.

His look of disappointment persisted in her mind.

Joan Williams

He emanated a sense of assurance and confidence and she had felt so safe with him. In every way, she conceded, he had been considerate and sensitive.

Kara allowed her mind to cover the scene when Nick had assisted her in undressing in the bathroom. She could have been embarrassed and victimized. Instead he had handled the situation beautifully. He had certainly made no demands upon her. Her heart skipped a beat at the remembrance of his hands gently and thoroughly sliding over her body. Even in pain she had been conscious of the magnetism between them.

Top marks for you, Kara. You just made an idiot of yourself.

Like a dimwit she had chosen to challenge his intent.

Kara walked into the bedroom and lay down on the bed. Her arm ached terrifically and because she had relied so heavily on Nick she had forgotten to take her medication. He had become her time-glass, her monitor, and she had given him permission to take charge.

Tears coursed through her closed eyelids. She willed herself to fall asleep and forget.

A soft voice whispering into her ear, caused her to jump in surprise.

"Please stop, darling. I behaved very badly. I was devastated at not pleasing you, when it was my sole intent. I'm not very good at this. Perhaps you can humor me for a while until I get the hang of things. Whatever you want is fine with me. The coat will be returned, if that is what you would prefer."

Kara turned over and put her arm around Nick's neck. The thought of his leaving had shocked her thoroughly. She didn't want to part from him in this way.

Nick's reaction was immediate.

He held Kara tenderly, drying her wet cheeks and smoothing her hair.

"Oh, Kara, my precious, everything will work out just as long as we are together."

She winced in his embrace and Nick stood up.

"You know, if I hadn't come back to give you these pills, I would have been on my way to a coffee shop or a cocktail lounge feeling sorry for myself, wondering how I could make things up with you. I've been in a cold sweat, scared that my clumsy attempts to please had driven

294

you away. I know you are not ready to hear it, but I love you Kara. That will not change."

He handed the pills to Kara, kissing her hand as he placed them into her palm. She put two of the pills into her mouth and he placed the glass of water to her trembling lips to drink. When she put the remaining two tablets into her mouth, she took the glass of water from Nick.

"Oh, I see," she queried, "you were going to walk out and leave me defenseless."

Tears sparkled on her eyelashes.

"No. I talked to Emma ten minutes ago, telling her that I might have to leave and asked her to check with you around seven to determine if you needed her to come over tonight. I don't plan on leaving until tomorrow, so there is no need for her to come, unless you want her here for your protection."

Kara's eyes gleamed.

"After dinner, I'd like to spend the evening alone," adding deliberately, "just with you."

She flushed at her own temerity.

Nick laughed unrestrictedly.

"You surprise me and I love it. Tell me more."

Before Kara could reply, Nick's restless mouth sought hers, sensuously entreating her participation. She was powerless to resist. Beneath the gossamer fabric her body clung to his, inviting his eager hands to explore.

Nick tore his mouth away from Kara's, gasping and breathing heavily.

Kara's capitulation had taken Nick completely by surprise. Her sexual innocence captivated and excited him beyond his wildest dreams. She had been responsive and eager, encouraging his advances in a delightfully naive manner, confirming the privileged information he had received through the hospital.

He would have to govern his emotions and curb his natural inclination to touch and caress her. He would have to keep himself in check. He was thankful that Jon at least did not appear to have a sexual hold over Kara and he could not be the one to take advantage of such an opportunity.

Kara slid out of bed and moved to the sanctuary of an easy chair in the living room, where she sat down and abstractedly began pleating with one hand the voluminous garment she was wearing. She looked pale, but composed.

"Would you like to speak with my parents about your trip to England and make arrangements to see them?"

Nick cleared his throat.

"If you don't mind, I would like to call them from London. When I'm through with the business I have to handle there, I will be able to schedule some time to visit them, if they want to see me."

Kara shrugged her shoulders. "As you wish."

Pursuing another thought Nick asked "Where would be a good place to stay locally during my visit?"

Immediately she responded.

"At the home of my parents."

Astonished he quickly countered.

"That would be too much of an imposition. I'd prefer to stay somewhere else."

Kara answered frankly, "Then without a doubt, 'The Black Bull Inn.' It is a four star hostelry and provides service par excellence. It is about fifteen miles from my parents' home."

Quietly she added.

"Jon and his friend, Leif Andersen, own it so perhaps you would prefer staying at the Queen Victoria Hotel, which is much nearer to my parents' home. The "Vic" is quite traditional and has a very good reputation. It just doesn't have the ambience of The Black Bull Inn."

Nick was surprised to learn about Jon's involvement with an hotel; he thought his total concentration was the farm.

"I'll play it by ear, Kara. Don't bother to alert anyone of my arrival, I can do it very easily from London once I know how my time is going. It's conceivable that I may not be able to make the journey north and will have to rely upon telephone calls."

He crossed his fingers. No way how.

Nick made a pot of coffee.

They were sitting close together on the settee, Kara's right arm next to Nick so that her injured limb would not be bumped while they talked. Occasionally Kara identified pictures in the photograph album lying on the table.

Nick was nervous about bringing the subject up, but he was anxious to know.

"Kara, I realize that you and Jon have known each other all your lives, but why in the very recent past has he decided that he wants you for his wife? Something which bothers me is that he has had all his life to get to know you and discover what an exceptional person you are and yet it is only within the last couple of months that he has proposed to you. He has been with you more than any man has a reasonable right to be, yet he did not commit himself. It perturbs me. Would you mind telling me how it all came about?"

Kara's intensely green eyes sought dark midnight black eyes.

"I'm not sure I can. I am still trying to work it out myself. I told Jon when he asked me to marry him that I had loved him all my life—and that is true. He has always been my protector, my friend, my idol, if you will. When my parents told me about his engagement to Angela, it hurt a little, but I thought that was because I would no longer be able to claim his time when I needed it. I was living a life I thoroughly enjoyed in California and I knew both Jon and Angela as friends and wished them well. It was only recently, when he kissed me with a depth of feeling I hadn't realized was there, that I wondered if he was the love I had waited for."

A faraway look came over Kara's face.

Nick's heart seemed to stop beating. This was not the way he wanted the conversation to go. He felt like snapping his fingers, anything to bring her back. If she thought this was awfully traumatic to relate, couldn't she imagine how devastating it was for him to hear?

As if in another world Kara softy continued.

"Roger was my first love and it was through Jon that I discovered how very inappropriate Roger was for me. Jon was outstanding."

Kara smiled in remembrance and went on to tell Nick the story.

Nick felt as if a frozen hand was squeezing his heart. Jon had behaved impeccably. He certainly had earned Kara's admiration. In addition to becoming the hounded incapacitated celebrity, Jon had also raised his stature in Kara's eyes.

That was a hard act to follow. How could he compete?

The sharp trill of the telephone startled both of them.

Nick picked up the receiver. Kara was watching his face as it started to register disbelief and astonishment.

"We'll be right there, please give me your address."

He hurriedly wrote something on a writing tablet and excitedly handed the instrument over to Kara.

"It's the Palm Springs police. They think they may have found your pearls."

Eagerly Kara responded to their questioning, describing the necklace further. She hung up, excited.

"Do you have anything to show them by way of proof?" Nick asked.

"The pearls are insured by Lloyds of London, but they also are listed on the codicil to my home-owner's policy. It won't take a minute to find—how stupid of me not to remember this."

Kara gave the policy to Nick and walked over to the album lying on the table. Turning the pages she pulled a large picture out of a page and handed it to Nick. It showed a close-up of Kara wearing the pearls.

"With a magnifying glass, perhaps the similarity can be established."

Kara's voice became eager.

"Oh, darling. Wouldn't it be wonderful if it was my necklace?"

She had carelessly thrown her right arm around Nick's waist, squeezing slightly in her excitement.

She was looking at the picture he held in his hand.

They looked at each other in amazement.

A blush started creeping over Kara's face.

Nick leaned down and rubbed his face against hers.

"With a little practice you're going to do just fine and I'm willing to tutor you every step of the way."

Kara stood still, neither avoiding his gaze nor encouraging his intimacy. She was shocked by the automatic response she had made and the feeling that it had been so right.

His endearments must be rubbing off on her.

She really would have to be more careful.

* * *

Before they set off for Palm Springs, Nick phoned Wendy, saying they would pick up the earring on their way to the police headquarters. She insisted that they come back afterwards for dinner and fill her in on the events. Kara located the large mauve velvet case in which the pearls belonged and put it, together with the insurance policy, into her handbag. She found a manila envelope in which to place the picture. While she was doing this Nick went into the kitchen, returning with the white cape. He slipped it around Kara's shoulders, kissing her protesting mouth as he did so.

"You look fantastic. It was made for you and it covers your arm very effectively."

There was a pause as Kara scrutinized the floor. Looking up her smile was warm as she softly replied, "Thank you."

If she had not been disabled Nick would have swung Kara off her feet. In the space of a few minutes she had not only let her defenses down and spoke to him with affection, but also had agreed to accept his gift.

He was Pegasus at his beloved's command. He would fly her to the moon if that was her desire.

Kara's heart lurched at the look of love radiating from Nick's attractive face and on impulse she took a step toward him offering her lips.

Tenderly enveloping her in the bulky garment, Nick solemnly claimed his reward, savoring to the fullest the soft, pliable mouth willingly submitted to him.

"Oh, Kara, I love you so much, please don't trifle with me. I couldn't bear it."

The tears in Nick's eyes brought tears to her own. She wished her heart would allow her to speak the words he wanted to hear.

Jon's pledge held her back.

Stopping in Rancho Mirage to collect the earring from Wendy, Nick informed her that he and Kara would not return for dinner. He had to leave for London the next morning and they had yet to go to the police headquarters in Palm Springs to identify what it was hoped would be Kara's pearls. Perhaps next time he was in southern California they could take her up on her invitation. Wendy kissed Kara's cheek, holding her hand until she promised to return also.

Finding the police headquarters on Tarquez Canyon Way was easily accomplished. Assisting Kara from the car, Nick noticed how pale she had become. Her green eyes were startlingly vibrant against her waxen cheeks and white bandages.

"Are you okay, sweetheart?"

She leaned against him for a moment as if to draw strength from his body. Carrying Kara's handbag and envelope in one hand, Nick took hold of her right hand comfortingly in his other.

They did not have to wait long to receive attention. Nick immediately recognized Lt. Ziegland as the officer who had come out to the hospital and was relieved to see him. They shook hands

He led them through a maze of corridors, stopping at a small room.

He motioned them to take a seat.

Riffling through the papers on the desk, he brought out a copy of the police report and proceeded asking more questions about the pearl necklace. Nick produced the photograph from the envelope and Kara took the insurance policy from her handbag. Nick also handed over the pearl earring, which they had just collected from Wendy.

"Please excuse me—I need to get something." Picking up the papers he had brought into the room, the officer left the two of them alone for several minutes. When he returned he had what looked like a bank security box in his hand. Laying all the items on the desk, he opened the metal box, carefully extracting a long string of pearls.

Nick watched Kara's face.

She was holding her breath and her face was taut.

Her face lit up. Flashing a dazzling smile first at Nick and then at Lt. Ziegland, Kara expectantly held out her hand toward the rope of pearls, but retracted it when she realized it had not been officially identified as her property.

"They look like mine. On the clasp the Olavssen crest should be embossed."

In dismay she looked at Nick.

"How silly of me, I didn't even think of that when I gave the description."

Taking a magnifying glass Jim Zeigland looked at the clasp on the pearls, offering both to Kara after doing so.

For the first time, he allowed a smile to interface with the business at hand.

Nick's grin reflected his relief at establishing claim to the pearls and he concentrated on watching Kara's eager face. Unable to manipulate both the pearls and the glass at the same time, Nick took the pearls, turning the clasp toward Kara as she viewed it through the glass.

Wordlessly she handed the magnifying glass to Nick, with a big smile on her face. Thank Heaven for that.

"This is obviously an incredibly unexpected event," Nick stated, "How on earth was this valuable piece of jewelry found in such a remarkably short space of time?"

Nick looked at Lt. Zeigland as he carefully laid the pearls and magnifying glass on the desk.

A huge grin covered the somewhat craggy features of Lt. Ziegland as he related the details.

"Rancho Mirage is an affluent, fairly quiet, community with citizens who monitor their own districts. Guards are on patrol in security gated areas and this is particularly necessary when special events take place. Mrs. Rutherford holds these functions quite frequently where important wealthy people attend and security guards are especially conscious of the lure of the criminal element."

Kara slipped her hand into Nick's and he gently squeezed it.

"Such was the case Friday evening. As it happened, the crime was not witnessed first-hand, but a guard patrolling the inside perimeter saw two men in the process of climbing over a wall. He tried to apprehend them, but they had used a rope to gain access and pulled it back to the other side in their escape. Using his walkie-talkie the guard contacted 911. At the same time he heard a car start and saw the lights turn on, going south on Thunderbird Terrace. With this information relayed to police precincts in the Palm Springs, Indio and Indian Wells districts and alerts going out to points north, a large networking system was mobilized."

Jim Zeigland shifted positions on the chair, leaning over to refer to a form laid in front of him.

"I'd like to say that the arrest was made shortly after that, but unfortunately, it didn't work out that way. We don't even know if the vehicle was identified at that particular time, or if the search was called off. What we do know is that for some minor law infraction, a 1978 Ford Ranger truck was pulled over by a motor cycle patrol officer just before reaching Calexico on the Mexican border. The inspecting officer saw part of a firearm protruding from under the seat. He called in a squad car. The team searched the suspect's vehicle, coming up with the pearls and a few other items of questionable ownership. This occurred Sunday morning, when according to this report, the suspects were returning to Mexicali where they lived. They had been entering the U.S. illegally for some time apparently and had become a little overconfident and careless, since their activities and travel had previously been restricted to night movement."

He examined the necklace briefly before transferring it into Kara's waiting hand.

"It's funny, but when they were questioned about the stolen articles they were carrying, they casually said the pearl necklace was intended for the girlfriend of one of them. Can you imagine that happening? They had absolutely no concept as to the real value of this item. The frightening part is that, give-or-take another hour, those pearls would have been in Mexico and you could have kissed them goodbye—forever."

Kara's hand trembled and Nick took the pearls from her as she reached into her purse for the velvet jewel box. Nick settled the necklace on the padded satin interior, together with the pearl earring picked up at Wendy's home earlier. He handed the box back to Kara, who returned it to her purse. She slipped her hand back into Nick's and he held it between both of his.

Kara signed the papers acknowledging receipt of the jewelry and they were free to leave.

On the way out, as Kara walked ahead of him, Nick quietly informed Lt. Zeigland that the reward money he had offered to pay for the return of the necklace be deposited to a worthy law enforcement cause. Nick asked that the chief make the decision and send details to his office so that a check could be mailed to them.

Kara turned and thanked the lieutenant and asked if it would be appropriate to send a check to the Widows and Orphans fund. He quickly looked at Nick who nodded his head in agreement with Kara's choice. Lt. Zeigland responded that an already magnanimous offer had just been made to it. Kara looked at Nick intently. Smiling at Lt. Zeigland she turned on her heel and started walking toward the exit.

A short time later Kara and Nick arrived back at the car. Nick firmly carrying the handbag as well as the picture.

"That was a very generous gesture, but there was no need to do that, Nick. I'm to blame and I'd like to repay you."

Settling the handbag and picture on the passenger side seat, Nick reached for Kara.

"Good, it's about time you paid your dues. Do you remember Shylock in "The Merchant of Venice?"

A half-smile came to Kara's lips and she nodded affirmatively.

"What I need is your heart, but it must be freely given. It is the only condition under which I can accept it and the only way you can pay any debt you feel I am owed."

He lightly brushed his lips against hers.

Kara did not reply.

Nick sighed and with a resigned look on his face, assisted Kara into the car.

It was just after seven and they had missed a meal.

"What do you want to do about dinner? Do you have any restaurant in mind?"

The look of unease on Kara's face confirmed his impression that the head bandage and cast would be a deterrent.

"Can we pick up something to eat on the way home?" she said.

It sounded so cozy after the disinterest shown to his heartfelt plea that Nick looked at Kara to hear the correction she invariably interposed when she became aware of a personal slip-of-the-tongue. If she had noticed, she did not comment.

He had seldom in his life felt so inadequate, impatient and frustrated. If she behaved this way with Jon, he could understand his lack of progress.

That was it!

Brightening at the idea, Nick thought he had hit upon the solution. Kara and Jon had been friends for so long and knew each other so well that despite Jon's attempts, she did not appear to have fallen under his spell.

Intuitively Nick was sure Kara could not love Jon. How could she? She did not demonstrate the recognizable traits. She was waiting for the three months to end so that she could come to a decision. If she loved him, she could not wait that long. She would already know.

Nick had deduced that Kara was not in touch personally with Jon. She did not phone or write to him. He had been the hunter, but he had failed to ensnare his object of pursuit. An important point was that Kara had not come to a decision regarding her feelings for Jon. No, she definitely was not in love with Jon. She just had not recognized or acknowledged the fact.

Nick smiled to himself, satisfied. She did not know it yet, but she had just been captured by a game hunter par excellence.

By the time they turned off at University Avenue, it was after eight o' clock and they were both hungry. Stopping at "The Great Wall" restaurant they picked up a variety of tantalizing dishes from the menu and then made haste back to the townhouse. While carrying the packages into the kitchen, he noticed how carefully Kara draped the cape over a hanger in the closet. He watched quietly in case she needed assistance. She was becoming more adept at doing things for herself. When she became conscious of Nick watching her, she smiled and mouthed a silent "Thank you," smoothing the length of the fabric to indicate her approval. The sweep of her hand was sensuous and Nick felt a thrill run through his body. She could turn him on so very easily. In fact under different circumstances, had she not been incapacitated, he would have willingly foregone the Chinese food for sustenance of another, more elusive, kind.

There were a couple of messages on Kara's answering machine. One was from Nick's secretary, Claudia, confirming his reservation on a United Airlines flight from LAX, connecting with the Concorde in New York, which would get him into London early Monday evening. Kara raised her eyebrows listening to the message. The second message was from Marcie inviting Kara out to her parent's home in Santa Barbara the next weekend.

They both set the table with the essential eating implements and Kara looked relaxed and happy. *Of course she had every right to be,* Nick reflected. *Her family's heirlooms had been restored to her unscathed. Perhaps that was why she looked so serene. If that were the case it had little to do with his involvement in her life.*

His thoughts were interrupted by Kara's teasing.

"So, you always book seat 64.A, except when you decide to take the Concorde? Sniffs of a double standard here, Mr. Prendergast. Perhaps you were just mixing with the common crowd for laughs."

Nick surveyed Kara watchfully. She was not aware that he had turned his itinerary upside down in order to remain with her a little longer and she did not need to know.

"I thought I would see how the other half lived. I'm doing some research on the caliber of the stewardesses, whether they are chosen for their efficiency or their looks."

He had a smile on his face as he made the remark, but Kara didn't seem to find it as amusing as he did.

The subject was changed.

"Kara, don't you think I ought to return your jewelry to your parents, so that they can have copies made for you to wear and keep the originals in a safe place?"

After a slight pause Kara nodded her head in agreement.

"You are right. It should have been done years ago. I intended having it done, but as a pampered only child I gave little thought to such mundane items as protecting irreplaceable family treasures." A pensive look passed over Kara's face. "I must have been a royal pain."

They smiled at each other, Nick did not believe a word of it; she was much too natural and normal.

"You could do another favor at the same time, if you don't mind," she said. "I have other jewelry which is of extremely sentimental value, which I would love to be able to wear again. I'd appreciate it if you could bring it back with you."

Nick's face set into a non-committal expression.

"Returning your pearls to your family is something which I feel is my duty, but I'm not sure that should anything happen to sentimental treasures how answerable I will be. They are the type of things which cannot be replaced."

Kara's eyelashes fluttered.

"The pieces I have in mind were given to me by my parents and grandparents as personal gifts at various times. In comparison to the pearls, they are insignificant, but to me personally they mean a great deal."

Nick released his breath slowly.

"Oh, I thought you meant things Jon had given you."

An amused expression came over Kara's face.

"Apart from the odd impractical birthday or Christmas gifts we gave each other, Jon and I did not usually exchange presents. He did give me a beautiful cameo for my 21st birthday—but I lost it. I never did have the courage to tell him."

Nick immediately responded that it would be no trouble bringing back whatever Kara needed.

As they were cleaning up, Nick grinned wryly. If Franc could see him participating in the household tasks that needed to be done, he would realize how hopelessly involved with Kara he had become.

Kara interrupted his thoughts.

"There's enough left for a party tomorrow." Kara looked crookedly at Nick. "Sure you don't want to stay?"

A somber look came over Nick's attractive features.

"I won't be back for at least five weeks and I honestly wish I didn't have to leave. Promise me you won't over-tax yourself during that time and that you will be very careful in everything you do."

Kara stopped her activities and looked at Nick earnestly.

"You really do care, don't you?"

Kara bit her lower lip.

"I have a confession to make, Nick. Ever since I met you, I have experienced the strangest feeling which has returned a couple of times. It is as if I have known you before and there is a nagging sense of urgency in bringing those memories back so that the puzzle fits together. It scares me. I don't want to change the way things are with us right now. It feels so safe."

Nick walked across the room and folded Kara into his arms.

"Is being safe of prime importance to you? Almost from the moment I first saw you, I knew without a shadow of a doubt that in you I had found my destiny and the feeling has intensified to the point where I can never voluntarily let you go. You will have to kick me out of your life, beloved, if you want to get rid of me. I do not have the strength or the inclination."

Softly caressing Kara's shoulder, as he gently laid soft kisses around her face, he asked.

"Why don't you want things to change? I want things to change very much. I want you to care for me as much as I care for you. I would even be satisfied if you loved me half as much as I love you."

Kara's lips parted at the tender declaration and without a moment's hesitation she sought Nick's compliant mouth. She kept taking him by surprise. He wanted all of her, but she had to make that conscious decision in a less emotional situation. It was an irrevocable contract he had in mind and despite the immediate temptation, he would bide his time until she was ready to make the long term permanent commitment.

Reluctantly Nick drew away from Kara.

"I'll need to leave very soon. There's some business I must attend to at the office before returning to my house and packing for the trip. The United flight leaves Los Angeles at 10:00 a.m. and my head will be in my hands if I miss it."

Nick packed most of the items he had accumulated in the past few days, leaving his toothbrush and shaving equipment in the guest bathroom, with a hand lettered sign: "Remove at risk. Owner temporarily out of the country, and hopefully only temporarily out of his mind."

Nick stood by the front door, with his briefcase and a hastily packed piece of luggage borrowed from Kara on the floor beside him.

"I'll give you a call from New York to make sure you are all right and that Emma has arrived."

"Really, Nick, there's no need. I'll be fine."

Kara looked at Nick and shook her head disapprovingly, but he saw tenderness in her expressive eyes that brought a glow to his own. His chest tightened as he fought against sweeping her into his arms, knowing he would not have the strength to let her go.

"I'll miss you, Nick. Have a safe trip and try to downplay my accident as much as possible. It will be quite a shock to my parents, but I know they will be relieved to have the pearls returned."

She lowered her gaze.

"Say 'hello' from me if you see Jon."

That reminder was like a douse of cold water.

"After leaving England, my time is scheduled for France and Japan. I'd like to stay in touch with you by phone from time to time. Okay?"

"That would be nice."

He turned up her face and kissed her lips gently.

"I can't get back soon enough. Think of me sometimes, Kara."

Her voice was husky, as she returned his kiss with seductively soft lips.

"Take care and thank you for all that you have done for me."

That had to be good enough for now.

Nick was thoughtful as he turned on the ignition.

Her final words almost sounded as if she were closing a book at the last chapter.

CHAPTER TWENTY TWO

The Concorde was like a stripped down racing bicycle, trim, lean, and utilitarian. Passengers were not paying for luxury and comfort, but for the ability to traverse the world at supersonic speed and save valuable time. This was always a consideration—time was money.

Nick conceded that by way of compensation for the austere interior, the meal served was of gourmet quality with caviar and lobster to entice the appetite. The three stewardesses attending to the needs of the passengers appeared to be more attractive and attentive than those on regular airline flights. They all expressed their eagerness in carrying out the passengers' wishes.

Nick's seat companion was a businessman with thick rimmed glasses, who briefly shook hands and immediately concentrated on working through a large dossier as soon as take-off had been achieved.

It took a huge effort on Nick's part to concentrate on what lay ahead in the next week. Repeatedly his mind relived the events since he and Kara met. Every minute he was leaving her farther and farther behind.

His briefcase was by his side as a reminder of the work that he should be immersed in, but he was reluctant to put Kara's face out of his mind.

He lay back in his chair, idly watching the man in the next seat.

Before the meal had been served Norman, beside him, ordered a bottle of the Russian vodka Stolichnaya and without protest a sealed bottle and a glass were immediately placed before him.

Nick watched in fascination as the contents slowly, but consistently, diminished. The man had an irritating habit of nervously running pudgy nail-bitten fingers through his thinning brown hair. What was particularly interesting to Nick was observing that the pages of the thick bound manual turned over with the same regularity. Curiosity won. Nick looked at his watch and set a couple of buttons and timed the frequency each page was turned. The man must be a speed reader. He was about to comment on his appraisal when without warning the man's head fell backwards and the spectacles tilted forward, slipping to the end of his nose.

Nick watched disquieted.

Had the fellow suffered a heart attack?

He waved a passing stewardess over.

"Is this man all right? He appeared to pass out."

At this point his services were not required.

Stepping closer the stewardess looked intently at the passenger, passing a wet finger beneath his nose. She cautiously slipped off the glasses, folded them and put them into the man's shirt pocket.

"It's okay. He travels this route quite often, usually passing out at about this time."

She held up the half empty bottle to indicate what time that was.

Looking at the man beside him, Nick pursed his mouth in reproach.

The stewardess interrupted Nick's thoughts.

"He's terrified of flying."

Nick commented dryly, "It must be very important for him to do so then."

"Yes," was the answer, "He has to regularly report to his father."

Nick looked puzzled, as if he had missed half the sentence, asking, "Do you know why?"

"His father owns the largest fleet of pleasure cruisers which operate around the Greek islands. He too is terrified of flying and refuses to leave his homeland. His son has no alternative but to visit him. This is the fastest way to get there."

Shrugging her shoulders after this remark, the stewardess put the empty glass on a tray with the depleted bottle of vodka and moved away.

Nick had traveled so frequently by plane that he had long forgotten any fears he might have started out with. A pang of pity for the scared man beside him dissipated when the man started snoring loudly. How could he attempt to sleep with that racket in his ears?

Nick stood up, stepping around the inert sleeper impatiently, heading toward the toilet area.

An eager eyed attendant followed him.

"Anything I can do, sir? Is there anything you want?"

Nick suddenly felt very drained and tired.

"Not a thing, thank you."

He wanted Kara. The phenomenal success of his business ventures had provided wealth and influence beyond his expectations. Success and recognition in the medical field had brought fame and dominance at the highest plateau attainable. Winning Kara, it appeared, was beyond his control and capability. She had to come to him in her own time.

Nick walked back to his seat with a glass of apple juice. He pulled out his schedule, looking it over to plan the best use of his time.

The snoring, interspersed with grunts, was very aggravating although Nick did feel a little more sympathetic to the poor fellow beside him after hearing about his problem. Taking earplugs out of his briefcase and inserting them, Nick tried to concentrate on his work schedule.

He was not in the mood and his thoughts wandered.

Nick wanted to meet Kara's parents, to explain about Kara's traumatic incident and the stolen pearls and their recovery, with the need for duplication. To placate Kara, Nick had finally agreed to say that they had met through his cousin, Wendy, but that they had known each other socially before this.

Most of all he wanted to meet Jon. To size him up without Jon knowing who he was.

★ ★ ★

The seminar held in London, which Nick was late in joining, was in full swing at the Claridge Hotel on Brook Street. It was a familiar scene to Nick. It ended late Wednesday afternoon, earlier than most of the seminars he held ended, but this was an abbreviated special symposium catering to physicians and specialists who had little time to waste. It was all serious business held for a much smaller group. To appease most of the attendees for not being present for the entire duration, Nick made arrangements for small groups to meet with him for breakfast and dinner, giving them all an opportunity to 'pick his brains' on a more personal level.

By the time Wednesday evening arrived and the seminar was over, Nick was exhausted.

Franc was still annoyed with Nick, feeling that he had behaved in a nonchalant manner, sloughing his responsibility off onto him. Franc could fill in for Nick at a pinch, he was familiar with Nick's program and routine, but it was not his area of specialization or responsibility. Nick was the one they all came to hear, in fact had paid top dollars for that privilege. Nick had the knowledge, the expertise, and the charisma. He carried the seminars almost single handedly. Franc, even though he was an eminent medical doctor in his own right, had chosen to become administrator, finance director and on infrequent occasions, such as this current symposium, fill in as back-up man. He had become much more interested in the joint ventures that the two of them had entered into. This touring lecture circuit was just one phase of their many enterprises.

Nick had intended traveling to northern England Thursday morning, as soon after the seminar as possible, having made arrangements to visit Kara's parents on the Friday. It would mean he had five free days, a luxury that seldom occurred. Franc was upset. Nick was usually so reliable and punctual. It still puzzled him regarding the circumstances for the delay. What was particularly aggravating was that Nick had offered no legitimate or acceptable explanation.

Having dinner together much later that night after the seminar ended, Franc put forward a suggestion.

"Since we are presenting the next seminar at Le Crillon on Tuesday why don't you travel back with me to the farm until then? The rest will be good for you and we do have much to discuss. Michelle and Fiona will be delighted to have your company."

Nick's face took on an obstinate expression that Franc recognized.

"Sorry, Franc, I've made other arrangements, but I will meet you in Paris."

Excusing himself, Nick left the table to phone The Black Bull Inn. He made reservations with arrival the next evening.

Franc looked at Nick speculatively when he returned. They had known each other a long time and Nick had something on his mind, which he was not willing to disclose. Perhaps if he had spent the weekend at his home, he would have relaxed sufficiently to confide in him.

Well, "sera, sera," all in good time.

They finished their meal and continued to discuss their mutual business affairs for the remainder of the evening.

They were nursing snifters of brandies in Nick's suite, when Franc questioned his friend.

"I meant to ask earlier, but you know how debilitating these seminars are, I forgot. How is Kara after the accident? You know the woman you took to Wendy's."

The unexpected inquiry shook Nick, even though he should have anticipated it.

Because so many women had passed through Nick's life in the last seven years, Franc had assumed that Kara was just another passing face. The unfortunate accident was sufficient reason for Franc to remember her and enquire about her welfare.

Swishing the liquid around in his glass, Nick responded.

"I'm traveling north tomorrow to meet her parents and return some valuable jewelry. I'll probably be seeing her fiancé at the same time."

There was a hurt twist to Nick's mouth.

Franc was observing him quietly.

"Answering your question, Kara's arm should be fine in several weeks and the stitches close to her hairline won't even be visible in a couple of months. Don Carmichael did his work well."

Abruptly Nick set down his glass.

"I'm ready to turn in. Will you meet me at Charles de Gaulle Airport as usual?"

Franc stood up also.

"Why don't you use the Bentley for your trip north? I can take a taxi to Gatwick and Michele will be picking me up at de Gaulle. Next week we'll meet you there."

Nick hesitated.

Their company-owned Bentley was a prestigious automobile, quite staid in its image and not exactly his choice for tooling around country lanes, but its luxurious appointments certainly would make the journey north more comfortable. If he did not take it, it would be left at the airport until a staff member went out to pick it up.

"Thanks. I'll do that."

✴ ✴ ✴

CHAPTER TWENTY THREE

It was a relaxing trip. So infrequently was time available to dawdle that by the time he reached Stratford-on-Avon, Nick was feeling in a holiday mood. He was ready for a leisurely breakfast at the charming Avonlea Hotel situated on the banks of the River Avon. On impulse he picked up a postcard of the historic hotel, in which the restaurant was located, from the display stand by the cash register. He wrote a few words and addressed it to Kara.

"Do you need stamps? I can let you have a few," the cashier asked Nick helpfully.

He purchased half a dozen.

"We have a mail pickup every afternoon if you would you like to leave it."

Nick handed over the postcard, smiling his thanks.

Starting the pattern for keeping in touch with Kara through postcards was a practical approach, Nick decided. He did not need reminders of Kara, she was in his thoughts constantly, but by using reverse psychology perhaps the postcards would serve as a reminder of him to her.

Feeling fortified by the substantial English breakfast termed 'mixed grill' Nick was ready to resume the journey northward, but first decided to take a picture of the Holy Trinity Church where the Bard, William Shakespeare was buried. Noticing it on the way in on Southern Lane he asked about it at the restaurant. He wished he had more time to delve into the history of this magnificent historical city. Perhaps sometime with Kara. It was a happy thought.

Nick continued driving at a leisurely pace with the City of York being his next stop. The countryside was lushly green and when he met up with the A.1 motorway at mid-morning it could by no stretch of the imagination be compared to the crowded, often bottlenecked freeways in southern California.

Removing his tie and loosening the top buttons on his shirt, Nick took a deep breath. He was in no hurry and set the overdrive at 45 kilometers. The haze of the bigger cities was being left behind. Farm areas, with their rolled up bales of hay, variegated barns, and flocks of meandering sheep provided serene, picturesque vignettes interspersed with passing hamlets and church spires. The sun's rays, occasionally penetrating the clouds, dramatically illuminated an area attracting the eye to its beauty.

He ticked off the cities as he passed: Cambridge, Nottingham, Sheffield, and Doncaster. Then he began seeing road signs which alerted that the City of York would be reached soon.

After the unaccustomed large breakfast Nick was in no rush for lunch. He parked the Bentley Shadow at the "Guy Fawkes' Hotel." Locking his passport into the glove compartment and slipping into his jacket, he went into the hotel's bar for a drink. The Lounge in the hotel was heavily paneled in dark oak, with a profusely carved bar section. The ceiling had overhead beams. Nick seated himself on a stool at the bar, noticing that most people were eating meals at small, round marble pub tables.

A red faced, tweedy-jacketed man was sitting further along the bar and he raised his mug of beer when Nick looked his way. Nick nodded and turned back to the bartender and ordered a pale ale. Studiously he looked around the walls, noting the proliferation of scenes attributed to the Guy Fawkes "Gunpowder Plot" period. Several sketches depicted various scenes showing Guy Fawkes, with his treacherous traitor band, attempting to blow up the Houses of Parliament in London on its first day in session. With King Charles in it. Guy de Maupassant, known as Guy Fawkes was born in York in the year 1570 and thus the pub featured the ancient tale describing his infamous activities.

Noting Nick's interest, the ruddy-faced fellow pushed his beer over and moved to the stool beside Nick.

"D'ya naw much about the legend o' Guy Fawkes?"

"Some." Nick responded. He pointed to the poem framed on the wall:

> Remember, remember, the 5th of November
> The Gunpowder Treason and plot;
> I see of no reason why Gunpowder Treason

Should ever be forgot.
Guy Fawkes, Guy Fawkes, 'Twas his intent.
To blow up the King and the Parliament.
Three score barrels of powder below.
Poor old England to overthrow.

For the next fifteen minutes Nick had to listen attentively to the narrative, which the self-appointed historian relayed in the dialect of the area. He stopped only to "Whet his whistle" as he said in accepting the ale ordered for him by Nick.

"So," said the narrator, "that's why we have a holiday every Fifth of November. That's when fireworks are set off and bonfires lit to burn likenesses of "the guy" to celebrate."

Having finished the beer and the tale, Nick's companion wiped the back of his hand across his mouth, nodded cursorily and departed.

Nick smiled as the bartender came over to pick up the empty glasses.

"Does this happen often?"

"Yes, sir, every day," was the reply. "But he does tell a good tale and it's worth the price of a beer, don't you think?"

Nick nodded, deposited a tip and returned to the car to retrieve his camera from the glove compartment.

Foregoing lunch meant he had more time to roam through this fascinating medieval city, with its ancient and glorious Minster and battlements. Kara had mentioned it as being one of her favorite places and Nick headed for a store that sold postcards. It was the usual touristy shop with "Greetings from York" and pictures of the Minster on almost everything it sold. He picked up an additional film for his camera and a couple of postcards. He saw a pack of playing cards, each with a different scene of York and its surrounds, which he included with his purchases. As he was waiting to be served he quickly jotted a few sentences onto a postcard, added Kara's mailing address and located a postage stamp. Watching him doing this, the sales clerk eyed him suspiciously. Once he had paid for his purchases, he was pleasantly told that there was a mailbox at the end of the street.

Looking along the cross street beside the mailbox Nick saw the twin peaks of the magnificent edifice rising into the sky. It was a breathtaking scene. He quickly focused his camera for a picture of the imposing cathedral.

For the next hour Nick strolled around the top of the city walls, parts of which dated back to Roman times, taking pictures of the changing views of the architectural details and ruins, the remains of some dating back two-thousand years. He climbed to the top of Clifford's Tower, taking pictures from the steep stairway of the amazing views of York. He loved it here. He could almost feel the history flowing through his veins. No wonder Kara found it so interesting.

Dodging the pedestrians and traffic meandering through narrow Whip-ma-Whop-ma Gate, he found his way via The Shambles to the entrance of the great cathedral.

Once inside the majestic structure, he tagged onto a guided tour for a short time and browsed around with the printed tour sheet in hand. The splendid stained-glass windows and impressive tombs, some dating back to the fourteenth and fifteenth centuries, were tributes to the artisans of that age. By the time he had decided that he could spend no more time there, he had developed a crick in his neck from the constant upward gazing.

A bulletin he had picked up in the gift shop, advertising an outstanding Viking exhibition, appealed to Nick's sense of tradition. It was a short walk away, he could fit it in. He stood in line at the Jorvik Viking Centre, paying three-pounds fifty for admittance. Apart from the postcard to Kara telling her where he was going, it was the best money he had spent all day. He came out of the display exhilarated and anxious to talk to Kara about it. Had she seen it? He carefully pocketed the booklet and receipt to show her. The reconstruction of York, which was called Jorvik by the Viking conquerors in AD 975, was started when ruins of the old city were discovered in the early 1970's. A vast number of original one-thousand year relics were incorporated into the 'new Jorvik museum.'

In walking back to his car Nick read the plaque on the St. Michel-le-Belfry Church indicating that Guy Fawkes had been baptized in that church on April 16, 1570, and recalled the accuracy of the beer drinking storyteller. For the umpteenth time Nick wished that he and Kara were sightseeing together and a wave of desolation rolled over him. He would store all these observations and keep them fresh to share with Kara.

The remainder of the journey to Darlington passed quickly. He had to stop and ask for directions to The Black Bull Inn, as it was somewhat off the beaten track. He arrived there just as dusk was starting to fall. The soft evening twilight transformed the old brick building, softening the steeply pitched roofline with its oddly assorted chimneys. Mullioned-windowpanes picked up the glow from the tall lamps starting to illuminate the parking lot and surrounding grounds and a welcoming glow issued from the interior.

Nick stepped out of the car and stretched, looking at the structure for a few minutes. It certainly was an interesting looking place, even in the uncertain light. A veritable piece of history. Kara had mentioned it was a few centuries old. He smiled to himself—almost brand new compared to some of the ancient cities he had just passed through.

So this was part of Kara and Jon's life.

It was not going to be easy, but he had to prepare himself and face the possible implications. He took the rolled up tie from his jacket pocket and put it around his neck, fastening it dexterously. Slipping on the jacket Nick retrieved his Rolleiflex camera, binoculars and passport from the glove compartment. Claiming his briefcase and carry-on luggage from the trunk Nick decided to leave his suitcase there. He would have it brought in later. The automatic doors locked as he walked away.

Once inside the Inn he made his way to the foyer, which was almost deserted. A pleasant-looking receptionist in a burgundy suit with a white bow-tied blouse welcomed him.

"Good evening, sir. Do you have a reservation?"

"Yes, for four nights. The name is Prendergast."

She tapped a few keys on the computer and glanced at Nick curiously. She took a set of keys from a panel underneath the counter on her side.

"Your suite is at the far side of the building. May we park your vehicle close to it, whilst the porter takes your luggage?"

Nick nodded in agreement.

She pressed a buzzer and almost immediately a man in a plum colored uniform entered the foyer, followed by a younger man in a white shirt and plum colored trousers.

Nick produced his car keys and held them out. The younger man took them and Nick half-smiled. He had expected the older man to drive his car. He would have preferred it that way.

"I would like to have the garment bag brought in, which is on the backseat as well as the suitcase in the trunk."

He picked up his briefcase and purposely reached for the carry-on bag. He would not allow them out of his sight.

With keys in hand, the receptionist gestured Nick toward the staircase.

"This hotel is on the National Trust Register. Because of this, modern conveniences such as lifts are not allowed to be installed. Fortunately your accommodation is on the first floor, so there's not too many stairs to climb."

She smiled apologetically.

Nick smiled in return but his amusement was in translating the British custom of numbering their floor levels differently to those of other countries in which he traveled.

The stairs led to several hallways, each pointing in different directions. Nick and the receptionist turned to the left.

The oak paneling below the wainscot level had taken on a mellowed gracious look. The white walls above it and the deep burgundy carpeting were most harmonious, giving an aura of quiet dignity. Old brass candelabras with white silk shades covering light bulbs were interspersed along the corridor, providing subdued lighting. Small tables, bearing dainty vases of fresh flowers, led the eyes along the hallway. It was charmingly simple.

Passing two uniformed waitresses in the process of taking covered dishes from a dumb-waiter and placing them on a serving trolley, Nick was reminded that he had missed lunch. Pangs of hunger assailed him as the tantalizing aroma reached his nostrils.

"Do I need to make a reservation for dinner?"

"Not tonight, sir. Thursdays are fairly quiet, unless we have some special event taking place. You may also have dinner sent up, if you wish."

By this time they had reached the end of a corridor with a large stained-glass window highlighted from behind by strategically placed outdoor lamps. It depicted a man, obviously of a religious order, following two altar boys bearing what looked like a miniature cathedral between them on a long tasseled salver.

"That looks interesting," Nick said. "Is there a story behind it?"

"I'm sure there is, sir, there is about most things here. You might like to ask Mr. Williams. He knows everything about the Inn."

Nick felt his heart thump. He was on Jon's territory and the fact was a little unsettling.

"Is he here at present?" Nick queried as the door was being opened.

She looked at her watch.

"Probably not yet. He is out most days, coming to the Inn around dinner time. Shall I leave a message for him, sir?"

"Not necessary, thank you."

She motioned her hand in obeisance and Nick walked before her into the lighted chambers.

Nick's suitcase had already been placed inside the door with his car keys on top. He picked up the keys and slipped them into his pocket and laid the carry-on bag on a settee. He placed the camera and binoculars on top of a table beside the settee. The sitting room was tastefully decorated with the burgundy and white theme still evident. An entertainment center, complete with a television set, VCR stereo equipment stood encased in a French armoire, the doors of which stood ajar.

The receptionist stood in the doorway observing Nick.

"We hope you will find everything satisfactory. Please call our service desk if anything further can be done to make your visit comfortable."

She smiled and quietly closed the door, leaving Nick alone to investigate his quarters further.

The suite he had been shown into was almost baronial in size. Picking up the suitcase Nick walked into a huge bedroom with a four-poster bed, swathed with damask draperies, which together with a massive wardrobe dominated the room. The wardrobe door was open and his garment bag was hanging on the metal rod. He placed the suitcase on a luggage stand and walked over to the floor length, heavy white lace curtains that ran across the room. Nick pulled the cord.

His lips pursed in a soundless whistle as the curtains ran silently across a track in the ceiling.

It was an area that could be used either as a workplace or an eating area. The room, turret shaped, had a table and four chairs arranged in front of six stained-glass windows. Prominently depicted on each window was a shield, bearing an exquisitely crafted family crest placed in its center. In the corner panes of each window different symbols were placed, but the diffused light prevented Nick from identifying them.

He quickly unpacked, putting his camera, binoculars, small jewelry case with the one earring and his passport into the top dresser drawer. He methodically arranged his clothing throughout the remaining drawers. He reminded himself that he needed to add the lone pearl earring to the velvet case containing the rest of the valuable set of pearls, which were locked in the built-in safe in the Bentley's trunk. It seemed that whenever he had access to either the earring or the rest of the pearls, one of the two items was not conveniently within easy reach.

The bed, double-size, was certainly an antique, Nick decided, running his hands lightly over the intricate smooth carvings. Queen and king-sized beds were modern inventions to accommodate the new heights and breadths to which modern man had reproduced. A burgundy and white striped duvet covered the goose down comforter and Nick anticipated a comfortable night's sleep. Upon further inspection Nick found a large tiled bathroom, which included a pedestal bath and hand held shower equipment. Functional, not lavish. The burgundy and white striped shower curtain was drawn back with a gold cord. In an alcove, a marble topped chest displayed an electric hot water pot, with packets of coffee, teabags, sugar and creamer and two cups. Nick smiled—Kara you should be here with me. Upon reflection, he decided, that probably would not be a good idea. In Jon's domain he definitely could be at a disadvantage.

Nick glanced at his watch. It was almost 7:30 p.m. No wonder his stomach was growling. Near the entrance was an easy chair and small round table, upon which lay the key to the suite. Picking it up, he slipped it onto the key chain with his car keys and dropped them into his jacket pocket. He looked around the sitting room before closing the door after himself, testing to ensure that it was locked.

Retracing his steps to the foyer, down the wide unevenly worn staircase, he saw the receptionist talking to the porter. She smiled.

"In which direction is the dining room?"

"Just follow me. I'll take you there."

The porter led the way.

This place seemed bigger than it looked from the outside. Conversationally the porter explained.

"There are three dining rooms, not counting the cars, but the one we are going to is usually used during the week when business is not as hectic as the weekends."

Nick did not quite understand the bit about the cars and thought the man's dialect must be the reason.

Double carved doors signaled the entrance and the porter threw them open for Nick's access. He saluted and turned on his heel and walked away, smiling when Nick slipped a bill into his hand.

It was a midsized room holding fifteen round tables. Nick waited in front of a pulpit-type desk, picking up a card from a receptacle showing that this was "The Nights of the Round" dining room.

Nick smiled to himself. Someone had a sense of humor. A pretty young woman in a long burgundy dress with a cape-like embroidered white collar approached him.

"Dinner for one, sir?"

He nodded.

Nick was conscious of the deferential approach. Jon had a well-trained staff, he conceded.

"As you can see you have a choice of tables. Do you have a preference?"

Nick waved in the direction of the fireplace, which was glowing invitingly; he was led to one of two tables placed in front. Nick had felt a distinct chill passing through the lobby and sitting in front of the fire brought a sense of relaxation. He was pleased that he could feel so in his opponent's province.

A menu written in old English calligraphy was given to Nick and he quickly perused it. Everything looked appetizing. He was starving. A waiter unobtrusively appeared at his side.

"Have you had time to decide, or should I return?"

Nick gave his order.

"The roasted lamb, with mint sauce, baby potatoes and peas—with a starter of chilled prawns and a green salad."

The waiter smiled, looking up from his writing.

"Anything to drink?"

"A bottle of Newcastle Brown Ale," he replied.

The surprise on the waiter's face was noticeable and Nick smiled to himself. If the Guy Fawkes conversation had not taken place, he would not have learned about this particular product, held in such high regard by northern England beer drinkers. That apparently was all the narrator would drink and Nick had committed the brand to memory to try it sometime.

Waiting for the waiter to return with the ale, Nick looked around the room. Six tables in addition to his were occupied. All with couples. Five of the couples were older people, who it seemed were regulars here. They called the waiters by name and appeared to know each other, smiling sporadically across the room. The other couple was distanced from everyone else, their table positioned in a bay window. They appeared to be much younger. The girl was flirting with her companion, leaning forward in animated discussion, sometimes running her hand along the man's arm to look deeply into his face. A couple of times he saw them kiss. For the British this was not their usual public behavior, particularly in so public an area. Nick dismissed the thoughts as the waiter approached with the ale and his "Starter" first course.

As he was finishing the entree with the perfectly presented pink tinged meat, and tantalizing mint sauce, Nick was surprised finding the man who had been sitting over by the window standing in front of his table. He had watched the two lovebirds leaving the dining area about fifteen minutes earlier and had idly wondered if they were newlyweds spending their honeymoon here. It would be very romantic to do so.

"May I join you?"

Nick gave the man a quizzical look as he placed the upturned fork with his knife on the empty plate.

"We have never met," the man continued, "but I understand you are a friend of Kara Olavssen."

Nick felt as if he had been punched in the stomach. He recognized Jon. He had not made the connection earlier seeing him with the girl in the subdued lighting when features had been too far away to distinguish.

Nick stood up and extended his right hand. He smiled pleasantly.

"Of course! You must be Jon. I recognize you now from photographs. I had no idea when we might catch up with each other. Kara asked me to give you a package which is in my room."

They shook hands and Nick waved Jon to take a seat.

Jon had a slightly aloof look on his face as he sat opposite Nick. They appraised each other.

Nick's self-confidence returned upon finally meeting Kara's suitor. His easy smile and composure showed it.

"What made you think I knew Kara?" Nick questioned.

"Aunt Silvia phoned a few minutes ago, indicating that you could arrive here tonight since she had checked the Queen Victoria Hotel and they were booked solidly for a computer convention. I noticed that you had already checked in here and Patsy, the receptionist, told me you were having dinner. It wasn't difficult to locate you."

As he said this, Jon smiled for the first time. It changed his appearance remarkably. From his tanned skin there was no doubt he was the outdoors, vigorous type, robust and exuding good health. His smile indicated a certain wholesome charm, replacing what Nick had thought was an arrogant expression.

A silence followed, with Jon breaking in.

"Look here, old chap, if you haven't anything else in mind would you care to join me in the cocktail lounge for a nightcap?"

He sounded sincere. Nick took him up on the invitation. "It would be my pleasure."

Nick had no intention of refusing. He had not traveled a quarter of the earth to turn down an offer like this. He in turn grinned, aware that Jon was eyeing the impeccable Saville Row jacket of his suit, and the Brook Brothers custom made white shirt with the gold cufflinks and tie tack secured to the couturier designed silk tie.

A slight frown creased Jon's good-looking face, but it immediately disappeared.

"Shall we go?" he asked politely.

Nick placed his burgundy linen napkin on the table.

"Whenever you are ready."

He pushed his chair back and rose to his feet.

The hostess smiled at Jon as he passed and then to Nick, who was following him, she nodded.

"As requested, your charges will be accumulated on your room statement."

Nick motioned in agreement. He had already signed the tab for the meal and continued walking after Jon.

Jon's limp was not as pronounced as Nick had expected. In fact he seemed to disguise it quite well. It really did not seem to be as great an impediment as Kara had led him to believe.

Music and muted conversation could be heard ahead of them and as they drew nearer Jon looked at Nick saying

"It shouldn't be overpoweringly noisy tonight—weekends are usually crowded and deafening. If my presence wasn't absolutely essential, this would be one place I'd definitely avoid."

Nick looked surprised at hearing this.

"Strange, coming from the proprietor, I suppose, but ever since Kara left, life has not been the same for me."

So this was his strategy, Nick thinks. *Too bad for Jon that he had already observed the flirtation with the girl earlier, which he must realize had been noticed.*

Jon led the way into the cocktail lounge. Several people called out a greeting as they made their way to a table in a corner, passing a male pianist in a dark suit and bow tie who nodded in recognition.

Jon unfastened the button on his jacket and settled back on the chair, thoroughly examining the handsome, debonair man, with the cosmopolitan demeanor seated opposite him. He looked away realizing that his intense scrutiny must appear rude.

"Do you travel to England often?" Jon asked.

"About every five or six weeks," Nick answered. "I have business to attend to in Europe and Asia." Casually placing his left arm along the back of the empty chair beside him, the custom-made rectangular four-karat diamond ring on his middle finger was displayed to advantage He noticed Jon's eyes immediately fasten on it and Nick experienced a perverse feeling of satisfaction. Territorial supremacy was a game he had often played. Nick was pleased he had impetuously worn the ring. It was one bequeathed to him by Walter, a friend and mentor who had died a couple of years earlier. Nick usually wore it as a physical reminder of his dear friend. Sometimes, such as now, it served as a good luck symbol.

"How long have you known Kara?" Jon asked. It was not a superficial question; the tightening of his facial muscles evidenced his concern.

"Just a short time. We met through my cousin Wendy."

Nick looked away toward the pianist. The question was one he had expected, but he had not anticipated being asked so soon. He wished he could put his cards on the table, but Kara had been insistent that Jon's feelings be spared. This was a misnomer.

Jon seemed to relax a little.

A cocktail waitress in a brief burgundy dress, with frilled white lace petticoats showing, approached and saucily asked Jon what his pleasure was. She leaned over and kissed him full on the mouth.

"Stop playing games, Angie, this is not the time or place and get out of that uniform."

Demurely she fluttered her eyelashes.

"Right this minute—sir?"

He looked away annoyed.

Surprised she asked.

"Something wrong, Jon?"

"Please summon a waiter. By the way, this is Nicholas, a friend of Kara's."

With interest Angela surveyed Nick, looking him over intently.

"Not bad at all."

She threw a mutinous look in Jon's direction as she left.

Nick gave Jon a penetrating look.

"The service appears to be exceptional around here."

Jon scowled.

"That is my ex-fiancée and she is making my life hell. Ever since she discovered how much I care for Kara, I have suddenly become a magnet to her. She spends more time here than she does in London, it seems."

From first impressions, it did appear to Nick in all fairness that the woman was the initiator.

A waiter appeared, attempting to restrain his heavy breathing. When the boss snapped his fingers, it paid to get your skates on. Silently he waited for Jon's command.

Addressing Nick, Jon said, "We have an excellent brandy, if you enjoy that as an after-dinner drink."

"Fine."

Jon ordered the waiter to bring a bottle of 'Charlemagne II'.

Nick smiled. "I couldn't have chosen better myself."

The waiter rushed off to carry out Jon's directions.

There was an awkwardly long pause. They both turned to listen to the pianist who was crooning a popular ballad.

Nick clenched his right hand into a ball. He and Kara had danced this number together at Wendy's party. It was sentimentally provoking and subtly yearning, there had been an immediate connection between them.

What a time to be reminded, Nick ironically thinks, sitting opposite the object of her affection.

Hearing Jon clear his throat brings Nick back from his musing.

"I understand you have arranged to meet Kara's parents tomorrow. Pardon me for asking, but is there a problem?"

Damn. Nick hid his annoyance. He had not been aware of the networking system in place here. He had been put on the spot. He was not about to disclose to Jon the real reason for his visit—Kara's parents primarily deserved that disclosure.

He fabricated slightly. "It's really a social visit. I seldom have the opportunity to travel further than London, so when Kara asked me to drop off jewelry, which she wanted to ensure was handed over to her parents, it seemed an appropriate time to do so. I'm taking advantage of the detour to have a mini-vacation."

That did cover certain true statements, while leaving much unsaid. Jon appeared to be satisfied with the explanation.

The waiter brought a tray to the table, offering the bottle for Jon's approval. He cursorily glanced at the label and had it presented to Nick who looked at it and said with a smile.

"Yes, thank you. I'm very familiar with the brand."

Jon poured a small amount into two large snifter glasses and handed one to Nick, who accepted it with a nod and held the glass to warm in his hand. Jon waved the waiter away, with a tight smile. Nick could see he was not at ease and wondered why. After all this was his arena.

When arms were placed around Nick's neck, he guessed the reason. For what length of time had she been listening to their conversation?

Angela's warm breath was on his neck.

"So you are Kara's friend. How nice."

Jon, focusing his gaze on Angela, remarked offhandedly "I think Nick must be returning Kara's pearls—they were the only jewelry she cared about. She mentioned one time that she seldom wore them in America and that perhaps she should not have taken them."

Nick was astonished to hear Jon voice this information and particularly disturbed that he seemed to know so much about Kara's inclinations. He put the untouched snifter on the table.

He needed to leave soon

Angela sidled around and sat on Nick's lap. She was wearing a long slinky dress in a white shiny fabric, which emphasized an extremely curvaceous body.

"Thanks for reminding me." Nick said, gently easing Angela to her feet. "Please excuse me. I must call Kara's parents and their telephone number is in my room."

"No need to bother."

Leaning over to the next table, Angela picked up a spotless paper wine coaster. She gave it to Jon who quickly wrote down a telephone number and handed it to Nick, who slipped it into his pocket. Aiming a smile in the direction of the two of them, Nick headed for the foyer.

What a dismal predicament. How could those two have been engaged and contemplating marriage? It seemed more like a love-hate relationship to Nick. Ruminating on the events of the past hour, Nick was not pleased that Jon had mentioned Kara's pearls. Was it to remind Nick of how well he knew Kara?

Nick phoned the number given to him. A voice announced "The Olavssen Residence" and upon hearing his name asked him to wait. A clear, refined voice spoke. It was Mrs. Olavssen.

"Nicholas how lovely to know that you have arrived safely. Did you have a good journey north?"

Nick hesitated for a moment. There was no mistaking the similarity in the voices of Kara and her mother. There was a natural warmth and sincerity.

"Thank you, yes. When would be a good time to come out to visit you tomorrow? My time is at your disposal."

"Let's do it fairly early—it is going to be a busy weekend for us. Ten a.m. all right?"

"Great." Nick answered.

In a subdued tone Mrs. Olavssen asked, "Was Kara well when you last saw her?"

"Kara looked marvelous to me."

He faltered. This was going to be difficult.

"There are some things which I need to discuss with you."

There was a pause at the other end and Kara's mother replied quietly.

"Very well. Until tomorrow. Goodnight, Nicholas." She hung up.

He wondered what the reception would be like once he had recounted the purpose of his visit. Nick smiled ruefully. In the last couple of hours he had never told so many half-truths.

Going back to the cocktail lounge Nick found Jon alone at the table, pouring more brandy into his empty goblet. He had a morose expression on his face. He looked at Nick as if he were an intruder. The glass of brandy was still untouched at Nick's place. He once again warmed it between his hands and raised it to Jon saying "Cheers."

Jon barely acknowledged the gesture.

The liquid slid down Nick's throat easily. It was like silk. He held the glass away, holding it up to examine the remaining lush dark amber mixture.

"Excellent choice. Thank you."

Jon looked bored.

Nick surveyed Jon through half-closed lids. Would it have made a difference if he had informed him that the award winning brandy came from his own vineyards; made from the wine of the St. Émillion, Colombard grapes. It was exported all over the world and he had drunk it in such remote places as The Forum Hotel in Petra, Jordan and El Sombrero in Acapulco, Mexico. That Jon had chosen it was a testament to its quality and popularity. It certainly was a great moneymaker.

There was a silence between the two men, each assessing the other. Jon stared at Nick studiously.

"How well do you know Kara?" his voice was curt.

Nick was surprised. A similar question had been asked earlier—had Jon been drinking heavily or was the uncertainty in waiting for Kara's answer getting to be too much for him?

There was a pause and Jon's voice toned down slightly.

"Forgive me for asking such a direct question, but I have never heard of you before. I'm sure I would not have forgotten your name if it had come up at some time. My interest is extremely personal. As far as I am concerned, Kara is my fiancée and I am curious to know what your role is in the scheme of things."

The words held an insolent tone and with an effort Nick managed to reply in a steady voice

"Does Kara consider herself engaged to you? She wears no ring."

He was trying to remain calm and polite. He really did not care for this man's attitude.

He saw Jon grasp the edge of the table, a look of anger momentarily clouding his face.

Nick continued. "As for your question, as far as I know, Kara regards me as a friend, but perhaps you should ask her, if there is doubt on your part."

Nick scrutinized his table companion's involuntary actions with interest. He observed the deep breath that Jon took in. *So he had been concerned, and rightfully so—the duel had just begun.* There was a relieved smile on Jon's face as he offered more brandy to Nick.

"No thanks. It's time to turn in. It's been a long, but interesting day."

He stood up.

"Thanks for your hospitality."

Jon nodded in recognition.

Nick turned and made his way out, walking past the pianist who was singing to two simpering matrons sitting at a table directly in front of him. The cocktail lounge and bar scene had seldom held much curiosity for Nick. With a sympathetic smile, he stuffed a generous tip into the container on top of the piano.

Angela saw Nick leave the cocktail lounge.

She had been hurrying to get back to the table and stopped to catch her breath. She had been quite intrigued by Kara's friend, Nick. Satomi had been on target when she had mentioned the charisma and magnetism he projected. Too late to discover more about him; she would have to wait for another opportunity.

She was about to return to Jon and his charms without delay.

★ ★ ★

Not wishing to run into Jon again before meeting Kara's parents, Nick phoned Room Service the next morning and ordered a simple breakfast to be delivered to his suite.

Standing with a cup of coffee in his hand he admired the view outside. The bow shaped window with the stained-glass inserts sparkled in the clear morning light. Through some of the translucent leaded-glass panes a wide expanse of lawn could be seen. A pond was visible in the distance and foothills were outlined against the horizon. It was an unobstructed view. Off to the right stood three burgundy and gold railway carriages, resting on railroad tracks. Quite intriguing. These must be the 'cars' that the porter mentioned. Nick looked at his watch. There was no time to get a closer look at them. Perhaps he could check them out later.

Last night, in a roundabout way, Nick had gained entry to his suite by using a more accessible entrance from outside. It appeared that there were several intersections that provided transition to the top floors of the Inn. The one nearest to his suite was quite close to a side entrance, very convenient to where the Bentley was parked. He could see the car from the turret window.

Nick was still slightly disturbed about the encounter he had had with Jon the previous evening. It certainly was not the run-of-the-mill kind. What with Angie in her seductive costume changing routine and Jon exhibiting an attitude problem, he was uncomfortable just thinking about it. Jon's wariness was difficult to fathom. Was it because of Angela's embarrassing demonstrations, or his fear of Nick's involvement with Kara?

Nick was puzzled. There definitely was something here that did not sit right.

Already dressed, he put on the jacket of a silver gray Barathea suit ready to leave. He adjusted the knot of the gray, white and black striped tie and passed self-inspection in the mirror.

Opening the top drawer of the dresser he looked for the small velvet box containing the pearl earring, which he had placed there last night. Frantically he searched around. He had taken it out of his carry-on bag last night, putting it with his passport, camera, and binoculars, so that he would not forget the small package. It had been an oversight not to include the earring with the rest of the pearls in the mauve velvet jeweler's case. Everything else was there. Nick looked in amazement. He was stunned. The predicament posed ominous problems.

Nick sat down on the settee reviewing the events of the previous evening from the time he had placed everything in the drawer, which was before he went down to dinner, to the time he arrived back in the room again. It was a total of almost two hours. Only two people could know about the earring, as far as he knew, and they were Jon and Angela. Jon had brought up the topic of Kara's pearls himself. Nick caught his breath at the implication. How could he possibly accuse either of them, particularly as he and Jon were together most of the time and Angela drifted in and out of his view with monotonous regularity.

Oh, good grief. What a mess!

The whole thing was becoming ridiculous. He certainly could not report a theft at this precise moment. He was already running late in starting out and the information that he had to pass on to the Olavssens' was startling enough without informing them of his ineptness in holding on to one earring—not a pair, for Heaven's sake, just one. He envisaged the local newspaper stepping in to blow things out of proportion once they heard about the disappearance. Nick decided to play it safe and wait for the right opportunity to inform Kara's parents of this implausible development.

Nick shook his head in disbelief.

After checking his back pocket for his wallet, he collected his passport, camera, and binoculars. On impulse he returned to the bathroom and picked up the clothes repair kit. There was a wine color, very close to that of the carpet. He ran a length between his fingers—a double strand about twelve inches long. He crouched down and carefully closed the door behind him, with the thread hanging out an inch above the floor. Using the miniature scissors on the Swiss Army knife that he always carried on a separate key chain, he carefully snipped the thread as close to the wood as he could manage. He hung the "Do not disturb" sign on the door handle and double-checked to make sure the door was locked.

In a somber mood he reached his car and opened the trunk to check on the security of the mauve velvet jewel case in the safe. Of course it was there. He glanced across at the Inn as he drove out of the parking lot and thought he saw a shadow pass across the turret window. He was becoming edgy.

The Bentley took wing. The superbly crafted automobile, with its powerful engine, effortlessly negotiated the narrow turns of the winding roads despite its size. Nick was in a hurry. He had committed the directions to memory and so it came as a surprise to find himself reaching the home of Kara's parents a few minutes before the appointed time. The wrought iron double gate to the property was open and with time to spare, he slowly proceeded along the twisting driveway noting the charming landscaping, displayed in an effortlessly casual manner.

He noticed a gardener working in a bed of ornamental bushes, who raised his trowel in greeting as he passed. That is what he liked about the English, their sense of understatement. This gardener probably worked very hard to produce a landscape that looked as if it had been left to nature.

Nick almost regretted emerging from the serenity of the long private driveway; it meant he had a difficult task to attend to very soon.

There in front of him stood a huge magnificent granite edifice, weathered by the centuries and standing in grandeur, secure and proud. With its towers and crenellated battlements it looked like a castle.

He was not prepared for this.

He laughed bitterly.

He had been so ultra-cautious in protecting his reputation, his position in life and his supersensitive values that he had judged Kara on his terms. For years he had been cognizant of the challenge he presented as a wealthy, eligible bachelor and it had become a matter of self-preservation to downplay the image. Kara, who worked with a desperate, needy population by choice and lived a satisfying simple lifestyle according to her own needs, could have indulged her every whim had she so chosen.

He was ashamed of his arrogance.

He sat quietly at the wheel, not quite ready to leave the car's shelter.

There was a movement to his right, which caused him to turn his head. The massive double doors were opening and a woman emerged looking toward his vehicle.

Nick looked at his watch.

The housekeeper was probably going to alert him that he was a little late. Stepping out of the car Nick made sure he heard it lock before moving away. Strange things have been happening to him lately.

With a smile on his face he quickly walked up the shallow stone steps to the open doorway.

"Hello, I'm Nicholas Prendergast. I believe I'm expected."

"Yes you are and welcome."

The enunciation was precise and genteel. The jade eyes confirmed who she was.

Nick was taken aback.

"Oh, this is a pleasure. I didn't expect you to be waiting for me. Am I very late?"

"Not at all. I was anxious to meet you. It is very unusual to receive Kara's emissary."

She leaned forward and took Nick's hand in both of hers. It was a warm gesture.

The unexpectedly hospitable greeting took Nick by surprise and he swallowed hard to suppress a flood of emotions that he was hard pressed to define. It was almost like meeting a long-lost friend.

Lord, this was a terrible start, feeling so vulnerable.

He managed a cautious smile.

She smiled in return and patted his hand.

"Come this way, Nicholas, my husband is in the garden. Let's join him there."

Courteously he followed her.

They walked through a large black and white marble foyer, with a huge crystal chandelier lowered from a high ceiling. Tapestries were displayed on two walls.

A maid stepped out of a room.

"Please bring refreshments to the Gazebo, Hilda."

The same marble hallway continued through the entire breadth of the building, ending in a conservatory, which led out to the garden. Nick opened the door and smiling her thanks, Kara's mother led the way down a tree-lined path.

She stopped at a white trellised building with a weathervane on top.

"Gus, Nicholas is here."

She looked along the winding pathway.

"He's not far away. I'm sure he will join us shortly."

Beckoning to Nick she walked up the steps into the gazebo and he followed after her. They sat down in deeply cushioned wicker chairs, placed around a wrought iron glass topped table. Almost immediately Kara's father appeared. He was holding a small bunch of white grapes.

"Look at these. They are getting bigger and better."

He sounded excited and Nick could not help grinning.

"Try some," he urged, holding the bunch out to Nick.

"Oh, darling, they haven't even been washed," Silvia Olavssen protested.

"Here, just rub the bloom off."

He rolled one around in his palm, revealing a shiny fruit, which he popped into his mouth. An expression of exquisite delight came over his face

"Hmm, wonderful. You must try some Nick."

Nick reached out and took one, rubbing it around in his palms as Kara's father had done.

He was dubious about his reaction, but as soon as he tasted the slightly tart juice on his tongue, with the fleshy fruit exploding in his mouth, he closed his eyes in ecstasy.

A smile surfaced as he reached for another grape.

"Wonderful. I think you have a winner."

In triumph Gustav Olavssen turned to his wife.

"I knew on sight, and instinctively, that Nick would appreciate the finer aspects of life."

He looked appraisingly at Nick.

"I'll bet you play Chess too."

Nick looked up in surprise.

"Kara told you."

"No." was the response. There was a brief pause and an eager question followed. "Does that mean you do?"

Nick nodded his head. This was quickly getting out of hand and they had not yet been formally introduced.

The maid appeared with a large tray.

Gus Olavssen placed the bunch of grapes on a napkin and removed the tray from her hands.

He smiled.

"Thank you, Hilda."

He carried the tray up the steps to the table and Hilda retreated to the house.

"Tea or coffee, Nicholas?"

"Coffee please. Black."

Mrs. Olavssen poured the steaming liquid into a fine china cup and handed the cup and saucer to Nick.

She automatically poured tea for her husband and herself, adding sugar and cream to both.

Before more niceties could take place, Nick hurriedly opened the conversation. He was too nervous to try to be nonchalant about this meeting.

He informed them in quiet tones that what he was about to tell them would come as a shock. It was not information he was happy to impart and that was why he wanted to talk to them in person.

Nick told them how he and Kara had met. He did not mind fibbing to Jon, but he could not start off that way with her parents. He told how he had taken Kara to his cousin's party in Rancho Mirage. At the time they were leaving, Kara went out to his car, while he collected his briefcase from the house. That was when the incident took place. He did not omit any of the important details. He informed them of Kara's injuries and he had difficulty controlling his voice at the recollection of finding her injured in the trunk of his car.

Nick's eyes were moist at the end of rehashing the painful incident to Kara's parents. It was still too clearly imprinted into his brain to speak unemotionally. He turned his head away and breathed deeply in order gain control of his feelings. It was a long time since he had broken down like this and the feeling of defenselessness returned strongly.

In a low voice he continued.

"I am particularly sorry to be the bearer of more bad news but, at the time of the accident, Kara was wearing the family pearls. They were stolen. Kara was naturally extremely distressed at the loss of these valuable heirlooms. I offered a reward. Miraculously, without needing this incentive, they were found against all odds. Kara wanted to have a duplicate set made, so that she could enjoy wearing them without worry. I offered to bring them back so that they could be kept with you for safety."

Looks of relief were shown on the faces of Kara's parents. Irreplaceable heirlooms they were, having belonged to past generations of the family, but their concern was for Kara's safety and her peace of mind. Had they been forever lost, they believed she would never have forgiven herself.

Nick was hesitant. There was still more he needed to admit. The phrase "In for a penny, in for a pound." seemed to fit precisely—being responsible for opening up this topic, he had to see it through to the end.

Here goes, Nick mused, how much bad news could they take?

Biting his lip, Nick said. "Unfortunately there's something else I have to disclose. I had hoped to clear the matter up myself when I returned to the Inn, but because of the limited evidence I believe the police need to be involved. There is no doubt that they will need to speak with you also."

The Olavssens' looked at Nick, appalled.

He continued speaking, with a troubled expression on his face.

"Between the time of my arrival at the Inn last night and the point of departure to come and visit you today, I left my room only once to have dinner, returning approximately two hours later. To my consternation I discovered a theft had taken place when the one pearl earring in a small velvet case I was bringing to you was found to be missing from a drawer. Nothing else had disappeared."

A gasp escaped from Silvia Olavssen.

Speaking quietly Nick continued.

"Unintentionally the single pearl earring became separated from the rope of pearls and the other earring since in the rush to catch a flight to London, I omitted replacing it with the others and packed it in my carry-on of which I never lost sight."

Shaking his head he added worriedly, "I'm having a problem grasping this turn of events."

A frown appeared on Gus Olavssen's brow.

"Who knew you had this jewelry with you?" he queried. Nick grew uneasy.

"Only Jon and perhaps Angela."

When the frown deepened, Nick hastened to explain further.

"As I am staying at The Black Bull Inn, Jon located me in the dining room and invited me to have a nightcap with him last night after dinner. At that time he asked about the purpose of my visit to you. Since the personal information I had to discuss with both of you was for your ears only and since I am not accustomed to telling falsehoods, I mentioned that I was returning jewelry from Kara and probably taking some back, which Kara had requested me to pick up. That way I could tell basic truths, without deliberately lying. Jon himself mentioned Kara's pearls and implied that they were what I was returning to you. About that time I could see Jon looking at someone behind me. It was only when I heard Angie's voice, as she put her arms around my neck, that I realized she must have been listening to everything I said."

Mrs. Olavssen tut, tutted.

"Her arms around your neck, indeed. Wasn't Jon concerned about that?"

Nick looked embarrassed.

"That just slipped out, I'm sorry. Jon did seem disturbed by her behavior."

Gus Olavssen coughed behind his hand.

"Yes, well I'm sure Jon can handle that. Now for the theft report. I will contact the local constabulary and have a plain clothed detective go to the Inn to see you. What is your room number, so that he can bypass the staff? What about six this evening, would that be a suitable time?"

Nick agreed to this. "That's fine, except the room doesn't have a number."

He pulled out his key chain and located the suite key. It was unusually shaped in an antique style.

"There's something engraved on it, but I can't make it out."

Kara's father held out his hand and Nick separated the door key from his key chain and passed it over.

"Excuse me. I'm going to get a magnifying glass."

A few minutes later they were all trying to decipher the lettering.

"Tyrrytt Tower, that is what it is." exclaimed Silvia Olavssen triumphantly, after they had passed the key and magnifying glass around the table several times.

"I painted a series of canvases for the previous owner of the Inn and during that time little bits of history were passed on to me. There was a story about 'Tyrrytt Tower.' I remember being intrigued with the name and also the story, which completely escapes my memory at the moment. One thing of which I am sure is that 'Tyrrytt Tower' was in that wing of the building."

"Well done, dear," said her husband, smiling fondly at her as he handed the key back to Nick, "and just which tower might that be?"

"It is the only one round in shape, which has six large stained-glass windows around it, with some kind of armor depicted, I believe—if memory serves me well."

Nodding his head, Nick joined in.

"I am occupying a suite with those very same windows in a semi-circle, as part of a circular addition to the bedroom. If there is only one section of the Inn built like this, then I'm sure 'Tyrrytt Tower' is where I am. Each window shows a different shield and sword, with family crests beautifully designed on them."

They sat and smiled at each other. One small mystery solved.

Gus Olavssen solemnly looked at his wife and Nick.

"These suspicions must be kept private. We have no legitimate leads to work with and, of course, cannot jump to conclusions. There has to be a logical explanation for the missing earring."

Both agreed with him.

With a contrite glance at both of them, Nick spoke quietly.

"I feel responsible for what has occurred and I would give a great deal to reverse the situation. Is there anything I can do to make amends?"

There was a long silence.

Nick looked down at his hands. They had cause to dislike him, an outsider bringing harmful elements into their daughter's life and creating disruption in their own.

"It is not a problem for which you should feel responsible."

Gus Olavssen looked over his spectacles at Nick.

"If anyone should be blamed, it is Kara. She made the decision to wear the confounded things in the first place and started off this mess."

Nick managed to restrain a smile. No one he knew could speak of something worth over a million pounds as "confounded things."

Gus looked over at his wife as if expecting some rhetoric from her.

"Quite so, dear. It was extremely imprudent of Kara to take such a foolish risk. So very unlike her, I might add."

She stopped and looked at Nick.

"Did Kara mention why she wore the pearls that night? Was it a gala occasion?"

Nick took a moment to think.

"Not really. Later on, when we were going over the details, Kara told me that the prospect of seeing me again had made her a little nervous."

Silvia Olavssen's astonishingly expressive sea green eyes observed Nick.

She shook her head.

"How unusual. Kara is normally quite self-assured. I think it meant she was a little uncertain of herself at the prospect of being with you. You must have had quite an affect upon her."

She saw Nick's eyes light up and she smiled. He was so obviously in love with their daughter.

He sighed and looked down at his clasped hands.

A small hand was laid gently over his own.

"You must care for Kara very much to come here prepared to endure our inquisition and wrath."

The soft voice startled him.

He had expected a deserved reprimand.

Nick looked up confused.

Both parents were looking at him searchingly.

"If I may be so bold, of what importance is Kara in your life?"

It was a protective father speaking.

"She means everything in the world to me." Nick confessed honestly.

✶ ✶ ✶

They sat, in typically English fashion, sipping tea, discussing the weather, the European Common Market and the recent terrorist hijacking of the Italian cruise ship 'Achille Lauro.' Nick's throat constricted. Civilization's cultural veneer in this well-bred family was obviously more pronounced than it was in his. He was not as much in control of his emotions as Kara's parents appeared to be.

After his emotional confession they had gracefully accepted what he had said at face value and closed the discussion. It was over and done with. They were too polite to rush an acquaintance of their daughter out of their home, even though he had surprised himself by admitting his love for Kara. Mrs. Olavssen had already informed him it was going to be a busy weekend for them and he was taking advantage of their time.

Nick was shaken out of his musings when Kara's mother said unexpectedly.

"Nicholas, on Sunday we are going to the beach for the day. Would you care to accompany us? It is one of Kara's favorite places and you might like to see it for yourself."

He saw Kara's father shoot a surprised look in his wife's direction.

He answered reluctantly.

"I've already taken up so much of your time. I wouldn't want to intrude further."

Nick was taken by surprise. He had come here fully expecting to be reprimanded and they were being impartial and charming.

Gus Olavssen stood up, and Nick had an overwhelming feeling that he was being dismissed. He rose to his feet also.

"Well, now that all the heavy stuff has been dispensed with," he glanced suspiciously at Nick and added in a mock threatening tone, *"and there are no more surprises in store for us, are there?"*

Very quietly Nick replied. "I sincerely hope not."

"Then how about a game of Chess?"

Relief flooded through Nick.

CHAPTER TWENTY FOUR

The time passed peacefully. The punching of the time clock and the chiming of the grandfather clock were the only sounds heard in the large, comfortable den. They were playing with the regulation Staunton chess pieces and for most of the time Nick had abstractedly moved the wooden carvings as if by rote. In wonderment he contrasted the events of the last two days. On one hand he may have made an enemy or two and on the other hand he had hopefully found two allies. He wondered if anyone had tampered with his suite again. Where would it all lead?

Hypothetically he traversed certain possibilities.

Nick's perambulations were shattered when Gus Olavssen delightedly pointed to Nick's side of the chess clock. It had expired. The game was over.

"Gotcha, Nick."

Nick attempted to look disappointed. Running out of time was a chess player's bugbear. In actuality the game had taken a backseat to his primary concerns, which he had been mentally reviewing.

Nick acknowledged defeat by offering his hand to indicate good sportsmanship at the loss.

Gus took the proffered hand and leaning over, patted Nick's shoulder.

"Good game, I really enjoyed it. I haven't played so well in years—it must have been the quality of the competition."

Given the extraordinary nature of the purpose of their meeting, Kara's father felt the morning had progressed quite nicely. He did not envisage a problem with the insurance company regarding the earring, but it would be a blow to lose one. It could not be duplicated. The most important aspect was that Kara had come out of this as well as she had. He admired Nick for bearing the blame for everything that took place and there was no doubt about the genuine devotion Nick had expressed for his daughter. Nick had been terribly upset about Kara's injuries and his sense of guilt seemed to hang heavily on him. Gus Olavssen chuckled silently to himself. Nick appeared to be quite smitten with Kara.

Mrs. Olavssen appeared.

"If lunch is postponed any longer, I will not take responsibility for Mrs. Taylor's actions. She has informed me that the soufflé is about to fall."

The gentle smile on her face belied the dramatic statement.

She slipped an arm around her husband's waist as they walked out of the den.

"Come on, Nicholas. Remember cook's warning."

She looked back laughing at him.

From the large dining room an atrium was visible in which the water from a fountain was gently cascading, providing a soothing sound. Despite its size the room had retained a cozy atmosphere that seemed to promote conversation and encourage relaxation. The dark furniture was polished until it shone like glass. The table was laid with linen placemats upon which three silver-rimmed china place settings rested, with the appropriate silver cutlery and Waterford crystal arranged around them. An enormous urn of fresh flowers dominated the other end.

Settling into their chairs, Silvia Olavssen looked across the table at their guest.

"Nicholas, I hope you don't mind, but I took the liberty of including you in our group which is attending the surprise birthday dinner party for Jon tomorrow evening. It is to celebrate his thirty-third birthday and it is being held in the railway coaches at The Black Bull Inn. As you are already staying there, please say you will accept."

Nick hesitated. It would give him another opportunity to observe Jon. Besides, seeing the railway coaches from his window had piqued his interest. What was most important, he was being specifically asked to join Kara's parents for the evening and how could he resist such an invitation.

"Are you sure I'll not be in the way? Kara gave me a gift to pass along to Jon, but I don't need to present it personally."

"I won't take no for an answer, Nicholas. It would delight us to have you as our guest."

He capitulated quickly. "In that case, thank you. I accept with pleasure."

As an afterthought Silvia added.

"I hope it won't be an imposition, but formal dress is required."

There was an apprehensive look in her eyes. As handsome as Nick looked in the impeccable suit he wore, it just would not be appropriate for Saturday's formal affair.

Nick contained a smile. The clothing she was referring to could almost be classified as his "night wear," so often did he wear dinner jackets and tuxedos. He already had a couple with him, packed for the trip to France.

"No problem, I assure you."

It was just after one o'clock and time for him to leave. The three of them walked back to his car. Accessing the trunk, Nick opened the safe. Removing the lavender velvet jewel case he solemnly handed it to Kara's mother, who quickly looked inside, nodded and closed the lid.

Silvia Olavssen reached up to kiss Nick's cheek saying, "I feel confident the other earring will be found, don't worry."

Nick walked around to the driver's side.

"We'll see you tomorrow, Nicholas, for cocktails in the Pullman?"

He agreed, taking her hand in his and pressing the dainty fingers gently.

The two men shook hands, with Gus Olavssen saying casually.

"Why don't you stay here overnight after the party, then we can all leave together Sunday morning for Wisherly? That way we won't waste time waiting for each other."

They were giving their approval.

Nick's grin, registering delight, was his answer.

He fell in love with them. Like daughter, like parents.

As he was starting to pull away, he had to lower the window to hear Kara's mother speaking.

"Please don't be late on Saturday, we want to try to keep it as much of a surprise as possible."

He waved and shook his head in acknowledgement.

Nick proceeded through town with a fatuous smile on his face. The visit had turned out so much better than he could have imagined. He would have to pick up a few items, to be ready for the change of events, but at the top of the list, there was a postcard to mail.

✴ ✴ ✴

Nick's euphoria faded somewhat when he parked the Bentley outside the side entrance to the Inn. He put his passport in the glove compartment and locked it. He carried packages up to the suite and approached the door almost stealthily. The "Do not disturb" sign was still displayed. He squatted down to examine the door more closely and ran his fingers along the lower edge of it. The slight feel of "something" stopped him. Retracing his fingers he sensitively located the thread. It was still in place. With mixed emotions he opened the door.

Entering the room warily Nick noted that the bed was unmade, so the room had not been serviced. He had some concern that during his absence the room might have been searched. Releasing his breath Nick quickly walked around the rooms, noting nothing unusual. Not that he had left anything worth stealing, but he felt as if he were being watched. He removed the 'Do not disturb' sign from the door handle.

He was tired. It had been an emotionally draining day, even though it had ended on a high note. He decided to take a shower, before the detective arrived. Afterward he would call Room Service and arrange to have a meal delivered. He still had some work to finish. Finally before going to bed he would phone Kara.

In that order.

He wanted to bring her up-to-date and fall asleep with her voice in his ears. He was missing her more than he had expected.

Nick put away his purchases and returned his camera and binoculars to the dresser drawer.

Could he be going crazy? The small velvet box was lying there. With a great deal of trepidation he picked up the box and lifted the lid. One lustrous pearl earring lay there. He snapped the top closed, breathing heavily.

He was definitely cracking up.

He realized the pressure of his normally rigorous schedule, plus the advent of Kara and the traumatic events leading to the present situation had affected him tremendously—both physically and emotionally, but how could he possibly overlook an object that should have been plainly visible?

Nick thought back to the morning's routine.

The jewelry box was definitely not there. He had meticulously looked in each corner of that particular drawer and he remembered going on to open each drawer in the dresser, in the event that he had abstractedly placed the box with other things. He was not a careless person. He traveled far too often and was too well organized to leave things to chance.

Nick reproached himself, realizing what he had just done. The shock of finding the little jewel case had sent caution to the wind. He had just placed more of his own fingerprints on the box. Would he have covered incriminating fingerprints that could have been left? He was annoyed with himself.

It was four-thirty. He should alert Kara's parents to this latest unaccountable occurrence.

Gus came on the line.

"This is absurd, but the earring has been returned. Put back in the drawer, from which it was taken. Can you believe that?"

The intake of breath at the other end of the line supported Nick's own feeling of disbelief.

"That's incredible, Nick. Are you absolutely sure you searched for the jewel case thoroughly when you thought it was missing?"

A note of irritation crept into Nick's voice.

"I have mentally walked through each sequence several times. The box was not in the dresser drawer where it had been placed. Of that I am totally convinced."

The tone of his voice left no room for doubt.

What should be done now? There was no theft to report, but that which needed to be addressed could be infinitely more threatening.

Gus cut into his thoughts.

"Lt. Leighton is the person coming to see you shortly, let me give him a call to check on a couple of things. He can then get in touch with you directly. Is that all right?"

"Fine. I'll be here."

The cocktail napkin, upon which Jon had written the Olavssen's telephone number, was on the nightstand beside the bed. He went to reach for it and quickly withdrew his hand—both Jon and Angela had touched it as well as himself.

Phoning the Service Desk Nick arranged for a carafe of coffee to be sent up to his suite. He settled down to do some work and wait for the lieutenant's call.

The phone's double trill broke through his concentration.

"Lt. Leighton here. Will it be convenient to see you in half-an-hour?"

Nick agreed.

"I will be bringing a forensic specialist with me to go over your rooms. Have you touched the box with the pearl in?"

Nick felt like a child caught sneaking candies out of a jar.

"Yes. I'm sorry. I didn't think."

The police officer sounded a little disappointed with his answer.

Of course he had to open the box to check that the earring was still there, so why was he apologizing?

"Well, please touch as little in the room as possible. We will be there very soon, dressed in outdoor clothing."

The telephone rang again.

Picking up the receiver Nick was surprised to hear Angela's voice.

"You're a difficult man to reach—I've been calling all day."

From the time Nick had discovered the alternate route around the Inn, he had little cause to pass the front desk. Sure that the receptionist or staff would inform him of messages, or that the red light on the telephone would indicate a waiting message, Nick contemplated if this was a ploy to discover if he was in his suite.

Nick's voice became guarded.

"Oh really!"

She was going to have to struggle through this conversation alone.

"Jon asked me to call and invite you out to the farm for dinner this evening, if you're free. There are a couple of things he thought you might be interested in seeing."

Nick was undecided. He did not trust either of them, but he was anxious to learn as much about the two of them as possible.

"It's only a few miles from where you are—I don't mind picking you up," she said persuasively.

"What time did Jon have in mind?"

"Around seven."

"Fine. I may be a little late, but if you give me directions I'll get there myself."

She proceeded to do so.

Nick was restless. He hoped the detectives would arrive promptly otherwise it would be a challenge to arrive at the farm by seven. He prowled around the chambers, finally standing in front of the windows, sipping a cup of coffee, waiting for the arrival of Lt. Leighton and his man.

He saw a nondescript vehicle pull in beside the Bentley and two men hurried out.

A soft knock on the door announced their arrival.

They stood outside with two badges displayed. He read their names and opened the door further to allow them access.

They were extremely efficient and polite.

While Lt. Leighton questioned Nick, writing everything down, Lt. Brown dusted the drawers, tables, doors, the jewelry box and other objects upon which incriminating evidence could have been left.

Kara's father must have explained the situation very well because, in having Nick recount every relevant detail, not an iota of disbelief or surprise was registered on the lieutenant's face.

Nick pointed to the paper wine coaster.

"This has been handled by both of the suspects."

Lt. Brown at least looked pleased.

The earring in its case was placed into a zippered plastic bag, together with the coaster.

"We need to take these should they be required as evidence, sir."

Lt. Leighton closed his folder and picked up the plastic bag as he addressed Nick.

"If we need to contact you, where can we do that?"

"I'm leaving for France in a few days. The necklace and the other earring have already been returned to the Olavssens'."

Nick pulled from his wallet two international business cards with telephone numbers and addresses of offices in several European cities. He gave one to each of the men.

"A message can be left at any of those numbers."

The two officers exchanged their official cards and respectfully said good night.

Rushing to meet the appointed time of seven o' clock, Nick showered and changed into a blue silk patterned shirt and navy blue slacks and blazer. He was ready to leave the Inn with only minutes to spare.

Nick arrived at the sign "Coppice Farm" shortly after seven.

Kara had mentioned how old the farmhouse was, but she had not prepared him for the historic impact that met his eyes. He felt as if he had stepped back in time. Even the surrounding gardens were in the style of the old world. He studied the view with pleasure. Before he had located the entrance, a door opened and Jon appeared. He seemed to block the entire space.

Nick walked along the path toward him, handing over a package that showed the rounded shapes of bottles. "Coals to Newcastle," he said smiling. He had brought over a few bottles from his private reserve, which he had stuffed into the trunk almost as an afterthought. He was going to ship a case of the product to Kara's father.

Jon looked intently at Nick, as if weighing him up. He took the package offered to him, tucking it under his arm and held the other hand out to shake.

"Glad you could come on such short notice. Hope it wasn't too much of an inconvenience."

"Not at all—I was undecided what to do about dinner. You helped make the decision."

Jon laughed spontaneously. Once again Nick noted how his smile completely transformed the somewhat disdainful features.

"I was standing outside admiring your farmhouse. There must be some wonderful tales to tell about a place as steeped in history as this must be."

Jon's face softened. Here was a subject dear to his heart.

"I planned on showing you around after dinner."

"Good."

"Come on in" Jon said moving aside, "but duck your head as you enter, otherwise you'll have a large bump to remind you the next time."

Jon closed the door after he entered and deposited the package on the hallstand by the doorway.

"The others are already here having cocktails."

As if on cue Angela walked into the living room with a champagne glass in her hand. Unlike the skimpy white gown that Nick had last seen her wearing she was dressed in a black turtleneck long sleeved gown, which fitted almost as closely as her skin. It certainly seemed to be more revealing than the white one, if that was possible. She stopped and smiled at Nick, tilting her head to one side and resting a hand on one hip.

"Welcome. You've arrived at precisely the right time. All the boring chit-chat is out of the way and we are ready for something more sophisticated."

She giggled, as if pleased with her own wittiness.

Jon swatted her on the rear, sending her back into the room from which she had just come.

They followed her.

Five people were sitting on high stools at a dramatic enclosed fourteenth century Gothic arch that had been converted into a bar. It still retained its integrity as an artifact crafted by skilled artisans of earlier times.

The conversation stopped as Angela, Jon and Nick entered the room. Interested faces looked at Nick.

Starting with the nearest couple Jon introduced his neighbors.

"Sergei and Vicki Dominick, they own the farm next door."

They held out their hands to shake.

"Martin and Ginnie Shrewsbury, they have the stables and riding club which you passed on the way here."

From the end of the bar they nodded their heads and smiled.

The fifth person looked at Nick through long black lashes. She had a bronze complexion, with elliptically shaped eyes and a demure expression, which belied the sinuous figure draped in a white chiffon tunic, with gold trimmed braid. She gave the impression of an Indian princess.

She looked to be the person most out of place in this rural setting, yet she had managed to transform the high barstool into a throne.

Jon turned to Nick as if offering the pièce de résistance.

"This is Satomi—she is a friend of Angie's and is not only the top model at Frazier's, but you will find her featured on almost every magazine cover internationally these days. But you probably know all of this. She is spending a few days in the area."

Nick look slightly puzzled.

Jon looked at Nick to watch his reaction.

She certainly was a ravishing woman.

Nick smiled at them all in the same non-committal way.

"Everyone, allow me to introduce you to Dr. Nicholas Prendergast, the world's eminent heart specialist and lecturer."

Nick's jaw tightened. So much for traveling incognito.

Jon walked around and pulled out the bar chair next to Satomi. She looked intently at Nick, scrutinizing him thoroughly as he sat down beside her.

"This is an unexpected pleasure. We almost met once before and I was hoping there would be another opportunity."

Her eyes sparkled with amusement as she noticed the puzzled expression on Nick's face.

"Le Duc du Paloma gave a cocktail party to which I was invited and Valencia Gambola was there with you."

Still no recognition appeared on Nick's face. She continued.

"A year July I was in Rome on an assignment and apparently you were giving a seminar at the same time at the Lycium."

He nodded his head remembering.

"Oh, yes, I'm with you now. Why did you say 'We almost met'?"

She pouted prettily.

"Le Duc said he would like us to meet and went off to find you, but Valencia no doubt decided that she wasn't willing to share you with the rest of the world, and the two of you were seen escaping through a side door. That was very naughty of you. I was most disappointed."

Nick's eyes narrowed. This woman was a game player

"Actually, if I recall accurately, I was the one who wanted to leave. I dislike those affairs immensely and a few months earlier I made a deal with Valencia, who by the way is distantly related to me. She agreed to accompany me to a couple of official functions during my stay in Rome and for doing so I gave her the use of my apartment on the Grand Canal in Venice for the August International Film Festival."

He could see the interest generated by that last statement.

Before he knew Kara this would have been added ammunition to activate whatever his desires were, but looking into Satomi's eager eyes, he felt the roles had reversed and he was the victim

"What would you like to drink?"

There was a jovial smile on Jon's face.

Ad-libbing Nick said, "There's a drink I particularly enjoy, in fact it's become a favorite. I believe it's been called 'Cloud Number Nine'." Under his breath Nick thanked Kara for being the inspiration and jogging his memory.

"Sounds wonderful," Satomi murmured, "I'd like to try it."

Jon looked at Nick.

"I haven't heard of that one—will you bartend? I'll supply the ingredients."

Nick acquiesced and walked behind the bar counter.

The ingredients were measured into a blender and Nick started it off until it frothed to the top. Wide bowl glasses were arranged on the counter and Nick half-filled six of them. It worked out perfectly.

Ginnie and Martin said they would stick with their Newcastle Brown Ale. Under different circumstances Nick would have preferred joining them, but the cocktail memories brought Kara back vividly close and he wanted to keep that picture of her with him. He remembered how they had begun to get to know each other when sipping the "Tequila Sunrise" cocktail and the warm protective feeling that still came to mind of when she had fallen asleep on his shoulder.

Nick brought his mind back to present company. He had a nagging feeling about Satomi. She was much too available. He recognized the strategy.

Another round of cocktails followed the first.

Nick wondered when the meal was going to be served. The hors d' oeuvre tray had stood empty since his arrival and no one seemed interested in having it replenished. Eight hours earlier he had had lunch with Kara's parents and he had been so preoccupied with the information he had passed on to them, that he had not done justice to the excellent meal. Now he regretted that omission. He felt slightly light-headed.

Angela clapped her hands.

"Dinner is ready to be served, everyone."

Nick shook his head. He was terribly tired. He would leave as soon as appropriately possible.

The group followed Jon and Angela along a narrow passageway to a large dining room.

"Oh, Angiela what a difference. It's really smashing."

Both Ginnie and Vicki apparently were enthralled with whatever changes had been made in the conversion of this room. Nick was not sure that he liked the green, yellow and white color scheme that Angie was being complimented on.

Nick personally found the furnishings ostentatious, certainly not in keeping with the dignified matriarchal image conjured up when he first saw the distinguished building from the outside.

Jon was nodding his head in agreement with the compliments aimed at Angela. Nick, remembering Kara's tastefully inviting townhouse, stayed silent.

Nameplates were displayed at each dinner place.

Nick and Satomi were seated side-by-side.

After a delectable salad had been served using produce from Jon's extensive garden, a maid appeared, offering a choice of roast beef, Chicken Cordon Bleu and brook trout on a large tray. A second maid followed on the heels of the first displaying a divided platter containing roasted and whipped potatoes, minted peas, glazed carrots and steamed asparagus. Nick was famished. He took a grilled trout and a portion of everything else. He would have to compliment Jon he certainly knew how to satisfy the appetite of his guests.

He was beginning to relax and feel comfortable with these strangers.

Nick felt a hand on his thigh.

Turning, he looked into the seductive eyes of Satomi.

"I'm staying at the Inn in the 'Cloister Wing'. If this meal doesn't fully satisfy your appetite, I have the perfect antidote. Please visit me tonight," she whispered.

Nick removed her hand.

"I have an enormous amount of work I must deal with tonight. Perhaps I can take a rain check."

Nick almost laughed out aloud at the expression of incredulity registered on Satomi's face.

Oh, Kara, how easily others pale in contrast, Nick thankfully conceded. He had fallen in love with Kara almost instantaneously and a great sense of peace filled him. Here he was with one of the most sought after models in Europe endeavoring to entice him and she had little effect on him. There was a time he would have enjoyed being diverted in this manner and would have played the game according to international rules. She had flawless features and the svelte body associated with her profession. Nick looked at her in a detached manner and compared her to Kara with the blazing jade eyes, alluring mouth, sensational curves and quick, droll mind. His temperature rose at the thought of her.

Satomi, you do not stand a chance.

He released his breath slowly. He had passed a very important test and in a ludicrous way he had Jon to thank for putting temptation in his path.

Jon was looking over at the two of them, heads close together, and when Nick happened to catch his glance he thought he saw a look of satisfaction reflected on his face.

Angela announced that desert and coffee would be served in the parlor. This was a small, quaint room, reserved for visitors in Victorian times. It was still furnished in the style of that era. This diversion gave everyone time to move around. Nick approved of this room. This was the way the whole farmhouse should look. Nick walked over to the window and stood looking out at the patio with its hanging lights. Jon joined him.

"I'd like to show you around soon and immediately after dessert may be as good a time as any."

Nick eyed Jon contemplatively. He was beginning to wonder when the reasons for his visit would be revealed. He had already deduced that Satomi was high on the list.

"I'll look forward to it."

Jon and Nick walked over to the stables, excusing themselves after finishing dessert.

They left the others chatting over coffee and liqueurs.

Jon led the way talking as they wended their way. "Do you have horses, Nick?"

"Yes. I have a farm and property in France and I ride most of the time I'm there."

Jon looked at Nick curiously. He was having a hard time measuring up this man who projected a sophisticated image and was certainly handsome enough to capture most feminine hearts. Satomi was completely entranced by him. He was concerned that perhaps Kara had become captivated with this man as well. Jon had been perturbed to find Nick to be the famous heart specialist and further alarmed to discover that Nick took his wealth for granted. Nick's debonair persona apparently fascinated almost everyone he came into contact with—it certainly had his guests in awe. He was someone to be reckoned with.

Inside the stables, Nick looked at the horses with interest as they walked along the center aisle with stalls on both sides, accompanied by snorts and neighs as they passed. Jon patted certain animals, mentioning pertinent information about them. "Lady Guinevere" has taken 'Best of Show' at the Harrogate Fair. "Fearless Freddie" has just been entered into his first show and "Kojak" is about to be sent out to stud."

They continued until they reached the stall they had been heading toward. With a soft whinny a bright-eyed tan colored mare came over and pressed her nose into Jon's outstretched hand. Nick reached out and patted her neck, inspecting the animal closely at the same time.

"What's the data on this one? She's a beauty."

Jon leaned against the wall, observing Nick stroking the filly's mane.

"Well, apart from the fact that "Kara's Karma" is potentially the best horse I have and by far the most expensive, she has won the most prestigious awards over the last couple of months. A month ago, Her Majesty the Queen, presented the "McCullough Cup" to her at the Edinburgh Horse Fair for the best in her class. It's Kara's horse."

Nick kept looking at the horse, continuing to stroke its sleek neck, despite being shaken by Jon's statement.

"What does Kara think about that?"

"She doesn't know yet. It's my wedding present. If that doesn't get her back here, nothing will. She loves this animal. It will be worth the 500,000 pounds I invested."

Nick froze on the spot. Jon sounded like a horse trader—money invested? Nick was disturbed by Jon's blunt disclosure.

Abruptly Nick gave the horse a final pat and turned around. Folding his arms across his chest and leaning back against the door frame he looked intently at Jon. "When do you intend telling Kara?"

"When she comes back to marry me, which I anticipate will be quite soon."

Jon had the look of a man sure of himself. Nick would not want to be playing baccarat with him right now. A coldness invaded Nick's senses that had nothing to do with the crisp night air.

Apart from a few trite declarations, Nick had heard no real sense of love and tenderness expressed for Kara in Jon's conversations. He had not asked about her—was that because he did not think Nick knew her well enough, or that he was afraid he knew her too well?

In a purposely cool tone Nick asked.

"Will Angela give her blessing to this alliance? She appears reluctant to let you go."

Jon looked as if he were about to answer and then changed his mind in the process, fumbling with a reply. "Angie is fully aware of the situation. She understands where I'm coming from and agrees. I foresee no problems."

What kind of a reply is that? Nick thinks grimly. *Jon is deliberately evading honest answers and clouding the issue. He is not ready to give up either Kara or Angela. In addition, Jon is trying to maneuver me into a situation with Satomi, just in case he needs extra ammunition against me.*

Clever, devious fellow, this Jon. Where was it all leading, and why?

Jon stood away from the door and looked at his watch.

"We should return to the others. Our conversation, of course, must remain private—I have your word on that?"

"That is your prerogative."

As they walked out of the stables Jon eyed Nick carefully before confessing, "Satomi is a very erotically talented person, I think you would enjoy being with her. She has expressed a definite interest in you, which believe me, old chap, is a rare compliment. She came back from town this afternoon, unusually excited about seeing you there."

Jon looked at Nick enquiringly.

Nick's heart dropped—where did she see him? Coming out of the jewelers? His mind raced. All right—there would be no problem on that score; he had also picked up gold horse-head cufflinks as Jon's birthday gift as well as the inexpensive set of pearls.

Nick shrugged his shoulders.

"I have not met Satomi before tonight, but she informed me that at one time our paths almost crossed. No doubt you heard her say that.

To fill you in on my intentions, so that you know where I stand, I've been a confirmed bachelor for some time and have finally found the woman I've been waiting for. With this in mind, I intend proposing to her just as soon as I return to California and look forward to changing my lifestyle completely. So in answer to your invitation, I am happily unavailable, thank you."

Curiosity was ill-disguised on Jon's face.

"It wouldn't be Kara's friend, Marcie?"

"It could be."

That should keep him guessing. His clipped words were aimed to discourage further questioning.

Jon persisted.

"Would it be presumptuous to ask who it is?"

"Yes. The lady is not yet aware of my intentions."

Nick looked Jon squarely in the face.

"Until I approach my future wife, there is nothing further I wish to disclose on this matter."

He spoke with icy finality.

Jon dropped the subject.

They returned to the house by a back door. Voices and laughter reached them. A game of Charades was in progress and Nick and Jon stood in the doorway, mugs of coffee in hand, watching until the game ended.

Nick suppressed a yawn; it was almost midnight, time to leave.

Angela had been making a pest of herself most of the evening taking pictures indiscriminately.

When Nick announced he was about to depart, she insisted on more poses from the group.

Seating Satomi between Jon and Nick she cajoled.

"Put your arm around Satomi, Nick, you have such a serious expression on your face. Relax! She's not going to bite you."

Reluctantly he complied. Satomi snuggled closer to him, smiling invitingly into his eyes.

Angela nodded approvingly.

Time was dragging and it was almost one in the morning before Nick could get away.

He stood in the doorway ready to leave the farmhouse.

Jon shook his hand.

"Thanks for coming. Would you mind dropping Satomi off at the Inn? She's staying there too."

Nick compressed his lips.

"Fine. Is Satomi ready?"

"I'm right here, Nick."

She had placed a stole around her shoulders and came out of the bedroom hallway with Angela. She had heard the last part of the conversation.

As they drove back to the Inn Nick asked conversationally.

"I understand from Jon that I missed seeing you in town this afternoon."

Satomi perked up.

"Yes. I was pulling into a parking space opposite 'The Wishing Well Card and Gift' shop as you were backing out."

No cause for alarm, he had just picked up a postcard for Kara.

Curious, Satomi asked, "Where will your next seminars be held? Perhaps we will meet again in our travels."

Now there was cause for alarm.

"I will be in Paris and Japan, but my seminars provide few social opportunities. Usually my time is fully absorbed. The people who attend want to get full value and so breakfast and dinner meetings usually become part of the package. Actually, it's a very work-intensive event with little free time."

Conversation ceased at this point with little spoken until Nick walked Satomi back to her suite.

"Please come in for a nightcap."

"Sorry, I'm ready for bed."

"So am I," she whispered temptingly.

Without warning she stepped close to Nick and put her arms around his neck, kissing him passionately on the mouth.

"Think about that through the night. I'll be here waiting for you."

Her husky voice and provocative eyes held a wealth of promise.

Gently disengaging himself from her embrace, Nick looked at Satomi thoughtfully.

"You are a beautiful, exciting woman and you have a great deal to offer some lucky man, but that cannot be me. My heart is elsewhere."

So saying, without waiting for a response, he turned on his heel and walked away. He did not see the tears appear in Satomi's eyes.

Ever since she had caught her first glimpse of Nick she had become infatuated with him, following his career and romantic involvements like a stupid teenager with a crush on a movie star.

She was sorry she had confided her feelings to Angie and Jon. That had been foolish, but she would not give up on Nick Prendergast.

CHAPTER TWENTY FIVE

Walking around the old town of Thirsk, with its beautiful ancient church and plethora of antiques shops was an unusual, but enjoyable, activity for Nick. Seldom was there time to spend in idle pursuits such as this, even though it had commenced with a purpose in mind. Browsing around the "Needle in a Haystack" antiques shop he came across just what he was looking for. An exquisitely carved cameo of a beautiful lady's head wearing an elaborate hat and holding a parasol had fallen from its velvet display mat and lay face down on the glass shelf. Curious, Nick asked what was hidden and when it was retrieved knew immediately that the gorgeous piece was perfect for Kara. It was set in an 18-karat gold frame, intricately and delicately designed. Suspended on a long gold chain Nick could imagine it around Kara's slender neck. Charging it to his American Express Gold credit card he was very satisfied with his purchase.

Sitting drinking tea and eating a scone at an outdoor café near St. Mary's church, Nick relished spending quiet time alone. He was not looking forward to Jon's birthday bash after the uncomfortable time spent at his home the night before. He was going because Kara's parents had invited him and he had promised to attend. He wanted to get to know them; in fact it was important for him to do so. There was much he needed to discuss with them. The time spent with them at the beach would, he hoped, provide that opportunity. Nick's spirits rose. The familiarity established so easily with Kara's parents defied explanation. They were the kind of parents he would have wished for himself.

Looking at his reflection in the armoire mirror later that day, Nick frowned. He was impeccably dressed in a custom-made dinner suit, but under the circumstances this could be a hindrance. He did not have the slightest interest in attracting feminine attention and he fervently wished that Satomi had resigned herself to his recent confession and would be concentrating her efforts elsewhere.

Nick walked downstairs, through the side exit of the Inn, and across the lawn to a cobblestone path that led to the railway coaches.

It was after seven at night and the cars seemed uninhabited until he opened a door and the hum of conversations reached him. A Major Domo stood waiting.

"May I see your invitation, sir?" he enquired politely.

Nick glanced at the clipboard in the man's hand.

"I'm with the Olavssen party—Nicholas Prendergast."

"Yes, of course, please come this way."

Nick found himself in a Pullman car festooned with balloons and paper decorations. A big sign read "Happy Birthday Jon." Most of the tables were occupied and a grin lit up his face when he saw Kara's mother coming toward him. She hugged him briefly.

"The lights are going to be put out in about fifteen minutes, so get a drink from the bar and join us at our table. Gus is watching out for you."

She nodded her head in the general direction. Noticing the two packages in Nick's hands, she asked, "Are they for Jon?"

"Yes. One is from Kara and the other one is from me."

"Allow me to put them with the rest of the gifts," she suggested, taking them from him.

Nick walked the remaining distance to join Kara's father who was rising to his feet at the sight of him. He had a smile on his face and an outstretched hand.

"Good to see you again, Nick."

He sounded genuinely pleased to see him once more.

Turning to the man by his side, who had also risen to his feet, he introduced Nick to Jon's father, Jim Williams, who glanced at him with interest and also held out his hand with a smile. Gus Olavssen placed a hand on Nick's shoulder.

"I've just been telling Jim how delighted I was to be matched with a chess player of your caliber yesterday."

Jim Williams sat down and picked up his drink.

"You must be pretty good to gain the respect of Gus. Do you play much?"

"Not anymore," Nick admitted," I wish I had more time. I used to play in my spare time when I was down at Oxford, which is where my rating peaked, but I am now going downhill."

Both of the older men looked at Nick with interest. Gus Olavssen was graduated from Cambridge University, the rival of Oxford University. No doubt there could be interesting conversations to look forward to between them in the future.

"Let's get a drink," Kara's father recommended, "before the place becomes noisy."

They maneuvered their way to the bar and Nick admired its impressive carving as they stood beside it.

"How long ago is it that these coaches were actually built?"

Gus Olavssen tapped his chin reflectively.

"Let me see. Jon discovered them in the old railway shunting terminal in Newcastle shortly after he went into partnership with Leif on this place. He was quite excited about them, even though they were decrepit and in need of extensive refurbishing. As far as I know, they had been there for some years, having been released from the main London Terminal. Don't quote me, but I think these Pullmans have to be over seventy years old."

Nick looked around with genuine interest.

"Their restoration appears to have been done exceptionally well."

"Oh, I agree," Nick's companion noted dryly, "Jon spares no expense when it comes to his obsessions."

Picking up their drinks they returned to the table to find Silvia, Satomi and Renata Williams there also. Irritated at being in close contact with Satomi again, Nick nonchalantly acknowledged Satomi with a nod. He certainly did not wish to have Satomi flirting with him or exploring his body in front of Kara's parents, as she seemed intent upon doing.

Already she was eyeing him in a lazily bold examination.

"This seat is reserved for you."

She patted the vacant chair between herself and Renata Williams.

Gus turned to Nick and introduced Renata, whose close inspection brought the feeling that his presence was not entirely approved—as if he were butting in on personal family festivities. Nick was dismayed. On one side was a woman who apparently lived life on her own terms without regard for social mores and on the other side a woman who looked as if she devoutly endorsed them.

"Satomi is taking time out of her busy modeling schedule to spend a few days with Angela and Jon." Gus explained.

Nick nodded absently.

"Yes, I know. We had dinner together last night."

The surprised expression on Mrs. Olavssen's face alerted Nick to his faux pas. Quickly he added, "We were seated next to each other at a dinner party held at Jon's farmhouse last night."

Did he detect a note of relief in her voice as she replied, "That's nice. We haven't had a chance to visit since the dining room was remodeled. We are anxious to see for ourselves the imaginative changes we understand Angela has made."

He glanced at Mrs. Williams to his right, whose sour expression did not give the impression that she was in agreement with this viewpoint.

Suddenly the lights went off and on a couple of times and those people standing around, rushed to their seats. The lights were turned off completely. In the darkness a few giggles could be heard and the whispers of others shushing them. Nick felt soft movements on his left thigh, stealthily moving higher. He took hold of the hand, moving it away from his leg at the same time lips touched his face.

"Stop that," he murmured fiercely, squeezing the fingers held tightly in his own.

The lights flashed on and everyone started yelling "Surprise" and "Happy Birthday" as Jon stood speechless in the doorway.

Most people had risen to their feet, clapping their hands, anxiously straining to see Jon's face. Except for Nick and Satomi. Mrs. Olavssen was staring at Nick and Satomi's hands entwined together.

Damn!

He released Satomi's fingers and glared at her. She snickered and opening her evening purse, removed a tissue and proceeded to wipe the lipstick traces from Nick's face.

"My aim wasn't very accurate, was it?"

He pushed her hand away reaching into his jacket pocket for a handkerchief.

Angela rushed over to Jon, giving him an affectionate kiss. His parents waited at the table, watching Angela share the spotlight with their son. Neither one of them looked particularly pleased, Nick noted. Jon had regained his composure by the time he reached his parents and kissed his mother affectionately and hugged his father briefly.

Satomi uncurled herself from the chair and sloped off toward Jon and chastely kissed his cheek, immediately returning to Nick's side with a smile, as if expecting to be rewarded for her modest behavior.

Jon and Angie started circulating among the assembled guests and Nick took the opportunity to walk back to the bar to get away from Satomi's suffocating closeness. Leaning against the counter, he was pleased when Kara's father joined him and asked, "Would you like to look around the other cars while all this jollity is taking place? We will be back before we are missed."

Gus noticed the look of relief on Nick's face.

Not much that happened escaped Gus Olavssen's scrutiny and he recognized a determined woman when he saw one.

"Sounds like a great idea."

They pressed their way through the crowded narrow space to the doorway. Nick did not look in Satomi's direction, but Silvia Olavssen did and witnessed the anger registered on the too perfect face.

They arrived back just as Jon and Angela were returning to their table. Satomi looked bored and her eyes were hard as she surveyed Nick. She would not accept Nick's negative conduct and determined to teach him a lesson should it not improve. On the way back to London, she would probably pay a quick visit to Lady Bassenthorpe—there was a woman who knew everything!

Tables in the other two dining cars had been festively set up for the meal and a porter, dressed in old style clothing, grandly announced the commencement of dinner.

For the first time Leif's smiling face appeared and Jon jestingly admonished him.

"Some friend you are, keeping me in the dark about all of this. Did you bribe the staff? I'm going to have to talk to them."

Jon patted Leif's shoulder amiably. The major part his friend had played in keeping this a secret must have been monumental. It had been a big enough task keeping Kara's welcome home party a secret, but at least he and Leif had worked on it together. For this special celebration Leif had to work on it almost single-handedly, without his assistance, and into the bargain making sure it was concealed from him.

Leif, with his enterprising staff, had outdone themselves in the creative preparation and imaginative presentation of each delectable item on the menu. The guests were pampered deliciously and sinfully, sating the body, and soothing the spirit.

Champagne flowed freely and when the birthday cake was slowly wheeled in front of Jon's table, all eyes were riveted on the masterpiece before them. It was an incredibly realistic model of Jon's farmhouse, complete with the formal front garden and horses grazing in the background. Jon was touched. He loved this farm home of his more than anything else. Leif stood smiling lopsidedly, aware of the affect upon his friend. Jon walked over and clasped him around the shoulders, hugging him to acknowledge his thanks.

Words failed him.

Nick looked around for Angela to observe her reaction, but she was nowhere in sight. He reached for his camera as Jon looked in his direction.

"How about something for posterity?"

Jon nodded.

Nick walked over and took a picture of Jon standing beside the cake, and another of Jon and Leif with the cake between them. Jon's parents strolled over and Nick took pictures of them also.

The huge wooden slab, upon which the cake rested, was carried over to a table. The lights dimmed slightly and the candles, placed to resemble fencing around the tableau, were lit. A rich contralto voice started singing "Happy Birthday" and everyone joined in.

Before the candles were blown out, the song was started again. Nick was so intent on observing the group around the festive table that he was taken by surprise when the top of the large paper-covered wagon, which had borne the cake into the room, suddenly burst open. Angela stood posing voluptuously in a skintight gold sequined gown, with long white gloves and wearing a blonde Marilyn Monroe-type wig. In a soft, breathless voice she cooed her way through the birthday song, with accompanying facial expressions and stances.

Enthusiastic applause broke out at its completion.

It had been a flawless performance and it took everyone by surprise. Jon had been looking at Angela in amazement and went to her, lifting her from the box and willingly receiving her kiss. Nick had automatically taken pictures, capturing the electrifying event.

Cries of, "Speech, speech," echoed through the railway car.

With his parents standing beside him, and Angela, hanging on to his arm Jon gave a brief speech, thanking Leif, his parents, Angela, and all friends for the outstanding surprise and insisting that everyone enjoy themselves.

Nick looked at Kara's parents.

They were sitting quietly, at ease, observing the action around them. They were such a gracious couple, Nick found his gaze returning to them unconsciously.

Nick flipped off the miniature Dictaphone recorder, which he had switched on discreetly. Before leaving his suite, he had impetuously reached for the tiny machine, deciding to do this as a memento for Kara, to show he was trying to be fair and honorable in this competition with his rival. Nick honestly had expected her name to come up in Jon's short speech, and he was troubled when it had not. Kara's name was constantly on his mind and emblazoned on his heart. It was not conceivable that love for her would become so insignificant that it was overlooked.

In retrospect, Nick mused, this could be an interesting tape to listen to.

The cake was ceremoniously cut and distributed, with more champagne flowing. Angela looked very happy and a shiver went through Nick. She looked like a bride at her own wedding reception.

He glanced at Kara's parents.

Gus Olavssen was quietly observing the scene, one arm casually draped around the shoulders of his wife, whose somber expression gave Nick the impression she was unsettled by the events. Nick sighed, perhaps their hopes were to see Jon and Kara married.

Was it just last night in the stables that Jon had expressed so strongly his intent to wed Kara in such positive tones that left no doubt of his purpose. Jon, with his arms around Angela, was making a mockery of his alleged love for Kara.

An annoyed look flashed across Nick's face.

He rose from the table.

"Please excuse me."

He walked over to the door, leading outside. He had to get out of there.

Standing outside, with his back against a tree, Nick stared at the new moon. It was just a faint sliver, but that same moon would be shining on Kara. Nick looked at his watch. It was almost nine-thirty, which would make it almost dawn in California. He had an urgent need to hear Kara's voice.

He was about to return to his suite at the Inn, when a hand placed on his arm caused him to flinch.

"Sorry, Nicholas, I was concerned about you. You looked a little upset in there and I could imagine how you felt, so I decided to find you and ask you to come for a walk with me."

Silvia Olavssen stood waiting for his response.

He roused himself and patted the hand that lay on his arm saying.

"That sounds like a good idea. I'm really not much of a party person," Nick broke off and looked intently at his rescuer, "what was that you said about imagining you knew how I felt?"

Kara's mother looked a little doubtful.

"Kara phoned us last night. She seemed very confused and I feel as if I am betraying her trust somewhat, but for the first time she mentioned Jon proposing to her and not being sure how she felt about him."

Nick's face tightened and Silvia's face displayed concern.

"After tonight's exhibition, I felt that Kara should be alerted to Jon's questionable behavior. Her father feels it is not our right to interfere at this point, since Kara has not made a decision. Jon, I'm sure, is aware of our observations, but he is not, after all, officially engaged to Kara."

Her usually soft voice held an icy edge.

"Jon will certainly realize that our consideration for the future happiness of our daughter will be judged on acceptable behavior and principals."

"Then you don't think Kara should be advised that her possible future husband suffers from the "out of sight, out of mind" syndrome?"

Mrs. Olavssen shrugged noncommittally.

"Unfortunately my hands are tied. Let's walk. It's a little chilly out here."

Immediately Nick removed his jacket and placed it around the narrow shoulders.

She smiled in appreciation, and snuggled into the warmth.

For a few minutes they walked along the smooth paths around the gardens without speaking. Stopping, Kara's mother took Nick's hand.

"It has worried me that the same phrase could be applied to you, too. I didn't realize you knew Satomi so well."

Nick halted in his tracks and looked deeply into the face that so closely resembled the one he loved most.

"I know you observed Satomi and me holding hands and saw her wiping the lipstick from my face. You also know that she and I sat together at dinner last night, but what you don't know is that I have not encouraged her in any way."

Nick looked uncomfortable.

He pulled Silvia's arm through the crook of his elbow and they commenced walking again.

"You know, I am becoming a little embarrassed by the personal nature of the conversations I have been having with you and your husband in the short time I have met you. I am a very private person, but it is important to me that you understand how serious I am about your daughter."

His voice was subdued as he persisted, "Last night I made a point of informing both Jon and Satomi that I am in love with a woman I hope will become my wife, without disclosing her name. It appears that Satomi has chosen to ignore what in essence was a warning to her. She has put me in an awkward situation, which she may believe is to her advantage. I have every intention of rectifying that should she persist."

Sighing, Nick's face registered dejection.

"I'm very sorry that this has occurred. I cannot predict or be accountable for Satomi's intentions or actions, but she has not been, nor will she be encouraged by me. Unfortunately, as she is a guest, as am I, her uncalled for behavior must be endured to a certain degree for the sake of propriety and the comfort level of the other guests."

Sympathy was reflected on Mrs. Olavssen's face.

"I empathize with what you are saying. I suppose because you are such a handsome, fascinating man that women are drawn to you magnetically."

A crooked smile appeared on Nick's face.

"If that is true, why has it not happened to your daughter? She appears to be able to live without me very easily."

Silvia chuckled.

"Well, she asked about you last night and she did sound concerned, especially when her father told her that one of the world's top models would be sitting at the same table with us tonight. Of course we didn't know at that time just how captivating you would be to that particular model."

She squeezed Nick's hand when she saw the look of dismay that came over his face.

"I suppose we should return to the cars before a search party is sent out looking for us. I have a lot of faith in Kara's judgment, Nicholas, and I am sufficiently optimistic in believing that both you and I will feel she has made the right choice."

Nick turned and gave her a quick hug; it helped having her on his side. She returned his jacket with a smile.

It felt very warm inside the Pullman and excited chatter met their ears as they entered. Gus Olavssen, even though he was talking to an older couple near the bar, was keeping a close watch on those leaving and entering by either the doors leading outside, or the tandem door leading into the other cars. His face brightened when he saw his wife coming through the door and Nick was touched to see the tenderness with which they greeted each other.

"The dancing has just started in Camelot Court and if you want to catch me whilst I am young and nimble, we'd better have the next dance."

It was said facetiously by Gus, much to his wife's delight.

"This really is an offer I can't refuse," she said, taking her husband's hand. "Keep a couple of slow numbers for me, please Nicholas."

He bowed slightly in answer.

Stiffening at the sight of Satomi making a beeline for him, with Jon, and Angela trailing after her, Nick fought the impulse to escape. Feeling more reassured after the conversation out in the garden, Nick had temporarily forgotten what a nuisance Satomi was.

"Oh, good! Nick, you're here. We've been searching the Inn for you."

He smiled woodenly; she just did not give up.

Satomi took his hand and started pulling him toward the door.

"Let's dance, the orchestra sounds fabulous.

Nick gritted his teeth, searching for an excuse.

Thump. A slap on the back from Jon.

"Ready, old chap? We'll spend an hour or so in the ballroom and then the younger crowd will be coming to my suite in the hotel to open the gifts and finish off the party there."

He was holding Angela's hand.

"Angie and I will join you in the ballroom shortly. She's been bubbling over with some news she can't hold back much longer."

Seeing the indecision on Nick's face, Jon asked.

"You're not going to desert me?"

"Of course he's not," Angela put in quickly, "he wouldn't want to spoil the fun."

Nick shrugged his shoulders. This was, after all, another opportunity to observe Jon, who was providing him with valuable ammunition.

The four of them walked across the lawn and through the Inn to the ballroom, where Jon and Angela parted company with Nick and Satomi. Camelot Court had been closed off to the public for the evening to allow Jon's guests to enjoy more privacy.

Satomi caught Nick's hand, and pulled him toward the dance floor.

"Mmm. One of my favorite numbers."

She placed a hand on each of Nick's shoulders, waiting impatiently for his touch. Even in this contrived setting, being so close to the man she had fantasized about nightly for so long was a dream come true.

Nick took Satomi's right hand from his shoulder, holding it firmly, while he placed his other hand lightly on the thin silk barely covering Satomi's back.

After a couple of dances with Satomi rubbing against him in an embarrassingly flagrant way, Nick was grateful when Silvia Olavssen came to rescue him.

"Will you still be sleeping overnight at our home after the dancing ends?"

"That would be good," he said, "unless you would prefer that I not."

A sly look entered the sparkling green eyes.

"Or you get a better offer?" A knowing smile followed this statement.

"We have been watching Satomi trying to seduce you on the dance floor and Gus said he is going to give you a medal if you reach our home intact."

Nick was amused. Silvia had brought some humor into the awkward situation and he was grateful to her. He allowed his body to relax. He was worn out trying to avert Satomi's brazen advances. She was not being very subtle in her attempts to lure him. He had to be on his guard constantly and he was sorry that he had agreed to attend Jon's private party. Clearing his throat and studying Silvia, he spoke quickly.

"There's going to be a party shortly in Jon's suite here at the Inn and they wouldn't take no for an answer. Jon will be opening the gifts at that time and, to be honest, I wanted to see his face when he opened Kara's gift."

A haunted look passed over Nick's saddened face. He must be masochistic wanting to watch the expressions of a two-faced man, a man without conscience.

He emitted a long sigh.

"How will I gain entry to your home? Will someone have to wait up for me?"

There was a pause before he continued. "Perhaps, I'd better stay at the Inn. It seems I am unnecessarily complicating things."

The second dance was ending.

Silvia patted Nick's arm.

"Let's discuss it before we leave. We are looking forward to your visit and there shouldn't be a problem. I thought you might feel comfortable using Kara's suite."

Nick almost whooped with joy. He would love to sleep in Kara's bed; it was a step closer to being with her.

He picked up the slim, elegantly gowned lady and swung her around, planting a kiss on her cheek after setting her carefully back on the floor.

There were a few surprised looks and Silvia Olavssen, with her usual aplomb, said airily.

"It's my dancing, you know. It gets them every time."

A beaming Nick led Kara's mother back to the edge of the dance floor where her husband was waiting.

"That was a rather daring maneuver you just exhibited, young man. Had I tried that, I would have been chastised."

He smiled as he spoke.

His wife hastened to explain.

"I just informed Nicholas that he could use Kara's chambers tonight—as you saw, he could hardly contain himself."

Nick had an ear-to-ear grin on his face.

"I'm going to the powder room, so you two behave yourselves whilst I'm gone." So saying Silvia drifted away.

"Would you like to take a stroll outside? I find it quite stifling in here."

Gus Olavssen loosened the front of his dinner jacket as if to emphasize his condition.

He had a serious expression on his face and Nick nodded in agreement. They walked past the reception area and out onto a loggia that held more of Jon's well-wishers. They were becoming noisy.

Gus guided Nick over to an almost deserted path.

"We had a phone call from Kara last night."

Nick nodded.

"So your wife informed me."

The stern expression on the older man's face left Nick with a sinking feeling. Was a lecture coming? Nick predicted Mr. Olavssens's deliberations. He would tell Nick how Jon, who had almost been a family member for so long, was his choice for Kara.

Nick would protest. Mr. Olavssen, did you not see how Jon behaved tonight in front of everyone, kissing and embracing Angela when he so recently proposed to Kara? Mr. Olavssen would reason, Jon is just sowing his wild oats. We have known all along that Kara and Jon were intended for each other.

Perspiration stood out on Nick's forehead.

They were almost back at the loggia entrance again, and the lanterns were shedding their glow.

Gus Olavssen was still talking and Nick had to refocus his thoughts to listen.

". . . and that was when she said she was confused about a marriage proposal which Jon had made to her a few days before she returned to California at the end of August. Kara said she had doubts that it could work out because whenever she thought about Jon she saw your face."

There! That was the reason for this private discussion. To be reminded that Jon had first claim and he was interfering with their plans. Nick was infuriated. In a quiet, tight voice he said,

"So that is why you are upset. You would prefer she marries Jon, and I am getting in the way. I'm sorry if I have ruined your plans, but I love Kara with all my heart. We have a lot in common and we could have an amazing life together. Besides, I will make a much more suitable husband for her than Jon."

Gus Olavssen peered at Nick over his glasses.

"I thought I just said that."

"What? What did you say?" Nick asked hoarsely.

"Already I like what I see of you, Nick, and I appreciate your honesty and straightforward approach. I want you to know that we don't approve of Jon's tactics. It is disappointing and degrading to observe this side of him. I obviously can't speak for Kara, but I hope she makes the right choice and that the best man wins."

The delight on Nick's face caused Gus Olavssen to take a step backward, raising his hands in caution.

"Please don't attempt to pick me up. I'm not as light as my wife and there are guests around who would think our behavior rather strange."

They started laughing and sat down on a bench until they had composed themselves once again.

Companionably they walked back to the dance hall, grinning now and again at their absurd behavior.

They saw Mrs. Olavssen dancing with Jon when they entered the room and she smiled happily when she saw them.

"I think a drink would be in order, don't you?"

Gus steered Nick over toward the bar.

They were almost there when Satomi and Angela intercepted them.

"We came to ask you to dance," Angela said, looking first at Nick and then at Gus Olavssen.

Nick turned to Gus. "I have already danced with Satomi this evening, so perhaps you should have the pleasure."

With that he took Angela's hand, leading her toward the dance floor. Satomi followed them, scowling. Gus trailed behind her, a smile of approval at Nick's manipulation hovering around his lips.

Angela had changed into a long rose pink flowered satin dress, which swayed around her as she moved. She appeared more subdued than at any time Nick had seen her.

"I was very impressed with your impersonation. It was very good."

She smiled rather wanly and closed her eyes. Nick was concerned.

"Are you feeling all right? You look a little tired. We could sit this dance out."

Angela responded quietly, "I do feel a little faint, there has been so much excitement getting ready for today and it does feel warm in this room."

Tucking her hand through his arm they walked through French doors, which led out to a patio. Angela sat down on a cushioned bench and Nick stood beside her.

"Would you like a cold drink?"

She shook her head.

"No thanks. I just feel tired and I guess a bit depressed. I thought this would be a wonderful evening, but it isn't turning out that way."

Nick looked at Angela in surprise. She had appeared so happy all evening.

"Funny isn't it, you think you know someone so well, and then kazoom, they suddenly turn into a stranger before your eyes."

Tears welled in Angela's eyes.

"What a mess!"

Nick handed Angela his crumpled handkerchief and she dabbed her eyes with it. Nick turned around when he heard footsteps behind him.

Jon stood looking at Angela as Satomi went over and sat beside her on the seat, putting an arm around her.

"I think we should leave, Angie baby. Why don't you stay with me at the Inn tonight, there's plenty of room in my suite."

Angela nodded looking miserable and forsaken.

He inadvertently had blundered into a very personal situation. Feeling awkward Nick said, "I hope you will forgive me if I say goodnight at this point. I have an important phone call to make to California."

He addressed this remark to Jon, who nodded absently, but he was acutely aware of Satomi's penetrating eyes on him. Smiling encouragingly at Angela, Nick hastily returned to the ballroom, inwardly shuddering at the capricious relationship which he had started to observe between Jon and Angela.

The Olavssens' were with a small group of friends when Nick joined them. Mrs. Olavssen put her arm around Nick's waist, as if she were accustomed to doing so.

"We are about to leave. What are your plans?"

"I am ready to leave also."

"Oh, good. Let's do it."

She went over and kissed the cheeks of Renata and Jim Williams and shook hands with several other people. Following her around was her husband. Nick stood waiting. He shook hands with a few people he had met before leaving the room on the trail of the Olavssens'.

Gus asked as they exited the room. "How about leaving your car here and traveling with us? You won't need your car tomorrow, since we will use a four-wheel drive to go to the beach."

"That's fine, but my luggage is in the trunk of my car. I'd like to stop off and collect it?"

Ten minutes later they were on the main road heading east to their home, "Velkoment."

Kara's mother insisted on taking over the backseat of their Rolls Royce limousine while Gus with Nick sat opposite her. Silvia promptly curled up, pulling a fur car rug around her shoulders and sighing in relief. She smiled at both men and closed her eyes. Loosening his jacket and taking off his bow tie, Gus smiled to see Nick doing the same thing.

"Pleased that is over, are you?"

Nick nodded his agreement. They settled down to a discussion of the current political issues and the international stock market.

The huge front doors of the mansion swung open at their approach.

"We're home, darling."

His wife was sound asleep.

Gus smiled at Nick, reaching over and gently rubbing his wife's shoulder. Silvia sat up and leaned back against the leather upholstery. Her eyes were closed.

"Don't waken me before eight, Gus, or you will have to bear the consequences."

"My wife gets very aggressive when she is deprived." Gus said softly.

Silvia Olavssen's eyes flew open and Nick's heart skipped a beat. For a moment he saw Kara in those fiery green eyes.

A boisterous laugh issued from Kara's father.

"When she is deprived of sleep, I obviously meant."

Silvia Olavssen shook her head slowly, trying not to smile at her husband's naughty playfulness. Nick's throat tightened. The warmth of their affection surrounded and included him.

Nick climbed out of the car as the other door was opened. The master of the house was home.

"The luggage in the boot is to be taken to Kara's suite."

Alfred, their chauffeur, looked with interest at this information.

"Is she coming home, sir?"

"No. Mr. Prendergast will occupy her bedroom overnight."

Gus placed an arm around his wife's waist and Nick watched them ascend the shallow granite steps. He took his briefcase from Alfred and followed them into the foyer.

"Is it too late for a brandy and a game of Chess?" Gus enquired.

Nick raised his eyebrows.

"I don't think you would stand a chance this time. Before I was at a disadvantage—I was preoccupied and quite frankly, scared to death. Right now I have a pressing telephone call to make, to California."

A mischievous smile lurked around his host's mouth.

"All right. I'll let you off the hook this time, but we must have another game before you leave. Correct?"

Nick nodded his head, covering his mouth to hide a yawn.

They all walked up the wide staircase together and Mrs. Olavssen sleepily said goodnight to Nick, rubbing her cheek against his. She went into a room through double doors and the two men continued walking along the wide corridor. Nick's luggage had been placed inside one of the rooms and the lights had been turned on. The down-filled comforter on the bed had been turned back.

"No rush to get up in the morning. Just come down when you are ready."

Gus Olavssen gently punched Nick on the arm as he was leaving.

"A telephone is by the bed—say hello to Kara for us."

Nick was smiling as he closed the door. Divesting himself of his jacket, he looked around the room with interest. So this was Kara's bedroom.

He could imagine her in this room and she felt very close to him. He had thought of only her from the time of leaving California to the arrival in this unfamiliar part of England. At last he was at peace, as if they were sharing this experience together.

It was after midnight, it would be just after 8:00 a.m. in California.

He went into the well-appointed blue and white bathroom and performed his nightly ablutions, changing into blue silk pajamas and switching off the light as he left. He opened the heavy velvet drapes and looked out. He could see the outline of trees and very little else. The moon had not reached its zenith. Nick settled himself on the bed, shoving a few decorative pillows behind his back.

Using his AT&T calling card he carefully dialed the international code and waited nervously. He felt as if he had been separated from Kara for an eternity. It was a direct connection. The phone rang several times. Nick was disappointed, Kara was not there. About to hang up, Kara sleepily spoke a soft "Hello."

In a cheerful voice Nick responded, "Hello darling, this is your private reporter checking in."

There was a pause before a breathless reply, "Oh, Nick, where are you?"

"Actually, my love, I am lying on your bed—I told your mother how much I missed you and she insisted that I sleep in your bed—for reassurance you understand?"

He could hear Kara laughing.

"You idiot! Really. Where are you?"

"Would I lie to you?"

Nick sounded aggrieved.

"If I said that the room I am in has very feminine white bedding, with a blue and white tiled fireplace and an elaborate white and gold French telephone with the number 638-502 on it, would that mean anything to you?"

There was an even longer interval of silence.

"I can't believe they would offer my suite when there are many others they could have chosen. What did you do to inveigle yourself into their good books?"

Nick sighed tiredly. Was she going to be difficult?

"I guess it was when I started telling them all about the trauma I had caused you in Rancho Mirage. You know, having your arm fractured and getting bonked on the head and then the pearls stolen. They thought I needed rewarding for putting their daughter through all of that and I suppose this is their way of punishing me."

Nick's sarcasm was evident. He had hoped, from indications during the conversations with her parents that she was missing him and would be willing to tell him so. He was aching for some sign from her, but she seemed very reluctant to come out of her cocoon.

He sighed audibly and changed the subject.

His voice held a serious undertone.

"Strange things are happening at The Black Bull Inn."

"Oh."

Kara's voice was subdued.

"Yes. I put the one ear-ring, still in its case, in my dresser drawer and when I was about to return it to your parents yesterday I discovered its absence."

"Oh, no, Nick."

He could hear the disbelief in Kara's voice. Nick continued,

"What is so amazing is that after the visit to your parents, I found that it had been returned. Right where I'd left it. Can you imagine that?"

Kara responded, incredulous at this turn of events. "Unbelievable. What do you think happened, Nick?"

"I've an idea and I'm trying to work something out. It's very sketchy at this point. Just a hunch, but I'll keep you informed."

A note of concern was in his voice. "By the way, darling, how's your arm and head? Is Emma looking after you properly?"

"My arm is feeling more comfortable, thank you, and the bandages are still in place. In answer to your question, Emma is terrific, I'm thinking of keeping her on permanently."

Nick smiled into the receiver.

"Good, I'm pleased about that. Say 'hi' to her. By the way are you receiving the postcards I've been sending?"

"Yes, we have. Emma can hardly wait for the postman to arrive. She is so excited following your trip."

"What about you?" he interrupted, "They are intended for you. Aren't I making them exciting enough to interest you? I can certainly change that—of course they probably will make Emma blush, if they are not censored by the U.S. Postal Service, but as long as they make you happy, I'll be glad to oblige."

"Nick, you know I didn't mean it like that," Kara protested. "I'm really enjoying following your travels. Very much."

He would have to be satisfied with that—or would he?

There was an awkward pause and Nick waited for Kara to speak. He had done most of the talking so far; Kara had contributed very little. He had more interesting conversations with his secretary discussing the morning's mail.

When she spoke, she asked if he had given the birthday package to Jon. She certainly brought him down to earth quickly.

He was beginning to get annoyed.

"Actually, Kara, I've seen Jon, Angela—and Satomi, several times since I arrived here on Thursday."

There was a distinct edginess to her voice.

"Oh, really and is the famous Satomi as beautiful in person as she is on the magazine covers?"

He deliberately waited a few moments before responding.

"Yes, she is. She's quite stunning."

He would let her think about that tidbit.

There was another long pause and Nick shook his head. It was like pulling teeth getting Kara to respond to him.

He tried another tack.

"You really didn't do Jon's farmhouse justice when you described it. I found it fascinating."

He immediately picked up the interest in Kara's voice.

"When did you go there?"

Finally he was starting to enjoy the conversation.

"Jon gave a dinner party Friday evening and invited me."

"Who was there?"

Nick went over the guest list and was amused when Kara said, "I suppose you and Satomi sat together."

He suppressed a chuckle. "How clever of you. How did you come to that conclusion?"

"Just a lucky guess, I suppose." She did not sound very pleased at her accuracy.

Nick decided to add fuel to the imaginary potential fire.

"Tonight there was a surprise birthday party for Jon at The Black Bull Inn where I'm staying. It took place in all three railway cars. It really was fun. Angela did a Marilyn Monroe impression, popping out of a cart to sing "Happy Birthday" to Jon—she was surprisingly good."

He waited tensely for Kara's reaction. Would she be jealous of the time Jon and Angela were spending together?

"No doubt you and Satomi were sitting together again." It was said crossly.

"You're absolutely right. Darling, you amaze me. You didn't mind, did you?"

"Of course not!"

Nick heard the catch in Kara's voice and he longed to hold her in his arms. He was being unkind, but he had to know. When was she going to realize her true feelings and admit them? She was so damned proud.

In a quiet voice Kara asked, "Why are you sleeping at my parent's home when you said you were staying at The Black Bull Inn?"

"Tomorrow we are all going to Cormorant Bay for the day and as your parents' guest it was decided that we could make an earlier start by being in one place from which to set out."

Nick could not hear Kara's next question, it was spoken softly.

"I'm sorry, Kara, I can't hear. You'll have to speak louder."

"It's not important. I just asked who was going to the beach."

"I was told to expect the usual crowd. I really don't know who they are."

"Will Satomi be there?"

A note of enthusiasm leaped into Nick's voice.

"Oh, yes. Apparently she has some sensational swimwear she intends showing off."

Nick started laughing heartily. He grabbed a pillow and rolled around, smothering his face in the soft goose-down filled fabric, to muffle his mirth.

Kara had hung up on him.

CHAPTER TWENTY SIX

In the large, impressive suite, lying in the huge bed with the comforting arms of her husband around her, Silvia told Gus about an incident that had occurred earlier in the evening.

"You probably don't remember, but I left you and Nicholas in the ballroom to go to the little girl's room."

He shook his head quizzically, wondering why such a normal function would be of such importance.

"Instead I decided to use the facilities in Jon's suite. I had Patsy, the receptionist, let me in. You know how I dislike using any public washroom."

He nodded. This he knew.

Silvia's voice took on an intensity that caused Gus to look at her closely.

"Well, when I was there, Angie and Satomi arrived and I could hear them talking in the living room. Satomi was urging Angie to be patient. She was positive that Jon loved her very much, despite his recent behavior. Things would improve—she felt sure of it, especially after the unexpected news Angie had communicated to Jon. As for Satomi, she was determined to get Nick into bed. He was the most brilliant, handsome and sexiest man she had ever set eyes on. The fact that he was famous and wealthy added considerably to his magnetism. She was convinced that if she could make love to him, and she knew precisely how to please a man completely, he would never want to leave her. To go ahead with her plans she needed Angie's assistance."

Silvia shivered.

"I couldn't believe that a woman so gorgeous had such insidious designs on Nick. She said she had targeted Nick for some time and this was the first opportunity she had had to carry out her intent. You know, now that I think about it, she sounded a little demented and quite obsessed."

Her husband asked, totally out of his depth. "Didn't they need to use the bathroom you were occupying?"

He was very concerned about his wife's escapade.

"Fortunately not. I was in the small two-piece powder room. The full sized bathroom is off Jon's bedroom, en suite. After a while I presume they moved into the bedroom because I couldn't hear them very clearly."

"Then what happened? What did you do?" Gus asked gravely, expecting to learn of her escape from the complicated situation.

"Well, I had to get down on my knees and press my ear to the opening on the bottom of the door."

Gus hugged his wife—partly in fear at the audacious risk she had taken and thankful that she seemed to have come through it unscathed. Ruefully he commented, "I didn't realize we had a Nancy Drew in the family. Nor that my wife was so influenced by another man that she was willing to get involved in a situation which, not only could have had serious repercussions, but that she would stoop so low."

His dig was met by a withering glance. Thirty-three years of marriage had enhanced not only the classical beauty, but also the determined character of Silvia LaBarbera Olavssen.

Changing to a more comfortable position against her husband's chest, Silvia questioned.

"Did you know that about Nicholas?"

"What? That he is sexy and handsome? Ask your daughter, she should know more about that than I do."

Silvia bit back a caustic comment before continuing the conversation.

"I think we should try to help Nicholas. I would not like to see him maneuvered into an embarrassing situation."

Gus laughed at Silvia's anxiety.

"Darling. Nick is an intelligent, sophisticated man. I'm sure he has had to cope with this type of thing before. I have a feeling he wants to have a serious discussion about his intentions regarding Kara before he leaves. I'll probably find out more when we go to the beach."

Returning to her original thoughts, Silvia persisted.

"It really did get my adrenaline going. I still feel that Nicholas needs our help, sweetheart. I have become quite fond of him. I only wish that Kara would wake up. You know she is not in love with Jon. I don't know how she can imagine that she is. They used to disagree on almost everything at one time, but I suppose she has forgotten about that."

She put an arm around her husband's still trim waist.

"I know this is silly, but wouldn't it be ideal if we could choose Nicholas to be the son we never had." Silvia snuggled into Gus's neck, leaving a trail of kisses.

"We don't have to call it quits yet." Gus enthusiastically responded. "Did I hear an invitation to keep on trying?"

Adoringly taking his wife into his arms, the nephew of former King Olav V of Norway, tenderly made love to the love of his life.

CHAPTER TWENTY SEVEN

They left for Wisherly at eight-thirty, after a substantial meal in a pleasant breakfast room. It overlooked a pond with blossoming lily pads clustered around its fringe and tall grasses around the perimeter, gently moving with Koi fish activity. Nick had an excellent night's sleep, waking refreshed and ready for whatever the day brought. He could handle anything in this feeling-good mood. His amiable humor was apparent and Kara's parents smiled knowingly at each other across the table. Kara and Nick must have had a very satisfactory conversation last night.

They reached Wisherly a little before nine-thirty. Gus Olavssen drove slowly along the "front" so that Nick could get an overview of the area. He pointed to the huge rock monoliths on the sand and the weathered shipwreck, recollecting anecdotes about Kara and her fascination with the Punch and Judy puppet show. He recalled what a tomboy she had been climbing the rocks and jumping over the tide pools, competing with Jon in whatever he did.

By the time they arrived at the beachhead Nick was anxious to see more. He leaped out of the Jeep and ran down the wooden stairs to the beach, immediately turning and running back up, two steps at a time.

He laughed breathlessly when he saw Kara's parents eyeing him dubiously.

"Sorry. I had to let off a little steam. I've really looked forward to being here and can't believe I've actually made it."

His smile was a little embarrassed upon realizing the spontaneity of his joie de vivre.

In his understated way Gus Olavssen responded, pushing his glasses on top of his balding head.

"That's great, Nick. By the time the luggage and cooler have been carried down to the houseboat, I'm quite sure the realization will have hit you."

They all started laughing.

It was amazing how well their personalities had meshed in such a short time.

Silvia made a pot of tea and they took their steaming mugs out onto the foredeck. Nick sat in a canvas deckchair and stretched out his legs. He sniffed the salt air and sighed blissfully.

"I've dreamed of this. I can certainly understand why Kara loves it here and I can't wait to explore the area myself."

Gus, turning around from leaning on the handrail suggested, "If you really want to become familiar with the territory we can take the speedboat out or get an appetite for lunch by walking over to the breakwater. You'll get some excellent pictures, it's a wonderful spot. It was one of Kara's favorites."

"Would it be too much for you to walk there? I could use the exercise and I don't mind going alone."

Nick's face showed concern. The peninsula jutted out some distance away, closing off the other end of the bay.

Silvia Olavssen laughed.

"Don't challenge him, Nicholas, or you may find yourself in a competition. Gus loves to walk, especially down here. He and Kara used to walk for miles, neither one of them admitting to sore limbs. They are both much too proud for their own good at times."

Nick noted this personal observation. He certainly could see this trait in Kara and endorsed her mother's comment.

They could hear cars pulling into the parking area and muffled conversation was beginning to filter down.

Gus suggested, "I'm ready to depart whenever you are."

Nick rose to his feet immediately.

"You might want to leave your jacket. The sun will be warming the area shortly."

Nick returned to his cabin, laying the coat on the bunk. He slipped on his sunglasses and slung his camera around his neck. The shorts and sports shirt should be cool enough.

Gus Olavssen kissed his wife and Nick unthinkingly swatted her casually on her bottom as he passed.

Silvia Olavssen burst out laughing, putting a hand over her mouth in an effort to hide her outburst.

"Stop getting smart with me, young man. You do not merit that privilege yet."

Nick was taken aback by his spontaneous action and held up his hands in an apologetic gesture.

Watching them walk away, a tiny smile lurked around Silvia Olavssen's mouth. She had been taken by surprise at Nick's small intimacy. It amazed her that from their first encounter with Nick, she and Gus had immediately bonded with him. It also appeared from the familiarity just taken by Nick, that he felt very comfortable being with them. The smile lingered.

Nick and Gus chatted in a general way for a while and when the conversation flagged, Nick looked directly at his companion.

"Sir, I realize you know very little about me and I want to thank you and your wife for making me feel so welcome, under unusual circumstances. I'll never forget it."

He had a very serious expression on his face.

"I have already indicated my feelings for your daughter and I will not rest until Kara becomes my wife. Having disclosed this, I think you are entitled to know more about me and this seems to be an appropriate time to do so."

Gus Olavssen smiled approvingly. He liked this fellow's forthright style.

Reminding how he and Kara had met and that almost instantaneously he knew they were destined for each other, Nick paused for a moment, looking slightly perturbed.

"Kara doesn't know very much about me and I'm afraid I must plead guilty to keeping her in the dark."

Gus Olavssen looked at Nick searchingly and retorted abruptly.

"Why was that? It sounds as if you had some reservations."

Nick was startled.

"No. Nothing like that. There's a long story involved which I have managed to submerge over the years."

He took a deep breath and bent down to pick up a shell.

He pushed his sunglasses on top of his head and examined the shell intently before speaking.

"It's been a long time since this Pandora's Box has been unlocked and I'm having difficulty getting started."

Nick's face had become tense and Gus Olavssen looked at him in alarm. He was baffled. What kind of deep secrets could be hidden in this young man's life?

Nick rubbed his forearm across his eyes and looking straight ahead said very quietly.

"When I was thirty-one, I was instrumental in performing an intricate heart operation which had been performed successfully by only one other surgeon and he lived in another country.

Observing Gus Olavssen's perplexed expression Nick stopped.

"I'm sorry. I have become so accustomed to being "a celebrity" and being recognized on sight that my conceit just got in the way. I automatically assumed you knew who I was."

Unexpectedly he grinned.

"I guess that was one of the reasons why it was so refreshing when Kara put so little stock in my name when we met. She put me in my place, without realizing it. Apart from my initial gut reaction that Kara and I belonged together, I think I was quite intrigued that she appeared to have a sufficiently strong personality that no matter what my name was, it would have been of little consequence."

A solemn expression cloaked Nick's features.

"I'm a doctor of medicine. Actually my specialty is heart transplant surgery. As I said, I was instrumental in performing an intricate heart operation under the supervision of a brilliant specialist. He was my mentor and friend and the only surgeon in the world to have effectively accomplished this procedure, until I followed in his footsteps. Shortly afterwards he acknowledged being afflicted with rheumatoid arthritis, which had started to impede his skills. He was devastated and so was I. He was like a big brother to me and neither one of us handled it very well. We had talked about going into business together. I was very close to his family. I visited them frequently in Europe."

Gus suddenly realized with a start who Nick was, but he refrained from voicing his surprise. Nick was so down-to-earth and likeable that he had disguised his fame well.

Nick stopped and looked pensive.

"I thought I knew him so well. Walter appeared to be coming to terms with his infirmity and had started to travel with Jane, his wife.

He said he was writing a book. The last time I saw him he was cheerful and optimistic. Totally unexpectedly he committed suicide a short time later. He simply could not go on with useless hands."

Nick did not seem to hear his companion's words of sympathy.

"By default, as a result of the exceptionally successful heart operations which followed, and I suppose because of my youth, there was a proliferation of flattering media coverage. I became a celebrity without realizing it or wanting the acclaim.

My business grew astronomically, circling the globe, and it was an honor being called upon by the Académie de Médecine to lecture on the subject. This has now become my way of life. I travel the world, giving seminars and lectures and performing open heart operations before select surgeons, as part of the teaching process, from time to time. But, oh, dear Heaven, I still miss Walter enormously."

Breathing a deep breath to relieve the tension, Gus Olavssen contemplates how shocking for Nick to lose such an important mentor and friend. At least it was a natural reaction for Nick to be devastated at the loss. If this is the problem of which Nick spoke, it is not an impossible barrier to overcome.

Nick cast a troubled look at Gus and said, "That's not all."

Gus had a sinking feeling. From the look on Nick's face, what was about to come was infinitely more serious than the narrative he had just listened to.

Sighing deeply Nick broke the silence.

"Several years before the period I've just talked about, I met Princess Serawin, the youngest daughter of Sheikh Abdullah bin Ibrahim of Saudi Bahria. She was being educated at the Sorbonne's University Pierre et Marie Curie" campus in Paris. Michele, who became the wife of my good friend François, introduced us when I was visiting them in Paris. We fell in love. François de Veaux and I have been friends from our medical student days at Magdalen College, Oxford, where we met.

I had been flying back and forth to Paris a couple of weekends each month, meeting Serawin at Michele and Franc's flat. We attended their wedding and had begun discussing marriage ourselves and our future together. I arranged to take my internship at the same hospital as Franc, so that Serawin's studies were not disrupted. It was only when I started looking for a place of my own that she took me to the penthouse suite, which occupied the whole upper floor of a small private hotel that had been purchased by her father. It had its own private elevator. It was there she revealed her true identity. Until that time I knew her as Fatima and so did Michele and François. They learned of her true identity at the private engagement party we gave. It was at that time that I moved into her apartment. We had known each other for about eight months."

Nick rubbed a hand across his brow.

"Since she was a prime kidnapping target she lived in a very restricted environment, having a housekeeper, cook and a live-in Eunuch-type guard and chauffer. Michele's father is the French Ambassador to Jordan and only because of that were Serawin and Michele allowed to become friends.

Serawin had no intention of returning to the suppressive lifestyle of her father's kingdom and we were so much in love we felt strong enough to face adversity. She phoned her father to tell him about our plans. He was absolutely furious and refused to listen to her. Two days later I found the apartment in shambles and Serawin and her attendants missing."

Nick pulled a handkerchief from a pocket and blew his nose.

The two men walked along silently.

Gus patted Nick on the shoulder, but did not speak.

Nick pulled his sunglasses down onto the bridge of his nose and with a quiver in his voice continued.

"Michele contacted her father in Amman and using diplomatic terminology he cautioned me to tread warily; I was facing a formidable and powerful enemy in the Sheikh. Their women were regarded as chattels, even princesses."

Nick shook his head, as if to deflect the distasteful thoughts being recalled.

"I went to the American Embassy in Paris and was firmly informed that they could provide no assistance or even suggestions. They intimated that their Embassy in Rumak was virtually a paper tiger, with little diplomatic immunity or authority. Since I travel on both American and British passports, I was met with the same outcome at the British Embassy."

Nick removed his sunglasses and wiped the misted glass lens on the fabric of his shirt tail.

He went on.

"That same day I received a frantic phone call from Serawin. She was crying uncontrollably and her words were so garbled I could hardly make out what she was saying. I'd switched the answering machine over to the record mode, and so I could go over and over it later until some sense could be made of it.

She was about to be taken to the royal physician for examination before being publicly betrothed to a cousin I knew she found repulsive. She begged me to come for her. The conversation was very brief and I have no idea how she managed to make a phone call out of a country so watchful and security controlled, but I suspect we played right into their hands.

I realized once they discovered she was no longer chaste that her life would be in danger. I was beside myself and crazy with worry. I managed to borrow a large sum of money from a wealthy patron. This was needed instantly to arrange private transportation and pay whatever bribes would be necessary in finding an escape route out of the unfamiliar Arab kingdom for the two of us."

Nick sank down on the sand, and put his face between his hands. This was more difficult than he had imagined. There was so much guilt to deal with.

His shoulders started shaking and Gus Olavssen dropped to his knees, patting the younger man's back.

"You don't have to say anything more, Nick. I didn't realize what a struggle this was going to be for you, dredging up such a traumatic period in your life."

They sat quietly for some time.

Nick shivered.

It had to be dealt with. He could not be like an ostrich burying its head in the sand, forever. It was not fair to Kara.

Looking toward the ocean and staring blankly, he persevered.

"Soldiers were scrutinizing every venue in and out of the country for foreigners and suspicious people. They had pictures of me, taken from the apartment I later discovered, and it didn't take them long to track me down. As it's one of the middle-eastern countries, I had adopted the common white disha dasha and the ghubra headgear as disguise, but my limited fluency in the Arabic language was a dead giveaway. It was a foolish attempt. My heart had taken over my brain. I was an easy target and on the third day there I was seized and thrown into a dungeon."

Nick rubbed away tears.

"For an intelligent, highly educated man, I was unbelievably naive. Serawin and I had expected the world to accept us on our terms."

Breathing deeply, in a shaky voice he resumed.

"I was in prison for almost three weeks, kept in chains the whole time, in isolation and at the mercy, or rather the whims, of soldiers in a brutal private army. They found my helplessness great entertainment. I learned later that my fate could have been unspeakably worse if it had not been for the intervention of The Red Cross and certain influential friends who constantly kept my plight in the glare of publicity. When the British Embassy got involved on my behalf, the American Embassy also stepped in."

Unsteadily a shell was retrieved from the sand.

The shell was discarded and Nick rubbed his hands together as if to bring back warmth.

"I was released with the warning never to set foot in the country again or my life would be in peril. My passport is stamped 'Entry Denied Permanently' to that country."

Nick's mouth contorted in pain.

"My worst moment was when I was informed that the Princess Serawin had killed herself. I didn't believe them for an instant and told them I'd never stop searching for her."

Sweat was gathering on Nick's forehead and in a voice that trembled he said softly.

"Once I was put on the Sheik's private jet, I was given a sealed box."

He stood up, agitated and shaking.

"They are monsters. Terrifying and evil!"

His lips curled contemptuously and his eyes spit out sparks like the words he spewed.

"The box contained Serawin's finger, with the engagement ring I gave her attached."

His clenched fist smacked his other hand and a fierce grimace surfaced at past remembrance.

"A card said 'Praise to Allah, she can now rest in peace, the offending member has been removed'."

A ragged gasp escaped.

"How could a father sanction such a deed? It actually lay on blood soaked white satin. I was in shock. I must have gone berserk, because when I came to I was in a straightjacket and remained that way for the rest of the flight."

Nick sat down abruptly, passing the back of his hand over his perspiring forehead.

"I was mentally, emotionally and spiritually paralyzed. Had they removed Serawin's finger to demonstrate how powerful their rules and convictions were? Was she actually still alive or had they removed someone else's finger and used the ring to convince me symbolically that they would stop at nothing to keep us apart?

I spent hours trying to rationalize their actions, but it all boiled down to how could they behave this way in the name of an unjust deity?"

A sob escaped from Nick he laid his head on his arms.

"It was awful. I explored every possibility I could find, hoping to discover a way to rescue Serawin, believing that a father could not be so callous. It was impossible to find the capital to back-up some of the hair-brained schemes I would have attempted if the money had been available.

The knowledge of my previous disastrous rescue attempt had preceded me. I was turned down by every banking establishment I approached and that is when I determined to become wealthy to the extent that I would never, NEVER need to ask anyone for financial assistance again. I vowed I would never, never be found so vulnerable and defenseless again."

He gulped and his voice shook as he continued.

"Two weeks later I received a newspaper clipping in Arabic from a friend who, unbeknown to me, had been in the country on business at the time all this happened. He had taken the risk of smuggling the article out in his luggage. It had been translated and it stated that Princess Serawin had succumbed to a childhood ailment and there would be a day of public lamentation for her. Her body would be on display at the Royal Tombs in the Garden of Allah. The article was dated the day after I left."

Nick raised his head, and stared blankly at the water.

"I have never forgiven myself for not trying harder to find her and the guilt persists."

The slap, slap of the approaching surf was the only sound heard.

It had taken a great effort to relate the entire sequence of events. For so long Nick had tried to block the memories from emerging and now, having relived the painful circumstances in detail, raw emotions had risen to the surface.

The two men sat together, one looking sightlessly ahead and the other miserably aware of the anguish encountered by the other.

Nick started talking in a tired voice.

"For so many years I have been convinced that the only true love in my life had been snatched away. It was a punishment I was willing to bear. I deliberately decided to devote my life to furthering my career in medicine, keeping myself constantly busy so that I would have little time to dwell on the past. It tore me up knowing that without financial solvency I had so little control over Serawin's well-being. Had I been wealthy, many doors would have automatically opened. There was no doubt in my mind that the situation could have been resolved and Serawin's life would not have been sacrificed. Lousy money, that's all it takes."

Nick shook his head wearily.

"It's very easy to build an empire and amass a fortune when there is little else of importance in one's life."

Contemplatively he added quietly.

"I didn't realize that in finding temporary consolation in the arms of prestigious women who made themselves ridiculously available, that I was becoming anaesthetized to real feelings."

Candidly he looked at Gus Olavssen.

"And then, unbelievably, I met Kara."

Suddenly Nick stood up and so did Gus. They faced each other.

"It scares me to death that I could lose Kara. For the first time in years I sleep peacefully. The face in my dreams is hers. You can't know how important that is. I have lived with nightmares for so long."

Nick looked anxious.

An arm slid across his shoulders.

"Kara knows none of this?"

Nick shook his head.

They once again started walking toward the promontory.

"You can see what a basket case I have become in discussing it with you for the first time in years. Remorse weighs heavily on my conscience. I keep thinking I could have done more to save Serawin and I can imagine Kara's reaction, the horror. Perhaps I have been very unrealistic expecting Kara to return my love. Conceivably she and Jon belong together and I am the intruder. If I was the cause for anything happening to her, I couldn't handle it, yet I couldn't go on without her. She is everything to me."

They walked in silence until they reached the rocky jutting breakwater.

They stood together surveying the 360 degree panoramic view.

Nick breathed in the tangy air as he looked out to the horizon where tiny Tinker Toy tankers were slowly moving, with yachts challenging their domination of the ocean.

Gus watched the relaxation that took place. First the tense body slackened and the facial features grew softer and less uptight.

Feeling himself under observation Nick turned and flashed a quick smile to his companion.

"I apologize for being so dramatic. I was overtaken by feelings that, for many years, have been kept under control. Apart from François and his wife, and my cousin Wendy, you are the only person with whom I have voluntarily discussed this period in my life."

Nick crouched down, hiding his face, allowing the fine sand to trickle through his fingers.

Gus Olavssen's face registered compassion.

He sat down, resting his back against a large rock.

"It's a great weight you have carried, Nick, and there are no apologies due. I feel I should be thanking you for trusting me with the account of your horrendous experience. Of course Kara will need to know about this. It obviously has left scars, but it is a burden she can help you bear. She is so like her mother, who has a great capacity for returning love immeasurably and, in my humble estimation, I believe that is what you need."

He stopped speaking and pursed his lips.

"There is just one problem that I can see."

Nick glanced up quickly from doodling in the sand.

"Kara has to be convinced that she is the person to meet your needs. In a way she is a bit like you. She was terribly hurt by a young love affair, vowing not to allow herself to become involved with anyone else. She appears willing to give her love, but seems confused right now, unclear about her own judgment. Jon took her unawares by proposing. He was always the brother, the friend and non-judgmental confidant and she doesn't know how to relate to him in this new role. She doesn't want to be hurt again and Jon is a very safe person for her. That may influence her thinking."

Nick looked at Kara's father with new respect.

He had described his daughter very well and Nick recognized the logic from his own knowledge of her. When Mr. Olavssen had mentioned Jon as being a safe person in Kara's opinion, a bell rang in his head. It was odd that Kara herself had used that expression in relation to the two of them. The phrase came back 'I don't want to change the way things are with us right now. It feels so safe'."

He was beginning to understand Kara very well.

As if the world's problems had been resolved, they smiled at each other and stood up, brushing off the sand clinging to their shorts.

Gus patted Nick on the back.

"If we hurry, we should get back in time for whatever food has been left."

"I'd like to take a couple of pictures first, if you don't mind. Would you walk over a few paces so I can place you with Wisherly in the background?"

The air had been cleared between them and Nick was relieved. It freed him to concentrate on pursuing Kara seriously. First, though, there were a few loose ends to tie up.

During the return trip to the picnic area, Nick discussed the method he wished to follow in an endeavor to resolve the mystery of the disappearing jewelry. It was a long shot, but worth trying.

Gus asked for permission to relay Nick's traumatic experience to his wife and Nick agreed. By the time they strolled up to the group arranged on blankets, they had re-established their easy relationship.

Nick saw immediately that Jon, Angela and Satomi were already there. As arranged, during lunch, Gus reminded Nick in a voice loud enough to be heard distinctly by those around them, "You do plan on staying overnight with us, don't you Nick?"

"Thanks. Yes I do, but first I'll feel better after putting some jewelry in my safe at the hotel. I've been keeping it in the car's trunk, but that's not a smart thing to do."

"Good. I thought you might try to get out of finishing our chess game."

Nick laughed.

"Dreamer."

They were clearing away the lunch items when Satomi, in a strikingly brief silver bikini, walked up behind Nick and put her hands over his eyes and pressed herself into his back.

"Guess who?"

Nick stiffened.

"How many guesses do I have?"

She dropped her hands, clenching them in annoyance.

"We are thinking of driving into town. Do you feel like coming?"

Nick's response was made quickly.

"Not right now, I'm looking forward to a swim as soon as lunch digests, but don't let me spoil your fun."

Satomi's face registered irritation. Having to beg this man to fall in with her invitations was annoying and rather insulting. She was not accustomed to being treated in such an off-hand manner.

Satomi wandered off and Silvia approached Nick.

"After turning down that outstanding offer," she looked at Satomi's undulating body retreating, "perhaps you would consider another. We are going into town for banana splits after the children play in the water for a while. Would you like to join us?"

"Sounds great to me. I was thinking of taking a swim soon, so it will work out very nicely."

Noticing the book sticking out of the beach bag carried over her arm Nick asked.

"Where are you off to?"

"I said I would supervise the younger children in the water for a while until the parents take over. I'd also like to try to finish this book."

"Do you mind waiting a few minutes? I'll change into my swim gear and carry a deckchair down there for you."

"That would be very nice. While you are getting ready, I'll dig out a few towels."

They found a spot close to the water.

This was the natural "swimming pool" that Kara had mentioned to him when recalling childhood memories of Cormorant Bay.

Nick stuck his toes in the water.

"Hey, it's not bad."

He shrugged out of the patterned beach jacket, showing a pair of muscular arms and a strong chest, with a small expanse of dark hair below the neckline. His body was lithe and the long legs were athletically developed. Silvia Olavssen's heart sank. As soon as Satomi saw this beautiful specimen, it would be difficult to keep her away.

If ever a man exuded sex appeal, this was he.

She sighed, wondering why she was trying so hard to protect Nick. He was a grown man. With his looks and savoir-faire he had obviously come across the "Satomi's" of the world before.

Silvia's husband was taking a nap. He had looked a little troubled at lunchtime and said he wanted to talk to her when she got back from playing "Lifeguard." She was sure it had to do with Nick and that worried her somewhat.

The children were having fun, splashing and floating around on inflated mattresses. Nick dove into the water, swimming strongly back and forth, suffering their attempts to distract him. After negotiating the obstacle course several times he finally succumbed. Before long he was carrying the younger ones around on his shoulders, allowing them to jump off into the water and catching them as they came up for air. They were like tadpoles in the water, completely at ease, swimming through his legs and standing on their hands with their legs waving above the water like reeds.

Silvia took a couple of pictures. He looked so boyish, with his agile body and big attractive grin. Silvia smiled fondly; Nick seemed to be enjoying himself as much as the children.

Silvia had no idea how long Satomi had been sitting behind her, but in turning around she saw the unabashed desire in her eyes. She shivered as she returned her gaze to the water.

Pam and Dave Bennett, holding a huge beach umbrella, joined Silvia.

"We'll take over, dear. Many thanks."

They waved to the youngster sitting on Nick's shoulders and he carried their son out of the water, depositing him on the sand and ruffling his wet hair after doing so.

"He looks a bit sunburned and I think I am too."

Nick's pained expression backed up his words.

He threw himself down on the towel spread out beside Silvia's chair.

"That must be the hardest way to keep in shape, I'm exhausted."

Closing his eyes, Nick lifted his face toward the sun smiling contentedly. He liked the paternal feeling that cavorting with the children in the water had evoked. A wash of tenderness engulfed him at the thought of sharing a child with Kara. Just the method of producing one was a thrill he could hardly wait for.

"Do you need to lie on most of the towel or can anyone join you?"

Silvia turned to see Satomi taking off her lacy jacket as she spoke, presenting a spectacular view of the length of her tanned body in doing so.

There were groups of people sitting and lying around. He could hardly make a big deal of her suggestion, when most of the men were eyeing him enviously. Nick moved over a little.

She sat down. Provocatively Satomi proceeded to apply suntan lotion to her body, starting with her feet and working her way upwards, each stroke a sensual caress.

Silvia watched in fascination. It was not only a type of self-worship, but almost as if a sacrifice was being prepared for the altar. She continued to watch with interest, surreptitiously glancing at Nick to watch his reactions.

At first he observed Satomi with a skeptical smile on his face and then his expression changed to boredom. Silvia heard rather than saw Nick turn over onto his stomach. When she peeked from around her book, she saw his head resting on his arms facing away from Satomi with his eyes closed and a look of repose on his face.

"What are you doing?" Nick was exasperated.

This statement immediately grabbed Silvia's attention.

"Gosh, you're jumpy, Nick. I'm just putting some sunscreen on your back." Satomi held up the bottle of suntan lotion to show Nick adding, "You'll be sorry otherwise."

Nick's lips shut tightly, allowing Satomi to finish spreading the cream she had already squirted onto his back.

Sensuously she caressed his shoulder blades, fluttering down the rib cage to the trim waist and in deepening circles back up to his neck. It felt very soothing and despite himself, Nick started to relax.

He looked up and saw Angela taking pictures.

Disapproval was registered on his face. Nick stood up abruptly.

"I've had as much . . . . sun as I can stand for one day."

Silvia Olavssen immediately said. "Yes. I have too."

Looking at the fob watch on her sundress, she added, "Besides, it's time for tea."

Nick picked up the deckchair and their belongings and strode purposefully toward the houseboats with long legged ease.

Silvia followed him, her thoughts dwelling on Satomi's tactics. *She certainly was intent on charming this man and even though he was not encouraging her, Silvia wondered for how much longer he would be able to resist Satomi's enticement. He was a virile, vigorous man, but he was human after all and susceptible to life's seductions as everyone else.*

They arrived back at the houseboat in time to find Gus setting a tray with glasses of iced tea. He had changed into beige twill trousers and a subdued checked sports shirt. He looked refreshed and affable.

"I saw you coming and thought this would hit the spot."

Silvia gravitated toward her husband like a homing pigeon.

"You're wonderful. You can almost read my mind."

She put both arms around him, leaning her head against his shoulder for an instant. Picking up the tray, she carried it to a small mesh table where cucumber, shrimp and creamed watercress sandwiches, together with fruit, were arranged.

Mrs. Taylor, the family cook, had packed food before they left and the cooler had kept everything invitingly chilled. A telescopic awning had been pulled over the deck and they sat quietly enjoying the cool refreshments and the welcome shade.

Gus broke the comfortable silence.

"Jon came over about half-an-hour ago. Said they had intended going into town, but he had to have a discussion with his parents. He asked if we would take Satomi into Wisherly with us."

In answer to his wife's frosty expression he retorted. "There was little I could do about it, dear."

She set down her glass.

"Is Angela coming too?"

Gus scratched his head.

"Actually, he didn't mention her. She's probably staying here with Jon."

Nick excused himself. There were documents he needed to look over. Signs of an approaching headache were evident.

Silvia Olavssen pushed a jar of Tylenol into Nick's hands when he opened the bedroom door when she knocked.

"We are going to rest for a while, so why don't you relax and perhaps the headache will disappear."

The unspoken look commiserated with him, as if acknowledging the reason for the headache.

Nick lay on the bunk, looking at the sky through the port window.

He had planned on informing Kara's parents of his background, but he had expected to do so in a clinically factual yet relaxed manner, in charge of the situation as he had become accustomed to doing in his professional life. Instead, in Gus Olavssen's presence, he had become agitated, completely losing his composure, with the horror of his memories surfacing to wash away his defenses. Looking back he was appalled at his outward display of weakness. He had worked so hard to build a protective barrier.

He was vexed at this lack of control.

He could handle Satomi. In fact it would be a pleasure to do so. She was making a nuisance of herself, and he was becoming irritated by her conspicuous, unwanted attention. Nick returned the unopened files to his briefcase. His head was still throbbing, despite the pills. What's more, he could feel the sunburn's hot glow developing.

He took a brief nap.

By the time he dressed and went out onto the deck, Satomi had arrived. She was sitting with Silvia and Gus under the awning, a drink in her hand, idly swinging a long bare leg, which was crossed over her knee.

They all rose to their feet as he closed the cabin door, giving the impression they had exhausted their conversation and were ready to leave immediately upon his appearance.

"Sorry if I kept you waiting."

Satomi's eyes lit up at the sight of him. In the white shorts set, trimmed in navy, with a crest on the breast pocket, Nick emanated health and vitality. He also looked terribly sexy.

Within a few minutes they were in the Jeep and bumping along the dirt track toward town.

Silvia Olavssen had taken charge of the seating arrangements.

Nick was sitting in the front passenger seat with her husband who was driving. Nick heard her say in her exquisitely refined voice.

"I thought this might be a good time to get to know each other. We haven't had an opportunity until now and I'd love to hear about your exciting career."

Nick did not miss the exasperation in Satomi's reluctant participation.

After a few desultory remarks the conversation in the back seats dried up. Not a peep was heard from that direction for the remainder of the drive into Wisherly.

Nick deduced that Kara's mother did not rate Satomi very highly in her appraisal. He was amused at the steps she was taking to keep her away from him. He gave her full marks for the diplomatic way in which she was handling things; she obviously thought he needed assistance.

Nick jumped out of the Jeep when it stopped and assisted Silvia Olavssen from the vehicle. She slipped her arm through his.

Gus Olavssen helped Satomi alight from his side.

"What would you like to do while we wait for the others to arrive, Nicholas? There's the Punch and Judy puppet show, a stroll around town or we could walk over to the Italian Gardens."

The few things she had listed made Satomi wince.

"I've never seen a Punch and Judy show. I'd like to do that. How about you Satomi?"

She shrugged her shoulders and raised her eyes toward the sky.

Nick's eyes were sparkling. If Franc could have heard him say that he would have gone into shock.

"I've brought my camera to take pictures." Nick voiced, reaching for the camera left on the vacated seat.

Silvia squeezed his arm.

"Let's go troops. Watch for traffic."

They all walked across the wide road to the esplanade and down concrete steps to the beach. Scratchy music was coming from a little hut-like building no more than five feet square. It had a carnival-style, multi-striped tent top and a roll-down curtain of the same striped canvas, covering what Nick was informed was the stage. Several adults, with a few children, were sitting on folding chairs arranged in rows in front of the little structure and they sat down and joined them.

Satomi looked very bored. She was placed between both of Kara's parents and Nick's mood lightened considerably. They felt like his guardian angels.

From the weather stained amplifier, perilously perched on a bracketed shelf, a booming voice crackled through the old equipment.

"Showtime in ten minutes. Come and take your seats to watch the oldest show on earth."

It was repeated several times.

Nick and Silvia Olavssen grinned at each other.

A little man, wearing a bowler hat, brought a step-stool to the front of the hut, placing it in the center to stand on while rolling up the curtain and fastening it at both ends with two wooden pegs.

Nick's lips twitched in amusement.

This certainly was different from the last stage performance he had attended, which was at the Teatro alla Scala in Milan. He had gone with a group of friends to watch Placido Domingo's inspired performance in "Don Giovani." For one thing, the stage was somewhat larger than this one!

Tickled with his own sense of humor, Nick became suddenly aware that his headache had disappeared.

The little man picked up the stool and hurried around to the back of the hut. Immediately up popped a puppet with a nose like a parrot, dressed in an outfit similar to that of a jester. A wide pointed collar with a bell on each apex hung around his neck. After skipping along the yard long stage, another puppet appeared. This was Judy. No sooner did Punch see her than he reached down and picked up a truncheon, which he held in both hands and whacked Judy over the head with it. The three children sitting in the front row gasped, after which they roared with laughter. Nick was somewhat puzzled. Punch was chasing Judy around the stage, causing the children to laugh louder and even the parents were starting to smile. A policeman appeared and dragged Punch away. An inner curtain came down, with scuffling behind the scenes. When it was hoisted Punch was seen in a black and white striped outfit, behind bars.

Nick was slightly nonplussed. The children seemed to be enjoying it a great deal and by the time it ended the adults were laughing too. It was very quaint, but he did not find the humor that the others did. It did not make sense and that perhaps was why he was so mystified by the actions that had taken place on the little platform. To increase his understanding, he would research the subject.

Silvia Olsen leaned over to Nick and whispered. "It really is fun entertainment for children, quite primitive in fact going back to the sixteenth century, but it's different. Kara used to be fascinated by it—came to see it whenever she could."

A lump came in Nick's throat.

How he would enjoy holding Kara's hand as they watched this centuries-old performance. His mind drifted off—he could imagine the fun in bringing their children here, and watching their little faces at the animated production. Lord, he was getting sloppily sentimental. He had not had this type of fantasy before. Cautiously he looked at the woman seated beside him to see if his thoughts had somehow projected themselves to her

All the characters returned to take a bow and the little man in the bowler hat rushed around to the front of the little building. Whipping the hat off his head it was passed around the audience for their donations before they had time to drift away.

Nick had taken a few pictures as the various characters presented themselves on the little rostrum. At the close of the entertainment, permission was given to take a picture of Kara's parents standing at each side of the booth. The little man obligingly stood behind the stage, displaying Punch and Judy, and a big smile. He had happily pocketed more money after the show than he had gathered in the past few days.

"Nick, stand over there with Satomi."

Gus Olavssen took the camera from Nick.

Instead of adopting the same pose, Satomi put her arm around Nick's waist and smiled alluringly at him. She was only a few inches shorter than he. For the first time he actually noticed what she was wearing. Tiny shorts, with slits cut up past the thigh and a brief halter-top, leaving little to the imagination. It startled him to see Satomi clad so scantily.

He must be walking around in a trance.

They wandered across the road again and Nick excused himself to go into a souvenir store. He had to pick up a couple of postcards. Gus Olavssen followed him in and started looking around, picking up items and putting them down again.

"Kara used to love these as a child."

He held up a stick of pink striped rock candy, with the name Wisherly running through it.

Nick held out his hand.

"I am unable to deny her anything."

There was a glint of amusement in his eyes as he purchased it and the postcards.

The dark brown eyes looked into the bespectacled ones. They were on the same wavelength. They enjoyed being together and it showed. They walked out of the shop laughing.

Mrs. Olavssen and Satomi were nowhere to be seen.

"They must have gone over to the ice cream parlor." Assessed Gus.

They found them there, together with the crowd from The Colony. It was a very lively group. Satomi was talking to a good-looking older man with wings of graying hair at his temples.

Nick was immediately relieved. It took the pressure off him. He slid into the booth beside Silvia Olavssen, with her husband sliding around the semi-circular booth to her other side.

They all ordered banana splits.

Nick decided to tell them a little about his plans for the evening.

"I purchased an inexpensive string of pearls and earrings and if I could borrow the original jewelry box, which I brought back from Kara, I will put them into the safe in my suite. I'll take a taxi back to the Inn and enter by the side door, which is seldom used. Then I'll wait."

A glimmer came into Nick's eyes.

"It's a silly game, but I have an intuitive feeling about doing this."

A look of alarm passed over Silvia Olavssen's aristocratic features and she patted Nick's hand.

"Do be careful. Is it really worth the risk?"

Scrutinizing Nick, Gus Olavssen said laconically.

"Do you need a gun?"

Silvia gasped. "Whatever made you say that?"

Agitatedly she twisted a paper napkin, looking at Nick.

"Please stay overnight with us. I can't bear the thought of violence taking place, with the possibility of you getting hurt."

A smile lurked around Nick's eyes.

"Thanks for that vote of confidence. I don't carry a gun, nor will I use one. The element of surprise will be to my advantage. I'm not worried, so please don't let this concern you. I have a feeling your incorrigible husband is adding his own sense of drama to a very simple situation."

Gus looked away sheepishly, like a young prankster caught in the act. Nick was right; his weird sense of humor had brought up a sinister possibility. He was sorry that he had spoken the thought.

Satomi swayed over to their table and leaning forward, with a direct view into her cleavage, announced, "I'm riding back with Bill Thompson and his group. Don't wait for me."

Nick suppressed a grin. She obviously did not relish the prospect of another backseat drive with Silvia Olavssen.

Soon afterwards, Nick and the Olavssens left the ice cream parlor and walked outside.

It would soon be dusk and time to leave this scenic little village. How quickly the last few hours had sped past. Once his mission to inform Gus of his background has taken place, Nick had enjoyed being here immensely. He genuinely cared for this couple. He thought he would have done so even if Kara had not been their daughter—but the fluttering in his stomach reminded him that in the intense green eyes of Silvia Olavssen he saw Kara and in the subtle, sophisticated, yet sometimes outlandish humor of Gus Olavssen he evidenced the distinctive humor passed on to his only child.

They arrived back at the houseboat and quickly packed and closed-up, retracting the awning, fastening portholes and securing doors. Nick could not believe how quickly he had adapted to the simple lifestyle here. He liked it. He would have found it a glimpse into Eden if Kara had been there with him. The thought intrigued him.

"I don't mind driving back."

Gus looked at Nick and a smile surfaced. He pulled out a key chain with two keys attached and handed them over.

"Can't let an opportunity like this pass, can we darling?" he said looking at his wife.

The two Olavssens' looked tired and Nick felt some remorse that they had put themselves out for him. He had dragged Gus miles across the beach, throwing him a curve by clobbering him with his depressing life story, which his daughter would need to know. Silvia had stepped in as his unsolicited guardian angel, protective to the point of wearing herself out with her fancy maneuvers to keep Satomi and himself apart.

They climbed up into the Jeep and immediately sat in the rear two seats and a smile tugged at Nick's mouth. They were so accustomed to being chauffeured that observing Nick in the driver's seat, they had automatically taken their usual places without question.

The drive back was uneventful and smooth. Conversation was minimal; they were all feeling a little tense. Nick became lost in his thoughts and when he looked into the rear mirror to ask for the code to open the wrought iron gates, he saw two heads, close together, sleeping peacefully.

The vehicle stopped smoothly, but even so it awoke Gus.

He yawned and nudged Silvia.

"Safely home again, darling, thanks to Nick."

The huge gates swung open and by the time the portico was reached they were both fully awake. Nick was pleased that they had trusted him sufficiently to relax so completely.

Mrs. Taylor, the cook, rustled up a delicious meal upon their return. Looking at his watch, Nick decided he could procrastinate no longer. It would soon be time to get over to the Inn.

The probability of having to stay awake through the night, merely acting on a hunch was not the smartest decision he had made, but he was committed to the project, even though he questioned the wisdom of it. The day was starting to take its toll.

Nick considered phoning Kara—he was still enthralled with the concept behind the phone hang-up, but he was in no real hurry to make the first conciliatory move. He smiled to himself. After all he had pride too.

There was just time for a game of Chess and that lasted longer than Nick had hoped. It was just after ten o' clock when Silvia handed over the empty velvet jewel case to Nick. Gus volunteered to have his chauffeur drop him off at the Inn, but Nick insisted on taking a taxi, which he would have drop him off before reaching The Black Bull Inn. It would not do to have the Olavssen's vehicle recognized at that time of night, especially as Nick had indicated his intention of staying with Kara's parents overnight.

Silvia hugged him fiercely around the waist.

"Take care, do you hear, nothing is worth a risk, so please don't take chances."

Gus put a hand on Nick's arm.

"Call if you need us, otherwise we will look forward to seeing you in the morning for breakfast."

He clasped Nick's shoulders as the taxi pulled up to the portico.

Nick left quickly.

The brief hug from Gus Olavssen had reminded Nick of his sunburn. He carefully sat upright in the taxi. These two special people were becoming the parents he had hardly known.

Nick's throat tightened. His only identification with his own parents was in an old photograph album sent to him by his grandfather when he was seven years old, after the plane crash in which they were killed. It was the only deliberately kind action he remembered his grandfather ever doing. After his daughter's death he had become estranged from Nick, closely adopting the lifestyle of a recluse. Nick was shunted off to exclusive private boarding schools around the world.

The attorney administering his parents' meager estate had informed him that his grandfather would spare no expense in having him educated at the finest academies, providing his grades merited the continuance. Diligently Nick had concentrated on his studies, hoping that by being on the Honors List consistently his grandfather would express an interest in him. Perhaps even want to see him. Nick's mouth twisted. What a futile hope! Even through medical school and during his internship, he doggedly had hoped to hear from his grandfather, sending letters, pictures and postcards to the only address he had—a post office box in Switzerland. Mr. Zermach, the attorney, who kept in touch through infrequent correspondence with Nick, said he reported Nick's progress at the twice-yearly meetings he had with his grandfather, so he knew the old man was still alive.

It was too late to cry over the 'might have been,' but a sense of deprivation invaded Nick's thoughts of what the two of them had lost.

Nick sighed and moved into a more comfortable position.

He was flying out of Newcastle International Airport the day after tomorrow and he fully expected to see Gus and Silvia Olavssen not only for breakfast, but also for the remainder of his time in England.

He counted on it very much.

* * *

CHAPTER TWENTY EIGHT

The taxi dropped Nick off just before reaching the Inn and without incident he found himself back in the Tyrrytt suite.

From the time he opened the door Nick used only a penlight flashlight, borrowed from the Olavssens, to find his way around the place. He put the inexpensive strand of pearls, with the matching earrings, into the velvet case and placed it into the safe, tumbling the lock.

Nick resigned himself to a long evening. Most probably quite uneventful, but the omen persisted. He could spare one sleepless night following up on a hunch.

Feeling his way through the armoire he found a pair of black slacks and by the same method searched the drawers for a black T-shirt. The white outfit would certainly be a giveaway.

He settled down beside the door inside the bathroom after changing his clothes. From this vantage point he could see through the bedroom to the front door and also from this position he would keep an eye on the bedroom safe.

The cool tiles on his back were soothing.

Searching through his clothing by touch had brought back the memories of Kara in the bathroom when he had undressed her and a rush of longing overcame him. He visualized the scene once more, improvising.

Cautiously he flicked on the interior light of his watch.

It was after 2:00 a.m. and he was having difficulty staying awake.

He put his head back against the wall, shifting his shoulders slightly to find cooler tiles. He would go over the day's events to keep awake. He had reached the Punch and Judy show part when he heard a squeak.

Blinking his eyes and shaking his head to focus his thoughts, Nick's senses became finely tuned. He deliberately breathed deeply and let his breath out slowly. He heard soft shuffling and looked toward the front door. He could not see a blasted thing. He would just have to lay low. Suddenly a diminished ray of light started making its way toward him, taking him by surprise. It was advancing from an unexpected direction. He was pleased to have chosen this camouflaged position in which to wait. The ambush should be in his favor.

The safe had been reached and Nick cautiously peered out. The figure was hardly discernible, only an exposed gloved hand was visible in the nebulous light. He was tempted to accost the intruder right there and then, but something held him back. He watched intrigued. Instead of the usual procedure being used—turning so many times this way and reversing, a key was being inserted to open the door of the safe. Nick had not noticed a keyhole there before. The safe was opened and the jewelry case removed. It was opened and the pearls were displayed.

Time to intercept!

Nick had been stealthily raising himself onto his stocking feet and without hesitating he rushed into the room and threw himself onto the intruder in a first-class Rugby tackle. He smacked the robber against the floor and pinned him there, waiting for retaliation.

There was none.

He was not prepared for the easy victory. He reached for his flashlight and turned it on, still hanging on to the arm of the interloper.

A black ski mask covered the face and Nick dragged it off, gasping as he saw Angela's countenance emerge. She had her eyes closed and it was obvious that Nick's lunge had stunned her.

He was about to walk around switching on the lights, when it occurred to him that Jon could not be far away. Where was he and why was Angela here alone? Was Jon on guard outside waiting?

Nick pulled Angela into the bathroom and closed the door.

There was no window in this room. He turned on the light and this, together with the cold marble floor, appeared to bring Angela around. She moaned, clasping the back of her head. She opened her eyes.

They looked at each other keenly and Angie turned her head away.

Softly Nick asked, "Why, Angie? Why did you do this?"

She lay with her eyes closed and tears started rolling down her cheeks.

"It was the only way I could think of."

Nick looked puzzled.

"To accomplish what?"

Angela lay still, the desperation in her voice had affected him.

"Please tell me, perhaps I can help."

She opened her eyes, still spilling with tears.

"I doubt it."

Attempting to sit up she said, "Jon doesn't know I'm here. Do you want to call the police, I'm totally responsible?"

"No. I don't want to do that. What I want to do is find out why you feel it necessary to steal. I'm puzzled. Is this a regular practice of yours? I recognize now that you must have taken the earring and returned it again. Is this being done as an idle new sport for the rich?"

Angie shuddered and laughed hollowly.

"If only that was it."

She immediately started sobbing again, her body shaking uncontrollably. Nick looked at her closely and put his arm around her shoulders. She looked as if she were about to go into shock.

"Listen to me, Angie. I only want to help, so take your time telling me why you are here. One thing for certain, we have to talk about it."

Her teeth were starting to chatter.

"I love Jon so muuuuuch."

She was shaking bodily.

Nick reached for a bath towel and pulled it down from its rod. He wrapped it firmly around her shoulders, tucking the ends in at the neckline.

"Go on."

"Jon asked his parents for another loan this weekend and they flatly refused. Told him it was about time he shaped up and took ownership of his responsibilities."

She dabbed at her eyes with a corner of the towel.

"At lunch I heard you say you had the Olavssen pearls and it seemed an easy way and the perfect opportunity to acquire most of the money Jon needs, without too much trouble. The pearls must be insured and a claim could be made out for them. Kara has so much, she would never miss them."

Nick looked at Angie, his eyes narrowing.

"I thought Jon was financially very secure. He has the farm with all its acreage and livestock and the Inn which seems to be doing very well."

Angie's frame shook.

"He has taken huge loans out on the farm and he and Leif still carry a large mortgage on The Black Bull Inn. That's all he has left. He hasn't been very good at managing money and I didn't know how badly until yesterday when he asked me to sell my engagement ring. That's when the idea to take the pearls occurred to me."

"How do you know so much about Kara's financial affairs?" Nick queried.

Looking flustered, Angie hesitated before replying.

"Jon's Godmother keeps him very well informed. She's known Kara's family from way back and has an abundance of information at her fingertips about them. Of course, Jon is familiar about lots of things too, growing up with Kara. His father and Kara's are involved in deals together as well."

Putting her hands over her face, Angela started sobbing noisily

"Now there's no other alternative but for Jon to marry Kara."

Nick could not believe his ears.

Jon was being forced into marrying Kara, the woman he would give up everything to possess, to become his wife and bear his children. It was so ridiculous a situation, he felt like laughing, albeit sardonically.

How would Kara feel knowing all of this?

He patted Angie's back absently, as his mind raced.

"I assume that Jon has been aware of this impending situation for some time since he proposed marriage to Kara several weeks ago. Did you know about that?"

She sniffed and answered almost inaudibly.

"Yes. Jon told me he was forced to do that. He was covering all bases, because the handwriting was on the wall. I've known for some time that he was gradually selling off properties that had been left to him. I thought that was because he didn't want to be bothered maintaining them any longer. I didn't think it would come to this."

She paused, and there was frustration in her voice as she continued.

"Jon spends money as if there's no tomorrow, you know, as if his bank account is the bottomless well. But he hadn't anticipated things getting out of hand like this. Buying the thoroughbred filly recently made things much worse. It cost a fortune and the surprise he intended was spoilt when he felt he had to admit that it was my wedding gift."

"He said that?" Nick abruptly interjected.

Angela's eyelids fluttered.

"Yes. He was very reluctant to reveal the secret before he had planned."

"When did he say that?"

Nick held his breath.

"He told me yesterday when he asked me to sell my engagement ring. He knew I was ticked off with him."

Was Jon hedging his bets? First the horse had been intended as Kara's wedding gift and now, obviously in an effort to placate Angela, it had been promised to her. Was this a ruse to cover Angela's fears while giving him more time to work on Kara? Jon's deviousness was becoming blatantly more apparent to Nick in the short time of their association.

"Jon loves me, I know it."

Angie turned to Nick with a look of anguish on her face.

"I'm over two months pregnant and there's no doubt that Jon is the father of my baby." Defensively she continued, "He wants it as much as I do."

Nick was shaken.

He rested against the wall and quickly sat up. The sunburn was really bothering him.

Looking at Angie contemplatively, Nick made a decision.

"Perhaps I can help you, but I must have a week or two to work some things out. Don't do anything foolish and in case you think you are getting out of this situation very lightly, I have all this on tape."

He held up the small Dictaphone recorder, which he had taken from his trouser pocket.

"Our conversation has been recorded and I will not hesitate to use it should I find it necessary."

Looking closely at Angela he asked.

"Where is Jon, by the way, if he doesn't know you are here?"

Angie looked away.

"He was so upset after the awful row with his parents that he decided to stay at "Much Ado" to think things over."

412

Nick looked perturbed.

"He wouldn't do anything stupid, would he, in a distraught frame of mind?"

Angie smiled faintly and shook her head.

"No. He assured me of that when I offered to stay with him. It was only when Satomi and I were being driven back to the Inn that I thought about the pearls and decided to stay overnight in Jon's suite rather than with Satomi."

"So that she wouldn't know what you were up to?" he asked.

Angie blinked and rose slowly to her feet.

"You can put the lights on, there's something you should see."

She opened the bathroom door and walked over to the long lace curtains and spread them further apart. A trap door stood open in the center of the room, directly underneath the table.

Nick shook his head—no wonder he had been such an easy victim.

He followed her and looking down into a circular staircase of narrow stone steps, leading into blackness said, "If this goes down to Jon's apartment, it has all the signs of a set-up."

"No, Nick. It wasn't like that at all. Jon would never stoop . . ." she stopped and looked shamefaced and quietly continued "as low as I have."

Nick looked at Angie with a guarded expression on his face. It appeared that Jon and Angie were well suited, but what an untenable situation they now found themselves dealing with. Confessing to a theft to salvage her life and protect the innocent babe could have become a costly and heartbreaking attempt by Angie, but for Jon to consider marrying Kara as a convenience was not only contemptible, it was wrong.

Nick tapped his foot impatiently, still deep in thought.

Kara was far too desirable to be married for her money alone. It was not only laughable, it was absurd. What if Jon had discovered he really did love Kara and her money would be a bonus to solve his problems? Was Jon putting Angela off until he was sure of Kara? Grimly Nick resolved to leave him with only one option and that would not include Kara in any way.

Standing beside the window Angie turned around to face Nick.

"This is the Inn's most requested room. It's usually called the "Honeymoon Suite;"—it's used most often for that occasion. It just happened to be free when you requested a large area to work in and this was the most suitable. There was no way to know you'd have Kara's jewelry with you."

A thought occurred to Nick.

"If you came up here and took the earring, didn't Jon know what you were doing?"

Shaking her head, Angie replied.

"No. I could see that you were about to make a telephone call in the lobby and Jon was waiting for you to return. I felt annoyed and insulted by the way you both behaved and I decided to play a joke, with the intent of telling you how I did it when I returned the jewelry to you. It would have been as much of a shock to Jon as it was to you. He thought he had the only key to the tower stairway. It was very easy to slip up to the room and unlock the bedroom safe, using my own duplicate keys. Even though the jewelry was not in the safe, you made no attempt to hide it and it didn't take much of a search to find it. I quickly looked in the box and grabbed it, high tailing it down the inner staircase and then hid it in the apartment until later. It was pretty close. I returned to the lounge and saw you leaving. Jon was ready to make up and we spent the rest of the night doing so."

"So what made you return the earring after stealing it? Again you took a risk." Nick asked.

"Well, it wasn't until the next morning, after Jon went over to the farm that I had a chance to look inside the box. I thought one earring must have become lodged underneath the satin and pried it up. Why would anyone just have one earring in a box? It didn't make sense. It was useless and certainly not worth being incriminated for and it was too late to try to explain. The porter saw you leave, so I knew the coast was clear to return it."

Nick looked at Angie sternly.

"You are not redeeming yourself at all. I'm quite upset about all of this and particularly your unruffled attitude. You seem to consider this a game. You don't recognize my anger because you don't know me well enough, but believe me, Angela, I am furious and quite disgusted. I do not take kindly to being deceived and I do not forget easily. The only reason I may decide to be of assistance is because it happens to fall in line with my own plans. Nothing more. Step out of line and you will discover my displeasure first-hand."

He patted his trouser pocket where the recorder lay, to add emphasis to his words.

"One more thing. You will not mention this escapade to Jon or anyone else. I need your word on this."

Angela regarded Nick uneasily.

His eyes had signaled his fury and the icy tone of his voice left no doubt regarding his intent. She believed everything he said and was more than ready to cooperate.

"I swear not to mention this to anyone. It will be a secret between the two of us," she whispered, "and thank you for taking it no further. I will never do anything like this again."

He picked up the flashlight that Angie had dropped.

"I'll escort you back—by the usual way."

Nick closed the trapdoor. The patterned carpet fitted perfectly.

"But I didn't bring the door key to Jon's suite. I didn't expect to use it."

"Okay," he said "is there a copy at the reception area we can pick up en route?"

Angela nodded her head affirmatively.

They walked silently back to the door of Jon's apartment, stopping briefly at the deserted reception area, where Angie picked up a duplicate key.

Nick walked into the room with Angela, who looked at him in alarm. He seemed calm right now, but she remembered the hostility in his eyes just a short time ago and wondered what he had in mind. He looked into the bedroom, noting the small opened door and walking over to it closed it firmly, locking it using the key still in the keyhole. He held the key in his hand.

"You were not intended to have this. I will take it for safe keeping as well as the key to the safe, as additional evidence. You can rest assured you will not be disturbed by me."

He nodded to Angela and left the room, waiting until he heard the door lock and chain in place before retracing his steps. Angela would have to return the duplicate key to Jon's suite back to the reception area.

Slipping the keys into his pocket Nick heard them clang against the recorder, which he took out with a smile. He was becoming very creative—it did not have a tape in it. The last one he had used at Jon's birthday party was taken out and he had intended replacing it while waiting for the intruder.

As he walked back to the tower, Nick ruminated on the eye-opening information just given by Angela. So she was pregnant and it appeared to have happened unintentionally. On the surface Jon seemed to want to do the honorable thing by marrying Angela, with the advent of the baby leading him in that direction. However was that what he really had in mind, taking into account his urgent need for money?

Kara said Jon's proposal had been unexpected. No doubt he was hoping to capitalize on her lifelong feelings for him, but he had taken her by surprise and her earlier romantic involvements had made her too cautious to give an immediate answer.

Angela said that Jon loved her and Nick recalled the way they had behaved when he first noticed them upon his arrival at the Inn and again at Jon's party. They had appeared to be in love, but it seemed of such a turbulent nature that he shuddered at the instability of it. To each his own. He could not handle the capriciousness.

Nick loved Kara without reservation and his impatience was in waiting for her to acknowledge what he could already see—she loved him. She just had not come to terms with it.

Nick's brow furrowed. Lady Bassenthorpe seemed to know far more about the Olavssen's financial situation than appeared seemly or appropriate. She certainly had no qualms imparting her knowledge to Jon.

Nick stopped in his tracks. The letter from her to Kara. Was Lady Bassenthorpe and Jon in collusion on this? Would Lady Bassenthorpe, knowing of Jon's serious lack of money, point out Kara's fortune and suggest this as a way to solve his problems? Nick had been told that Lady Bassenthorpe would stop at nothing to accommodate Jon's every whim. She had, after all, written quite a convincing letter to Kara, begging her to consider Jon's initial proposal. A thoughtful expression came over Nick's face. Kara must be an extremely wealthy woman if, as Angela had intimated, her pearls could be regarded as baubles. It also placed Jon in the role of fortune hunter.

In this reflective mood, there was something else that was bothering Nick. That beautiful horse should not be used as part of a blackmail scheme. No matter what the outcome of all this was, the horse would belong to Kara. He vowed that it would be so and there would be no strings attached. She had already laid claim to it in her heart.

Glancing at his watch, Nick picked up his pace. It was almost four in the morning and he had been meandering through a maze of corridors at the Inn for almost an hour, while his brain thundered around, working on ideas to run past Franc.

Back in his suite, with all of the lights turned on, he examined the open safe. It had a tumble lock, which he had used to close it, but at the side of the handle to open the safe was a brass nameplate. With a little pressure applied to it, Nick pushed it aside to find a keyhole. He closed the safe door and used the key he took from Angela to open it again. He heard the soft whirring of a bolt being released. This was the way to override the tumbler action. Very ingenious.

Nick sat back on his heels and whistled softly.

Was the purpose of this to rob wealthy visitors in the 'good old days'? Surely it was not a practice nowadays.

In a thoughtful mood Nick reflected on both possibilities. Perhaps he should discuss this with Gus Olavssen.

In a few hours he would need to look refreshed and halfway presentable, if Kara's parents were going to start considering him as an eligible suitor for their daughter's hand.

The telephone awakened him.

It rang several times before Nick reached for it, sighing.

His sunburn hurt like hell. That would teach him for staying out in the sun longer than he should. Also in grappling on the floor with Angela he had banged his shoulder and it was stiff and sore.

What a start to the day.

"Yes." He responded curtly, looking at his watch.

It was just after seven and he could easily have slept for a few more hours.

"I couldn't go to bed without apologizing to you, Nick."

He felt as if his heart had stopped beating.

"Kara?" he whispered.

"Who else were you expecting?" was the soft, teasing reply.

"Certainly not you, my love, not after the way we parted on the telephone a couple of nights ago."

"That's why I'm calling."

There was a pause and the tremulous voice started speaking quickly.

"I'm sorry for hanging up on you. It was very childish of me. I hadn't realized how much I was missing you until I heard your voice again and I wanted to tell you that, but when you started going on and on about Satomi, I couldn't handle it." She gave a little embarrassed laugh. "I suppose it could be said that I was in a state of envy. I wanted so much for it to be me who was with you."

A thankful smile spread across Nick's face. She was starting to communicate with him.

He lay back very carefully on the pillow, making himself as comfortable as the sunburn would allow.

He was going to get as much mileage out of this conversation as possible.

"Nick are you still there?"

He deliberately yawned.

"Sorry. You woke me up and I had a very late night."

There was a catch in Kara's voice.

"With Satomi?"

Was this really happening? He could hardly speak. He could not take a chance on this being a dream.

"Sorry for teasing you, darling, I was with your parents all day at the beach and left them around ten at night. Please forget about Satomi, she means absolutely nothing to me and I don't want to waste time discussing her, but I do have a lot to say to you."

He turned over onto his stomach, feeling an ache that had nothing to do with his shoulder.

He heard a click, and thought Kara must have hung up on him again.

Startled, he cried out her name, and she immediately responded.

"I'm here, Nick."

He frowned, was someone listening in?

"Kara, I'm going to be spending the remainder of my time in England at your parents' home. In fact I'm checking out of here in a couple of hours. I'd like to phone you from there tonight, about eleven, which will make it 7:00 a.m. your time. Is that too early—it's a workday for you? I had the feeling someone was listening in to our conversation just now and what I have to say to you is very, very private—in fact, my darling, for your ears only."

He heard the relief in Kara's voice and a warm glow suffused him.

"I'll be waiting, sweetheart," she said, and his heart soared.

She cared. She actually cared for him.

"I love you, Kara. Goodbye, my precious, sweet dreams. I'll be talking to you soon."

Nick was shaking as he hung up the receiver.

It was too good to be true, but it would be weeks before he would be back in California. How could he exist without Kara for that length of time? This must change.

He stretched out on the bed, luxuriating in his thoughts. Kara had missed him. He hugged a pillow—things could only get better in the future. Nick allowed his imagination to dominate his thoughts for a while.

He phoned the private number that Gus had given him. Unexpectedly Silvia answered. She sounded cheered hearing his voice.

"It's about time. We were ready to come looking for you."

Nick laughed, pleased.

"Sorry. Blame your daughter—she just phoned me. I'm so thrilled I feel like celebrating. How about coming out to brunch with me this morning? I could pick you up in about an hour."

Her laugh made him smile; he could detect the same delightful peal that Kara's voice projected.

"Too late, my dear. Breakfast will be served on the terrace in half an hour. We are waiting for you, so put your seven league boots on. We will take you up on dinner though. There is a charming country place where I think you will enjoy their imaginative menu."

As if an afterthought, which Nick knew camouflaged her real concern, she asked

"Did you catch the person who tried to take Kara's pearl earring?"

Nick crossed his fingers.

"No. I guess I'm not cut out to be a detective."

Nick replaced the phone in its cradle. Who would have thought things would turn out this way? Kara had almost admitted she loved him; he had promised to play a game of Chess with Gus; Silvia had already declared her intentions that she was on his side and tonight there would be the phone call to Kara.

He jumped out of bed, elated. Even the sunburn and sore shoulder did little to dampen his high spirits. Shaving, he mentally reviewed the business he would discuss with Frank. Most of it would need to be accomplished quickly and stealthily. Franc could do it. He had every confidence in his friend and business partner.

Nick stood looking at his reflection in the mirror, the electric shaver poised in his hand. What would he have done without Franc—always being there for him all this time? Michele too had given her friendship without reservation. He leaned his forehead against the mirror. What a selfish, arrogant simpleton he had become. He loved these friends and over the years it was almost as if he had tried to kill their affection and respect.

Nick muttered a vow as he tapped his head against the mirror. He would be seeing them soon and this would give him an opportunity to begin making amends.

Nick quickly packed his belongings, carefully surveying the rooms before leaving. He walked down the back stairs with his luggage, placing it into the trunk of the Bentley. He did not have time to wait for a porter. He went to the front desk and handed over his American Express Gold card.

It was going to be a lovely day, after all.

CHAPTER TWENTY NINE

Franc and Michele with their four years old daughter, Fiona, were waiting for Nick in the VIP lounge of the Charles de Gaulle Airport, northeast of Paris.

Franc studied his friend carefully, watching as he walked toward them from the Customs area. There was something different about him, which he could not pin down. He had acquired a tan, which looked terrific, but that was not the reason. Maybe they would have time to relax and get close again. For the past few years Nick had become steadily more businesslike in their relationship. It hurt Franc more than he was willing to admit, to find their friendship crumbling.

Fiona ran to Nick.

"Oncle Neek," she screamed.

He managed to hastily set his briefcase and luggage down as she threw herself into his arms. He hugged her affectionately and kissed her cheek.

"You are getting so big and so beautiful, just like your mama."

Michele approached Nick, taking his face into her hands and kissing him lightly on the lips.

"Did François let the cat out of the bag then?"

She patted her slightly protruding stomach.

"Oh, no. That was my sloppy French. I have been thinking in English for the past few months and I'm not back into gear yet. Give me a break, Michele. You know how I have to concentrate."

Nick held her away from him, eyeing her up and down. "Will I be Godfather again?"

Michele smiled. "But of course."

She touched Nick's sunburned nose delicately.

"You look fantastic. Your mini vacation must have agreed with you."

He nodded and looked over at his long-time friend and stood Fiona on the carpet.

"It's good to come back."

He walked over and clasped his friend tightly.

Franc eagerly reciprocated the hug and Nick grimaced as he did so.

"You can see how easily I became sunburned. It made me realize what little time I spend outdoors. I hope your invitation still stands to spend next weekend at the farm."

With a short laugh Franc said in delight.

"It's about time."

Silently Franc said to himself, *for whatever reason, welcome back Nick.*

They were all staying at the Hôtel de Crillon. It was Nick's favorite hotel in Paris. It overlooked the place de la Concorde and was founded in 1909 by the champagne family Taittinger, neighbors of his at one of his vineyards. The regal old hotel was elegant and imposing. Fresh urns of flowers, tapestries, marble sculptures, ornate Louis XVI mirrors met the eyes at every turn. It bespoke wealth and luxury and was a haven after the grueling hours he and Franc put in at the seminars. Michele and Fiona were staying overnight in the palatial two-bedroom suite, leaving the next morning by train for their farm on the outskirts of Paris. Their overseer would be there to meet them. It was a trip that delighted Fiona.

Franc had the forethought to make reservations for dinner at the 'Jules Verne' restaurant, which had a magnificent view of the river Seine and the surrounding area from the third floor of the Eiffel Tower. It was Michele's 35th birthday the next weekend and this celebration had been planned while they could all be together in the city. Fiona was excited. She looked like a little porcelain doll in a pink and white dotted gauze dress, with a large lace collar and white patent shoes and purse.

Nick could hardly refrain from smiling whenever he looked at her. He took her dainty hand after getting out of the taxi and together they walked to the elevators. Franc and Michele smiled happily at each other. Whatever had taken place lately with Nick was bringing him back to life.

Michele whispered to her husband.

"Don't grill Nick too much. I'm sure he'll tell us all about it at the weekend. I can hardly wait."

She squeezed François' hand in anticipation.

The first day of each seminar was usually the most boring for Nick and this, his third day in Paris was no different from all the other "first day's" that started the sessions. He was pleased that at least the first two days in Paris had been spent leisurely with his friends.

Familiar with Nick's "first day's boredom" Franc offered his assistance occasionally, reviewing the agenda with the wide assortment of registrants; Hospital department heads and interns, university medical center professors and students, interested medical administrators and also certain specialized sectors of the news media. He usually went over some of the statistical information and source handouts and gave a preparatory run-down of the textbook written by Nick, which would be used in conjunction with the lectures. Today had been no exception and when the preliminary session ended, Franc suggested going to a nightclub or the theater to relax. Nick shook his head.

"Let's have an early supper in the dining room of the hotel and then relax in the suite. I want to make a phone call to California around eleven."

Franc waited for Nick to expand on this piece of information, but he adroitly switched the subject and went on to other things.

Franc was puzzled. Nick phoned California often. He had offices, property, and businesses there, but it had never been a big deal before. From Nick's tone of voice, there was a special reason for calling at a precise time and he was not ready to disclose it.

They had almost finished their meal in 'Les Ambassadeurs,' one of the three outstanding restaurants at The Crillon, when Franc's gaze focused on a gorgeous, exotic woman, who was deliberately walking over to their table.

"Nick how wonderful and what a coincidence."

She bent down and kissed Nick on the lips.

Franc was impressed. She certainly was a beauty, but they all seemed to manage to find Nick.

Catching him off-guard was Nick's harsh answering tone.

"What are you doing here?"

"Work, work, work, darling, that's all I do."

Instinctively Franc pulled out a chair, and Satomi sank into it gracefully.

Nick glared at him.

"By the look of you, our weekend together did no harm—in fact you look rather cute with your sunburned nose. I know I'm being naughty, but how's the rest of you?"

She threw her head back and laughed, as if sharing a deep secret.

Nick looked annoyed. He laid his napkin on the tablecloth and stood up.

"We were about to leave. There's still work to do, so if you will excuse us."

Franc hurriedly stood up also.

Satomi shrugged her shoulders.

"Perhaps we could have dinner tomorrow evening? I am staying here for a few days."

"That's not possible. I have business dinners scheduled for the remainder of the week."

Satomi looked at Nick resentfully. He would regret this public renunciation. Who the hell did he think he was anyway? The maître d'hôtel was heading in their direction and diners were staring. They were causing a ruckus in the dignified, exclusive dining room.

The three of them hurried out of the room in a group.

As they entered the marble foyer they were approached by a man.

"Hi, Dr. Prendergast. How are you?"

When Nick turned to look at him, Satomi ran her arm through Nick's and a picture was taken of their exit from the restaurant. A couple of other photographers' bulbs lit up the area. Satomi withdrew her arm. It probably would not make the headlines, but it should make a newsworthy article and that was her intention.

She smiled brilliantly at the closest photographer as he moved away. He was quite cute and she would be seeing him later.

Nick said in a low, conversational tone.

"If this harassment continues, I will deal with it in a manner which will be most embarrassing and unpleasant for you."

His eyes were icy. "Do you get my message?"

So be it. Satomi's eyes blazed at him, as she hissed.

"You'll regret this, believe me."

Franc walked between them and took Nick's elbow, ushering him toward the private elevator.

Once in the suite, Franc poured a stiff brandy for each of them.

"Who was Miss Sweetness Personified and what was that all about?"

He handed the crystal snifter to Nick.

"In a nutshell, she seems to have a crush on me—apparently has seen me around for some time. She is a top-flight model and I guess does not take rejection easily. I met her about a week ago and hoped I'd seen the last of her."

Franc rolled his eyes.

"Had enough of her charms, I suppose."

Nick looked at him sharply.

"I never touched her, or wanted to. Ever since I met Kara, I've had absolutely no desire to be with anyone else. It's a long story, my friend, and I'd like to fill you in, since I hope you will be our Best Man. I don't like throwing this at you all at once, but the Japanese seminars are due to start next week and there's some business which must be dealt with immediately. Since it could play a pivotal role in whether my future happiness is secured or not, Franc, I really need your help."

The imploring look on Nick's face tugged at Franc's composure.

The years had rolled back, and François de Veaux breathed a sigh of relief. It had been a long time since Nick had asked any favors of him, or discussed his private life. They still depended on each other.

"Of course. What is it you wish to discuss?"

The two friends met on companionable ground.

★ ★ ★

CHAPTER THIRTY

He hated being so far away from Kara.

Nick pushed his work papers aside and rubbed his eyes. He was rapidly losing his power of concentration. His appetite had also deserted him and he was tired and worried.

He was halfway through the Japanese tour and things were not going well.

He was in Tokyo and it was hot and sticky. The seminar being held in the Komamoto Tower would conclude the next day and Nick was impatient for it to do so. Franc was pursuing the business transactions that Nick had asked him to concentrate on and these required his full attention, so Nick carried the seminars and their workshops entirely on his own shoulders.

Franc had checked in earlier that evening, informing Nick that the negotiations were going well and once again Nick was grateful for the financial acumen of his partner and friend. They were in touch with each other a couple of times a day, but there never seemed to be the right time for Nick to broach a recent development that had raised his concern about Kara. He was becoming quite exhausted by the heavy itinerary and the inability to take charge of his personal affairs.

From the time Kara had started opening up to him, Nick had prearranged their calls, as he often had business dinners after the seminars. The high point of his day was in looking forward to the phone time they could spend together. He was impatient to get back to California and the thought of spending another six days in Japan aggravated him daily.

His last phone call to Kara a couple of nights ago had left him vaguely apprehensive. She had sounded uncommunicative and when Nick asked if there was anything wrong, she said she thought she was getting a cold. He was anxious to talk to her this evening and dinner with a couple of professors from UCLA's medical center, on sabbatical in Tokyo, was rushed through. He had to get back to his hotel in time to make the call.

Reaching Kara's home answering machine was very disappointing to Nick. He left a message saying he would be waiting impatiently for her call.

He fell asleep on the bed, fully dressed. It was 3:00 a.m. when he awoke and checked with the night operator for messages. There was none. It was Friday afternoon in California and he phoned "Working it Out."

He was told that Kara had left for the weekend. They were sorry they had no idea where she could be reached.

What was going on? He started panicking.

Nick settled down a little when he remembered that Kara had mentioned spending the weekend with Marcie and her parents in Santa Barbara, but it was strange that she had not been available to take his calls. They had not planned on contacting each other over the weekend, as he would be traveling to Osaka in the southern part of Japan, and setting up for the seminar to take place on Monday. He had arranged to call Kara at night, after the first day's session ended, and he would just have to leave it at that.

The weather was not quite as hot in Osaka, but as usual the first day's opening session had left Nick irritable and exhausted.

When he phoned Kara's townhouse that evening, a long distance operator intercepted his call saying that the number was no longer in service, filling Nick with dread. Something was very wrong.

He waited until she was likely to be at the office and taking into consideration the time differential, phoned her there. Surprisingly he reached her, feeling unsteady at the sound of her voice.

He was sleeping badly and the days seemed interminably long.

"Hi darling. I called your townhouse a short time ago and the operator informed me that the number was no longer in use. What's up?"

"Oh, er, I decided to get an unlisted number."

She cleared her throat.

"Haven't you gotten over your cold yet?"

Nick's voice was softly solicitous.

Her voice seemed a little fuzzy.

"I'm okay. The clients have started calling me at home and I decided I needed more privacy."

The conversation ceased.

"You sound a little upset. Are you all right, sweet?"

Brightly. "Yes. Fine. I really should dash I was about to go into a meeting when you called. Talk to you soon."

Nick sighed.

"Just a minute Kara, I don't have your new number."

There was a pause.

A little breathlessly she said. "483-0020" and hung up.

Nick sat with the telephone receiver in his hand.

It had been a disturbingly brief telephone conversation. Not much had been said, but what was left unsaid filled him with foreboding.

Replacing the telephone receiver and sitting down, Nick began mulling over the discussions with Kara of the past several days.

Kara had sounded indifferent and detached. Was she tiring of him? Could she be having second thoughts about their unusual relationship? Perhaps his extended business trips were not to her liking and she had decided his lifestyle would not fit in with her own. He was filled with self-doubts.

The phone rang and Nick eagerly answered it, hoping to find Kara being her usual teasing self at the other end, wanting to make amends, just as he did.

It was Franc.

His voice was buoyant and upbeat.

"Good news, Nick—in fact excellent news. Everything you asked for has been negotiated successfully. I have to attend to some of the closing documentation so won't keep you, but before I fax the details, here's a summary.

The horse will be transported to 'Chateau Vineyards' as you stipulated. Should be there within the month. Had to settle on $25,000 more than anticipated, but it's certainly worth it. A beautiful animal. Just a minute."

Papers rustled. Franc continued, "Next. You'll have controlling interest in The Black Bull Inn and then the old farmhouse," Nick heard pages rustling again.

"Oh, yes. You'll hold a 60% mortgage, with a final balloon clause if you care to exercise it. Everything's been signed, without Jon or, in the case of The Black Bull Inn, his partner knowing the identity of the actual purchaser and investor. I used one of our companies as the 'Holding' company."

Pride of achievement was evident in Franc's voice.

Nick pulled himself together and managed to infuse some enthusiasm into his response.

"Great, Franc. You did a fantastic job. Let's celebrate soon."

"You okay, Nick? You sound tired. Are you overdoing things?"

Sometimes breakfast meetings and dinner conferences extended the workday to eighteen hours, much too strenuous for Nick to carry alone over a ten days span. Franc was concerned.

"It's been a long day—you know how that is." Nick yawned. "In fact I'm going to turn in as soon as we're through.

That sounded more normal, hearing Nick's positive response, but Franc knew Nick too well to be reassured. Nick had sounded more than tired—depressed.

Still worried, Franc suggested,

"Can you manage the rest of the seminar alone? I can catch a flight out as soon as this stuff is completed."

"There's just two more days here. Not worth it, Franc. But thanks. Goodnight, my friend."

Nick should have been jubilant with the news from Franc, but it was overshadowed by disturbing feelings, which were growing in magnitude each day that he was away from Kara. She was retreating from his life.

Recently at night he had started having nightmares, similar to those experienced during the destructively traumatic time with Serawin. Shuddering from the anguish felt so dramatically while asleep, he would see Kara in dangerous situations unable to rescue her. Sometimes threatening figures held him back from reaching her when she was crying for help. The worst times were new to his nightmare sequences—he would see her in the arms of a faceless man whose intimacies she encouraged. He would wake up in a cold sweat.

Nick thought he was going crazy. He could wait no longer. It was still afternoon in California and he phoned the new unlisted telephone number that Kara had given to him. At least he could leave a loving message on her answering machine.

"Apex Janitorial Service."

Yes, that was their number. It had been theirs ever since they started the business three years ago. Nick was devastated. Kara had deliberately mislead him. Without delay Nick phoned "Working it Out" to be told that Kara had left for an appointment and could not be reached.

Nick squeezed his eyelids together. Kara was walking out of his life and there did not seem to be a damn thing he could do about it.

In desperation he phoned Kara's parents. The phone rang several times and in looking at his watch and making the mental calculations he realized the household would still be sleeping.

Hurriedly he hung up.

He was frantic.

Next day he ended the seminar perfunctorily and took the Concorde to New York. His secretary, Claudia, had arranged for a private plane to fly him into Riverside's Flabob Airport after arrival at the Ontario International Airport in California. The Flabob basically consisted of a long landing strip in the middle of acres of land, running parallel to Mt. Rubidoux. A rental car would be waiting for him there. Within half-an-hour of landing at Flabob, Nick had reached Kara's townhouse and rang the doorbell, searching for the key which he had not returned. Emma answered the door and stood as if paralyzed seeing Nick standing before her.

Then her mouth dropped open.

"Kara's not here. She left for England two days ago. Didn't you know?"

Nick shook his head, with a grim expression on his face. Of course she had not mentioned it, she knew he would be back in California soon and had no intention of being here.

Nick's worst fears were beginning to be activated.

Emma invited Nick in.

"Would you like a cup of tea or coffee? It won't take long to make."

He shook his head. Hemlock would be more appropriate.

"I'll use the phone Emma, I have to call my secretary."

Emma went into the kitchen.

Nick idly fingered Kara's mail left on top of a bureau as he talked to Claudia.

"For the next week, I'm going to be out of the country. Put me on a United/American Airlines flight, whatever, in time to catch the

Concorde out of New York tomorrow. Also coordinate the arrival of the Concorde with a connecting flight from London to Newcastle. Have a limousine service in Newcastle pick me up at the airport. You'll have the flight information to pass on to them. As for my appointments here, please cancel or change them, with apologies. Sorry, Claudia. I owe you one."

As he hung up he pulled out from the pile of mail a small manila envelope that was sticking out. It had no return address, but bore a Paris postmark. It was dated five days earlier. He moved it around in his fingers. The contents were proportional and stiff. It was not a letter. He put it on top of the collection.

Nick walked into the familiar blue and white kitchen, almost expecting to see Kara there. Emma had made a pot of tea and Nick smiled tiredly as she handed over a cup and saucer.

"As you know I've been away for over a month and it took me by surprise that Kara would leave for England and not let me know her plans. Do you know why she left so hurriedly, Emma?"

Emma looked a bit upset.

"Not really. Kara did not confide in me, but a short time after you left, someone called Jon started calling quite often from England. They often had lengthy conversations, but Kara seemed to be all right, she didn't look sad or happy after talking to him. Then about a week ago something arrived in the mail from Paris, which upset her very much. It felt like pictures to me, so I thought it might have come from you. But it made her miserable for days and she cried in her room for two solid nights when she came home from work. I could hear her. Just after that she said she was going to England and that it was a good time for me to visit my daughter in Portland for my annual holiday."

Emma looked at Nick with compassion. He looked deflated and defenseless. Emma's heart went out to him.

"Why the rush and so much secrecy?"

Nick's face was a study in misery.

"I don't know, but she did seem to be in a hurry to get to England. She packed very quickly, trying to smile, saying this was supposed to be a very happy occasion. But she didn't seem very happy. She also said it was about time she made up her mind and this would be a good time to do so. I have no idea what she meant. Half the time she seemed to be talking to herself."

Emma sighed and looked down at the table. These young people complicated their lives unnecessarily.

Nick jumped up suddenly, startling Emma.

Walking over to the stack of mail, he grimly tore open the manila envelope. Thoughts had been shuttling around in his head, as Emma spoke.

Pictures fell out. He quickly glanced at them and went back and closely inspected each very carefully. They were all of Satomi and himself. The two of them on Jon's settee, pictures of her rubbing sun tan lotion on his back, one of her with her hands over his eyes in that damned tiny bikini (he had not realized this one had been taken), and a newspaper picture with an article indicating that they were following each other around the world. The caption read "Love will find a Way— Playboy finds Playmate." Satomi was quoted as saying she expected to have some exciting plans to disclose when she joined Nick in Tokyo. Oh, right! Why had Franc not come across this in the newspaper? He usually looked out for this type of nonsense.

A printed note included with the pictures read "A duplicate set, in case you mislaid the others."

So his hunch had been on target. Pictures had already been sent to Kara.

Nick was livid. Satomi, the witch, was carrying out her threat.

The evidence in Nick's hands was hateful and he could understand Kara's frame of mind to some extent, but how could she believe all this crap? Could she not have confronted him, at least to tell him what a scoundrel he was, if she believed the whole manufactured situation was true?

Her love could not be as strong as he had hoped.

He immediately phoned Kara's parents. Was Kara there?

Silvia Olavssen's fluttery evasive answers told him what he wanted to know. He could accept them wanting to protect their daughter, faced with this shattering pseudo-evidence.

He had to get back to L.A. to get a change of wardrobe and deal with some urgent business he had postponed. The next step was to find Kara as quickly as possible.

Standing in the doorway Nick said to Emma.

"Please don't mention I've been here, if Kara phones. You know I wouldn't do anything in the world to hurt her. If everything goes according to plan and she hasn't already done anything foolish, she will soon be Kara Prendergast for the rest of her life."

Emma patted his arm.

"As soon as you go I'm leaving for Portland, so no one will ever know you have been here."

She reached over and kissed Nick's cheek.

"Good luck. It's time something right happened for the two of you."

A sorrowful look was reflected in her eyes.

* * *

It was the longest trip Nick had ever made, as far as his patience and anxiety levels were concerned. He traveled on American Airlines to New York by First Class where he shaved and changed on the plane. He was shocked by his appearance in the mirror. He was so tense that each delay he encountered added more pressure to his already screaming nerves and physical endurance. It was impossible to rest on the American Airlines flight and also on the Concorde. The couple of large brandies he had downed, as usual in the hope that they would serve as sleep inducers, once again had not. He had not really expected they would, but his exhausted and troubled mind cried out for relief.

By the time he had changed planes and was met at the Newcastle International Airport by the limousine service chauffeur, he was ready to drop. Again sleep persisted in eluding him. Just when he felt the desire to rest his eyes, alarm would furtively galvanize his wild imagination and terror would strike, temporarily renewing his strength and willpower.

Nick arrived at the Olavssen's huge oak doors apprehensive and uncertain of his reception. He must see Kara and no one was going to stop him.

Martin, the butler, flustered by Nick's demanding tone, called over Hilda as she was passing through the foyer.

"Why, Mr. Nick. Was Her Ladyship expecting you?"

"I don't think so, but please let her know I'm here, Hilda. It is very important."

He spoke quietly, with a tight expression on his face.

Her Ladyship, who the hell was that? He shook his head in annoyance. He was much too distressed and exhausted to deal with Hilda's sense of humor right now.

"Oh, dear, they left for the church with Miss Kara about an hour ago."

Nick swayed and clutched the large brass door handle to stand upright. He could not have traveled this distance to find his efforts in vain.

"Which church?" he asked hoarsely.

She gave a name, which Nick did not immediately recognize.

"Where's that?"

"It's the old church in Thirsk."

Nick's face cleared slightly. That was the place where he shopped and found the cameo for Kara. Yes, he remembered the beautiful old church.

"Thanks," he muttered, dashing back to the limousine.

"Drive as fast as possible, without being stopped and you will earn an extra two hundred pounds. We are going to St Mary's Church in the center of Thirsk."

The man drove like a madman. Nick clung to the handle above the car door as they drifted around curves in the road, passing trucks and cars on impossible grades and shooting along winding country roads like a bat out of Hell. They reached the church, pulling into the driveway and Nick recognized the Olavssen's silver gray Rolls Royce standing outside.

Oh, no. Please Kara, do not let our love end like this.

With a wildly beating heart, Nick entered the church and stood looking toward the Nave.

There were about a dozen people in the chancel, with several people sitting in the pews. Far fewer people than could have been expected, but it obviously had been arranged very quickly. It was very quiet and his leather-soled shoes alerted everyone in the wedding party to his presence.

A silence descended as they turned and looked at him.

Nick saw only Kara. She looked so beautiful, the sight of her brought tears to his eyes. She was in a slim fitting white suit, with a draped scarf that cascaded down her back.

Please give me just a few minutes to explain everything, my love. He felt his lips moving, but his throat was constricted—speech failed him.

He rested his hand on top of a pew and stood hesitantly, waiting.

434

If this was what Kara really wanted, she probably would hate him for intruding on the most private and personal occasion one could solemnize. She certainly had not wanted him here.

It was a turning point from which she specifically had intended excluding him. Jon was looking at him intently with a questioning expression on his face and a lump of almost insurmountable proportions seemed to lodge in Nick's throat.

He had no right being here. He could have saved himself much heartache by accepting Kara's rejection.

Nick suddenly experienced a feeling like no other—he was empty, drained of life.

He turned and began moving slowly away, back toward the arched stone portico, where his vehicle was waiting.

"Nick, oh, Nick."

It sounded so much like Kara's voice—like a fresh blow to his heart. He could hear her voice everywhere. He looked over his shoulder to see Silvia Olavssen hurrying after him.

He sighed and turned to meet her. She was probably angry at his unprecedented arrival, particularly if she thought he had been cheating on her daughter.

He had traveled so far to tell Kara that he loved her and he was too late.

Silvia Olavssen was drawing near and Nick pressed his lips together tightly in an effort to hide his despair. He could imagine Kara aging so well. She had a sweet smile on her face and he wondered if she felt some affection for him, after all. Was she coming to say goodbye?

Nick could not speak, he could not move. He was frozen to the ground as if turned into a marble statue.

"Please come back into the church, Nicholas, it's almost over and . . . ."

He could not bear to witness the scene.

A weakness flooded his body. He could fight back no longer. He did not have the strength to go on without Kara.

A thankful blackness enveloped him.

Before the startled eyes of Kara's mother, Nick collapsed on the ground.

✱ ✱ ✱

CHAPTER THIRTY ONE

It was an unfamiliar room in which he awoke.

Nick's head ached and he closed his eyes to block out the pain.

Heaviness settled upon him.

He attempted getting out of bed, but his head suddenly seemed to weigh a ton. He lay back on the pillow groaning. A cool pack was immediately applied to his forehead.

"You really clobbered yourself when you fell, young man, you scared us to death."

He looked into beautiful green eyes.

Kara's mother was sitting by his side on the bed, holding his hand.

"Dr. Klaussen left a prescription for you, but said the best medicine would be to allow you to sleep for as long as you wished."

Events were struggling to return to his memory.

She looked at her watch.

"I think you must have set a record, Nicholas, you have more than slept the clock around."

He did not know of what she was speaking. It all sounded very inconsequential, but she had a lovely voice and it was nice having a friendly hand in his.

He closed his eyes and gently pressed the satiny smooth fingers.

Sighing deeply, he threw an arm over his eyes and bleakly confided to his bedside companion. "Why did she leave? Didn't she know how much I love her? How could I look at another woman when she has claimed me so completely? I thought she knew that."

Nick turned his head away and his voice quivered.

A shudder ran through his body and an anguished expression flooded his face.

"I need you so much, Kara. Don't leave me now."

He turned over in his restlessness, groaning from the effort.

"I can't live without you. Please . . ."

A sob escaped as he burrowed his head in the pillow.

During this soliloquy tears ran uncontrollably down the face of the distraught young woman standing at the foot of the bed. She motioned as if to go to the man, but a finger over the mouth of the lady by the bed restrained her.

Nick's shoulders shuddered and he rolled over onto his back. He was becoming unmanageably restive. He churned around on the bed, sighing and wincing with each move of his head. Moaning pathetically, he lurched over onto his stomach.

"So little faith in me. So little."

Sighing deeply he clutched the pillow, sinking his head into it. The two women watched as the involuntary activity decreased and slow, steady breathing took place, relaxing the tormented figure on the bed.

Placing a comforting arm around the shaking shoulders of the younger woman, the two of them walked out of the bedroom together. Silvia nodded her head to the crisply dressed nurse, who arose from the chair outside the door and entered the bedroom to resume her duties, a bedpan in her hand.

"There's nothing we can do right now, Kara. According to Dr. Klaussen, Nicholas had reached the point of exhaustion where his mind blacked out. He was unable to handle a particular crisis and this is nature's way of recompensing, giving him a well-deserved respite, so that he can regroup his thoughts and energy and get on with his life."

Kara looked back into the room, unwilling to leave.

"The nurse is very competent, darling, Nicholas will be fine."

Kara's mother smiled understandingly at the reluctance shown on her daughter's face.

They had all come a long way in the last 24 hours when in horror Silvia had watched Nick collapse on the gravel path.

She remembered it well.

✶ ✶ ✶

She had rushed back into the church calling for assistance.

When the group hurried outside the limousine chauffeur was bent over Nick.

"He told me he hadn't slept for almost three days. He was very agitated and upset. It's a wonder he didn't konk out before now."

He looked reprovingly at the group.

"Where did you pick him up?" Gus Olavssen queried.

"I met him at the Newcastle Airport. He'd taken the Concorde from New York to London, Guv'nor." said the man. "He was in a helluva hurry to get here, very impatient. Didn't say much. Sounded as if he'd done a helluva lot of traveling in the past few days—setting a record, to my way of thinking. Japan to California and then New York and on to London and up north. I reckoned up—about twenty five thousand miles in less than three days."

His face reflected how impressed he was.

Gus spoke over his shoulder.

"Kara, phone Dr. Klaussen's office from my car phone and have him or his assistant meet us at the house."

With the careful handling by Jon and his future Best Man, Leif, Nick was moved to the backseat of the limousine. Kara climbed into the front with the chauffeur to direct him, looking back at Nick constantly.

The lock of hair, which insisted on falling over his forehead, had shaken itself loose and Kara automatically reached over to brush it back into place. She studied his face. It was so strong and handsome. She could feel his lips on hers and his hands caressing her body. Just as they had done with Satomi.

A tormented expression flitted across Kara's face and she closed her eyes to extinguish his perfidious face. He should not have come here. It was too late for them now. It was over.

The men carried Nick to a guest room and Kara went into the lounge. She would have nothing to do with him.

Jon stood in the doorway for a while watching Kara's reflection in the glossy window.

He observed her quietly.

"So this is the man who has stolen your heart?"

Kara swung around.

"No," she replied curtly, turning away again.

There was a bitter twist to her mouth.

Jon walked over to Kara turning her gently into his arms.

"You know you could never get away with lying to me, Scooter."

Tears welled in Kara's eyes as she asked.

"For how long has Nick been having an affair with Satomi?"

Jon stepped back a pace, shocked.

"Satomi?"

He laughed in remembrance.

"From where did you get that preposterous idea? He seemed to dislike her immensely. She told Angie that she intended snaring him, but he refused to allow her near. He told me he was in love with someone else and intended marrying her as soon as she agreed, once he got back to Calif . . . ."

He looked closely at Kara.

"It was you, wasn't it?"

Kara's face blanched.

"He said that?"

"Yes, and he certainly convinced me he was serious. Mother was sitting next to Satomi and Nick at my party and she was disgusted with the way Satomi threw herself at Nick. Perhaps you had better talk to your parents if you want more information. They spent a lot of time with him. As a matter of fact it rather irked me that he hit it off with your parents right away."

Jon turned with a big smile to look at Angela as she walked into the room.

Glancing curiously at Kara and Jon she asked, "Am I interrupting something?"

Jon put his arm around her waist.

"No. I was telling Kara about Satomi's quest to get Nick into bed."

Angela looked with interest at Kara. How was she involved in this?

"What do you want to know?"

"I want you to tell Kara everything."

Jon squeezed Angie's waist to emphasize his request.

She started speaking, looking at Jon with a puzzled expression as she did so.

"Since Satomi saw Nick in Rome last year, she has had an almost fanatical craving for him. Because they travel internationally their paths cross from time to time, but Nick apparently never noticed Satomi and she zealously started tracking him down. He is quite a celebrity in his own right and she followed his career and personal life by keeping a scrapbook. She took it everywhere. She subscribed to several worldwide newspapers and magazines, so she could keep track of him."

Angela stopped and looked at Jon. There was a perplexed look on her face.

He nodded, encouraging her to continue.

"Well, the more she found out about him, the more impressed she was, and also the more determined she became to captivate him. He lives a very prestigious lifestyle as one of the world's most wealthy and eligible bachelors and she talked about him as if she knew him well."

Angela tittered nervously.

"She was kind of irrational when it came to Nick. There was no doubt in her mind that once he met her, he would fall in love with her."

Angela noticed how pale Kara had become and shuffled uncomfortably, looking at Jon for guidance.

"Go on, please." Kara said, feeling as if her voice was being pulled from her toes.

Jon motioned in agreement.

"When Nick phoned to register at the Inn, I was the one who took the reservation. I asked him if he was Dr. Nicholas Prendergast, the famous surgeon and lecturer, and he said he was and expected this information to be regarded as confidential. This was a personal vacation and he wished to relax. I was so excited. I immediately phoned Satomi and she flew up right away. I don't think anything could have stopped her from meeting him."

Kara sat down abruptly on the arm of a big easy chair. She had a thoughtful look on her face. So, he was the brilliant surgeon the newspapers reminded the world about and she had not even made the connection. The newspaper picture she had received referred only to his playboy image. She wondered if he had deliberately held back his identity from her. It suddenly occurred to her that he probably thought she would be swayed by what he was rather than who he was. She smiled, that seemed like Nick. She had just learned of one woman who was so intrigued that she would stop at nothing in an attempt to attract him.

Kara slid into the depth of the chair with a brave expression pasted on her face.

At once she could understand the ease with which he had taken charge. He had been so efficient and masterful. She thought of the things he had done for her in such a brief period and smiled inwardly at the recollection. He had treated her as his private patient, reminding her to take medicine and monitoring her well-being; scrutinizing Gina and Emma so thoroughly with her welfare in mind when interviewing them. Without protest he had changed his international itinerary in order to take her to Palm Springs to identify her pearl necklace.

Oh, so much he had done for her without complaint or the expectancy of being recompensed, financially or physically.

Kara bit her lip.

Most of all she could remember clearly the sensitivity and gentleness with which he had removed her clothing in the bathroom and the discreet and solicitous manner employed to avoid her embarrassment.

Kara bit her lower lip harder.

This was when she had started falling in love with him.

She laid her head between her hands and to the consternation of Jon and Angela, tears started falling rapidly through her fingers wetting the couturier white ensemble she was wearing.

Sniffing and wiping her hands across her eyes, Kara reached for the purse standing beside the chair and pulled out a package and handed it to Jon wordlessly.

She stood up and stiltedly walked over to a tissue box, extracting a couple of sheets and swiping at her eyes. Pulling several more she started blotting the front of her jacket.

Mystified, Jon opened the envelope with Angela leaning over his shoulder. They looked at Kara with alarm as each picture was revealed.

In a contrite voice Angela whispered, "Oh, Kara, I'm so sorry. I took most of these pictures, but I didn't know they would be used like this. Satomi asked me to take pictures of her and Nick together because she wanted to have something to remember him by."

Jon held up a picture toward Kara.

"This one, for example, originally had the three of us on it. I was sitting at the other side of Satomi on the settee at the farm."

Kara took the print from Jon and looked at it carefully—she recognized part of the antique mirror on the wall in the background, which she had not noticed previously.

"What about the others?"

"Well, Satomi snuck up on Nick and put her hands over his eyes. He was very calm, but let her know that he wasn't into playing games. On another, without permission, Satomi put sun-cream on Nick's back and he actually got quite angry with both of us about that, since she was dragging out the pleasure. I annoyed him by taking a picture."

Jon and Angela looked at Kara with sympathy.

Jon spoke.

"Obviously we can't comment on the newspaper cutting, but it does look genuine. What can we say, Kara? You must give Nick a chance, he was chased shamelessly by Satomi and he really didn't encourage her."

They looked at each other sorrowfully.

Kara heard the doorbell clang. It would be Dr. Klaussen or his assistant.

"Sorry we can't stay longer. There are still things we have to accomplish and unless we can help in any way, we really do have to leave."

Jon patted Kara on the arm.

They both kissed her on the cheek.

"Give us a call tonight, dear, if you need to talk."

He chucked Kara under the chin.

"You look as if you need a good night's sleep, Scooter."

He smiled at Angela and gave her a quick hug. They were getting married tomorrow and she was starting to flag under the strain of getting this quick, but elaborate, wedding together.

Martin, the butler, hurried into the room. He seemed quite disturbed.

"Ma'am there's a group of people at the door asking for you."

Kara raised her eyebrows. Seldom was she addressed as "Ma'am."

"Shall I say you are not receiving?"

Kara shook her head. She would see them.

In the foyer she looked into the huge Louis XVI mirror. The white suit she had worn to the wedding rehearsal still looked fresh and the tearstains were not too noticeable. Only her eyes reflected the anguish that was tearing her apart.

Kara stood looking at the man, woman and child standing in the doorway.

It was François. She recognized him immediately.

"Comment allez vous, François?" She spoke automatically.

He looked at her, shaken. She had spoken fluently in his language.

"Mademoiselle Kara. Excuse me for calling upon you without invitation."

Kara smiled sadly. "Please come in."

François was agitated. His best friend and partner had to all intents and purposes disappeared and the woman he was in love with lived in a mansion and spoke French.

She led the way into the lounge and rang the bell.

"Hilda, please bring refreshments."

François was truly unnerved and before he was invited to be seated, he started blurting out his concerns to Kara in a mixture of French and English.

"Have you seen Nick? Did he contact you from Japan? Has he phoned recently?"

The questions were asked with anxiety written on his face and reflected in his voice. Standing beside her husband, Michele's hazel eyes displayed concern. She added, "We are very worried about Nicholas."

Kara sighed.

"Yes. Nick is here and under medical attention."

With alacrity Franc stated, "I would like to see him, s'il vous plait."

Kara understood Franc's concern, but she needed time with Nick's friends first.

"I am learning things today for the first time and I find them very disturbing. Please sit down. We need to talk."

Fiona was looking bored.

Kara rang for the upstairs maid and Janet, the youngest maid in the household, appeared.

Turning to Fiona and speaking in French Kara said, "When I was around your age, I used the playroom a great deal. There is a big dolls house that you can walk inside, with furniture and a real china tea service to play with. Would you like to have milk and cookies up there with Janet?"

Fiona shook her head up and down vigorously, looking over at her parents for permission before eagerly taking Janet's hand.

To Janet Kara said.

"Fiona would like to play in the dollhouse. Please ask Mrs. Taylor to provide you with milk and cookies before going up there."

She smiled at Fiona as she was led away and turned back to her guests.

"How were you able to locate me? I was in California when we first met, Franc—we barely spoke to each other."

Briefly Franc explained. "Nick seemed lethargic toward the end of the Japanese tour and I was concerned when unable to reach him at any of our reliable telephone numbers there. I phoned Claudia at the Beverley Hills office who said Nick had cancelled his work appointments for a week and asked her to get him to Newcastle International Airport by the fastest possible method. From there he wanted a chauffeured limousine waiting to take him to your home. Nick made it sound like an emergency and she said she has not heard from him since. Claudia also had no idea of the address where Nick was heading."

Franc stopped speaking, taking time to get his thoughts together.

"Remembering that Nick used the Bentley to travel to northern England for a few days, I phoned from Paris and had one of my assistants in London search the Bentley for anything he could find relating to that trip. He found a business card of Lieutenant Leighton and faxed a copy of it to me. I phoned the lieutenant, who said Nick told him he would be staying with the Olavssens' at "Velkoment" and here we are."

Hilda brought in a tray holding refreshments. The conversation ceased temporarily as Kara poured coffee for Michele and Franc and tea for herself. Dainty sandwiches and petit fours were declined. Laying her head against the blue silk settee, Kara closed her eyes to get the past into perspective.

With an effort she started from the time she met François at Wendy's home, recounting the assault; the stolen pearls; her fractured arm and head wound; her blossoming awareness of Nick; the introduction of Satomi, and finally the receipt of the pictures, which had completely destroyed her.

"Would you permit me to see the pictures?"

Franc was terribly polite and proper.

"Yes. They are here." Kara was reaching for her purse as she spoke.

Once again the manila envelope was produced and Kara handed it to Franc. She sat back, sipping tea and watching his face as he observed each picture. A couple of times he looked up, as if about to make a comment.

Silently he handed the package to his wife.

He waited until she had looked them over, hearing the intake of breath when she came to the final pictures.

Michele shook her head, skepticism plainly written on her face as she handed the envelope back to Kara.

Franc shrugged his shoulders, gloom showing through his strained features.

"I am shocked. What is there to say?"

Michele nodded her head briskly in agreement. She was ready to defend this exceptional friend of theirs, who had confided just three weeks earlier how stunned he was at finding Kara, declaring they were perfect for each other. He was riding on Cloud 9.

Franc reached over and with a reassuring smile, took his wife's hand in his own and patted it. He would take care of this.

Involuntarily Kara burst out laughing. They turned to look at her in surprise.

François affectionately had called his wife "his baby with a baby." They had forgotten how well Kara spoke their language.

They agreed to continue the conversation in the French patois.

"It usually takes over a year to set up Nick's itinerary." Franc explained. "He travels around the world, either lecturing or performing select transplant operations. During the recent trip to Paris for a seminar, Satomi "bumped" into us at dinner. Nick was furious and I assume she was insulted because he would not agree to see her. It was not a pretty scene. The next day apparently there was a picture of the two of them in the newspaper, with their arms linked together. I did not see the picture. I learned of it in retrospect and thought it was just a publicity stunt."

Franc spread his palms open in a helpless gesture. A disapproving frown was on his face.

"I was witness to what took place just minutes earlier in the dining room." He shook his head in exasperation. "I also was with the two of them when the picture was taken. It goes to show how this sort of thing gets out of hand. If Nick had agreed to her type of blackmail, none of this would have been world-wide news. But there is no way that Nick would compromise his ethics."

Franc looked at Kara with concern.

"The picture sent to you of Nick and Satomi was not the same as the one I eventually saw that was published in the newspaper "Vive la France." It was all a set-up, Kara. Please don't judge Nick on this one episode. Nick is linked with so many famous women, whether or not he was actually with them, that he has become accustomed to ignoring most articles attributed to his conquests. Most of the time he isn't even aware of what is written about him."

Franc glanced at Michele, whose large hazel eyes projected distress. She interjected.

"Kara. When we met Nick after his trip to England, both François and I saw immediately there was something different about him. Something special. He was, for the first time in years, happy and excited. There was a new energy and vitality about him. We have known Nick a long time and our concern for him has been steadily increasing ever since Serawin's terrible tragedy."

A bewildered expression clouded Kara's face.

Hastily Michele looked at Franc.

They both looked at Kara.

"Has Nick told you about Serawin?"

Kara took a deep breath. This was leading up to something serious. There was a reason for their probing.

"No."

Immediately Michele went over and sat on the loveseat beside Kara, taking both of her hands into her own.

"It happened a long time ago, ma cherie, but it is a part of Nick's life and you must be informed of the devastation he has had to overcome, to become the person he is today and the person he can become because of you."

Kara drew a quivering breath and squeezed Michele's fingers.

"I must know everything. Please."

Franc was studying Kara directly and it was a few moments before he nodded imperceptibly.

Settling back in his chair, he fitted his hands together in a steeple shape. It was a long time since he had to consciously bring this episode to mind. It brought back painful memories.

There was a deep silence in the room.

With a quick intake of breath Franc started speaking. His eyes were fixed on his hands.

Kara clung to Michele as the story progressed, the two of them silently sobbing together.

Kara was deeply ashamed of herself. This man, who loved her so much without reservation, had a depth of character that would have put the Saints to shame. He had suffered so much. Her knight in shining armor had appeared and she failed to recognize him. She had been so blind, playing her own childish games.

Kara drew a shuddering breath, drawing strength from Michele's firm grip.

Had she destroyed his love?

Kara was mortified. Would Nick ever want to see her again? They had known so little about each other, but he had been ready to take her as she was and she was not whom she had first appeared to be.

She had made this trip back to England as a type of catharsis, to put some distance between the two of them and to renounce his traitorous love. All she had heard from the time of his unexpected arrival was in his favor, honorable and perceptive, revealing much more about the man than he would ever disclose.

Kara offered the box of tissues to Michele and took a couple of sheets herself.

"I'm going up to see Nick. Would you care to join me?"

The agitation in Kara's voice was barely concealed.

Michele and Franc quickly rose to their feet.

Franc spoke hesitantly.

"You know, I have been very concerned about Nick for a couple of weeks. Toward the end of his Tokyo tour he was very worried about not being able to get in touch with you. I had to come on strong for him to confide in me and his despondency brought back the bad vibes connected to the Princess Serawin ordeal. I couldn't have handled it. I don't know how he did. He must have been totally devastated having to go through such a trial once again, alone."

Franc looked remorsefully at Kara—he had spoken out of turn. Kara was guilt stricken and her face showed it.

"I'm sorry, Kara. I'm not usually so blunt, but Nick is my best friend and quite frankly he has suffered enough to last two lifetimes.

What he needs is someone who will truly love him and be committed to a permanent relationship—just as he is to you."

He took Kara's hand into his own and pressed it gently.

Kara's eyes filled with tears and her voice trembled.

"I've been such a dimwit, but you can rest assured. If Nick hasn't changed his mind, he will have no doubt as to how I feel about him and I'll spend the rest of my life convincing him of that."

Beaming her approval, Michele leaned over and kissed Kara's cheek.

CHAPTER THIRTY TWO

Kara's mother was sitting beside Nick's bed talking to Dr. Klaussen. She smiled easily at Kara and her entourage as they entered the room. It did not disturb her that her daughter had marched in with two complete strangers.

Lars Klaussen turned to face Kara.

"Your young man seems to be in excellent health, apart from the fact that he will need a recuperation period, once he decides to join the real world again. He probably will need some TLC to get back on his feet again, but Kara I'm sure you can handle that very well. Probably the tonic he needs, what!"

He kissed Silvia's cheek and in his usual agreeable way, showered a smile over Michele and Franc on his way out, throwing the words over his shoulder.

"You know where to reach me if there is a problem."

Immediately Kara went over to the bed and took Nick's hand in her own. What a remarkable man he was. She blinked tears away. Of all the women he could choose he had selected her and she, like the idiot she was proving to be, had used his heart like a ping pong ball.

Humbled, Kara leaned over the bed and softly kissed Nick on the lips.

"Please wake up soon, darling, so I can tell you how much I love you."

Kara looked over at the three people scrutinizing her. Did she say that out aloud?

With a flustered grin, she waved her arm feebly as she announced.

"Oh, Michele and François, this is my mother, Lady Silvia Olavssen. Mother, Michele and François de Veaux are special friends of Nick. They traveled here from Paris, with their little daughter, Fiona, to make sure Nick was all right."

They all laughed at the expression on Kara's face. She looked as if she had been interrupted in the middle of an important assignment and wished to return to unfinished business.

Silvia rose from the delicate bedroom chair, turning to Michele and Franc.

"If you have no other plans for the weekend, it would be our pleasure to have you stay here with us. It will be no problem accommodating you and you will be able to keep an eye on Nicholas. Once he regains full consciousness, he will doubtlessly be delighted to have you close by."

As usual her manner was gracious and pleasing.

She led them out of the room, leaving Kara with Nick. She would keep them busy for a while.

Kara was reluctant to leave Nick's side. She did not want to be parted from him for an instant. A roguish smile flitted across her mouth.

She walked over to the door and locked it.

Kara kissed Nick's face, in tender little movements. For the first time there was an urgent need to convey her love to him. She hoped she would have the right to exercise that privilege for the rest of her life.

Taking Nick's long, capable hand into her own she sat at his side, stroking it affectionately as she spoke aloud to his slumbering form.

"So much has taken place in the short time we have known each other, dearest, and yet it seems as if we've known each other forever. From the start I thought you were a very handsome man—far too good looking to have much else in your favor."

A wry frown surfaced and she tossed her head slightly.

"How wrong I was. I admit it. I've been wrong before, you know. Just look at every romantic episode in my life so far. At my age and with my track record you have to admit being a bit cynical is not entirely out of line."

A soft smile wreathed Kara's face.

"But you, Dr. Nicholas Seymour Prendergast, certainly have a way with you. The strength of your love captured me. I love you so very, very much Nick."

Kara lightly traced Nick's slightly parted lips with the tip of her index finger.

Did his eyelids flutter?

Kara sat very still, hardly breathing, waiting.

He grunted and shifted his shoulders slightly. His eyes remained closed.

Kara patted his hand and drifted off in thought, returning to soliloquize again.

"Would it have upset you, sweet, to know that Jon started phoning me after you left for Paris? He asked if I had seriously considered his proposal and come to a decision. The first time I put him off. I was very newly in love with you and still uncertain about our future together. Once you started phoning me from Paris and Tokyo, there was no doubt that I had fallen under your spell. The next time he called, I couldn't have married him for any reason, so certain I was of my love for you."

A troubled frown creased Kara's forehead and she closed her eyes, lowering her voice to a whisper.

"When the pictures arrived from Paris while you were in Tokyo, I was devastated. My love was still too fragile to be challenged. How could you tell me you loved me and be having an affair with Satomi at the same time? I was almost ready to believe that I had made a mistake and given my love to the wrong man again—this time a playboy."

Tears trickled down Kara's face.

"Darling, I've never felt this way about anyone before with such certainty and I'm sorry for doubting you. It won't happen again. I promise."

She wanted to be closer, to feel Nick's body aligned with hers, to draw comfort from him. She longed to touch him.

Walking around the bed, Kara slid off her pumps and crawled on top of the bed beside Nick. She rubbed her cheek against his shoulder and gently placed her right arm around him, conscious that her left arm, beneath her, ached. It was still weak from the accident injury. Still, she would be with Nick for just a few minutes before joining guests gathering downstairs.

The memories of the times he had held and caressed her body came back in a gush of exquisite ecstasy. She reached up and put her lips to Nick's ear.

"I've been such a fool, my love. Please come back to me, I've missed you so much."

At last she had identified the need within her and the love that had taken over her life.

Contentedly Kara nestled close to Nick, a blissful smile on her lips as she fell asleep.

She raised her head and looked at her watch. Her left arm was stiff and glued to her side. How could it be six in the morning? She had just rested beside Nick for a moment.

Kara restrained a chuckle. She had spent the night with Nick and he did not know it.

Kara slid quietly off the bed. She hoped there would be a time when she could tease him about this. With a rueful twist to her lips she started rubbing her left arm vigorously, working on bringing back the circulation.

Her elegant Balenciaga suit was creased beyond recognition. Her eyes twinkled. It had been put to good use. The therapeutic benefit derived from being with Nick was well worth its exorbitant price.

The nurse was coming along the corridor, medication in hand. She tightened her lips in astonishment at the sight of Kara leaving her patient's room, in rumpled clothing, with shoes slung over her fingers and an absurd smile drifting across her face.

Kara looked back at the door she had just closed and noticed the 'Do not disturb' sign. Thanks, mama.

Kara greeted everyone in the breakfast room with a radiant smile. She had showered and changed and was ready and eager to meet the new day.

She had quickly looked in on Nick a few minutes earlier. He had appeared calm and was breathing easily. He looked devastatingly handsome and even the coarse beard, which was sprouting, added a wickedly enticing feature.

She had whispered to him.

"Hurry and wake up, slow poke. How are we going to catch up on lost time if you continue to waste precious time oblivious to the opportunities we have."

She lightly touched her eager lips to his, wishing he would respond. Guiltily she looked over her shoulder when she heard the padded soles of the medical shoes approaching.

Kara carried a glass of orange juice out to the terrace. Hilda had offered to serve breakfast there, but Kara declined. She was still on an emotional high. Yesterday had been a remarkable day. It felt as if she had gone through an intensive learning experience with instructors bent on educating her and grading her for her perception, understanding and commitment. She was still waiting for the outcome, a judgment of some sort.

Michele joined Kara beneath the large umbrella of the glass patio table, bringing with her a croissant and fruit on a plate.

"Are we going to be in the way? This must be an awkward time for us to be here with a wedding taking place today."

Kara smiled congenially. She automatically switched to the French language.

"No problem. I'm still hoping that Nick will recover soon and I'm sure he will be very pleased to find you here."

Looking down at her hands she said hesitantly.

"I'm sorry for deserting you last night, Michele. I hope you didn't feel abandoned, but I really needed to be with Nick. I hadn't anticipated falling asleep on his bed."

Michele's smile was warm and empathetic.

Hilda walked over with a tray, and placed a steaming cup of coffee, on its saucer, in front of Kara. Hilda motioned the carafe toward Michele, who smiled her acceptance. After filling her cup, the silver coffee pot was placed on a pad at Kara's right hand.

Michele picked up the conversation.

"I understand how you feel. New love is astonishing. It keeps us suspended between humbleness and hope. François told me how much Nick relied on the telephone calls with you in Paris. They shared a suite and Nick insisted on being prompt, no matter what kind of business arrangement they were involved in, in order to be available to talk to you. François also said he didn't know when Nick would have had the opportunity to be with Satomi, since he was barely out of his sight."

She handed over a sheet of paper.

"Franc wanted you to see this. Last night we played Bridge with your parents and we quite naturally talked about you and Nick. Your father took Franc to his den and Franc phoned the editor of "Vive La

France" and made arrangements to have a copy of the article they published about Nick and Satomi faxed here. Voila."

Kara looked down at the article held shakily in her hand and drew an involuntary quick breath.

There were three figures shown, not just two. The caption read "Dr. Nicholas Prendergast, famous heart specialist with his partner, Dr. François de Veaux and Mrs. de Veaux exiting the tony Les Ambassadeurs Restaurant."

She flashed a swift glance over at Michele, only to find her trying hard to suppress a wide grin.

"Isn't it perfect retribution? Satomi's name was not only omitted, but she was mistakenly given mine, thereby leaving Nick's reputation clear and defeating her purpose. When François saw the article he was incensed at having Satomi connected to our family name, but then the funny side hit us. Satomi's objective for a wide newspaper coverage failed and she must have had a fit. The best she could do was by probably having the original newspaper picture 'doctored'."

Kara smiled weakly. Satomi certainly was a determined woman.

"Thank you. It's very reassuring knowing that Nick has two very loyal friends. It would be my pleasure to earn your friendship too."

Over coffee cups their eyes met and they smiled.

Amusement sparkled between them.

There was no doubt they would become friends. They knew it right then.

Speaking with a serious expression on her face, Michele stated, "We appreciate your parent's hospitality, Kara. They have made us feel very welcome." Staring into space she added, "And it's good to know that Nick will have a lovely family to call his own at last."

She sighed and turned her attention to the half consumed croissant.

With interest kindled, Kara willingly fell for the bait.

"What do you mean 'Nick getting a family of his own'?"

Michele looked up, as if surprised by the question.

With a suspicious expression on her face Kara remarked.

"I suppose another insight into Nick's background is about to be revealed."

Michele nodded gravely. Some things had to be dragged out of Nick and this was one of them. His grandfather was a fable unto himself.

Kara refilled their coffee cups and gazed steadily at her table companion.

"Go on. After yesterday, nothing will surprise me."

CHAPTER THIRTY THREE

Angela and Jon's wedding was scheduled to take place at one in the afternoon.

Jon was spending the last few days as a bachelor at the farmhouse with Leif, who was enjoying the brief role as Best Man. The Reception to be held at The Black Bull Inn had been planned to include the entire staff. They would be on staggered shifts so that they all could be part of the celebration for some of the time. There was great excitement around the usually dignified hostelry. Crews of decorators had been contracted to festoon and embellish the main building, the railway carriages and the grounds to bring an air of festivity and celebration to the property. Lemon, green and white bows and floral arrangements were displayed and grouped everywhere. Ribbons and banners fluttered from unlikely locations.

Going over later in the morning to assist in setting up the display of wedding gifts received, Kara was overwhelmed with the efforts being made. It must be costing Jon a great deal of money. She wondered about Jon's truthfulness in explaining the lemon, green and white color scheme at the farmhouse. Had he become an expert deceiver?

Angela was still in a robe when Kara returned to her parents' home. "Donald of Doncaster" had finished styling Angela's auburn hair into a riot of ringlets and flat curls and they were talking comfortably over mugs of coffee.

Kara nodded approval as she encircled Angela.

"Absolutely perfect with your gown and coronet of rosebuds. You'll look gorgeous."

Don smiled with pleasure.

"I have time to dress your hair too, if you wish."

Kara shook her head and smiled as she helped herself to coffee from the serving cart.

"I'm so accustomed to doing it myself, for better or worse, that with a high society coiffure I feel like a Barbie doll with an attitude." She laughed outright. "I also think I act the part, too. It goes to my head in more ways than one."

They laughed light-heartedly at her self-deprecation. Kara's good manners were as inborn as the diluted royal blood that flowed through her veins.

Sunlight was streaking into her mother's studio apartment that had been temporarily commandeered to take care of any last minute wedding activity. Genna, one of Don's beauticians, had already wrapped Angela's nails and was ready to start on Kara's. It was the only concession she had made to being fussed over.

"The Inn is looking smashing, Angie. Your wedding is going to be the society event of the year."

Angela looked mildly pleased, but not glowing as Kara imagined a bride should.

Don had packed his equipment away and was helping Genna clean up.

Waiting for the machine to finish drying her nails, Kara looked over at Angela, sitting in an upright position with her eyes closed and neck stiffly erect.

"We should be starting to get dressed soon. Your gown and veil have been taken to Nona Stephenssohns's suite and my things should be there also. You may need some assistance from Hilda and Janet and I'll call them when you're ready. Jackie is dressing at her parents' home and then being chauffeured here in their Daimler, which will be used to get the bridesmaids to church. Which, of course, you know. I must be feeling a little nervous, prattling on like this."

Angela smiled faintly.

As they walked through the corridors on their way to the guest suites in the south wing of the building, Kara inspected Angela's face surreptitiously. Where was the flush of excitement and the radiance expected on the face of a prospective bride? There was little to indicate this in Angela. With a jolt Kara recognized a clue that Angela was exhibiting—she was scared.

Kara motioned Angela into the pleasant, sunlit rooms and walked over to the elaborate pearl encrusted gown, hanging in its clear vinyl casing outside the armoire. Over a year earlier Angela had designed and expertly made the gown. Finally the day for its wearing had arrived. What a circuitous route they, and it, had traveled in reaching this fateful day.

From the time of Kara's return to carry out the express function as bridesmaid, Angela had made a real effort to return to a friendly relationship with Kara. Over the past two days they had become more attuned to each other as they recognized their separate and totally different priorities.

"Your gown is breathtaking, Angie. You'll make a beautiful bride." Kara enthused admiring the soon-to-be-worn garment.

Somewhat despondent about the lack of enthusiasm emanating from Angie, she gave her a quick hug.

"I'm going to bathe and then I'll come back to help."

Sighing, Kara barely avoided shoving her newly tipped nails into her jeans pockets as she strode quickly to her chambers. If it was her wedding day and she was marrying Nick she would be delirious with joy, ready to scatter her feelings of love and delight over the world.

Something was wrong with Angie. She would test the waters soon.

Kara and Angela had changed into the long silk petticoats, with the flounced hems and little conversation had taken place between them. They were applying makeup when a little reluctantly Kara decided to broach the subject that had been bothering her.

"Aren't your parents coming to your wedding, Angie?"

Susan and Bart were a distinct part of her life and she could not imagine them missing out on Angela's important day.

Angela's voice quivered.

"We gave them so little time. They had already planned an important viticulture trip to Australia, touring the vineyards for three weeks. We'll join them there for a few days of our honeymoon."

Her lips trembled. She was still shaken by the rapidity of the events that had taken place over the last two weeks and the amazing way things had turned out, but she yearned for the comforting arms of her parents. In a flood of emotion she blurted out.

"Kara, the reason we had to rush into this wedding is because I'm over three months pregnant. Jon had encountered some serious financial problems and Nick stepped in to resolve them. He made everything possible."

With guilt-ridden eyes she clapped a hand over her mouth.

Kara stopped applying lipstick, her hand held in mid-air. She stared at Angela through the mirror.

"Nick did what?"

Angela shook her head in disbelief.

"I can't believe I said that. I promised Nick I'd never mention this subject to anyone, not even Jon. I guess it's because I'm so nervous and it seems like a miracle took place."

The lipstick case was laid on the dressing table tray and Kara turned to face Angela, determined to pursue the subject.

"Why would Nick get involved in Jon's affairs?"

Angie blinked her eyelids nervously.

"It's a long story, but to keep it brief, I inadvertently confessed to Nick that I was pregnant with Jon's baby, but that Jon had proposed to you because he was seriously in debt."

Kara's eyes widened in astonishment and she shook her head in disbelief.

"That is a remarkable admission to make, Angela. It covers a range of sensitive areas one would expect to discuss only in strict confidence with a limited number of people. Yet somehow you have managed to divulge all of this to Nick? I'm completely mystified."

Kara glared in exasperation.

"How could that possibly happen?"

Tears threatened to fall and spoil Angela's beautifully made-up face and Kara remorsefully grabbed a handful of tissues and held them against her lower lids taking up the overflow.

"I'm sorry. You shocked me."

Thoughtfully Kara pondered Angela's words.

"So Nick made arrangements to straighten things out for the two of you?"

A loud sniff came from Angela.

"Yes. He said he would get involved, only because it happened to be in line with his own plans."

Comprehension was dawning on Kara.

Nick was indeed a very resourceful and determined man.

"Just what would have happened **if** I had fallen in love with Jon?"

Angela gasped and grasped Kara's hand.

"Oh, Kara, I would have died. I love Jon so much and I know things will work out for us eventually. Right now I'm still in shock and very confused. Everything has happened so fast."

A troubled look stole over her face.

"Jon has always had a special place for you and I envied you for that. He told me he attempted to fall in love with you, but because you have been friends for so long, it didn't happen. He is such a handsome man and a wonderful lover and you were together so much." Her voice faltered. "I've been jealous wondering whether you fell under his spell. I have no right to ask, but did you?"

Angela's eyes flickered anxiously to Kara.

Looking intently at Angela and studying the suspense displayed on her face, Kara knew she could never have had blind faith in Jon. She was already questioning the wisdom of spending a fortune on this wedding, which they apparently could ill afford. It was because of Nick's largesse that they could proceed in such a lavish fashion. Slowly she shook her head and patted the hand that held hers, a faint smile illuminating her face.

"I tried to, but Nick wouldn't allow it."

They burst out laughing shakily. It eased the tension and they returned to complete their toilet in companionable, but wary silence. This was hardly uplifting, wedding day talk.

Angela did look lovely, Kara mused, her eyes straying to her in the mirror. There was one secret that would be kept from her forever. Angie would never know that Jon had phoned California several times in an attempt to change Kara's mind about marrying him. Even the shock of receiving the pictures from Satomi had emphasized how hopelessly in love with Nick she was.

The only way she would attend his wedding, she told Jon, was in the role of bridesmaid. Kara smiled at her reflection. Nick had a knack for making wishes come true.

Please let Nick still love me. Anxious nephrite eyes stared back at Kara through the mirror.

Hilda and Janet brought in refreshments.

They complimented Angela on how lovely she looked and admired her beautiful wedding gown. Hilda had known Jon from the time he was a small boy and she teased Angela as they assisted her in dressing.

The stress that Angela had encountered during the past months had been of sufficient magnitude to restrain an increase in her body measurements. The gown fitted perfectly.

Kara changed into the lemon chiffon bridesmaid gown, which had been speedily designed by Jackie and hurriedly executed by the Frazier workshop. It swayed around her effortlessly, outlining her body as she moved. Jackie would be wearing a replica in sage green chiffon. Satomi had deliberately not been invited to participate and in a huff had taken herself off to Europe.

Absently brushing her cheeks with apricot blush, Kara was deep in thought. If Nick had stepped in to provide the financial solution, which Jon had desperately needed, he knew that Angela was pregnant with Jon's child. Nick could have used that information against Jon at any time. Nick would have realized that Kara, in good conscience, could not have married a man knowing that another woman was carrying his child.

Kara sat down sharply, as if someone had jammed a stick against the back of her knees.

Angela, Hilda, and Janet in the midst of their preparations glanced over at Kara, who smiled and picked up a glass of mineral water as convincingly unconcerned as she could muster.

Her thought process whirled. Nick had not used that knowledge to his advantage. He had waited for Kara to make up her own mind about him. It had to be her decision. What an honorable, unselfish and intrepid lover he was proving to be. Kara's heart felt as if it was pounding through her whole body—she had to see him before she left for the church.

Leaving Nona Stephenssohns's suite, she held up her long skirts and ran along the corridors.

✳ ✳ ✳

There was a movement in the room and Nick slowly opened his eyes, turning toward the sound. He was so tired. He could sleep forever.

An incredibly sublime woman was coming toward him, looking at him with a tenderness he could not immediately comprehend. She was in a billowing lemon gown, which floated around her as she moved.

"Are you an angel?" he asked hoarsely, reaching out his hands in wonder to touch her.

She leaned forward and kissed his lips in a soft, lingering caress.

He had to be in heaven.

His outstretched hands encircled a body, which was not only heavenly, but also warm and enticing. What was even more tantalizing and electrifying was that his touches seemed to stimulate a reaction that he found both gratifying and breathtaking.

Gently Nick swept her even closer into his arms, murmuring endearments that fell from his lips like dewdrops. He kissed and touched her reverently and she responded like a rain-starved flower.

He started shaking.

He must be hallucinating again.

Did one ever recognize when one had reached the height of supreme madness?

He lay back on the pillow trying to suppress the agitation.

Darkness was starting to engulf him and he was spinning out of control.

Again a mouth closed over his.

"Darling, I have to leave, but I will be back soon."

Nick gingerly shook the head that threatened to float off into space, so lightheaded had it become.

The same angelic face hovered over him and he sighed in satisfaction. He even swallowed, without protest, the evil liquid poured down his throat.

If this were being dead, it was not so bad after all.

He turned onto his side and slept peacefully.

"You must return to the Reception, darling, since you are a conspicuous part of the wedding party. I will accompany you. Your father is waiting for a telephone call and will join us later."

Kara showed reluctance at her mother's suggestion.

They had left the wedding festivities for a short time when the dancing commenced.

"Nick is in very good hands here with Nurse Armstrong and she has instructions to telephone us at The Black Bull Inn should Nick come around fully."

Kara's face was mutinous. "Yes, but . . ."

Silvia played her trump card, "If the de Veaux' family feel they can take time away to enjoy a little relaxation, then surely you can be persuaded too."

Taking Kara's arm and leading her down the wide staircase, Lady Olavssen said with a touch of wonder in her voice.

"Isn't it strange how this young man has come into our lives and in such a short time established himself as a permanent fixture?"

Kara looked stricken.

"Unless he decides I'm not worth all he has gone through so cruelly and needlessly."

Silvia Olavssen lightly touched her daughter's cheek with her fingers.

"I think Nicholas knows what he wants and he is a very obstinate man."

She smiled knowingly at her daughter.

463

CHAPTER THIRTY FOUR

Nick awoke and looked around the unfamiliar room.

He could not remember a darned thing and he certainly did not recall checking into this hotel. He had no idea where he was.

He looked at his watch it was Saturday, the 22nd, and it was 7:00 p.m. Great. That helped. Knowing what year it was might be helpful too.

Groggily he edged out of bed and went to the bathroom.

He looked in the mirror. Did he always look so scruffy? He ran his hand tentatively over the unkempt growth of hair on his face.

He put a robe over his pajamas and left the room. He walked sluggishly down a wide hallway and clasping the handrail for support, trod carefully down the stairs that led into a large marble floor foyer. Looking over his shoulder he noticed a woman in a white uniform briskly following him. What kind of a place was this? Maybe he really was crazy. Things were beginning to look a little familiar, so he must have been here before. Perhaps he even belonged here.

A maid in a black and white uniform smiled at Nick.

"Hello, Mr. Nick, glad to see you up and about."

She turned her head away to hide a smile; he looked quite the Buccaneer with that stubble.

"Would you like something to eat?"

He shook his head. He turned into a corridor and was walking along it, when a door opened.

"Nick, I was about to come and check on you. How do you feel?"

Gosh, these people were attentive and they appeared to know him well. He must be a regular here.

He wished he knew.

"I guess I feel all right, but to be honest, I don't seem to remember where I am."

He saw the man look at him sharply.

He was trying to be candid and this man looked at him as if he were an imbecile.

The man waved away the nurse as she approached.

"Come and sit down for a minute. I have a phone call to make, but I'll be right back."

When the man returned, Nick was standing beside the French windows looking out into the garden. He could see a pond and a gazebo in the background.

"It is very peaceful. Do I live here?"

"No, but you are always welcome." the reply was made solemnly.

Coughing a little nervously, the gentle faced man continued.

"I have been invited to a party and a certain young lady has specifically requested that you and I attend together. Do you feel up to it?"

Nick shrugged his shoulders. "I feel very tired. Is it necessary?"

Gus looked sympathetic.

"Yes. I hope you will find the effort worthwhile."

Nick went back to his room and found a tray holding a glass of orange juice and a sandwich on the little antique table by the window. He consumed it slowly as he shaved. He found he needed this sustenance after the tiring chore of showering

Feeling a little better, he changed into a dark blue suit with a white shirt and blue and burgundy patterned tie. This was hard work. He wondered if the suit belonged to him, it seemed slightly loose.

Forty-five minutes later they were seated in the backseat of a chauffeured vehicle.

"Where are we going?" He asked.

"To The Black Bull Inn."

Gus Olavssen was a little alarmed that no recognition was shown.

Nick lay back on the seat. He was tired; just getting dressed had been a major effort.

Gus Olavssen looked at Nick with concern. Dr. Lars Klaussen had suggested trying this type of shock treatment on Nick and he had agreed to go along with it, but maybe it would not work and what then?

He was distressed that things had turned out this way. Nick had not deserved being dealt this hand and no matter what the outcome he was determined to assist in whatever way he could to resolve the situation.

Lights were blazing from the windows of the old structure and the outdoor areas of The Black Bull Inn were illuminated fully. They drew up to the front entrance where a large white banner, with green and yellow lettering, was draped over the threshold.

It read. "Congratulations Angela and Jonathan."

Nick glanced at it without interest.

Gus guided Nick up the main stairway and endeavored to carry on a conversation with him as they walked along the oak paneled corridor. Nick was too preoccupied looking around, narrowing his eyes as if to recall something important. They stopped at the end of the corridor and Gus tapped on a door. Immediately it was opened.

Gently Nick was shoved inside.

He stood a little nervously with his back against the door, staring into the room. It was strangely welcoming. The most beautiful woman he had ever seen stood before him. She was in a floating diaphanous gown, which looked vaguely familiar. He tried to bring back the memory and his heart thudded in anticipation. She was smiling as if she knew him very well, looking him over as if to memorize every detail about him.

A hot flush stole over his body at her examination. He struggled to maintain his composure. There was something so compelling about this woman—he could not take his eyes away from her. He was drawn to her magnetically and inevitably.

Nick closed his eyes and breathed raggedly.

There was only one woman in the world who could affect him this way and she was married to someone else.

He had witnessed the wedding taking place.

He placed a hand over his wildly beating heart as if to arrest its motion.

He tried to rid himself of the image conjured up in his mind's eye, which was indelibly embossed on his heart. He could never forget her face, it was the dearest memory he had.

There was a pounding in his head and his heartbeats felt like physical blows. There was a strangling constriction in his throat and a breathless tightness in his chest.

The same image was, in fact, standing before him.

A feeling of indescribable, unbelievable joy filled him.

His eyes opened in wonder and Nick stared in disbelief.

"Kara," he rasped, opening his arms.

She needed no further command. She was in his embrace in an instant, kissing him ardently, entwining her arms around his neck and gasping at the ferociousness of his grip, as he pulled her tightly against him as if he would never let her go.

"Am I dreaming?" he whispered.

"Oh, Kara, I've held you like this so often, in my imagination, I can't believe this is actually happening. You feel wonderful, beloved."

He slid his hands down to her hips and pulled her even closer, searching for her lips to join them together further.

With an intake of breath, he ran his hand down her left arm, and held up her hand.

It was ring-less.

He raised it to his lips.

Groaning, Nick swung Kara up into his arms and unsteadily carried her over to the four-poster bed, depositing her on the striped coverlet. He stood looking down at her, examining her face for a sign of rejection. She held out her arms and her eyes glowed with encouragement.

Nick slipped off his jacket and jubilantly accepted her invitation. Kara's superb body captivated him completely and his kisses and eager hands drew gasps from her, but she pressed closer, as impatient to receive his caresses, as he was to dispense them.

"I love you, darling, you must know that."

Nick pulled away from Kara's delectable body, kissing her softly on her lips and moving down to the hollow in her throat.

Drawing in a deep breath he gently brought Kara very close. It was a deliberate move; he wanted her to feel how very much he desired her.

"More than anything else in the world, I want you for my wife. I am denying myself the greatest gift you could give me by waiting until you make that commitment. I am determined not to make that same mistake again. You have to want to be mine as much as I want to belong to you. It does have a limited timeframe though, I can wait for you only a short time—before I lose my mind completely." He said in desperation.

Kara snuggled closer into Nick's arms, a rush of contentment overtaking her.

"I adore you."

She kissed his chin.

"I idolize you."

She kissed his eyelids.

She took his face between her hands and tenderly whispered.

"And I will love you forever."

Her soft inviting lips sought his and he lay mesmerized. She gently moved her mouth against his, delicately probing with her eager tongue. Nick gasped and sank his face into the cloud of silky blonde hair. He could not stand much more.

She was really making it difficult for him to remain honorable.

"Kara, you have to help me on this. I want you so desperately and my primitive urges cannot be suppressed indefinitely, you know. I've waited for you for such a long time I don't want to spoil things."

Raw, unadulterated love shone on Nick's face.

The telephone rang, and they both sat up instantly and guiltily.

Kara took hold of the receiver.

"Hello." She said huskily.

She curled her nose at Nick, who was stroking her hip and breathing heavily.

"Oh, yes, everything is perfect."

She was quiet for a few moments.

"We will be down in fifteen minutes." There was a pause before she replied. "Oh, all right, five minutes."

She giggled as she hung up.

"They are checking up on us. Apparently they trust you less now that you are back to normal than they did when you didn't know who you were. Perhaps I should have said I was still working on the problem."

Her sly smile compelled Nick to pull Kara back into his arms. This was going to be the toughest time to endure, but what a reward to look forward to.

✱ ✱ ✱

Two mornings after Jon and Angela's wedding day, as Nick, Kara and her parents were finishing breakfast Nick grinned at Kara and looking at her father stated,

"It's a beautiful morning. Do you care for a stroll in the garden?"

Gus Olavssen looked out at the dreary overcast gray sky and peered closely at Nick. Slipping his glasses from the top of his head onto his nose, he looked out of the window again.

He was about to make a comment, when a smart jab from his wife suddenly activated his thought process.

"Oh, yes, indeed, yes."

He stood up, smiling broadly.

"Hilda, bring fresh coffee out to the carriage house, please."

Smiling at Silvia Olavssen, Nick bent down and kissed Kara softly and sweetly, whispering in her ear.

"If he turns me down, you'd better be prepared to elope."

Kara's eyes twinkled. She had the greatest urge to drag this exceptional, sexy man to her bedroom and keep him there for the rest of her life. She longed to belong to him completely.

Kara and her mother watched the two men walk out of sight along the winding path.

Kara smiled at her mother.

"Nick insisted on going the formal route. He said he has never done this before and wanted to start off the right way. He was quite nervous and I told him that the two of them would be in the same boat, since this would be the first time for daddy too. I hope it helped."

She sipped the coffee, looking expectantly at her mother across the table.

"Well, he certainly shouldn't be worried. Your father and I approved of him from the start. I watched him at the beach playing with the children in the water and even earlier than that I subconsciously hoped my daughter would recognize what a treasure awaited her. I couldn't believe you would even consider marriage to Jon—don't you remember how you constantly quarreled whenever you were together more than a few hours?"

Kara laughed.

"Yes, I suppose we did. Don't worry—it was just a temporary case of insanity. Once Nick appeared on the scene, I had difficulty remembering what Jon looked like."

She shook her head in wonder.

Silvia leaned over and patted her daughter's hand fondly.

"From the first time we met Nicholas, he told us what his intentions were as far as you were concerned and I was so touched. He was so sincere and utterly believable, I wanted to hug him and wish him good luck. When he said you meant everything in the world to him, I was shattered by his intensity and vulnerability. I felt like pledging you to him by proxy."

Kara burst out laughing and looked at her mother in amazement.

"Mother, I believe you are a little in love with Nick yourself."

"What nonsense." Silvia reached for a tissue; she was becoming quite maudlin.

A smile hovered around Kara's mouth. She had never seen her mother in this mushy condition before and it surprised her to see how strongly she had bonded with Nick.

"Are you going to be one of those mothers who sobs their way through the entire wedding ceremony, or are you getting it out of your system now?"

Indignation rose swiftly to her mother's face, until she saw the gently teasing expression conveyed by Kara.

"You are so right for each other, Kara, and you look so perfect together. I have dreamed that the right man would come along for you and, my darling love, I really think he has. You're right, I am getting morbidly sentimental."

Tears were trembling as Kara took her mother's hand and held it gently. They sat quietly waiting for their men to return.

With his hand on Nick's shoulder, Gus Olavssen was listening attentively to Nick as they walked back to the breakfast room. Kara's face lit up as she watched these two uncommon men in her life so at ease with each other.

Nick shot a smile to Kara, upon seeing her observing them through the window and her father winked. Nick opened the door and Gus walked over to his wife, placing an enthusiastic kiss on her lips.

"Nick was absolutely right, dearest. It is a beautiful day."

Turning to Kara he took her hand and pressed it lovingly.

"As your mother and I obviously know, Nick could not have chosen a more suitable wife for himself than you, my darling, but what we couldn't foresee was that you in your wisdom would choose not only the most appropriate husband for yourself, but a man who is as close to being a son as we could ever hope for." Turning to his wife he joked. "Unless you have any surprises for me in the near future, dear?"

Kara was tickled to see color rise to her mother's face.

"I'd prefer to wait for grandchildren, thank you, since we couldn't possibly improve on our only production."

Nick went and kissed Silvia's cheek and a delighted smile spread across her face.

Kara's face registered approval. *They really do care for Nick, as he does for them,* she happily realized.

Yes, this future husband of hers has been well-worth waiting for.

Nick responded.

"For my part I will do the very best I can to carry out your wishes, with Kara's consent and participation, of course."

Nick beamed and moved over to Kara's chair and started rolling his thumbs along her shoulders, as he had done out on the patio of her home a few months earlier.

Happiness possessed Kara she closed her eyes, placing both of her hands over Nick's as he continued to caress her with his hands and eyes. Then, as now, she was aware of his strength and gentleness and love.

"There's only one objection that I can envisage."

It was said by Gus unexpectedly.

They all looked at him, waiting.

"It will take Kara and her mother every minute of the next three weeks to get this wedding arranged."

Silvia Olavssen's delighted smile faded to undisguised dismay.

Nick sighed and walked over to the window. There probably would be a great harangue, with everyone growing heated and upset. They should have married quietly and returned with their surprise announcement.

Silvia stood up and walked over to her husband as if to object, but he held up a hand and continued.

"Nick made it a condition. He said it was either that or the two of them were going to elope. He has some business to attend to and will be away for a couple of weeks. When he returns he will not be responsible for his actions if his bride-to-be is not waiting, flowers in hand, ready for the dash down the aisle."

His hand was still held up as if swearing an oath.

Nick was impressed with Gus Olavssen's inventiveness.

Shaking her head dubiously, Kara's mother looked questioningly at Kara.

"It certainly will be a challenge."

In a pondering tone she continued, "Of course we could set up a marquee in the huge area at the back of the tennis court and I'm certain your Uncle Henry will be delighted to officiate at the ceremony. There still is time to post the Bans. Kara, do you think there is sufficient time for Leif to cater the whole affair?"

Kara sat fascinated. She looked at Nick.

"I think what your bossy future mother-in-law is saying is 'Yes, we can do it'."

He was shocked. That was it.

Kara's parents were facing him, with Kara sitting at the table behind them. She stuck out the tip of her tongue and wiggled it at him sensuously.

It took all of his poise not to burst out laughing. From where did she come up with these provocative lures? He could hardly keep his hands off her as it was, without being extended such a tempting invitation. He had waited a lifetime for her and he would wait that long again, if he could be sure Kara would be there for him.

Three weeks would probably seem that long.

CHAPTER THIRTY FIVE

It appeared to Nick that the past couple of days had been hectic ones for everyone except for him.

Upon his return to the Olavssens' home he had barely seen Kara and when he did there were always other people around. An observation he made was that Norwegian people must be very prolific. Perhaps it was the early bedtimes promoted by the long, cold, dark winters. In any event, there were enough relatives and friends coming around, dropping off wedding gifts and looking him over, to make him wonder how many hands he would have to shake and how many kisses would be expected of him at their wedding. All these strangers were making him nervous.

Already he could see it was going to be a very exhausting time. He should have gone with his initial instinct and eloped with Kara and come back and faced the music.

His own guest list was quite brief and he had taken care of it. Franc was to be his Best Man and Kara specifically had asked Michele to be her Matron-of-Honor and Fiona her Flower Maiden. Marcie was flying in the day before the wedding to have her Chief Bridesmaid gown fitted properly. Wendy and Gerard were thrilled to attend and Claudia was dumbfounded, but enraptured, it was like a fairy story. Dr. Don Campbell and his wife, Ann, were astounded and charmed by the romance of it all. Emma would be attending with her unmarried daughter and they planned on staying for an extra week to tour Britain. Claudia had taken care of the travel, hotel arrangements and expenses for everyone on Nick's list. It was his way of thanking them.

An invitation had been sent to a certain post office box in Switzerland, but that was merely a formality. Nothing was expected to come of it. Nothing ever had before.

Each day Nick talked to Franc, who was delighted that at last he would be Best Man for his friend. They discussed their many joint ventures and it was Franc who sounded Nick out about an idea that he had been contemplating for the past few weeks.

"Where are you and Kara planning on living?"

For the first time Nick expressed concern.

"Franc, I was thinking of giving up the lecture circuit. It's starting to get a little tiring and quite honestly, I don't want to be away from Kara in the future. I will, of course, have to fulfill the engagements made through the end of the year and that is going to be tough."

Franc coughed and said quietly, "This may be a good time to discuss a few things I've been deliberating."

"Go ahead, mon ami."

"Nick, having said what you just did, you can appreciate that because Michele is due to have the baby in a few months and Fiona is about to start school, that I'm having doubts about being away from them so frequently. I'd like to be a full-time daddy and husband."

There was a lengthy pause.

Nick's voice held doubt when he responded, "I don't know how I would get along without you, Franc. For so long we have worked together spectacularly. I couldn't have asked for a better organizer and friend." Nick sighed. "To reiterate my previous statement, perhaps now is the time to get out of this particular field."

"That is not what I'm driving at, Nick. Please listen." A trace of irritation was in Franc's voice. "Here I am about to suggest a fantastic opportunity and you are turning it down without consideration. I'm surprised at you."

"Okay, I'm listening," was the uninterested response.

Franc's enthusiasm was unmistakable.

"There is an incredible female I met recently. She is knock-em dead beautiful, sensational figure, chic dresser. You'd love her. She speaks Parisian French, precise and very classy and also a couple of other languages I understand. In addition to all this, she is very smart and I don't think it would take her long to become familiar with the data I deal with at the seminars, particularly if you coached her personally."

Nick interrupted crossly.

"You have got to be out of your mind, Franc, to come up with a proposition like this. Just imagine what Kara's response would be to such an asinine idea."

"Well, that was my next question—why don't you ask her?"

Nick snorted, about to express his annoyance, when he realized his friend was trying to tell him something.

"Kara speaks French?"

"Like a native, my friend. She even mentioned the dull conversation you and I had at Wendy's party."

Nick started laughing. He banged the arm of the chair, overjoyed.

Things were improving rapidly. He could visualize the direction Franc's ideas were leading him.

It would be a tremendous opportunity to work and travel together; to introduce Kara to his favorite places; to explore new countries and to make love in every one of them. It was, in fact, a fantastic idea. With her natural intelligence and quick grasp of new information, Kara would be the perfect partner for him.

"Thank you, my very dear friend. What would I do without your astuteness and ingeniousness? I'll take it from here and hope for only positive results."

He was brought back to earth when Franc chuckled.

"Michele and Fiona are driving me crazy. Michele was thrilled to be asked to be Kara's Matron-of-Honor, but her changing waistline is proving to be a challenge to the seamstress who is becoming quite proficient, if not exhausted, with inventing new draping methods."

There was a pause and another chuckle.

"Fiona is so excited. She has paraded before me so many times trying to settle on the Flower Maiden dress she will wear that I have a feeling the outfits will be worn out before your wedding day."

He laughed infectiously.

"You know what she said, Nick? She thought whichever dress she wears as Flower Maiden would be pretty enough to wear for her first day of school. What a girl."

They laughed together.

Nick was in a happy frame of mind when he went out into the garden after the stimulating conversation with Franc.

A plan had been forming from the time he had served on the ad hoc committee that approved the State contract for Kara's "Working it Out" facility. Hearing from Franc of Kara's command of several languages was akin to putting the last piece of the jigsaw puzzle into place, He must be ready and very thorough in his assessment before presenting it to Kara for her consideration.

He leaned back against the bench.

Doing the lecture circuit would be good for a year or two. It would give them time to have fun and travel in a work-paid environment. Kara would be fantastic as his intermediary and confidante. She would be his 'Ace-in-the-hole.' He could imagine the affect she would have on those unsuspecting seminar attendees who expected a staid, though illuminative series of lectures, to find this gorgeous gal walking them through the various phases, speaking to them in their own language. Delighted with his thoughts, Nick laughed out aloud, hitting his palm against his forehead. How they would envy him.

Nick closed his eyes and dreamed.

A floating leaf brushed his cheek and he opened his eyes, smiling.

He left one dream behind to cross the threshold into the supreme dream linking Kara to him irrevocably once they were married.

For some time Nick had contemplated the need for clinics to serve a special population. His nephew Gerald being part of that group. Kara had discussed Angela's sister, Barbara, and he was almost certain that her symptoms were identical to those of Gerald. He was anxious to have Kara's input as she was already involved in working with people with special disabilities. He had learned a great deal about Kara from the time he had served on the ad hoc committee for the State. She would be a formidable partner. She was so knowledgeable and clever in this field. She would be an integral part of the operation. Partners in every sense of the word.

A frown crossed Nick's brow.

Was she so career oriented that children would not have a place in her life?

His heart took a dive. He wanted so badly to have children with Kara—to raise their own family.

Glancing out of the library window where she was sitting at a desk going over some lists, Kara noticed Nick lounging on a garden bench.

He looked relaxed. His long legs were sprawled halfway across the path and a happy, dreamy expression was on his face. Kara caught her breath. He was so magnetic and masculine. He just had to kiss her and she was under his spell. She pushed her chair back, she had to go out and sample more of his magic.

His eyes opened dreamily as she kissed him.

He pulled her down onto his lap.

"I was thinking about you."

"Were you, darling? I hoped you were. You were looking much too sexy to be left alone."

"Kara, how do you feel about having children?"

His unexpected statement took her by surprise.

She looked at him seriously.

"How much thought have you given to this?"

"Enough."

"Then tell me where you're coming from."

He moved her bodily closer to him.

"You told me that you had appointed Marcie as Vice President of your company, so that she could take charge during your absence and you felt very comfortable about that. Right?"

Kara nodded.

"This is very sudden, and you obviously need to give it some thought, but would you consider taking over from Franc and traveling with me for two to three weeks every six weeks or so. It is my profession, darling, and my itinerary is set up for the next year. After a couple of trial runs, there's no doubt in my mind that you'll be fantastic."

He looked at her sideways.

"Particularly since you will have an opportunity to use the languages you have so successfully concealed."

Kara was pensive for a moment before answering, "Not deliberately, Nick, I just never found the proper time to use them."

She paused,

"That is, except with Michele and Franc."

He hugged her fiercely.

"You're perfect. Perfect for me. It will break my heart to be parted from you and a couple of weeks can seem like an eternity. I really need you with me."

Nick burrowed his head in Kara's breasts. She absently smoothed his hair as she thought about what he had said.

"Will this be a way of life for us?"

He raised his head.

"Definitely not—I have other plans. Plans that I hope you will feel as excited about as I do, but, to get back to babies."

Nick's mouth captured Kara's. Slowly he moved his lips around, sliding his tongue through her open lips. Their hot breath intermingled.

"What do you think?"

Kara gulped.

"About what?"

"Babies, darling—you want ours, don't you?"

"Yes, oh, yes, Nick." She clung to him. "But when will we have time, if we are traveling so frequently?"

Nick crushed her closer. A surge of love overtook him. Kara had, without words, agreed to accompany him on the journeys he was committed to make. He was so very fortunate.

His voice was huskily persuasive.

"We can start planning our family, once the lecture itinerary has been fulfilled and the clinics are starting to run smoothly. California would be the most logical place to start out with the medical centers since at first you will probably want to be near "Working it Out." The clinics and medical centers are needed everywhere in the world, darling. We don't have to be restricted geographically."

Nick leaned forward to kiss Kara, but her palms against his chest stopped him from getting closer.

"Clinics and medical centers?" she squeaked.

"Mmm. Right. Oh, darling, you feel so good, you smell so sexy. Maybe we should just concentrate on making babies."

His lusty intention was evident, as he removed her hands from his throbbing chest.

Kara pushed Nick away and shoved her hair from her eyes.

"I came out here to give you one small kiss and tell you in an uncomplicated way that I love you and suddenly I'm propositioned. Clinics and babies? Nick, an explanation is necessary. Right now!"

"Okay, killjoy, but only if I can hold you closer."

Smiling faintly Kara put her arms around Nick's neck, as he encompassed her waist and laid a tender kiss on her nose.

"We should be partners in everything we do, Kara, both in our private and business lives. I love you so much, my beloved. With your brilliance and compassion in your field and my, um, brilliance and resourcefulness in mine, the combination will be dynamic and bound for success. Tomorrow you will meet Gerald, Wendy's son. He is very special to me and has lived his life battling serious autistic debility. Just as Barbara, Angela's sister and some of your own clients have. Our clinics would be designed primarily to help them and others combat similar life-style obstacles."

The passion of his conviction glowed from his dark eyes.

"We really could make a difference, precious. I already know what you have done, but your potential and talent have barely been tested. You are capable of so much more, Kara. Together we can do it and think how very satisfying it will be working on projects that are important to both of us."

Kara raised glistening eyes to Nick. She was completely entranced.

"Oh, Nick, it sounds wonderful. You must have read my mind and my heart."

Nick kissed Kara's eyelids and moved to the luscious waiting mouth, which had captivated him from the start.

"But, we still haven't talked about babies."

Gruffly he responded.

"If they look like you, I want a dozen."

Kara started giggling.

"I meant when? My biological time clock is ticking."

Nick looked at Kara seriously, tilting her chin to look into her eyes.

"I'd love to say now, immediately, but we need two years to get the foundation for our plans in place. How do you feel about that?"

Anxiously Nick searched Kara's face for dissent. She remained silent.

"By that time you'll just be thirty-three. In this day and age that still allows us time to have, let's see—at least three or four children."

Kara skewed her body closer.

"Thank you, doctor. That'll be acceptable, as long as you promise we'll have lots of practice sessions beforehand."

Nick closed his eyes. Kara should not see the intensity of his love for her at this point. The power of it scared him.

When he opened his eyes, he found grave green eyes looking at him solemnly.

"Are you sure about me, and us, and all this?"

"More than anything in my life—you are all I'll ever need."

✷ ✷ ✷

CHAPTER THIRTY SIX

Nick prowled around the granite Viking fortress, excited and restless.

Kara had returned to her tasks in the library after the satisfyingly impromptu, but important, rendezvous they had on the garden seat.

Ironically it left Nick wanting more. They had so much to discuss, but the basic foundation had been laid. How could he wait another day when he was filled with so many ideas and plans for their future? He needed Kara's opinions and he was anxious to harvest her thoughts.

At least Kara's father was usually available to use as a sounding board, otherwise he could have died of loneliness in this place and no one would have noticed. Tossing his gloomy thoughts, Nick went looking for Gus Olavssen. He had a plan he wanted to check out with him.

Settled in comfortable leather easy chairs in the den, the two men faced each other, informal and relaxed. They needed no obligatory warm-up conversation; they had established an easy relationship, with trust and respect cementing the bond.

Candidly Nick opened the conversation.

"I have some vineyards in the Loire Valley which have received many awards. I have been thinking of introducing a new strain of grape for a special anniversary commemorative along the way. Do you feel your hybrid could qualify?"

Gus, the vintner, responded.

"I have faith in it and I have high hopes, but I'm not an expert, much as I would like to be. I'm excited with the quality and the yield, but then I'm prejudiced. You tasted the product a few months ago, what did you think of it?"

Nick took charge.

"I was very impressed; so much so that I had research done on samples. The report came back today."

He offered a padded manila envelope to Gus and noted the look of interest as he accepted it.

"This is a private venture on my own land and now that, in effect, the go-ahead has been given, I would like you to consider something I have to say."

Gus looked at Nick's earnest face and smiled. How he looked forward to these conversations with him. Sometimes Nick used him as a sounding board and at other times sought his advice. It did not matter in which capacity Nick chose to utilize him—he simply enjoyed watching the gears in this young man's shrewd mind at work.

"Fire away."

He reached for a pipe.

"There are about 500 fallow acres, which are in the process of being plowed and cultivated, even as we speak. Special vines will need to be ordered for delivery soon. My problem is that, as excited as I am about this venture, there is only one person I feel is capable of running this show with me. I really need his expertise and judgment, since he already has actually tested the varietal strain I plan on using."

Gus replaced his pipe on the stand beside his chair and gave his full attention to Nick.

"I anticipate the soil and climate will be much more compatible in the Loire Valley than here in the colder north country and I have no doubt the vines will thrive there. The funds I am investing will back up my conviction. Since I play the "Money Game" seriously, I don't expect this to be a losing proposition."

Nick grinned widely at Gus.

"Having said that to prepare the groundwork and to convince you of my credibility, I would like to make you an offer. By way of inducement my proposal would be to offer the partnership in a new winery, with the brand name "P&O Vineyards.""

Gus looked steadily at Nick, a peculiar expression slowly appearing. Hesitantly he said,

"I really don't think—"

"And, of course," Nick said, over-ruling Gus' nervous response, "For easier commuting a company plane will be at the disposal of the new managing director."

The sharp intake of breath alerted Nick that Gus did not appear to be comfortable with this last piece of information.

Joan Williams

"Nick, really. I hardly think all this—" his breathing was becoming a little irregular.

Nick determinedly pushed on,

"And also included would be the full use of the "Chateau Vineyard." It is one of my homes."

Gus stood up.

"Dammit, Nick. Let me get a word in."

Nick stood up also. Had he made a mistake, assuming Gus Olavssen was as interested in this project as he had hoped? Was this going to become an issue between them? Doggedly he persevered.

"And my last offer is that the managing director may also see more of his daughter than in the past, since she will be spending almost as much time in Europe as she will in California."

A wavering smile broke across Gus' features.

"Lord. You don't take 'no' for an answer do you? All I was going to say was that I would do it as a favor. This is something I've wanted to do for some time. A project close to my heart. I just needed a shove in the right direction. Of course there is one stipulation."

He looked rather sheepishly at Nick.

"That you change the P&O to O&P."

He smiled uncertainly before continuing.

"Just to make it alphabetically correct, of course."

The smile faltered.

"It does stand for Olavssen and Prendergast, doesn't it?"

Nick laughed.

"No, it stands for Old and Persnickety."

Nick lightly punched Gus on the arm and laughed in relief. For a moment, he thought he had misjudged this man he had come to love without reservation. They would work well together.

Gus joined in, thumping Nick's shoulder in reciprocation, saying,

"If this is your method of extortion, I should have held out for better terms."

Nick's eyes sparkled.

"You're right. I would have used all bribery methods at my disposal and conversely I would have agreed to almost any condition you cared to throw in. I was even prepared to bring in your future grandchildren as my next bargaining tool."

Gus was completely snared. This was a dream come true.

He beamed at Nick.

"I think a drink is called for, don't you?"

Nick grinned back.

"Good, and then let's relax over a game of Chess. I have a premonition you are going to lose this one."

The world was finally coming to order.

CHAPTER THIRTY SEVEN

Nick was starting to pack in readiness to move into the Tyrrytt suite that day. The wedding was taking place tomorrow and if he saw the bride in her finery before the marriage ceremony took place it would put a hex on their life together. Right!

He sighed. He would go along with all the superstitions and old wives tales. He still had work to attend to, but was unable to concentrate fully on anything. Kara dominated his thoughts.

He was on his way to his bedroom with additional items to be packed when he caught a glimpse of Kara going into hers. He discreetly followed in after her and closed the door, putting his camera and binoculars on top of a chest of drawers.

"Hello. My name is Nicholas Prendergast. What's yours?"

Kara turned. She had so many things on her mind; there were still last-minute things to attend to. The woeful look on Nick's face brought home how negligent she had become ever since his return. At least they had sorted out some important decisions, which made her extremely happy. She walked over to him and put her arms around his neck. She was wearing a muted patterned silk dress, with a swathed bodice and slim skirt and it took little imagination on Nick's part to envisage the delectable body beneath.

Kara's hair was growing longer and she looked more alluring than ever, with a sexy flowing style that moved sensuously as she turned her head. Nick ran his fingers through her silken hair. He could not look at her without wanting to touch her and he wanted her all the time.

Wordlessly he took her into his arms, they fit together so well. He adored her and was impatient for tomorrow to arrive, when he could finally, legally, claim her and whisk her off so they could be alone.

"Hi there stranger," Kara said rubbing her nose against his.

She took his bottom lip and gently pressed it with her teeth and urged his mouth open with her tongue. She was full of surprises.

He held her away.

"Where are you getting all this coquettish stuff from?"

Kara looked down demurely.

"I decided that I had better read some books before we are married. I wouldn't want you to be disappointed in me."

Laughing delightedly Nick lightly scooped her up, carrying her over to the bed. Gently he kissed Kara's lips as he laid her on the white bedspread. He lay down beside her, tracing her lips with a finger.

"Darling, it's going to be the greatest delight of my life to introduce you to a special world which only you and I will share. I can hardly wait to be your husband, your lover, your teacher."

He started kissing Kara more passionately as his desire grew. She turned toward him pressing herself against him as her arms slid around his neck.

"I want it so much, too, Nick. I love you so much. I ache for you to hold me, to touch me."

Nick pressed his head into Kara's neck. She smelled intoxicatingly seductive. He kissed around the smooth jaw line and fastened his mouth over hers. He slid his hand down her back, bringing her to him forcefully.

"Do you remember when I undressed you in your bathroom?"

"I'll never forget it." she whispered huskily.

"Well, I told myself at that time that I could never go through that kind of a test again. I wanted you desperately then and I want you even more urgently now.

It would give me the greatest thrill to make love to you right this minute, but I know I would regret it."

A hurt looked passed across Kara's tense face. Was Nick saying that he loved her, but that he could control his emotions to the point where his cravings for her could be suppressed at will? Kara's love and desire for Nick were steadily growing with the passing of each day. She was convinced beyond doubt that she had found the perfect mate, but was she the right one for Nick if he could curb his feelings for her so easily? It was a devastating thought and Kara looked in panic at Nick, who was staring at her thoughtfully.

He spoke quietly. "Darling, I hope you will forgive me for not discussing with you earlier a part of my life that sat heavily on my heart for a long time and for which I was hounded by guilt. Since coming in to my life you have thankfully eliminated the unhappy memories that have clouded my life for so long. I'd like to tell you about it, because the traumatic experience forever changed my outlook on life and molded the man I am today."

Kara looked at Nick intently. Was he about to divulge a side of his character that she could not accept?

Placing an arm around Kara's shoulders as they lay side-by-side on the bed, Nick tenderly kissed Kara on the lips. He closed his eyes to marshal his thoughts before beginning.

"A long time ago, before I realized how perfect love could be with you, I met and fell in love with a young woman called Serawin. At that time, she was my first and only love. She was a very rare person."

He clasped Kara tighter and looked deep into compassionate green eyes. Kara's body relaxed against his and she placed her lips on his neck and whispered.

"Before you go further, I want you to know that I have already heard about this from Franc, but I want to hear it from you. Whatever you say, you will never get away from me—it has taken me too long to find you. I intend holding on to you forever."

With a sigh he rested his cheek against Kara's hair and started recalling the painful time, which was amazingly slipping away from him. Kara had taken over his mind, his body and his world.

At the close of his story, Kara reached up, teary eyed, and kissed Nick on the lips tremulously.

"What a tragic experience. Thank you for telling me, darling. I'll never forget it."

She wiped her eyes with a tissue.

Kara had listened to narratives from both François and her father, each time devastated by the telling. A sense of purpose filled her. If it took the remainder of her life she would prove how much she loved this astonishing man.

Turning into Nick's arms, Kara put her arms around his neck, ready to demonstrate her affection.

Nick kissed Kara gently and then to her surprise, he slid off the bed and stood up abruptly.

"We have been absent from your guests downstairs for some time and I'm getting low on temptation resistance."

He held out his hand, and helped her off the bed.

He pressed a kiss on Kara's temple.

"Tomorrow we will be married and I can hardly wait. When we do make love for the first time it will be the right time and it will be wonderful. I intend spending the rest of my life establishing without a doubt that you are the love of my life."

He trembled as he spoke.

"We may never leave the bedroom."

Kara laughed in relief. She needed this assurance from the man who it appeared could have any woman he chose—and unbelievably he had chosen her.

It was a dizzying thought.

She took Nick's face between her slender hands.

"I've always been able to improvise. I just may surprise you, my love, given the right ambience and instructor."

Kara provocatively claimed Nick's mouth, sending shivers through his body. She moved away with a saucy smile on her lips, observing the ardor appearing in Nick's eyes as he ran his eyes over her curvaceous figure.

"Besides," she added with a mischievous look on her face, "I have to remember that you are still in a recuperative state and undue exertion should be avoided. What's more—I'm not sure you could handle my physical demands right now since a great deal of stamina and energy would need to be expended."

Seeing the warning look on Nick's face, Kara dashed for the bedroom door.

Wagging her finger at him, she said.

"You started this by saying you wanted to wait, I gave you an opportunity and you blew it."

As Kara started opening the door, Nick pushed it closed, taking Kara into his arms again.

A whimsical smile came over his face.

"I don't think you realize how much power you hold over me. I just have to touch you, as I'm doing now and I become totally defenseless and vulnerable, but not impotent. Definitely not impotent! For one more day I shall have to worship you from a distance and that will do wonders for my libido. So don't worry about my prowess. By the time we are finally married, I hope to not only prove to you that you are the only woman I could ever love, but demonstrate beyond a shadow of a doubt, how thoroughly we belong together, and that I am the only man you will ever need."

He kissed her long and tenderly, deliberately restraining the passion that was ready to display itself again.

As an afterthought he whispered.

"Or I shall die happy in the attempt."

CHAPTER THIRTY EIGHT

The quintet of musicians, seated on a raised platform festooned with blue ribbons, orchids, and silver bells, began playing Johan Sebastian Bach's "Air on a G String." The whisper of excited voices reached Nick and Franc as they stood listening to the gently calming music.

They smiled briefly at each other before turning from the festooned podium toward the assembled guests who had risen to their feet. Rows of chairs had been placed on both sides of a wide column of trellised arches decked with white roses and blue and white satin ribbons, which were gently fluttering in the slight breeze that had just sprung up.

From his vantage point Nick could see all the way through the arch of flowers to the two leading figures, slowly proceeding through the scenic corridor, with a retinue of figures in floating blue gowns following them.

They were too far away for their features to be seen clearly, but Nick's heart started thumping at the sight of Kara. This woman who was about to become his wife. His soul mate.

The magnificence of the gown she was wearing could be seen even from where he stood. It sparkled in the shafts of sunlight, which were interspersed through the arches as she passed beneath them. The tiara, resting on the shining gold hair, sent out its own brilliant prisms.

He could not take his eyes from her. He was hypnotized by the radiance she projected.

She was utterly breathtaking.

The heavily encrusted train was carefully draped behind Kara as she serenely took her place by Nick's side on the carpeted rostrum. Her luminous green eyes held his and a tiny smile hovered around her lips. He swallowed hard as he took her hand. He had not anticipated becoming so patently emotional.

He could smell her distinctive perfume, it invaded his senses.

Looking down at the sculptured bodice, artfully displaying the contours of Kara's rounded breasts, Nick unconsciously squeezed the fingers, entwined in his. Breathing was suddenly difficult.

His life seemed to be held in limbo, as he observed her perfection.

The service that followed, dedicating one to the other, seemed like a dream. He was entranced with Kara's flawless features. Her shy smile and clear, breathless responses touched his heart and he clung to her hands, drawing strength from the trusting glances she gave him.

Uncle Henry's message bound them together in God's love and the bonds of love taking them into eternity. He blessed their marriage.

They were man and wife. Uncle Henry, Vicar and Dean of The Grange Parochial College, proudly announced: "Please welcome into your midst the newly wedded couple Dr. and Mrs. Prendergast, Kara and Nicholas."

Spontaneous applause broke out.

Nick's startled look brought a smile to Kara's face, which she hid behind the slim hand, so recently graced with the wide gold band.

Nick felt as if his heart would burst as he took Kara into his arms. Their kiss was soft and loving and when she opened her eyes to look at her new husband, Kara saw an expression of joy that set her aglow. Tears of happiness lurked behind her eyelids.

Holding hands they threaded their way past their guests and through the floral arches to the strains on Mendelssohn's "Wedding March."

Lady Silvia Olavssen's eyes were in a constantly turbid condition and her husband patted her hand from time to time consolingly, aware of the emotions so close to the surface. A lump seemed to be stuck in his own throat, which was threatening to choke him. Thank God he had only one daughter and that one was hopefully committed for a lifetime to the man she had just married.

"Did I look as beautiful in my wedding gown as Kara looks in it today?"

It was still a source of wonder to Kara's mother that the wedding gown, which she had worn for her marriage to Gus, that had been carefully stored for thirty-three years, was being worn by her own daughter on this her wedding day. Upon inspection of the superb workmanship and design of her mother's gown, Kara said she would be honored to wear it. Amazingly, with minor adjustments, it fitted perfectly. Lady Silvia Olavssen hoped she would live to see it being worn again by a future grand-daughter.

Pressing his wife's hand, Gus whispered in her ear, "There never was a more beautiful bride than you, my love. I am indeed a fortunate man to experience it again today through our beautiful daughter."

Kara and Nick, with their attendants, made their way to the gazebo where photographers and news reporters had scurried after the ceremony.

For the first time Nick was conscious of the people around him.

Bemused he looked with interest at Gus, who was dressed in a gray swallow tailed formal suit, with a black and gray ascot tucked in at the neck. He wore a diplomatic sash across his chest, decorated with medals and insignia, indicating his place in the Norwegian Royal House. A gray top hat completed his outfit, which was tucked carelessly into the crook of his elbow.

He looked distinguished and aristocratic and very much at ease in this regalia and Nick was stunned for a moment. He had to look at him twice. Was this the man with whom he spoke so freely and effortlessly as they lounged casually in jeans? Nick had been so completely overwhelmed at the sight of his stunning bride that he had barely noticed her father in his finery

Nick stood uncertain, staring at him.

Gus gave a big wink and saluted the bridal pair.

Kara waved in return and put an arm around Nick's waist.

"Even though he'd never admit it, daddy does enjoy acting the part every now and again. Mother teases him about the trace of blue blood manifesting itself, but we forgive him—he'll settle down in a day or so. This is a happy day for them too, you know."

She leaned against Nick and whispered.

"You look so handsome, darling. I'm having a hard time keeping my hands off you."

Nick groaned softly, looking at his watch and murmuring in her ear.

"We've been married exactly eighty-seven minutes and I'm slowly dying for want of you. How soon can we get away? The plane is fueled and the pilot is on standby. You have only to say the word."

Kara curled her nose impishly.

"After the videos and pictures have been taken and our guests have passed through the Receiving Line, the toasts and meal come next and then the dancing will commence. After that we can steal away."

Nick snorted disbelievingly.

"Steal away? Right! We'll be an old married couple by then."

Kara turned her face away to disguise her grin. Nick's impatience was starting to emerge.

The photographers were assembling the wedding party for group pictures and Kara stood up on her toes and kissed Nick quickly.

"Just behave yourself for a few hours, sweetheart, and when it's acceptably appropriate to leave, I'll give you a big wink and we can say our adieux immediately. Agreed?

Nick nodded his head and laughed.

"Whatever you say, darling, but I warn you not to flutter your lashes at me, or I'll take that as a signal and transport you to another planet before anyone knows what has happened."

He took Kara's hand and placed his lips on the gold band shining brightly. Flashes from cameras witnessed the event.

Straightening, he smiled at his bride.

"I'm at your command, Queen of my Heart."

They joined the waiting group.

Furtively Nick glanced at his watch.

Despite his eagerness to depart, Nick had enjoyed the witty speech that Franc as Best Man had made and even his massacred terminology had lent a genuine glimpse into their friendship. With the pathos capable only in the gestures of a true Gallic, Franc described the act of destiny that brought Kara and Nick together. It was a real love story emphasized by the tear he discretely brushed away with his little finger.

Nick squeezed Kara's hand as the extravagant sighs of guests filtered around the huge canvas marquee at the close of Franc's romantic toast to the newlyweds.

They continued to hold hands as Kara's father responded.

"It would take a better man than me to top that tender and true account which Franc has just related. So I will not attempt to do so. Instead I want to welcome Nick into the family."

Turning to the bridal couple, he said to his son-in-law.

"We have waited a long time for you, Nick. Welcome, son."

Nick blinked quickly. The intimate disclosure took him by surprise.

"Lady Olavssen and I have known from the day Kara was born to us, that we were blessed. We have never thought otherwise and Kara has not given us cause to feel differently. She is our golden girl, our delight, the perpetuation of our dreams and hopes."

He blew his nose, stuffing the handkerchief back into his trouser pocket.

"She has not disappointed us and in continuing this propensity she has chosen as her husband a man who already has found a place in our hearts. He has further delighted my wife and me by assuring us that, with Kara's participation, he anticipates and intends multiplying the family. So eager was he to commence on this project that I feel I must give him a word of warning."

With a quizzical expression on his face he looked at Nick.

"I hope you will keep in mind that we have only twenty guest rooms, Nick."

There was a general roar of laughter, with ribald comments bandied around. Kara blushed and looked at her father in astonishment. His tongue was really loosening up. She had never seen him so full of mischief.

Nick leaned over and kissed Kara full on the mouth, adding fuel to fire.

This activated applause.

Gus held up his hand.

"Before my pleasant obligation is fulfilled, on a more serious note, I would like to select a few telegrams from the huge collection you see in front of me. Franc would normally have dealt with these, but he felt I was a little more experienced with the English language."

More laughter ensued.

"They all basically express the same content—best wishes for a long and happily married life. There's one from Prime Minister John Majors and also ex-Prime Minister Margaret Thatcher. Another is from President and Mrs. Ronald Reagan. There is a remarkable collection from world renowned personalities and dignitaries, as well as from special people in Kara and Nick's lives—heart patients, people with disabilities who have bonded with Kara and Nick, specialists in both of their fields of endeavor. They will all be posted around the room for your inspection, since there are far too many to read."

Gus handed the box containing the telegrams and wedding cards to Marcie and he continued.

"Out of all of these exceptional congratulatory messages, there is one which was received a few hours ago from Switzerland. It was sealed with instructions that it be read only at the wedding reception."

Marcie slit the envelope and handed it to Gus.

"Here it is."

All eyes were upon him and he cleared his throat.

Nick's face tensed and he grasped Kara's hand firmly.

Gus read:

"In order to attend this exceptionally happy occasion I would have broken down all my stupid barriers. Sorry, Nicholas, my doctors will not permit me to travel. You have made an excellent choice in Kara—a reflection of the man who has made me so proud over the years—despite my resistance to acknowledge that. Did you know I played 'pat-a-cake' with Kara as an infant? Her parents are well known to me. Nicholas, please let me make amends. Come and visit. I beg you. Sincere best wishes to a most brilliant grandson and his equally dazzling wife, from a very remorseful and foolish grandfather.

(sender) Marquis Philipe Fitzpatrick."

Tears gathered in Nick's eyes and Kara flung her arms around his neck.

"Oh darling—what a shock. But isn't it wonderful? At long last he is asking for forgiveness.

Taking Nick's face into her hands she asked apprehensively.

"Are you all right?"

Nick laid his head against Kara's cheek, facing away from the guests.

His voice was blurred.

"What a time to hear from him—how melodramatic."

He brushed a tear away with his hand.

"I'd like to get to know him, Nick, please." Kara's voice was cajoling.

He was silent for a while before responding.

"My first impulse is to tell him to go to Hell. I have managed my life quite well without him being a part of it. But that is my pride talking and despite his eccentric ways, I suppose he has done what he felt he had to do. What is most important to me now is that, even though he and I have a lot to work out between us, he will have the opportunity to get to know you and hopefully be around for his great-grandchildren."

Kara and Nick stayed silent within each other's arms, cheek-to-cheek, oblivious of all else.

There was an uneasy stillness in the room.

The Bride and Groom looked dejected and the wedding party at the Head Table sat with strained expressions. They were confused.

Kissing Kara on the cheek, Nick rose to his feet.

His smile was a little forced.

"Dear parents, honored guests, relatives, and friends, Kara and I thank you for attending the celebration of our marriage. Your presence has provided the caring that we have become accustomed to receive from you and upon which we rely heavily. You have made it an exceptionally happy occasion for us and an experience we will truly treasure."

Gently pulling Kara to her feet, he placed a possessive arm around her waist, and pulled her as close as the bouffant gown would allow.

"You have heard about our unusual courtship and so it should not be a surprise that today, our wedding day, is no different. True to form it has turned out to be a most unusual day."

He smiled gently at Kara, who intertwined her fingers through Nick's hand, only to find it trembling. Quickly she looked at him, but his face was composed and calm.

"A short time ago a telegram was read which took me completely by surprise. It was totally unexpected and, in fact, came as a shock. It was from the grandfather I have never met.

Gasps of surprise reached Kara and Nick from the assembled guests.

"Contrary to the impression given, the telegram from my grandfather has brought one of the happiest reconciliations imaginable. After years of trying to get the attention of a man whom I would like to be an important part of my life, I guess at last I actually did something right. I married Kara. I know that isn't totally accurate, but that is what I have to assume since this is the first response I have had from him since I was seven years of age. It appears that at last he is ready to repair our relationship and I should give the credit to Kara for this turn of events."

The row of faces across the Head Table suddenly perked up and smiles appeared.

The guests straightened up in their seats and waiters circulated, refilling wine glasses.

"This then is a very happy day for my wife and me."

Kara looked momentarily puzzled and giggled upon recognizing her new title.

"I think I have a late bloomer here, folks."

Laughter met Nick's fond banter and a wave of relief rolled around the room. All was well.

Nick's voice turned serious.

"There are some acknowledgements I would like to make. My thanks go most devotedly to Kara's parents. Without their combined efforts, I would not be married to the woman for whom I have waited so long."

A relaxed sigh echoed around the cavernous domed marquee.

"I would especially like to recognize the way Lady Olavssen took me under her wing. From the moment we met I felt I was in touch with a kindred spirit. She gave me the impression she liked me and it was very easy for me to love her, as I already did her daughter."

"Conveying that impression to Kara's father was more difficult. I distinctly remember how horrified he was when he conceded that I *might* be a suitable suitor for his daughter's hand, as long as I didn't try to pick him up and hug him, as I had done with his wife."

Nick smiled appreciatively over in the Olavssen's direction.

Laughter rumbled from one end of the room to the other, and Gus Olavssen raised his champagne flute in recognition.

Nick and Kara grinned at each other.

"It is with extreme pleasure that we welcome His Excellency, M. Bertrand de Fitzhugh, French Ambassador to the Kingdom of Jordan and his wife Andrea Bascombe-de Fitzhugh, who flew in from that country just a few hours ago. Their daughter, Michele, is a special part of our wedding party.

"Our attendants deserve special mention and it is my great pleasure to introduce them. Franc, please stand with Michele and Fiona."

The three rose dutifully to their feet.

"For the enlightenment of those I have just recently met, I was left an orphan at an early age and I lived a very solitary lifestyle until I met Franc and then Michele. Franc and I are business partners and I value his loyal friendship and business acumen more than words can express. Both Michele and Franc have provided a steadying influence that has sustained me through some very difficult times. I value their friendship deeply and it fills me with joy seeing them embrace Kara with the same closeness."

He raised Kara's hand to his lips and looked along the table.

"Marcie."

She stood.

"What I know about you is through Kara and I thank you for being the good friend and confidante that you have become. She has relied heavily upon you and that is why you are such an important part of her life. In many ways, you are to Kara the counterpart of what Franc is to me. I look forward to getting to know you back in California."

They smiled warmly at each other.

Nick looked at the list before him.

"Yesterday I met Lavinia and Beryl for the first time and we haven't had the opportunity to chat very much, but, given time we will. That's a promise."

Nick continued,

"Since it has been intimated that Kara and I are destined to have a large family, I'm pleased that the dollhouse Kara favored as a child will be retained for our children's use. If all these children enjoy it as much as she did and use it as frequently as she did, they may decide to live here, with their grandparents indefinitely. It is far too large a unit to be kept anywhere else but in a home with at least twenty guest rooms. Lord Olavssen has kindly offered this accommodation to our children—unconditionally."

Amused laughter followed.

Gus wagged his finger at Nick.

"Touché."

Nick was grinning from ear to ear.

Kara sat down, but Nick immediately drew her to her feet again, saying for all to hear.

"We are in this together, my love, and I want you right here beside me where you belong."

Contentedly she slipped her arm around Nick's waist and laid her head against his shoulder.

"Because none of us wish to prolong this phase any longer than we must and because some of us have more important things to do . . . ."

Nick looked down to see Kara shaking her head with an uncertain smile on her face. How these men of hers were having fun with the One-upmanship game.

". . . I just wish to thank a few more people for traveling so far to share this special day with us. Please stand as I mention your name. My only cousin Wendy Rutherford and her son, Gerald, have come from Rancho Mirage, California. As have Dr. Don Carmichael and his charming wife, Ann. Special kudos should be given to Claudia, my long suffering Major Domo, who has tolerated so much and amazingly survived it all. Thanks, Claudia. Emma—where is Emma?"

Emma stood up slowly, reluctant to face the limelight.

"Sincere thanks are due to Emma. She was there when Kara and I desperately needed her and we are going to find her invaluable when all the Prendergast children start coming along. Right, Emma?"

She impetuously blew Nick a kiss and surprised at her frivolous action, sat down heavily.

Nick winked at her and clapping followed.

"Do you have anything to add, darling?"

Kara shook her head emphatically.

"Then, once again, thank you for making this a wonderful day for Kara and me."

Gus Olavssen stood up tapping a wine glass to gain attention.

"After the meal and before the dancing commences, please assemble in the rose garden where the cake cutting ceremony will take place. Thank you."

Kara and Nick stood by the blue and white chiffon draped doorway and briefly conversed with guests as they straggled out to the rose arbor.

Nick looked at Kara and said under his breath.

"How can you look so innocently beautiful, yet so sinfully sexy all at the same time? Now that our duties have been performed, I'm anxious to leave."

In a desperate tone he added, "Surely it's time."

Kara sighed. It had been a long day and she was more than ready to leave, but the cake cutting ritual needed to be photographed for posterity. At the same time the tables and chairs were being rearranged inside the marquee and the portable dance floor installed. An army of trained technicians was already at work.

Stretching her hand to caress Nick's handsome face, Kara noticed with pleasure how the unfamiliar band of gold shone brightly in the stray beams of the strobe lights being tested in the huge tent.

"Two more hours' max., sweet. I'm so tired I could sleep for a week."

Nick looked at her aghast.

"There is no way, my love. That is not part of my nocturnal plans for you."

Kara leaned against him, laughing weakly.

"Is that a threat or a promise? Maybe I'll sleep through it all," she teased.

Disbelief was written over Nick's face as he forcefully pulled her against him.

"What I have in mind to do with you will leave you begging for more. Sleep will be the furthermost thought from your mind. I promise."

He dipped down, hungrily kissing Kara's waiting mouth.

Fretting, he protested.

"When are we getting out of these clothes? I can't get near you for all the stuff we are wearing and it is just a matter of time before I spear myself on that damned, er, lovely headdress."

Kara smiled at the intensity of his aggravation.

Resignation was in Nick's voice as he added, "If I don't get to hold you properly very soon, Kara, I won't be held responsible for my actions."

Kara's luminous eyes expressed her own tormented want. She held Nick's hands. His sensuality and increasing need were beginning to excite her.

"I promise we will leave shortly after the dancing commences."

They could hear the orchestra starting to tune-up.

Nick carefully coiled Kara's train over his arm and together they joined their guests in the rose garden.

Nick felt as if his facial muscles had frozen into a synthetic smile.

The photographers were still hanging around, waiting to take their endless pictures. Thankfully their assignment was almost finished.

Guests were claiming tables around the dance floor. The bar area was crowded.

Kara was talking with friends at the edge of the dance floor and Nick could not keep his eyes away from her. She was so gorgeous. He caught his breath whenever he looked at her. From time-to-time he could hear her laughter and he automatically smiled at the sound.

Michele, Franc, and Fiona were sitting at the table with him, but he may as well have been there alone. He had eyes only for his bride.

Keeping a straight face Franc interrupted Nick's thoughts, tapping him on the arm.

"I don't expect you to look at me, but please listen. I may not have a chance to talk to you for a while."

Briefly Nick looked at Franc, smiled, and turning his gaze back to Kara said, "Go ahead, please tell me."

"The groom is attending to the horse and will continue to exercise it daily, waiting to be informed when you wish Kara to see it. It's being stabled near the hunting lodge, so when you come up for air, you'll know where it will be."

Nick smiled his thanks. Franc had arranged everything and the best part had been left to Nick. He was excited at the prospect of showing his wedding gift to Kara. The horse, which she had expressed great attachment for, would be hers. He wanted Kara to rename it, to put the past behind them.

Thinking of the arrangements made, Nick smiled happily to himself. Instead of using the chateau, as first intended, he decided to have the hunting lodge readied. It was far enough away from civilization to be completely private, yet sufficiently convenient to allow the plane to land nearby. Only two servants, a married couple, would be available to attend to their immediate needs. He wanted to ensure their honeymoon would be quiet and uninterrupted. As long as Kara wished to stay there, everything else would take a backseat.

Michele tittered.

She had been watching Kara and Nick ever since they were pronounced man and wife. She had never seen Nick so totally bewitched, blatantly displaying his happiness. Even when mixing with the guests, his eyes searched for Kara constantly and his love was plainly reflected there.

Michele nudged Nick.

"You'd better get ready, they're about to play your song."

Nick navigated his way through to Kara slipping his arm eagerly around her waist. He smiled at Wendy and Gerald, who were part of the group.

The orchestra leader rapped on the microphone to attract attention.

"Ladies and gentlemen, it is my pleasure to request the bride and groom to introduce this evening's dancing with the traditional "Bridal Waltz." Kara and Nick if you will."

A hush fell over the room.

Leading Kara to the center of the floor, they stood facing each other.

Kara looked at Nick shyly. Yes, they truly belonged together now. Her heart fluttered as the realization hit her.

Kara started looping the long, heavy train over her arm and Nick bent over to assist, smiling and stepping back when it was securely looped into place.

The introductory bars of the melody started and Kara turned her face to meet that of her waiting husband and the look of love radiated there stopped Nick in his tracks. He took Kara into his arms and kissed her with a depth of feeling and reverence that left them both trembling.

There was silence followed by enthusiastic applause.

The tender moment had taken everyone by surprise.

The music began again.

Nick and Kara started dancing, unable to take their eyes from each other.

Suddenly the tempo of the music changed.

For a moment a puzzled frown appeared on Kara's face. A seductive tango was being played and Nick smiled at Kara's perplexed expression.

He spoke into her ear.

"I don't waltz very well and I am still upset that George managed to dance this number with you, when I do it so much better. The orchestra leader is humoring me. Okay darling?"

The tune was "Jealousy."

Kara's lips parted and she smiled a small secret smile. This new husband of hers was so unpredictable and innovative. She was looking forward to their lives together. To think that she had thought she could live without him.

Nick returned the smile. He was about to embark on the most glorious mission of his life. It would, in fact, become the most satisfactory endeavor he had ever participated in. Kara deserved his full attention and it would be his purpose and reward to be her faithful and devoted husband.

Nick's pulse raced.

Kara was privately making love to him on the dance floor with those fabulous eyes traveling over him, with the way her hand caressed when she touched him and in the way her body tempted his as they came together.

She was driving him crazy.

He grinned. She would be an extraordinary pupil—she had so much potential.

Only the beguiling music broke the silence in the room.

The two dancers were perfectly attuned to each other; they accomplished the intricate steps with precision and grace. The delight in each other's performance was expressed clearly on their faces. Kara started improvising, wonderment reflected on her face when Nick deftly followed and matched her movements. Nick laughed, this was one dance she could not embarrass him in executing.

Silvia Olavssen dabbed at her eyes.

"Don't they look wonderful together? Kara has indeed found her Prince Charming. Were we ever so much in love, Gus?"

"Do you question it, beloved?"

Gus Olavssen's glasses had clouded over and he pushed them up to their usual position on top of his head as he took his wife's hand into his own.

Silvia Olavssen was overjoyed with Nick, the new addition to their family, and from the way Gus had been going around shaking hands and chortling happily with everyone, he must feel the same way too. She reached for her handkerchief again.

Kara surveyed her husband with awe as the dance came to a close. What other surprises did he have in store for her?

Nick pressed Kara close for a passing moment, before releasing her to her father for their dance together.

"You are so very beautiful, Kara. I am physically aching to make love to you. Please take pity on me."

"You're not alone, sweet," she muttered.

He walked over to Kara's mother to claim their special dance. He also claimed her to replace the mother he had hardly known.

"Are you spending your honeymoon at the Chateau?"

Nick smirked.

"Good try! Should there be an emergency Pierre, my butler, can get a message to me. That's all I'm telling you. I have waited too long for time alone with Kara and I'm going to make the most of it."

He looked like the cat about to get the cream.

His mother-in-law burst out laughing.

"With that expression on your face, I think my unsuspecting daughter ought to be warned. I never did give her that special little pre-nuptial talk mothers and daughters are supposed to have."

Amused glances passed between them.

"Don't worry about Kara. She is very safe with me; I will treasure her always. You should, perhaps, be more concerned about me. Your daughter has been testing me almost daily, anxious to experiment with the dangerous knowledge gained from the 'self-help' books she felt were so necessary for her enlightenment."

He eyed his dancing partner shrewdly.

"Yes. Perhaps you should have talked to Kara after all. But with my protection in mind."

Silvia nodded her head, smiling. She was happy that she and Nick were so at ease with each other. It had been thus from their first meeting. She was convinced that Nick had been destined to meet Kara. Already her imagination was taking flight—what a story to pass on to all the grandchildren she hoped would come along and spend special time with them.

The music ended and picking her up, Nick turned around a few times with Silvia in his arms.

"Thank you for being you, dearest mother-in-law."

He set her down on the floor with a hug and kissed her cheek.

They had an audience watching them.

Silvia waved her hand carelessly.

"He does it all the time. It's got to be my dancing."

Laughter met this pronouncement and Nick bowed over her hand.

Kara approached Nick with outstretched hands and a delighted smile on her face. They kissed and she slid her arms around Nick's waist, squeezing tightly.

The music began and Nick was ready to dance with his wife again, but Franc claimed the honor.

Nick held out his hand to Michele with a smile and they moved into a slow dance.

"I bet the night will pass far more quickly for you than this day has." Michele said, looking slyly at Nick.

"That's an understatement. I don't know for how much longer I can keep this up."

He winced as if in pain.

A sobering thought hit Nick, and he trod on a blue satin clad foot at the recollection. She yelped.

"Sorry Michele."

He had intended explaining to Kara the responsibility he had assumed for Serawin's death because their love had been predominantly of a physical nature, spontaneous and immature, without benefit of marriage; because they chose to ignore cultural mores the penalty had been disastrous. The lesson learned had ingrained itself into Nick's conscience and he resolved that this would not happen again, no matter the cost. He vowed that until he could claim Kara as his wife she would remain safe in his keeping

She had been testing him to the limit lately.

He looked over at Kara once again and inwardly trembled at the emergence of her passion relayed to him through the jade green eyes. The love that had become so exclusive to them was being confirmed, leaving no room for doubt.

Slowly and deliberately she winked.

He trod on Michele's foot again.

"Sorry about that. Would you like to sit this one out? I'm not doing well am I?"

Michele agreed on both counts.

Kara started walking toward Nick, meeting him at the edge of the parquet floor.

Her eyes were mistily tender. She looked young and vulnerable.

Nick blinked his eyelids quickly. He took a deep breath and smiled lovingly at his wife.

It was time to leave.

They had a life to start together.

The End